COLD RUNS THE BLOOD

by

Elliot Thorpe

Grosvenor House
Publishing Limited

This book is published by
Grosvenor House Publishing Ltd
28-30 High Street, Guildford, Surrey, GU1 3EL.
www.grosvenorhousepublishing.co.uk

A CIP record for this book
is available from the British Library

ISBN 978-1-78148-633-7

Acknowledgments, nods, waves and thanks to my family and to Mark Blackwell, Neil Feist, Lee Foster, Dan Griffiths, Nick Heady, Ronda Hopper, Tamsin Keeley, Gail Martin, Richard McTighe, Lucy Parrado, Juan Peña Núñez, Dane Pestano, Edward Robinson, Gary Russell, Kenny Smith, Neal Smith, Paul Tonks and Sam Toomer.

For Julie

e all have something to say in life. As
riters perhaps we have more to say than
sual. And while we may not be able
o change the world, we can aspire to
ulfill our dreams – and maybe even
nspire others to fulfill theirs.
nd with that outlook, anything is possible.
ood fortune on your journey, Julie
nd don't forget me when you top the
estseller list!

6/8/14

For my parents, without whom…

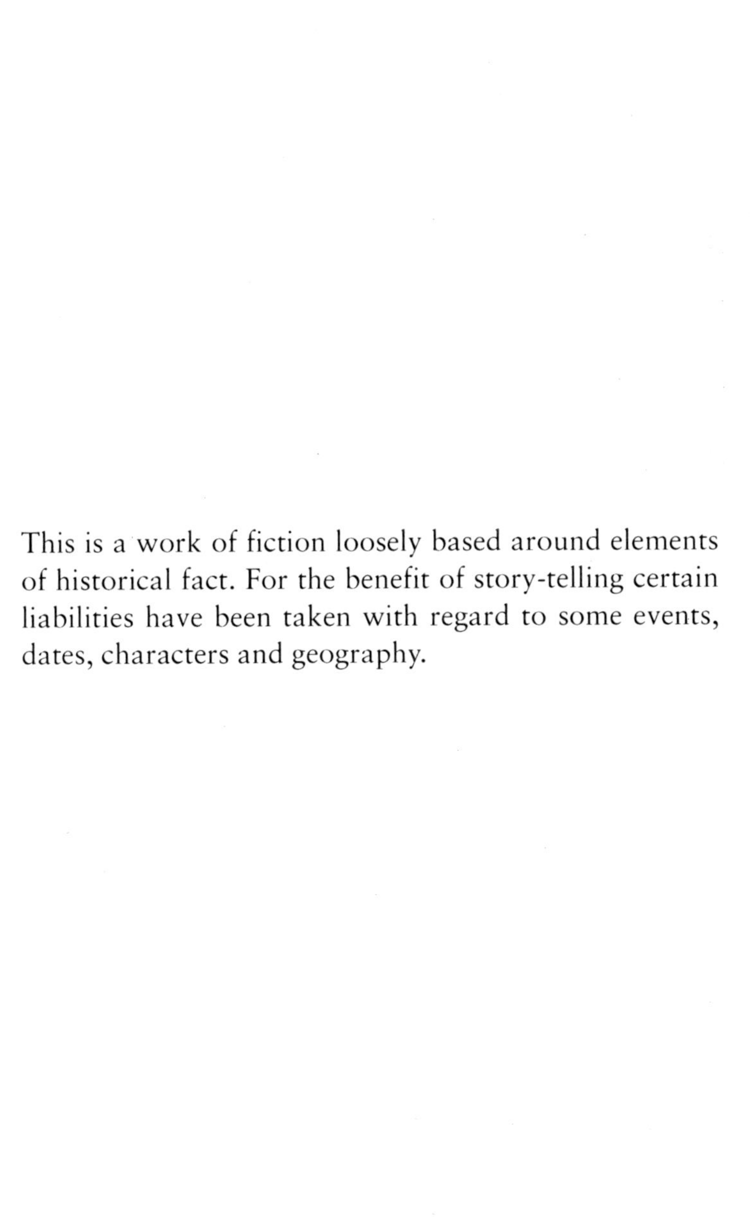

This is a work of fiction loosely based around elements of historical fact. For the benefit of story-telling certain liabilities have been taken with regard to some events, dates, characters and geography.

Prologue

Once upon a time, Agatha Weiss was told that everybody dies.

She never quite believed it, never quite understood why that should be so. It seemed unjust and unfair. As she grew up and watched those around her succumb to the wrath and demands of their oppressors (of which there were many) that unfairness she had harboured developed into an understanding.

Death, it seemed in her developing mind, was not an end but a release from the torment of life.

Yet her journey into adulthood had taken her down a path many considered blasphemous. It was this journey that allowed her to stand defiant against those oppressors and reignite her opinion that death should not be the end.

And even now, on the day of her execution, she held tight to that belief.

Agatha had received the briefest of trials following a brutal incarceration of almost three years. Eventually found guilty of witchcraft, she would burn at the stake to cleanse her of the evil that her judges had said had consumed her all her life. To save her from casting any bedevilling spells, they had removed her fingers from her hands. When that wasn't considered enough, they removed her hands from her wrists.

She was bound now by heavy wet rope to the thick, shaven tree trunk fixed upright in the centre of the town square. It rose up from a pointed base of wood and kindling. Her elbows and ankles were raw where the bindings cut into her flesh.

An obscenity had been brutally carved into her forehead by zealous guards, her long black hair shorn, almost scalping her in places.

Three holy men stood out from the crowd, cassocks a dirty cream and reeking of stale piss.

From upon her funeral pyre she looked down at them, at Bishop Sigmirului. The disgust on his old, lined face was evident. His two priests moved to flank him, both holding burning torches.

The market place was surrounded on all sides by the two-storey buildings that made up the town hall and the burgomaster's residency. Archways and narrow windows looked out upon the wide cobbled square, each filled with local traders plying their wares: hot foods, exotic spices and silks from the east and trinkets from the north. Shepherds herded their flocks as pick-pockets slipped unheard between the seething mass of people.

Agatha could see from upon her pyre right out through the largest of the archways, the one that singly allowed entrance and exit to the town of Bistritz.

She was positioned there to taunt her, to show her the physical way out as oppose to the spiritual one that was to happen once the instruction within the *lex Cornelia de sicariis et veneficis* had been carried out to completion.

Sigmirului opened his Bible and met Weiss' eyes with a sneering glare.

"No Christian should make or render any devotion to the deities of the trivium, where three roads meet. No more devilish charms at springs or trees or crossroads for you, fallen child." He wiped away Agatha's fresh spittle from his cheek. He signed the cross in the air before her. "We purify your sins with the power of the flame. We banish your soul before the might of God."

The priests either side of him leant forward and thrust the torches into the base of the pyre. Immediately the kindling caught and the fire spread quickly, making easy work of the dry fuel. Smoke rose up into the cool May air.

Agatha struggled against her bonds, the low flames catching beneath her. She could feel the growing warmth on the soles of her bare, sore feet.

"Lady of Darkness, Dark Isis of spell, blessed Marise, eternal Mother, hear me and help me."

The noise from the crowd surrounding the pyre was becoming so riotous that none could truly hear Agatha's words, which was just as well. Whether she actually was a witch or not was hardly the matter. No one would dare question if she was through fear of being condemned for supporting a heathen and being tortured and executed themselves. And there was nothing like a good public execution to make a town forget about its troubles: the Ottoman Turks were forever attempting to invade, control and turn the town but found that the path to Bistritz was strewn with more dangers that even the Sultan could conjure up. And so, time after time, the Turks were driven back and back again.

There *was* the argument that the Turks were well-aware of the superstition rife in these lands and so would simply sit back and watch their enemy trial and execute themselves into extinction.

Certainly the Sultan's spies went back to Constantinople almost on a weekly basis to tell of events such as what was happening in Bistritz today.

"Let the tongue of these God's children be numb, and powerless to speak the evil, to speak the untrue! Let their voices fail and throats close on the harmful words, by the power of the Dark Lady! It is you, Sigmirului, who will burn on Judgement Day!"

The heat of the flames caught Weiss' voice in her throat as they jumped and licked around her. She was determined not to scream, not to show her enemy Sigmirului and his brethren that what they were doing was beyond agonising. She knew what she was and the power that she wielded and she knew that she would die with that knowledge. The only time she was prepared to scream was as she reached the final moments of death, consumed by the agonies of the burning - and only then it would be in defiance of her executioners.

Through the flames, smoke and pain, Weiss could make out Sigmirului still chanting his pointless words, could see the crowds ecstatic with the sight of her roasting before them. Yet amid all the confusion, one figure stood out just then and Weiss could not help but stare.

For those moments, her excruciating drawn-out death was forgotten. There were no flames, no embers licking at her. Just this woman before her. Passive. Unflinching. Beautiful like the sun in a waterfall.

Agatha was not sure if she had seen her alluring face before. But a burning canker deep within her mind told her it was Marise herself, come to take her away from this wretched life to face Caleb the Undead on the battleground of insanity.

She blinked and then the woman was gone – the last thing Agatha ever saw as the agony returned.

The flames blinded her in a fury of light and her skin began to roast.

Chapter 1

As if defying the uncompromisingly harsh winter, the Dambovita Citadel imposed itself upon the white landscape, a colossus of a place that had once sang out with a Wallachian voice.

Now occupied by the Ottoman Turks, it still retained its position as the commercial hub of the country. The additional military advantage of the Turks holding the Citadel as their own was something that the Wallachian forces, driven back to the palace at Târgoviste, were acutely aware of: they had fortified the Citadel themselves some years before.

Târgoviste was a good three days' ride north-west and the proximity of the two mighty armies had led to a stalemate, only punctuated by occasional skirmishes on the outlying provinces.

As a result, the Turks controlled much of the south and continually looked keenly northwards, waiting for the moment to strike, reinstate Basarab Laiota as the Prince of Wallachia and bring Vlad Dracula to his knees.

The janissaries and sipahis stationed permanently at Dambovita greeted the return of their commander, their *amir*, with all the honours befitting a man of his status.

It was a pity that Yozgatli Tanyel had little time for such pomp, but he recognised the positive effect it had on the men, all a long way from home and all suffering from the seemingly-permanent intense cold.

He briefly acknowledged their salutes and cheers as he dismounted.

His horse, as weary as he was, disappeared into the multitude of stables and smithies as it was led away by an attendant squire.

Tanyel shuddered through his thick furs as a biting wind whipped up and across the ramparts of the Citadel.

It was a typical Wallachian November, the chill intense, the sky a dull morose grey, even at this midday hour. They were still full with the Russian snows that had arrived early this year. It made him long even more for the warm breezes that coursed across the scimitar-shaped Golden Horn, the natural harbour laying east to the glory that was Constantinople.

Working his way swiftly through the maze of crowded streets, Tanyel paused at the great double doors that would convey him to the epicentre of his people's occupancy. To find solace within was paramount to him – but there was something incessantly wrong about seeking comfort in a place that still reeked of the Wallachian.

The two dutiful guards opened the court's doors to him. Tanyel ignored them as he passed through.

At once he was pounced upon by a bent, gnarled figure in shabby clothes, an apron covered in all manner of stains hanging loose from the flaccid neck. This was Isak, senior servant to the Governor and of such an age to have been witness to the building of this damnable place.

"Welcome, my Lord," the man croaked, bowing, "The Governor has been expecting you for at least an hour now."

As the doors thundered to a close behind him, shutting out the chill, Tanyel glared at the old man, his unfeeling eyes boring into Isak's watery pupils.

"We are both well aware of his need for punctuality," Tanyel spat. He didn't particularly care for this Isak. He had too much history and too many associates to be taken into any great confidence yet Tanyel had to admit that such a position was useful and Isak had certainly been forthcoming in the past about certain subjects.

"Indeed, sir. Shall I inform him of your arrival?" Isak shuffled across the stone floor to a second set of doors.

"No. That will not be necessary. If the Governor has been waiting for all that time, far be it for me to make him wait any longer."

Isak nodded and beckoned Tanyel to the inner doors. The old man struck them once with surprising strength and waited. A muffled reply came from within and Isak swung the heavy doors inwards.

Tanyel stepped through as Isak moved off to other duties. He was surprised to find the usually morose Governor Tarih-i-al-Osman laughing and talking animatedly with a man unknown to Tanyel – but who seemed to be very well acquainted with the Governor. They stood near a raised dais, on which rested four chairs: two obtusely carved thrones bookended by simpler, smaller affairs.

As Tarih-i-al-Osman finally noticed Tanyel standing in the doorway, he motioned the other man into silence, greeting Tanyel with open palms.

"Ah, Yozgatli," Tarih-i-al-Osman began, a slight lisp playing over his words, "come and sit with us. In a moment we eat."

"Governor...?" Tanyel began, eyeing the other man with caution.

"This, Tanyel, is Ismael. He honours us with his presence, bringing gifts from our home in Turkey."

The man named as Ismael bowed gracefully, his long face pale and clean shaven. His white eyes were shocking in their paleness.

"The honour is ours to welcome you, Ismael," Tanyel said, bowing in return. "May you bring happiness to our Citadel."

"And this, my friend, is the commander of my army: Lord Yozgatli Tanyel." Tarih-i-al-Osman patted both his visitors on their equally broad shoulders, motioning for them to sit. Ismael did so without hesitation behind the long wooden table, the centrepiece of the hall.

Tanyel was suspiciously wary of the man's casual demeanour. Trust was something earned with difficulty, Tanyel had long ago learnt, and this stranger from their homeland was no exception. Unfortunately, Tarih-i-al-Osman was notorious for confiding in too many people, a quality which made Tanyel sceptical of any new visitor to the Citadel, especially in the delicate climate of the Wallachian uprising. The Sultan, it seemed, had more faith in Tarih-i-al-Osman than was deemed necessary.

"I was just commenting to your Governor, Lord Tanyel, how impressive this architecture is," Ismael ventured, tilting his head slightly as he spoke and gesturing at the hall around him.

"Wallachian by design," Tanyel countered. "Surely you must be aware of that?"

"The Wallachians are undeniably talented, but have no logic when it comes to fortification." Tanyel shifted in his seat, looking away from the odd stare Ismael was giving him. "The *voivode* himself is responsible for most of the work here, yes?"

Tanyel suddenly stood, right hand at the hilt of his scimitar. "You will not talk of that Wallachian devil in the presence of the Governor."

Ismael, realising his error, immediately moved back in his seat, hands raised in a gesture of submission. "I wished no offence, my Lords. I was to merely note the clumsiness of the fortification. It is now seventeen years since the *voivode* made this the stronghold. We should be wary of its pitfalls."

"Are you suggesting that the Wallachians have an advantage?" Tarih-i-al-Osman offered, tapping the table with a knife, impatient more that his belly was growling than with Ismael's line of reasoning. "My army waits. There can be no threat from the Shipka Plains."

"You know of their whereabouts?" Ismael countered, eyes widening with the information.

Tanyel, ever cautious, stepped in before his count could reveal more information. "There was a sighting, nothing more. Bathory and the *voivode* have probably moved their armies on from there by now. We have no need to worry."

Ismael nodded again, as though absorbing the words with relish.

"There can be but such an insignificant threat to us. The superior Turkish army will not cower in front of merchants and barbarian kings." Tanyel returned Ismael's nod with a smile, the expression turning into an alert stare as the large double doors were suddenly flung open. High above them, in the rafters, the impressive wooden candelabra swung gently with the sudden rush of air.

Two thick-set soldiers burst through the wide doorway, dragging between them a dazed and bloodied smaller man. Breathing heavily under his weight, they staggered to a halt a few paces away from the table. Tanyel and Ismael rose simultaneously. Tarih-i-al-Osman followed suit a moment later.

"What is the meaning of this?" Tanyel growled, throwing the captive a poisonous glare. "Who is this man?"

"A Wallachian soldier, my Lord," gasped one of the new arrivals, a man-at-arms no older than the poor soul he had in his grip. "He was unconscious when we found him by the river."

"But why bring him here?" Tarih-i-al-Osman moved towards the captive, pushing the boy's head back with a grip of his chin. The young Wallachian's head lolled back on his chest as the Governor let go. "He is a worthless brute. I do not desire his company. Remove him."

"But my Lord..." the soldier endeavoured.

"You heard the Governor," Tanyel hissed, "take him away."

"But he has treasure," the soldier uttered hastily, lest he be punished for insubordination.

Tarih-i-al-Osman breathed out sharply between his teeth.

Tanyel looked sceptical. "What form does this treasure take, soldier?"

The Wallachian crumpled to the floor as the grip around his shoulders eased. Blood from his wounds seeped onto the stone.

Reaching into a sack on his back, the first soldier removed an object, the sight of which made even Tanyel gasp. It was a box no larger than a small loaf of bread adorned with intricate lines of silver, specific geometric shapes intertwined and crossing over each other and delicately worked into the highly polished mahogany surface.

The burning candles around the hall bounced their light off the object, giving it an odd glow, almost like a halo.

Tarih-i-al-Osman removed his right glove, tentatively reaching out to touch the object. Its surface was incredibly smooth, as if the markings weren't even there. The Governor, having the sensation as though fine sand was being poured over his fingertips, drew away from the object, instead kneeling at the shoulder of the Wallachian. He pushed the man over onto his back, the delirious man groaning.

"Where did you get this?" Tarih-i-al-Osman whispered, mouth close to the man's ear. He could feel his own warm breath bouncing off from the prone figure's skin as the man twitched. The man's bloodied, dry lips parted, as though he was attempting to speak. Tarih-i-al-Osman moved his own ear to the man's mouth, straining to hear.

"He will say nothing tonight," Ismael advised, waved quiet by Tanyel, also eager to know of this peculiar treasure's origins.

"It is a most dazzling sight." Tarih-i-al-Osman drew his lips back over blackened teeth in a smile, hypnotised by the object. "It is beautiful – a *kutu* unlike anything hoarded before from these savage Catholics."

"I agree, my Lord," Tanyel responded, taking the object from the first soldier's grasp. He weighed it between his large hands. "It is unlikely that the Catholics could produce such work."

Tarih-i-al-Osman nodded. The thought of presenting this to the Sultan sent a wave of excitement across his round shoulders. "This miserable soul must know of its history."

"A spell below will loosen his tongue," suggested Ismael. "If he is unwilling to talk then a more persuasive method will have to be adopted."

Tarih-i-al-Osman agreed, eager to submit the Wallachian to the kiss of the whip in the dungeons deep below them. Tanyel looked at Ismael from out of the corner of his eye. The stranger's comment did not seem to fit well coming from his mouth. It was as if this Ismael was trying to impress them.

"Take him away. Do with him what you will – after we have eaten, of course," Tarih-i-al-Osman said.

Tanyel raised an eyebrow. If anything, the Governor was infamous for his gargantuan feasts and he was not about to miss such an advantage.

Isak returned to the Hall with two full carafes of wine as the Wallachian prisoner was taken away. The wine lapped against the inside of the bottles as Isak shifted unsteadily on his bunyoned feet, glancing once, expressionless, in the prisoner's direction.

"Is he not too old?" Ismael commented to the Governor, not without the old servant's earshot.

"He has been in service here for many years. I would not even dare to dismiss lest the Citadel fall to dust!"

Tarih-i-al-Osman had grown fond of Isak, giving the old man certain privileges in the process. It was said that Isak was present when Radu and his older brother Vlad became enemies and that Radu rescued Isak from impalement, Isak in turn secreting Radu in Turkey until Vlad's rage had subsided.

The meal came and went and the wine flowed freely and the box now sat in the greasy palms of the corpulent Governor.

Tanyel, drawn to the object with a surprising desire, ran gloved fingers across the pitted surface of the long table. He eyed the *kutu* in Tarih-i-al-Osman's hands with envy. It was peculiar that such a treasure would have been protected by a mere foot soldier and Tanyel wondered if the Catholic had not actually stolen the box or - no, perhaps the *kutu* had *discovered* the Wallachian.

Yozgatli Tanyel frowned inwardly at the odd thought so dismissed the notion, turning his thoughts instead to the interrogation he would oversee once the wine had been consumed.

The Wallachian had been badly beaten and it was likely that the commander's men had been zealous in taking advantage of the Wallachian's solitude when they had found him. No matter, the commander shrugged, pulling a carafe near to fill his tankard full. The creature was only, after all, just a Catholic so it was of no consequence.

Chapter 2

"*Cogitatio stulti peccatum est et abominatio hominum detractor*. It is a deep laceration. But you are young and it will heal."

Brother Verrecchia cradled his left shin, trying to hide the tears from his elder. The young monk had a low pain threshold and the wound left him sobbing silently, not even the icy ground on which he was sitting detracting him. Yet he did feel foolish positioned there, amidst the thick snowfall that blanketed the dense, surrounding forest. A yellow moon was cowering behind the tops of the high trees, giving the deeper parts of the woodland a sickly glow. Branches drooped under the weight of the snow, like pale crests along the backs of knotted fingers. The biting wind whipped up, Verrecchia's shudder becoming real as he felt its cold caress.

Facing along the edge of a narrow stream, he had come close to ending his fall in that freezing stretch of water and, as he looked into it, he recognised his good fortune. Father Apollinari, kneeling by his young protégé, dabbed the wound with a handful of snow. He ripped a length of his habit away at the hem and bandaged Verrecchia's leg tightly. "The cold will pull the blood back into your body away from the opening and ease the bleeding. I suggest we collect our belongings and attempt to continue our journey."

"How much further have we to go?" asked Verrecchia, wincing with the sudden pressure.

Apollinari stood. He was a tall man - beyond six feet - and, from Verrecchia's prone position, he seemed much taller at that moment. "A day. Perhaps three now on foot."

Verrecchia did not like to complain, having learnt over these last few months that Apollinari had little tolerance for self pity. Instead he allowed himself to be helped up by the Abbot and be led back away from the stream. Apollinari slowed, cautious not to add strain to Verrecchia's injury. Up ahead, a wagon was positioned awkwardly by a rough path with one wheel shorn off. Apollinari peered over into the ditch running along the other side of the path. "The damage seems to be worse than we thought. We certainly took enough of a jolt. No wonder you were thrown clear. "

"Where's the wheel gone, Father?"

"It's not down there," Apollinari replied, nodding towards the stream. He returned his attention to the cart. "It may have rolled away."

Apollinari, circling the cart as Verrecchia wobbled unsteadily on his own, placed a hand on the wagon's snapped axle. He could feel the splintered wood against his palm.

"Careful, Father, please" warned Verrecchia. "It doesn't look very–"

The cart jolted and suddenly slipped off the road into the ditch with a loud crunch, causing Apollinari to stumble back. Clouds of light snow settled as it came to rest on its side. A flurry of birds went overhead, squawking in indignation at being disturbed from their roost.

"...sturdy." Verrecchia teetered and collapsed to the ground next to Apollinari, his wound getting the better of him.

"About as sturdy as you are. Are you alright?" Apollinari helped Verrecchia to the edge of the road, not far from the large boulder that had interrupted their progress when the cart struck it. Verrecchia nodded, a frown playing across his face as his leg throbbed. "It is no wonder in this meagre light that we couldn't avoid the obstacle. Still, we have come this far without any hindrance so we should perhaps be grateful."

Verrecchia nodded and breathed out slowly, looking back along the road in the direction that they had come from. The Basilica of the Holy Trinity of Saccargia nestled in a peaceful orchard towards the north of Sardinia seemed such a long way away now. He wondered if he would ever see his home again. They had been travelling for weeks, crossing many countries and forever heading east. It had only been since Bistritz, where Apollinari had left Verrecchia under the care of the local priest while he saw to other church duties for two days, that they had started to head in a more southerly direction. Apollinari had not spoken of events during those forty-eight hours and Verrecchia knew better than to ask.

As clouds in the night sky passed overhead, so the moon was able to give some light and, further along the road, to their right, Apollinari noticed movement around the curve of the track. The faint sound of spurs and hooves became louder. "It is as I thought. We appear to be on a main highway."

Verrecchia followed his gaze, making out five riders easing their mounts to a steady canter as they came into view.

"Do you think they'll be friendly?"

"That's more than one horse - and in unison, too. They could be soldiers and able to offer us some assistance," Apollinari responded, smiling. "There's only one way to find out."

The lead horseman pulled his ride to a stop in front of them, the beast whinnying.

"What is your business here?" the man bellowed, drawing his sword. He was a large man, but that could have been the thick furs and heavy cloak he was wearing over his armour. His face was ruddy with the cold, lips straight and taut. A heavy moustache curled over his mouth and down each side, stopping under his chin. Dark eyes peered at them from under the fur headgear.

By their uniforms, Apollinari reasoned they were not Turks.

"Good evening, my son. I am Father Apollinari from Saccargia. This is Brother Verrecchia."

"Hello," Verrecchia said, doing his best not to look worried as the horses gathered around them.

"What are you doing here?" the soldier asked again, wielding his sword threateningly.

Backing away slightly, Apollinari drew up to his full height. "We are headed for the monastery at Snagov. We have suffered an accident. Our cart. It lies at the bottom of this ditch." Apollinari motioned with a chilly hand to the wreck beneath them.

The soldier moved his sword to Apollinari's neck. "You have business at Snagov?"

Father Apollinari raised his arms. "We pose no threat if that is what you are asking."

"No one travels through Vlasie at this time of night." The soldier dismounted, ruby-red cloak flowing.

"We are on God's business," Verrecchia offered, voice quaking as he stood, trying to keep calm as a lower-ranking soldier checked the horse's reins. The monks' animal snorted.

"Absolutely," the Apollinari confirmed. "We mean no harm."

"If you have any sense then you will know that Vlasie is not fond of newcomers," the first soldier explained. "And the Turk is fond of keeping vigil in these forests. You should be careful who hears you preach the Lord's word."

"We will bear that in mind."

"I am a captain in the Prince's army, Alexandru Popescu."

"We are fortunate indeed to have been met by such an exemplary convoy. We have been travelling for a while and have become unsure of our surroundings," Apollinari stressed. "But you say this is Vlasie?"

"It is. You are not far from Snagov. You have an audience with the Abbot?"

"Yes, with Father Shandor. You are acquainted with him?"

"Not through choice." Popescu circled Apollinari as the monk helped Verrecchia to his feet. "How is it that you know him?"

"I have never personally met the Abbot before but we have exchanged letters."

"Are you senior to him?"

"At Snagov, Father Shandor remains at the head. But any news from the Vatican I am able to impose upon him."

"You come from the Pope?" Popescu squinted at him for a moment then motioned for his men to retreat.

He remounted his horse, sword sheathed once more. "These roads are treacherous. Cut-throats abound. We will escort you to Snagov."

"You are most kind."

"Kindness has nothing to do with it, Father Apollinari. The Prince demands the curfew is maintained."

Apollinari took none of Popescu's bravado with any great concern. The monk was nearing the end of his third decade and had seen far too many military commanders come and go. This Popescu was no different and his attitude was bullish. Nevertheless he seemed efficient and soon his men had secured the monks' weary horse to one of their own.

Apollinari felt the cold more these days and was silently relieved that their journey to Snagov would be made a little easier by Popescu's presence. Pulling his cowl up and around his greying temples, Apollinari hauled himself up into the back of the covered wagon that formed part of Popescu's caravan. Verrecchia struggled up behind him. The younger man looked at the hooded monk and Apollinari sensed a question was about to form.

"Who is the Prince, Father?"

Grey eyes steeled either side of a strong Roman nose. The neatly trimmed beard crinkled slightly as Apollinari pursed his lips. "The Prince, young Roberto, is a formidable Wallachian leader in these parts. His notoriety precedes him but one cannot discount the fact that the towns and cities are safer places since he reclaimed the throne."

"Why?"

"Because no one dares to defy his wrath. His lands remain secure."

With a few muffled shouts and the stomping of hooves on the frozen ground, the caravan moved off.

"But Popescu said that the Turks and bandits roamed the forest. Surely that will make our undertaking far harder?"

"Policing the outskirts of the towns is never an easy task. Look at how we were warned off in Hungary."

"No robber would dare steal from a monk!"

"Oh, Roberto, if only I had your naivety!" Apollinari laughed and placed a hand on Verrecchia's shoulder. "I'm afraid the average bandit has little to fear from attacking God's messengers. But have no fear yourself. We shall be safe enough with Popescu and his men. Sit back and watch the sunrise."

With that, Apollinari settled back against the heavy trunks in the back of the wagon and closed his eyes, opening one again briefly to watch Verrecchia shuffle where he sat to see more clearly the world go by. All thoughts of Verrecchia's wounded leg were gone for that moment while twilight slowly came upon them.

In a deeper part of the Vlasie, the gentle rhythmic tapping of the pots suspended from either side of the gypsy caravan heralded the ever-onwards motion of the small procession that cut a trail through the thick woods on the outskirts of Târgoviste.

It was a garishly-painted affair, albeit faded and peeling after years of exposure to the Wallachian elements. Its curved roof was green and black with either mould or dirt or both, the true colour underneath it long since obscured.

Now that winter had enveloped the land, very little was disturbed by the clattering of the caravan. Hibernation insured the relative peace and protection required by the forest's mammalian summer creatures: only the birds and insects left to forage, save for the large animals, the family of which included the grey wolf among its denizens. But even they knew to steer clear of the incumbent dangers, afraid of the strangeness and unpredictability of human-kind that often ventured deep into the trees. Little did they realise, of course, that man was more often than not fearful of them than the wolves were of man. Man was also considerably more unwary of the wolves' intuition and carefully plotted hunting grounds.

Only occasionally, when it was necessary, did the wolves dare to approach the habitat of these bigger creatures: when food became short and less easy to track, especially during the winter months.

As dawn came slowly upon the day, so the wolves gathered, calling to each other with that unnerving yet strangely compelling howl, recognising the possibility of a catch as the caravan slowed to a halt. The icy clearing was large, yet still overshadowed by the monolithic trees.

Bruno, the wagon's driver, jumped down from his perch and reached for his cudgel.

"Mr Zucco!" he called, walking along the side of the once brightly painted wagon, snow crunching underfoot. "Mr Zucco!"

"Yes, yes," a muffled response came, from within the caravan, and the occupant poked a red bulbous nose from out of the shutters to the rear. "I'm not deaf."

"Are you sure staying here will be safe?"

"Hobgoblins and what-have-you don't frighten me," Zucco scolded, easing his great bulk out and onto the

ladder at the foot of the entrance. He pulled the heavy blanket tighter around his shoulders. "See to the horses."
Bruno hurried back to the tired horses, hooking nose bags over both of them, all the while cautiously glancing around him. The dark trees loomed, and the howl of a lone wolf sent a shiver down the superstitious spine of the gypsy.
Zucco stepped onto the ground and headed towards Bruno, striking the curved wall of the caravan with enough force to wake the dead.

"Come on, wake up you old bitch!" he called, halting in his tracks, and curled fat fingers over his belt. "We're stopping here for a night."
When no response was met, he struck the caravan again, this time causing colourful language to emanate from inside. His long-suffering wife hit back from within, cursing Zucco's parentage, and eventually removed herself into the clearing.
A skewed ginger wig atop her head and thick, greasy make-up smudged beyond any recognisable signs of glamour, Marta Zucco glared at the sloping back of her husband. "What's all the bellowing for? This place always looks the bloody same to me."

"Everywhere looks the same to you." Zucco turned, ignoring his wife's constant snarling glare, and headed towards the second wagon fixed behind the first. The heavy sheet fixed over it did not easily disguise the fact that it was a cage on wheels. Nor did the drape deaden the clatter of the obese man's cane against the bars. "Wake up! Wake up! Can't have you sleeping all day. You could be dead in there."
Nothing appeared to stir from the cage, so Zucco called out again.

"Leave him alone, Ygor," Mrs Zucco retorted. "The poor little devil'll be frightened half out of his skin before you're through."

"As long as he can perform, I don't really care." Zucco continued to strike the cage until a shuffling could be heard through the sacking.

"That's better. Alive after all, eh?" Zucco looked back towards his wife, whose face was still framed in a wrinkled glare. "And what are you looking at?"

Marta pulled her tattered shawl over her shoulders. "It's cold out here. Where's the fire?"

"Bruno!" Zucco bellowed.

"Yes, Mr Zucco?" Bruno sheepishly returned.

"Get the stove going."

"Right away, Mr Zucco," the servant said, placing his cudgel against a shoddy wheel. Bruno moved off towards a small collection of felled branches nearby.

"And Bruno...get some dinner."

Bruno frowned, not in the least bit happy about his last order. Getting dinner meant venturing into the woods, and even moving to get a fire started didn't ease his worries about the surroundings.

A short distance away, closer to the caravan than the wolf was comfortable with, the beast eyed the three humans warily. One had moved away, and the other two seemed to be engaged in some sort of communication.

The wolf's interpretation failed to register this as a heated argument between a husband and his wife who were more than sick of the sight of each other, yet both stubborn, and probably too insecure, to walk away from the wedlock.

Padding gently along a fallen trunk, the wolf sat, yellow eyes glinting in the dusk. The first of the three humans had constructed a fire now, and had set off again, this time further away from the other two. The wolf took this as an opportunity not to be missed, so howled long and deep, instructing his pack to advance.

The lone human stopped to look around him and gripped his cudgel with white knuckles, perfectly willing to return to the camp and lie to Zucco about not having found a scrap of anything edible.

But Zucco saw Bruno pause through piggy eyes, and bellowed after his servant, causing both Bruno and the advancing wolf to tense. Bruno swallowed hard and nodded back towards Zucco, who uttered some curse that was too inaudible for Bruno to make out.

Stepping forward, Bruno shuddered at the thought of going any deeper into the trees. Nevertheless in he went and the air closed around him.

The animals had sense, Bruno decided as he took out his dagger, to stay as far away from the ogre Zucco as possible. How wrong Bruno was.

The wolf lunged and all Bruno saw was the flash of teeth and claws, a snarl in his face followed by the dank breath of the animal. Hitting the ground with force, Bruno attempted to regain his breath and slice at the wolf, but he was far too slow, and within seconds the first wolf had been joined by others.

The man screamed as glistening teeth and razor-like claws ripped through his threadbare clothes and into his flesh. Continuing to scream, Bruno was soon entirely smothered by fur and blood, unable to even move, but just lay there and be torn to shreds. His knife lay unused in the snow, inches from his twitching fingers.

“What’s that damn idiot servant of yours up to this time?” Zucco spat towards his wife, who shrugged.

"Hadn't you better go and look?"

Zucco waved a nonchalant hand in Bruno's general direction; himself more scared of the dark woods than Bruno. "He's probably been given the shakes by a rabbit. He'll be back in a moment, and he better have some dinner or I'll skin him alive."

Even if the threat had meaning, there would have been no need for Zucco to do so, for the wolves had done the job for him.

Dead now. Bruno's mutilated body was no longer in one piece, body parts scattered all and sundry in the frantic kill. The attack was easy, but the victim was unable to sustain the entire pack. The first wolf growled from the bottom of his blood-drenched throat and moved off towards the camp. Others followed, circling the clearing, the danger of the fire dismissed from their focus.

"What's up with you, then?" Zucco called out towards the hooded cage, as the bars shook violently. Its inhabitant seemed to sense the impending danger, but was unable to make the idiot Zucco understand. Suddenly the covering was flung back from the cage, and Zucco's swollen face leered in. "A bit uppity, my lovely, are we? Bruno frighten you with his squealing, did he?"

The inhabitant, whose home was the tiny cage, let out a stifled cry as two wolves appeared on the edge of the clearing and swung back and forth on the bars. Zucco remained oblivious to the warnings.

"Perhaps he wants some exercise, Ygor," Marta offered, grinning at the cage with blackened teeth. "He's been chained up in there for days."

"You don't know what you're talking about, woman. He's an animal. Has no idea of what he wants."

"I wouldn't be so sure, Ygor. He looks a bit agitated. What do you reckon?"

Marta pursed her lips, and made a noise towards the cage as though she was comforting a small child.

"Well, a couple of minutes, I suppose. But no more. Can't have him spoilt. Useless to us then, he'll be."

Marta clapped her hands gleefully as Zucco unlocked the cage door, tying the inhabitant's long collar around a bar.

"Don't worry about that, Ygor, he's not going to run off. Are you my pet?"

The inhabitant smiled at Marta and the old woman scrunched up her wart-covered nose. With the cage door wide open, and the collar loose, the way was clear. But there was hesitation and a fearful look beyond the Zuccos to the wolves.

"Now what's up? Door's open but he won't budge. Stupid animal."

Zucco poked his cane through the bars just as he heard his wife scream. Spinning to face her, he stood, fat jaws agape, as a large grey wolf bounded towards him. This time Zucco screamed and fumbled to close the cage door. But his fingers were cold and they struggled to grip the lock.

The wolf skidded to a halt a few feet away, as if hesitant to come any closer. It looked beyond the man and into the cage. It didn't like what it saw. A deep growl entered its throat.

"Bruno! Bruno! Where are you, you miserable scrote?" Still holding onto the cage door, Zucco kicked out at the wolf while scanning their surroundings for any sign of Bruno. "Get out of here! Away! Away! Marta, get back inside..."

The wolf turned its attention to the woman.

"Slowly!" Zucco hissed.

Marta shuffled ungainly back into the caravan, heavy pleated skirts held tightly in a knarled fist. The wolf watched her as three more of the pack slowly padded towards them, eyes bright and alert.

"Ygor, don't you go do nothing stupid now."

"Just get inside and shut the door." He gingerly let go of the cage and raised his hands to the wolves. "See? Nothing here. Nothing to eat."

The nearest wolf bared its fangs and growled again and its companions quickened their pace and began bounding across the clearing.

"Blessed Marise, help me!" Zucco yelled and threw his arms to cover his face.

A loud *crack* reverberated around the clearing as the wolves dropped back, startled. Panting and hungry, they still kept their prey in sight.

The noise echoed again and the wolves scampered some distance away. A third sounding and the animals finally retreated back into the forest.

Zucco exhaled hard, his breath visible in the icy air. Unable to comprehend how close he had come to being torn apart where he stood, he looked out to the trees and could have sworn he had seen a woman looking straight back at him, long dark tresses clutching at her shoulders. If it hadn't been such an absurd picture, he would have sworn that the wolves were sitting calmly at her ankles as though they were domesticated dogs.

But as soon as Zucco remembered to blink, both the woman and the wolves had gone.

Chapter 3

As dawn rose, Popescu's squad moved steadily east, the covered wagon flanked on either side by ten mounts, their riders wearing full battle dress.

The soldiers' head-dress, nowhere near as elaborate and outstanding as Popescu's with its curves and ornaments, consisted simply of a three-piece metal helmet and chain mail from the back falling over their shoulders across a thick fur tunic. Underneath a breast plate glinted in the dawn sun. Heavy leather trousers kept their thighs and legs warm and protected, strong knee-length boots gripping either side of their horses. Their swords swung at their sides, smaller knives present only at their owners' choice.

The wagon, pulled along by a pair of horses, one behind the other, dipped and rocked as they moved north along the uneven Wallachian plains. The monks' horse was tethered behind.

Apollinari, attempting to stay upright in the rear of the wagon, wedged himself against the heavy trunks and tapped one with strong fingers.

"What are these boxes for, Father?"

The wagon lurched again as a pothole was avoided.

"They're coffers to pay for the military. It's customary for the rich to subsidise the war and I would be surprised if these chests aren't full to the brim with jewels, gold – anything of value that the Wallachian tax collectors can take from the Boyars."

From without the wagon, Popescu called for the entourage to halt.

"What's going on?"

"I don't know, Roberto. Stay here."

With that, Apollinari jumped out from the back of the cart more agilely than Verrecchia would have given the older monk credit for.

Apollinari knew Popescu would not entertain a conversation about why they had stopped so suddenly. Resigned to his ignorance, he took in his surroundings.

Snow had left the ground white, trees and bushes sparse and bare. Up ahead, the arc of the Carpathians rose like a great spined beast, the pinnacle of each mountain lost in the clouded, snowy atmosphere.

There was a sudden flash of movement in the skeletal woodland. Apollinari strained his eyes to see, convinced that the movement was not an animal.

He glanced at Popescu to see if anyone else had noticed. There was nothing to indicate they had but, nevertheless, Popescu's men had their arbalests drawn and were scanning the distance.

"Move forward. Cover the wagon."

Popescu's order was immediately carried out as foot soldiers, flanked by half the mounted troops, fanned out across the plain. Apollinari pulled his cowl up around his head as the biting wind ripped through him. Suddenly a cry from one of the foot soldiers drew the others to him, including Apollinari. Popescu pulled his horse up to where they grouped.

"What is it?"

A lieutenant, lowering his arbalest, turned to face his captain. "It's a body, my Lord."

"A vagabond's?"

The lieutenant crouched by the dismembered figure lying on blood-tainted snow. Amid the torn flesh and caked robes, flashes of gold appeared. The robes themselves were heavy, embroidered and deep-coloured.

"A nobleman. He has his gold about him still."

"Not attacked for his wealth, then."

"Wolves have had him."

Apollinari knelt on his haunches next to the lieutenant. "No. I don't think so."

"Look at his wounds. He's been ripped apart. There's a leg over there."

Apollinari followed Popescu's pointing sword with a frown, then looked back at the corpse before them.

"That is what we're meant to think, Captain Popescu." He pulled back the robes to reveal an open chest, organs raw and congealed. "There are no teeth marks, no claw marks. And he's not been eaten."

"Killed, dismembered but not robbed. Why?"

"This is the main trade route to Târgoviste. He's been left here as a sign."

"For who?"

"Superstitious locals. To frighten them off. To stop them returning this way."

Popescu dismounted, his armour clunking as he hit the ground. "Avoiding this road would add half a day's ride."

"There's no blood around him. Only that which has since seeped out beneath where he lays. He didn't die in this spot. He was brought here." Apollinari stood and stretched his back. Removing his hood and rubbing the back of his neck, he met Popescu's eye. "What would be the benefit of delaying traders, travellers, whoever?"

"A more circuitous route would take them through the deeper parts of the forest. At night, that would not be a welcome proposition. Târgoviste relies on its trading."

"No traders, no buyers, no Târgoviste."

"Indeed. This is the Turk's doing. Word would have spread of this corpse already. Remove it, lieutenant, all of it. Put it on the back of the wagon."

Before Apollinari could respond, the dead boyar had been collected up. The Abbot rushed back to the wagon and retook his seat by the patient Verrecchia.

"Roberto, if you are squeamish, you may need to spend the rest of our journey deep in meditation. And with your eyes closed."

"Why, Father? What is-"

The gruesome corpse and its separated limb flew up in the back of the cart and came to a rest with a heavy thump atop the caskets. Verrecchia scrabbled back in horror but there was little place to retreat to in the cramped rear of the wagon.

"A fellow passenger," Apollinari murmured. "At least he'll be quiet."

The Wallachian prisoner raised his head, the raw skin across his shoulders burning. Manacled by wrists and neck to the cold, damp wall of a cell, his raised arms had gone numb. He had been whipped, beaten and humiliated by the guards permanently stationed in the dungeon. He had never been asked any questions.

But now Tanyel had arrived, sweeping into the cell after a murmured conversation in the corridor outside with the chief gaoler. In a gloved hand he grasped a poker. It hissed as its orange tip met with Tanyel's spittle.

The resultant steam formed crescents in the air as the large man swung the iron in tight circles

"Count Tarih-i-al-Osman prefers the lash. This, however, is much more effective."

"What do you want of me?" the Wallachian croaked, blood clogging the back of his throat. "I cannot offer you anything."

"On the contrary, you have many things to offer us." Tanyel lunged forward with the iron causing the prisoner to flinch back, striking his head on the rough wall. "... such as the origin of your gift."

"I found it," he gasped, "I know nothing of its history."

"Do you expect me to believe that?"

"It's true. I saw a light..."

"A light?" Tanyel outlined the young soldier's features with the poker inches away from his captive's face. "Are you prone to such visions?"

The Wallachian blinked his good eye, following Tanyel across the room as the captain returned the iron to the coals.

"What's your name?" Tanyel sat on a stool positioned some feet away. "I'm afraid the masters here have very little time for small talk. More inclined to get on with things, so to speak."

"Rintoul," croaked the prisoner.

"Tell me, Rintoul...are you aware that we know of your army's location? It would take very little time for my men to capture some of your fellow soldiers." Tanyel removed the poker again, moving back towards the soldier. "Perhaps they will be more...forthcoming in their answers."

"It was only I who found it. The others did not come with me."

"That bodes well," Tanyel laughed. "A Wallachian contingent not aware of its own men's movements. Still, it would be no effort to remove some of them."

"No, they don't know," Rintoul insisted. He flinched away from Tanyel again, the manacles cutting into his flesh. "Do what you will with me. I can tell you no more."

"Oh, but I think you can. You see, I can be very persuasive when I want to be." Tanyel clenched Rintoul's bruised neck with his free hand and pressed the poker against his mouth. The Wallachian screamed, the iron burning his tongue, his lips. His vision blurred, seeing only an orange glow and hearing nothing but his own laboured breathing.

Tanyel replaced the poker in the fire, dusting his hands down on his tunic.

"Do you see now how I get what I want?"

Rintoul shook, his throbbing jaw hanging open. All he could think of now was the man standing before him with that wretched smile, and, if he were free, how he would sink his fingers into his eye sockets. He opened both eyes and began to sob, a whine building around his vocal chords.

The chief gaoler came into the cell just then, Rintoul's cry rising through the dank, narrow corridors.

"My Lord, do you wish me to stay?" The squat, stocky man, whose neck was as wide as his bald head glared at Rintoul, the prisoner shuddering and lurching against his manacles.

Tanyel thought about this for a moment then shook his head. "No. He can cause little harm. A few pitiful cries can do no wrong."

"Very well, my Lord."

"Ah, but one thing..."

"Yes, my Lord," Ekvan replied before he left the cell.

"A drink. Wine for me and something more... *interesting* for our guest."

Some moments later a guard appeared with a tankard of wine in one hand and a jug of brewed henbane in the other. The wine he gave to Tanyel, who downed it swiftly and carelessly, the henbane he placed carefully on the damp floor against the wall.

Wiping his mouth and chin, Tanyel thrust the tankard back into the soldier's grip.

"More."

The guard rushed away, leaving Tanyel alone with Rintoul once more. He lifted the jug from the floor and sniffed at its contents. It was vile to say the least and reminded Tanyel of the sickly-sweet aroma of putrefying flesh.

In a swift movement, Tanyel had Rintoul by the jaw and began pouring the liquid into his mouth. Rintoul gagged and wrestled his head from Tanyel's grip, spitting the henbane into his captor's face.

"Drink!" Tanyel hissed and tried again.

Rintoul tried to crane his neck but Tanyel's grip was firm. Rintoul allowed some of the henbane into his mouth and stopped struggling. Tanyel nodded and stepped back – but was immediately showered again by Rintoul's further expectoration.

Angry, Tanyel struck Rintoul across the jaw with his free hand. "You *will* drink!"

"You drink it..." Rintoul gasped. "You drink the filth!"

Tanyel ordered Rintoul to be unchained from the wall and taken to a larger part of the dungeon where he could be held flat, prone and unable to move.

"Now we will see who will drink this..."

On his back on a heavy wooden table and fixed down by six guards, Rintoul had little choice now as Tanyel poured the henbane into his mouth. Clamping Rintoul's jaw tight shut with both hands, Tanyel cracked Rintoul's head hard on the table causing Rintoul to gasp and swallow the vile concoction, choking him as it passed his scorched lips and tongue.

Tanyel released his grip. "Hang him back up."

Chapter 4

One of the largest monasteries in the Wallachian principalities, Snagov stood proud on its own island, its walls encompassing the entire body of land from length to width.

Foreboding in its size, the buildings proper were built by slaved zyganies and toppled boyars to be impregnable, their blood and pain mixed with the daub holding the massive supporting stones in place.

In addition to the main chapel, there were cloisters for meditation, dormitories for the monks and farms and outbuildings for visiting dignitaries. A prison, little used, stood away from the main complex. A solitary watch-tower containing a small bell overlooked the whole island. It was from this watchtower that Popescu's entourage was seen coming through the thinning woodland to the nearest opposite bank to the island. The wooden ferry brought it over the lake from the mainland, a slow process carried out time and again.

Eventually, once it was safe on the island, the caravan circled to a stop in the main courtyard. The drawbridge connected to the jetty rose back to its secure place flush against the exterior wall.

From an outbuilding came a large built man in his fifties, his habit fitting well across his wide shoulders and rounded belly. A well-tended grey beard, the only hair on his head save for his bushy eyebrows, covered his strong jaw below a beaky nose. Startling blue eyes looked out, ever inquisitive, from his lined face.

Those eyes came to rest on Apollinari who was climbing out of the back of the covered wagon but soon shifted to Popescu who, by this time, has dismounted his horse.

"Welcome back," the man intoned, the biting wind coursing across the island taking his breath away. He grasped Popescu by the arm. "Are you collecting stray monks, now?"

Popescu glared at Apollinari who was engrossed in dusting himself down. Verrecchia looked nervous, unsteady, never having been one to enjoy being on water. "These we found on the road through Vlasie. They appear to have gotten lost." Popescu leaned in close to the man. "The elder of the two has...a way about him. A way that isn't usual for your kind."

The large man thought for a moment and clasped his hands together in front of him. "Welcome strangers."

"Ah," Apollinari began, lowering his hood, "you must be Abbot Shandor. I'm Father Apollinari from Saccargia. My companion here is Brother Verrecchia. You're not expecting us but I am here bringing news from Bistritz."

The Abbot shook Apollinari's hand warmly and smiled at both the new arrivals. "News that concerns us here at Snagov? Please, tell on."

Apollinari looked around him, glancing at Popescu briefly. "This is Church business, Shandor."

"Ah, yes. We may be more comfortable inside."

Popescu's anger flashed in his eyes, but he knew, though a series of mistakes as a young lieutenant, that it was not right to question a Holy Father's decisions while on consecrated ground. He gritted his teeth and watched the three penitents walk towards the main building, taking no notice of the watchtower bell that had just started ringing to notify the monastery of more visitors wishing to cross to the island.

Sipping at a large bowl of warm milk, Apollinari made himself comfortable at the lengthy table in the refectory, its top white with years of determined scrubbing. The great fireplace behind him was already blazing like a forge, the day's bread baking in the huge oven. Apollinari breathed in deeply, savouring the aroma of the rising dough.

"I do not wish to prevaricate," he said, wiping away milk from his top lip with an index finger. "I have been asked to come here by Bishop Sigmirului."

Shandor frowned, shifting away from the fireplace's mantel against which he was leaning.

"It seems he has a problem which requires some careful attention."

"How does that concern me? We have little to do with Bistritz here. We do not share flock and I only know the Bishop by reputation."

"Nevertheless, he seems to consider his problem to also be yours."

"And yours too, if he has involved you. I hasten to suggest that the Bishop's problems are financial."

Apollinari smiled through sips, placing the earthenware bowl back on the table with a clunk. From the thick folds of his habit he produced a letter, rolled and sealed with wax. "Surely men in our position have little use for such conceit?"

"Our order cannot survive on faith alone. It costs to maintain our existence." Shandor sat in a vacant chair and took the letter offered to him. "But the Bishop is notorious for his...*spending*."

Apollinari watched Shandor break the seal and absorb the content of the letter, noticing furrows of worry cross his face. Silently, Shandor rolled up the letter and placed it on the fire. The two holy men watched it curl and crumble to ash.

Shandor clasped his hands together and stared for quite a long while at Apollinari, who was more than happy to continue drinking his milk.

As he drained the last few drops, Apollinari looked up at Shandor. "There are some things you have to reveal, aren't there? Some things you've had to keep to yourself for some time."

Shandor looked pained. This Apollinari was oddly perceptive. He wondered if he could trust him. Yet if Shandor tried to keep silent, he had a feeling that Apollinari would not leave it at that. "Come with me."

As they left the kitchen, the smell of baking bread slowly receded. Apollinari followed Shandor down a series of corridors and narrow passageways, always sloping gently downwards. They eventually reached a pair of narrow double doors.

"There is nothing untoward happening amongst the order, my brother, but in the world many new things are occurring," Shandor said finally, as he removed a set of keys from under his robes, chose one in particular and unlocked the right door. He waved Apollinari forward, the younger man frowning at the Abbot as he darted into the gloom.

Shandor handed him a burning torch from behind the door, keeping another one for himself. Waving it carefully around him, Apollinari could just make out the thick, swollen buttresses evenly spaced across the cavern. Deducing that they were in the deepest part of the monastery, he pushed against one of the supports, the stone ice cold under his palm.

"A wine cellar?" Apollinari commented.

"Not quite."

Shandor pointed across the low-ceilinged room. Following the direction of the Abbot's finger, Apollinari headed off, to arrive at an antechamber, its walls a different pallor to the main cavern. The ceiling was higher and Apollinari's torch picked out the bases of a series of iron cradles along the three walls. Placing his torch in the nearest one, Shandor doing likewise, Apollinari's eyes became accustomed to the sudden brightness the higher flames projected.

"Are we under the lake now?"

"Yes. The island is littered with catacombs that fan out beyond the island's perimeter."

With shadows bouncing around him in the claustrophobic chamber, he could clearly make out, along the opposite wall to the doorway, a collection from what seemed like a museum's storeroom. Lengths of carved wood were stacked in the corner, ornately decorated wooden chests and equally bland crates became surrogate tabletops for an incredible array of the most beautiful gold and silver goblets and plates Apollinari had ever seen. He tentatively picked up a small chalice, an incredibly smooth finish under his touch.

"No wonder you keep these hidden from view." He replaced the goblet. To the right of the crates he noticed more treasures: foot long statuettes, ornamental daggers, a perfect crystal replica of a human skull, the light from the flames dancing across its curved surface. Apollinari took a look at the vaulted ceiling, following the line back into the main cavern. "What is this place used for?"

"We keep the boyars' riches here when our enemies strike," Shandor explained, pulling a torch back from out of its cradle. "The Turks currently infest Dambovita."

"I take it Popescu bringing more treasures for you to store implies a battle is soon to be had?" Apollinari questioned, following Shandor across to the double doors.

"That is not for me to assume," Shandor said while swinging open the doors. "But our Prince does intend to reclaim the throne of Wallachia from the Sultan. The outcome is clear. The Turks will be forced out."

"But why show me all this?" asked Apollinari, arms wide. "Are you implying Sigmirului has less than you? Boasting does not become you, Shandor."

"No, no. Not at all. As I said, we have collected these treasures on behalf of the boyars. We know exactly what is in here – except that." Shandor raised his torch and Apollinari saw, against the far wall, a wooden box taller, wider and longer than any of the others.

Apollinari's voice caught in his throat. Swallowing hard, he could not speak and hoped Shandor had not noticed his agitation. He tried to remain calm as he stepped forward, his body throwing an undulating shadow across the box itself. The monk clasped his hands together to stop them from shaking but he wanted to reach out and touch it. He coughed twice to clear his throat.

"Have you tried to open it?" He hoped Shandor hadn't. That privilege he wanted for himself.

Shandor stood next to him and moved his palm gently across the casket. Apollinari wanted o pull Shandor's hand away but keep a tight grip on his own.

"It's sealed," Shandor replied. "it defies all attempts."

Apollinari was inwardly relieved. "When did your monks bring it here?"

"They didn't."

Apollinari frowned "Then how did you come by it?"

"I sent Brother Aret down here for our regular weekly inventory. He came back and reported its arrival."

"Clearly it passed the through without your knowledge."

"No. Between myself and Aret, everything that enters and leaves this chamber is accounted for. No other monk recalls it arriving."

Apollinari turned away from the crate but felt his gaze being drawn to it. "Who beyond the brotherhood know about these caverns?"

"None. It is part of our order to maintain our privacy. The boyars trust us to guard their treasures but do not know where we store them."

"Then you have an infiltrator, Shandor. Someone who knows and likes your security and privacy."

In a small clearing in the woods, hidden from view from the open Wallachian plains, a fire was burning. Over the heat, a boar roasted slowly, its juices dribbling over the flames that spat and jumped in reaction.

A woman leant over the boar, tearing off a piece of charred flesh with filthy hands. Ravenously, she bit into the dry meat. While it tasted more of charcoal than pork, it had been the first meat the group had caught in some days so she was grateful for any taste other than berries and vegetables.

She knew she was being watched but, as one of four siblings she had grown up accustomed to a lack of solitude. Claudia was naturally blonde, as tall as the average man and considered herself to always have been older than she actually was.

Behind her, Refik leant against a tree. He found her presence uncomfortable but was willing to tolerate her for as long as she was useful. He had to admit that her contributions had been rewarding for them but wondered how far she would go. He moved towards her, knowing that his manner and attitude towards her put her on edge. This he enjoyed, the toying with her, pushing her to react.

"Woman," he began, seeing her form tense, "share the meat will you. The fat will make you ugly if you take it all for yourself."

As much as she hated rising to his taunts, Claudia found it difficult to ignore them. "Then perhaps you'll be in good company. But you know the rules: whoever finds food eats first. I wonder why you have never eaten first, Refik?"

Claudia stood, throwing her piece of meat into the fire. She sighed quietly, making sure Refik didn't notice. She'd been here for longer than she cared to remember, living with these bandits. As Refik stared at her, a leer across his scarred face, she recalled her first day here, after she had woken in the forest; the last thing she remembered being asleep on her bed.

It had been a cold morning and, disorientated, she'd stumbled into the clearing where the bandits were hiding out. They'd surrounded her, swearing, laughing, and pushing her around. A few punches and kicks had ensured she was soon bound tight.

"What are you going to do with me?" Claudia had spat, wondering why she had even bothered to enquire when the outcome was likely. One of the bandits - the one she assumed was the leader - spread his arms wide and theatrically bowed.

"What would you have us do with you, fair lady?" he returned, laughing with the others. "A prize such as you would be hard to relinquish, especially one that has walked so carefree into our world."

"We'll keep her," another bandit proffered. "Who will miss her?"

"What if she's somebody important?" came an intelligent point to the rear of the group. "They might come looking for her."

"We can bargain. Get jewels," the second bandit suggested.

"What if she's the Sultan's bride?" Chants of disapproval spun around the circle. "Or the *voivode*'s current favourite?"

At this, the group fell into hushed whispers. Even as outlaws, they knew that crossing the Prince was capital enough to warrant impalement. Stealing his monies was bad enough, but to take his woman as well?

Claudia had detected an air of uncertainty as the group played this game around her. She played back as best she could.

"What will become of you when he finds out you have harmed me?" She left the thought hanging in the early morning air.

"She bluffs," the second man blurted. "She wants us to let her go."

"Well of course she does, idiot," the leader chided. "But what if she's telling the truth?"

"Kill her now and be done with it." The second bandit pulled his leader away from the main group. "Jurat, we can dump her body. Nobody will know."

"The Wallachians will," Jurat advised. "If she *is* important, Popescu will be sent to reclaim her. But she is a treasure though, I must admit."

"Popescu is a coward." Refik glared at Claudia over Jurat's broad shoulders. "We should use her as we please and then..." He made a cut-throat gesture, ensuring Claudia saw it.

"Yet perhaps your first suggestion is more worthwhile." Refik frowned. "But that was before we knew she might be the *voivode*'s."

"We can return her to Popescu ourselves - and come away heavier in purse."

"Popescu will not agree to that. You know how he bargains. He would slit our throats as soon as she is under his guard." Refik snatched a piece of meat from a colleague. At his colleague's complaint, Refik struck the man across the face will a gloved hand. "He will be in better favour with the *voivode* if he manages to kill us."

"Do you doubt our own skills? We can easily escape Popescu's men. Look at how we ambushed his own caravans in the past."

"I don't trust him," Refik stated, closing the chest and sitting heavily. "And neither should you."

Jurat nodded in silent agreement. Once a confidant of Popescu's, their friendship had been shattered over a mistake Popescu blamed Jurat for.

"It was a long time ago, Refik," Jurat whispered.

"Time has not healed this wound," Refik stated. "You did not kill him when we had the chance before. Why don't you save us all from this maudlin and end his life?"

"There will be chances again, I'm sure," Jurat reasoned. To change the subject, he moved towards Claudia. He gently touched her right cheek, feeling her soft hair against his fingertips. Smiling, Jurat leaned close to her and whispered: "I will let nothing harm you, not even Refik."

Claudia frowned, surprised by his words. This was an odd change of mood and she was unsure whether to trust him. "I'm relieved to hear it," she responded, just as quietly. "So am I being set free?"

"Unfortunately not. You are far too valuable to me."

"You?" Claudia glanced around her at the other bandits, especially Refik still seated on the chest. "What about the others?"

"They are cut-throats," he said, looking beyond Claudia at the forest, his eyes glazed. "I do not belong to them. They mean nothing to me."

"But they look up to you, don't they?" She glanced at Refik, not sure that this was true in his case. "You are their leader, Jurat. Don't you owe them something no matter how barbaric they may be?"

"I have helped them gain wealth through our ambushes. That's all."

"But what can you do with the money? Surely the boyars and the hierarchy know you to be thieves? You can't spend it here." Claudia raised her bound wrists to Jurat. "Please untie me. I can't exactly go anywhere now, can I?"

"I suppose not," Jurat agreed. "And you do speak wisely."

Jurat introduced himself and Claudia did likewise as she rubbed her aching wrists.

Refik stood.

"What are you doing?" he spat, grabbing Claudia's arms. "Are you mad, Jurat?"

"She will not run, Refik," Jurat responded, pushing Refik away.

"Can you be sure?" Refik stepped back, unsheathing his sword. "I do not trust her."

"But I do," Jurat calmly replied. "Now put away your weapon." Defiant, Refik never moved, but stood where he was, brandishing his sword in Claudia's direction. "Who is leader here, Refik? Put your weapon away."

Refik sneered, facing away from Jurat as his leader took Claudia by the hand and led her to the fire and the meat cooking on top. Watching the two, Refik made a small motion with his free hand, the other bandits taking note. They whispered to each other, nodding.

"Jurat," Refik said, Jurat's attention caught.

"What now, my friend?"

"She is *our* prize, not yours alone, *friend*."

"Of course, Refik," Jurat agreed, suddenly aware of the other bandits moving closer. "Are you now plotting against me?"

"It is you who plots," Refik countered, his sword raised. "You came among us, willing to live as we do, and now this...this *woman* has clouded your judgement."

"Refik, all I have done is welcome her to the group. How can that be a plot?"

"She is a woman. They are not to be trusted."

"Am I not allowed to speak?" Claudia's face tingled as she turned away from the fire. Refik snarled at her, the tip of his sword at her chest.

"Know your place, female."

"Fuck you."

"Claudia," Jurat warned, two bandits blocking his path to her. "Refik, if you harm her, the *voivode* will seek his revenge."

Refik circled around Claudia, tracing his sword along the ground near her feet. He shot Jurat a warning look then leaned close to Claudia's ear. She could feel his lips touching her hair and she grimaced. "I'm willing to gamble that the Prince isn't even aware of your existence."

"Are you willing to take that bet?"

"You bluff." Refik traced a finger across the back of Claudia's neck. "Do you know of the story of the mistress who attempted to lift him from a black mood? She dared tell him a lie that she was with child, just to keep him by her side. He told her that it would not happen, that she was not pregnant. Insisting that it were true and hoping that the *voivode* would be glad, she was adamant in her tale." Refik moved both hands down her back to her waist, feeling her tense under her clothes. "Then he cut her open from groin to chest to see for himself."

Claudia lowered her head. The relish with which Refik had spoken had left her with little hope. Should she, by some course of inexplicable fate, escape from these men then the degree of safety she would find elsewhere seemed slim.

But perhaps the *voivode*'s enemies would help her find her way home, or maybe Jurat could be convinced she was important and keep her alive. She sensed an ally in

Jurat, but Jurat had to ensure that Refik wouldn't kill them both.

It had been a long, difficult struggle to ingratiate herself into the group, particularly with Refik, but as the weeks had gone by, Jurat had eventually soothed the viciousness of his lieutenant's manner. Claudia had more than proved her worth to the group, leading scouting parties and raids on villages, hunting for food and provisions. Her sex had meant she had an advantage because most villagers could not comprehend that a woman would ever be an outlaw.

And after all this time, she still thought, every day, of home. She wondered if she'd ever see it again, if her family was out there looking for her. Surreptitiously, during some raids, she'd described them to various villagers in the hope they'd caught sight of them. But it was to no avail.

Knowing them as she did, of course, they'd more than likely be trying to rub shoulders with the local gentry than skulking around muddy village huts so in the last few days she had decided to try and find a way to one of the nearest cities. Jurat had been supportive of her and she couldn't wait for him to return later today from a raid to tell him what she had seen.

Chapter 5

In the shadowy dungeon complex of the Dambovita Citadel came cries of anguish.

The day was young and already Tanyel was with the prisoner.

Strapped to a rack, the cogs locked in one position, was Rintoul or, at least, the thing that used to be Rintoul. Over the course of the night, the torture had progressed until now the pitiful Wallachian was a misshapen mess of a man: arms and hips disjointed, hands bent like a severe arthritic's, legs twisted and useless. His shoulder blades had almost popped out of alignment, as though an extra pair of bones was trying to break out. His face was bloodied, pitted and scarred, wax dropped from a heavy candle clumped to his blackened skin. His eyes were swollen and black from repeated strikes to the skull.

Tanyel stood at the head of the rack, biting into an apple. Stroking Rintoul's lank hair with his free hand, he smiled, juice rolling across his bottom lip. Tanyel had enjoyed the torture, ignoring his own fatigue. The initial strength Rintoul had displayed had eased and Tanyel felt certain he could not break free from the tighter restraints. Tanyel could not determine whether the henbane had given Rintoul visions during the night or not.

Requesting an audience here with Tarih-i-al-Osman, Tanyel felt he could persuade the Governor to somehow use Rintoul against the Wallachians. If they understood that the Turks themselves had inflicted such torment then perhaps the Wallachians would not be so bold in attempting to reclaim the Citadel. Tarih-i-al-Osman entered a short while later, still looking as though he needed another night's sleep.

"At such an immoral hour, Tanyel, this better be worth my time," the count noted, lisp reducing the sternness in his tone. "You kept most of the Citadel awake last night with your tactics. You appear even better than the *voivode* at inflicting pain."

"With respect, Governor, I do believe I was given free reign." Tanyel motioned for Tarih-i-al-Osman to view Rintoul. The Governor did so, initially gagging into his palm at the sight.

"Great Allah, man, whatever have you done?" Daring to go no nearer the prisoner, Tarih-i-al-Osman stood a distance away, shuffling in his velvet slippers. "Are you sure this was not your doing?"

"Indeed not. I returned to him this morning and he had these." Tanyel prised open Rintoul's mouth, indicating unusually sharp canines within.

"Has anything else altered?"

"Other than what the rack has done, no."

"Destroy it." Tarih-i-al-Osman's command was plain. "The thing is positively hideous."

"If I may make a suggestion..."

Tarih-i-al-Osman glanced up at the commander. "Do not even consider keeping *that* in my palace."

Tanyel raised an eyebrow. Palace! The Governor had made himself a virtual king in the Citadel since he had been appointed as its overseer and it riled Tanyel to see the flatulent boor striding around as though he was royalty. The Sultan was the only one to have that right and Tanyel could only long for the day when Tarih-i-al-Osman, in effect an overbearing accountant, was cut down to size.

"Why did you summon me?"

"Governor, if you are having such a reaction, think how the Wallachian infidels will respond when they see such men at the head of our army."

The Governor spluttered over his own saliva at this. "Are you ready to suggest to the Catholics that the good soldiers of Islam are ruled by such devils?"

"Not at all." Tanyel threw the apple core into the brazier. It hissed defiantly in the coals. "But why not make them believe we can *create* such demons?"

The Governor's piggy eyes widened as he realised what Lord Tanyel was suggesting. He clapped his hands together. "We would be invincible! They wouldn't dare attempt to reclaim the Citadel back!" But then he frowned, tongue sliding across his bottom lip in consternation. "How do you hope to make more like this?" He indicated towards Rintoul slowly, as if worried the action would anger the sleeping man.

"The clue must be in the henbane. Perhaps this is the effect is has on the Catholic. We will have legions of these fanged men at our command. We can turn the Catholics on each other." Tanyel stroked Rintoul's forehead. "Demons to destroy demons."

"When shall you start?"

"Why not now? I will bring some of the prisoners up from the cells. They will make excellent guinea pigs."

"Oh, how wonderful!" Tarih-i-al-Osman smiled inanely. "Wallachian prisoners turned into these creatures to destroy their own people! I shall send word to the Sultan straight away and tell him."

"And what of the *kutu*?"

"The trinket box?" Tarih-i-al-Osman twitched like a mongrel with a flea. He had no wish to share that little gift with anyone. "It is safe."

No more than ten-foot square, Apollinari's room was sparse and he expected no less from the penitents that usually occupied it. Shandor was kind enough to offer Apollinari and Verrecchia a dormitory to themselves for the night, the brothers often having the burden of sharing their simple surroundings – four or even five to the tiny rooms. A small candle sat forlornly on the little window sill, its wax collected in the holder in an obtuse mass of grey and yellow. Apollinari picked up the Bible from the bookshelf above the left single bed, its companion mirroring the position on the right. The narrow window made reading difficult, even at this bright hour, so Apollinari gently closed the beautifully decorated tome and replaced it. He looked around him, considering their situation.

"Are you alright, Father?"

"Yes, Roberto. A good night's sleep always makes me fresh for the day ahead."

And there was silence again. Verrecchia sat on one of the beds and watched his mentor who lay back on the other. Apollinari's his chest rose and fell slowly through measured breathing, his mouth opening and closing every now and again as though he was about to speak but thought better of it.

After a while, Apollinari looked over to Roberto. The narrow bed creaked under his weight.

"How is your leg?"

"Sore. But the infirmary was very attentive. They told me I need to rest to stave off any infection."

"Then you should heed their words and…"

Apollinari's voiced tailed off as he looked casually at Verrecchia's leg then beyond it. The bed Verrecchia was perched upon was slightly away from the wall. He jumped up then knelt on the floor, the fine layer of straw crunching under his knees. Apollinari noted the bed had been moved quite regularly, the hay around its feet ground into the stone floor in a neat semi-circle.

"Father?"

Slipping quickly to the door, Apollinari popped his head into the corridor. Certain no one was nearby, he turned back to Verrecchia. "Stand up."

Apollinari began to haul Verrecchia's bed away from the wall. It was heavier than it looked but nevertheless, he made quick work of moving it to an acute angle to the wall. Revealed to Apollinari like some kind of undiscovered painting was a long low gap in the wall, just below the line of the slats on the bed.

"Stay here, Roberto."

Apollinari did not wait for his novice's perturbed reply and squeezed through, pulling the bed back to the wall in the process.

The gap opened up into a constricting bolthole, Apollinari confronted by a sharp corner.

Barely able to straighten up, Apollinari sidled along, his breathing disturbing the cobwebs along the wall in front of his nose.

He could hear Verrecchia's worried calls from the room and replied back, reassuring the young monk that he was fine.

The bolthole continued for a short distance until, after three steps down, Apollinari came upon a door much narrower than his shoulders. The little door opened stiffly outwards with a rheumatoid creak and he squeezed through.

A rush of cold air and a smell of incense burnt his nostrils.

It was the monastery's main cruciform basilica and he was standing on the high balcony that ran around the interior. Arrow slits gave meagre light from the outside but allowed shafts of pure winter sunlight to cut through the close air. Craning his neck to look through the nearest slit, Apollinari could see the rest of the monastery complex backed by the tops of the deciduous trees across the island, the undersides of the lean branches highlighted by reflections off the lake. He watched an eagle dance across the pinnacle of the trees, its considerable wingspan reaching into the sky as it climbed.

Turning his attention to the interior of the basilica, Apollinari saw huge candles placed at measured intervals around the building, in between the pews and pillars. A massive stone cross, carved with incredible detail, sat atop the imposing altar at the apse and the low fence-like arrangement kept it within the iconostasis and separate from the nave.

The place was devoid of anyone save Popescu kneeling in a pew, head bowed and clasped hands against his forehead. His thick dark hair showered over his shoulders.

Carefully and quietly, Apollinari trod to the winding staircase a little way from where he'd emerged from the bolthole, and descended to the lower level, moving up the nave to the solitary soldier.

He stood a few pews back so as not to encroach on Popescu's worship and waited.

Eventually, Popescu stood and moved to the iconostasis, pausing on the lower of the three shallow steps and crossed himself, kissing his rosaries normally kept tucked beneath his armour before turning away.

Apollinari standing there, his dark robes even blacker in the gloom, made Popescu tense briefly. A single, narrow sunbeam from a high arrow slit glared in his eyes.

"You monks are perfectly adapted to sneaking around."

"We are required to express our humility and reverence and silence is one such way." Apollinari moved to kneel on the steps, said a simple prayer and returned his attention back to the soldier. "I did not consider you to be wholly fearful of God and would not have expected to find you here."

"My own Lord desires it and I have no desire to defy his wishes."

"You pray at the request of another?"

Popescu nodded, tidying the sword kept at his waist.

"And who is your earthly deity?"

"Prince Vlad of Wallachia."

Apollinari pursed his lips. "A formidable master indeed. I understand why you would carry out his instructions to the letter. How long have you served him?"

"Twelve tours, now. I enjoy my position and know that I am privileged."

"Your allegiance does you credit, Popescu." Apollinari began to walk up the chapel's aisle to the main door, Popescu a step behind. "Where are you headed from here?"

"Back to my Lord's army."

Apollinari stopped and turned, facing the taller man. "Before you depart, I wonder if you will be able to assist me?"

Popescu was suspicious. "Why would you ask something of me?"

"This area is your jurisdiction. The safety of the monks, the boyars, the gentry: all your responsibility. Shandor, as effective an Abbot as he is, seems to have a problem and I do not understand how this can be so – for a man in his position."

Popescu seemed to brighten at this, as if amused by the notion that Shandor had suffered some form of indiscretion.

"Indeed? Tell me more."

Chapter 6

Verrecchia had sat in the little room for a while until he realised that Apollinari was not coming back through the bolt hole anytime soon. Deciding to explore his surroundings, he worked his way through the maze of gloomy corridors to reach the main courtyard outside, finding a garishly painted and battered caravan stationed some distance away from Popescu's own entourage. A smaller covered wagon sat nearby.

The sun was shining but there was still a biting chill which touched his skin even through the layers of his heavy black cassock.

The gypsy with the caravan had lit a small fire and Verrecchia took advantage of the heat by introducing himself and happily sat when a place was offered.

"Shouldn't you be praying or something?" Zucco enquired, tethering the horses to the hitch rail once the wagon had been secured. He could feel the stare of the soldiers on his back as he tried his best to go about his business with an air on nonchalance. "Want some food, boy?"

Verrecchia shook his head as he watched Zucco cut then throw some vegetables into a small, charred cooking pot and nestled it securely in the fire.

"How old are you? Fourteen? Fifteen?"

"I reach my seventeenth birthday in January."

"You don't sound like you're from around here."

"Neither do you."

Zucco grumbled under his breath and sat on his haunches. "We travel."

"What's under there?" asked Verrecchia, the covered box-shaped wagon piquing his curiosity so much so that he could remain silent about it no longer.

"Like animals, do you? I guess you have to being in your profession. Love to all and all that." The gypsy made sure the pot was steady before moving away from the fire. "What's under here stays under here and only comes out when I say so, you understand?"

He and Apollinari had met their fair share of travellers since they had left their own monastery but Zucco was gruff and overbearing in his manner and Verrecchia was somewhat wary of the gypsy. He had no wish to upset the man by pushing any further as to what was under the canvas so nodded in silence.

"Where are your travels taking you?"

Zucco squinted and looked across the island to the west wall. "To Craiova. Eventually. If the wife will let me." He came and sat back down at the fire, large frame heavy and uncomfortable.

"Your wife?"

"She's in there." He thumbed behind him towards the painted caravan. "Sick as a dog. Needs nursing day and night."

"What's wrong with her?"

Verrecchia should have known better than to ask for Zucco immediately launched into a tirade of foul-mouthed descriptions of what he thought was exactly was wrong with his wife. When he finished, he shoved a grubby finger into the stew, testing the temperature.

"Sure you don't want food?" Zucco shrugged as Verrecchia shook his head. "Fair enough. So you're travelling too, eh? Pilgrimage?"

"Not exactly. I am a novice and this is part of my training."

"Who you travelling with?"

"Father Apollinari. We are from the Benedictine Order."

"Anyone else?"

"No."

"Where is he now, this Apollinari?"

"He is here. I must assume he has business with the Abbot, still." Verrecchia decided not to mention boltholes.

"Does he beat you?"

"No!" Verrecchia was shocked at this. "He is a kind man."

Zucco eased himself where he sat and prodded the fire with a stick. "You're a long way from home. Italian?"

"Sardinian."

"How long have you known Apollinari?"

"A year, perhaps two."

"And you say he looks after you?"

"Yes. Of course."

Zucco nodded. "Good. Not a violent man, then."

"Why are you asking this? I don't feel it is because you are concerned for my welfare. After all, you do not know me."

"That's right. But you seem like a nice boy. My wife, like I said, she's not well. We came here for her to be treated."

"Treated?"

"That's what you monks do, isn't it? Heal the sick?"

"That is part of our duty, yes."

"Part of *your* duty, then?"

"I am being trained in the ways of medicine. I know a little."

"Enough to help?"

"I think the monks here would do a better job. They have access to the local herbs and potions."

Zucco looked at Verrecchia conspiratorially. "I don't trust these monks. Do *you*?"

"I have no reason to *not* trust them." Verrecchia stood, uneasy with the way the conversation was going. He glanced back at the main building over his shoulder, hoping Apollinari had seen him. "Why? Don't you?"

Zucco stood too, his wide frame blocking Verrecchia from the soldiers' view some distance away. "Fear of God? Who knows?"

He moved forward suddenly and stepped over the fire. Verrecchia stood his ground and did not move, even when Zucco was inches away from him. Sparks from the disturbed embers dissipated into the cold air like wayward sprites.

"But *you're* going to help me."

"I...I don't think I can."

"Get in the caravan," Zucco hissed

Verrecchia could smell Zucco's rank breath, the gaps between black teeth cavernous as the gypsy drew back his lips and leered.

"I need to see if Father Apollinari needs any assistance."

As the young monk turned away, Zucco grabbed his arm. Verrecchia cried out but Zucco snarled at him to be quiet.

"Everything alright, there?"

This was from one of the soldiers, their view of the monk still blocked by Zucco's great bulk.

"Yeah, we're all fine here," Zucco called. "The young lad just caught himself on the fire, is all."

The soldiers returned to their own private conversations and gave Zucco not a second thought.

"Now, my young boy, get in that caravan now. And heal my sick wife."

Verrecchia, realising he had little choice, moved quickly to the back of the caravan and mounted the few steps. Inside, he was met with an overpowering aroma of perfume. All around him, the cramped interior was nothing more than a bed, with more blankets and coverings than was necessary. The curved walls were adorned with dried heather, small animal skins and lengths of waxy cord.

It took him some moments to register Zucco's wife sitting on the bed, amid all the layers, ginger wig lopsided and make-up thick and garish. If she was naked from the waist down Verrecchia didn't dare look but she was certainly disrobed from the waist up. Her pale, corpulent breasts sagged heavy on her chest, swollen tips pointing downwards and brushing against her large belly.

"I...I..." Verrecchia simply did not know what to say and averted his eyes back to her face.

"Here's a nice little surprise," Marta said, voice harsh and low.

Verrecchia winced briefly from an acute pain to the back of his head before he blacked out, Zucco standing behind him with the cosh that dealt the blow in his hands.

Almost before Jurat had made himself comfortable around the fire, Claudia approached him, determined to get him to listen. He was the leader of the group and all decisions and plans had to be made through him. She saw him visibly sigh as she knelt beside him.

"Hello, Claudia," he breathed, his smile lost under fatigue and dirt. "I trust you and Refik have managed to keep away from each others' throats while I've been away."

"Leave him behind again and I'll kill him," Claudia grunted. "I really need to speak to you."

Jurat leaned over to the roast and tore a leg off. With his mouth full, he motioned for Claudia to continue.

"I've seen him," she began, "at least – I think it was him..."

"Your uncle?" Jurat pulled a length of gristle from his mouth and threw it aside. "Are you sure? If this is another of your mistakes..."

Claudia ignored the threat, knowing it meant nothing. "It must have been him."

"Did he see you? Did he recognise you?"

"I was too far away."

"Why didn't you go to him?" Jurat stood and stretched, asking a nearby colleague for a drink. "You've been waiting for this moment forever."

"I know where he was headed. I followed him for a time. Come with me - I won't be able to do it alone."

"And where was he going?" Jurat downed a pig's bladder of wine and gave the empty container back to his colleague.

"To Snagov."

"And why would you need me to go with you? You've been there before so they won't exactly refuse you entrance, will they?"

Claudia looked at the fire then back at Jurat, seeing his kind eyes hidden behind years of hiding out as an outlaw in the Vlasie forest. Their relationship had developed over the months, even though he was damned annoying. She wouldn't have gone so far as saying she had fallen in love with him but the attraction was strong and she found she missed him more often than not whenever he was gone for days on a hunt or a raid. But even so, she knew she had to tread carefully with this subject for it wasn't the first time that she'd thought she spotted her uncle in a moment of desperation – only to find her leads were false.

"Popescu is at Snagov, too."

For that moment, it was like she'd betrayed him. His whole face and body language changed towards her and he snarled as he stalked away. Gritting her teeth she followed him and pulled at his shoulder.

"Don't walk away from me."

He looked down at her hands, telling her with his expression to let go – but she didn't.

"If he was with Popescu then he is either in league with him, or..." He turned to face her and led her back to the fire. "Claudia, he could be his prisoner in which case even all of us together can't help you."

"No. it's not like that. I don't think so, anyway. But I've got to go to be sure."

"Then you try and convince Refik. You know what he's like."

"You're our leader. *You* convince him." Claudia clenched her fists and kicked at the embers. Sparks flew out back across her feet. "Then I go alone. Yes, I'll go in disguise."

Jurat laughed gently. "Popescu will see straight through you and execute you on the spot – or do something to you first *then* execute you." He sat down again and pulled Claudia close to him. It seemed an age ago that she used to flinch at such closeness with him. Now she welcomed his affections, however clumsy or animalistic they were. "How long have you been with us? Half a year?"

"Certainly since before the winter. What's that got to do with anything?"

"I've come to depend on you, Claudia. You're a worthy addition to our little band. To walk straight into Popescu's grip is suicide."

"This isn't my home, Jurat. We've had this conversation over – and my only way home is with my uncle."

"It means this much to you? You would really return with him?"

Claudia rubbed her eyes. She was tired because, even after all this time, she always had to sleep with one eye open simply because people like Refik couldn't be trusted. Jurat she knew would never hurt her but his faith in her made him almost like her captor than colleague. Letting her go would be very hard.

"I have to try – and alone if need be."

Jurat made a noise under his breath as though he was growling at her. "What was Popescu doing when you saw him?"

"He was with his men and a wagon."

Jurat stood and rubbed his chin. "A wagon, eh? Did it look heavy?"

"It was cutting deep trenches in the snow."

"Weighed down with heavy coffers, no doubt."

Claudia caught on to his pattern of thought and jumped up next to him. "Full of money for a cut-throat band of outlaws to ambush and steal? Do you think Refik would agree?"

"Refik may be a mad bastard but he is also greedy. His honour among us would not allow him to refuse. He *will* agree – and then we can get into Snagov and find your uncle."

Rintoul was alone in his cell. He had been moved back there, unstrapped from the rack, his joints dislocated and on fire. There were no windows here and he had no idea if it was day or night but there was a fog, a mist, hanging just above the cold floor where he lay and glowing in the light from the flaming torches in the corridor. He was not sure if the mist was his vision until he coughed (in itself an effort) and saw the vapours shift and curl like Bedouin silk in the breeze.

A shadow fell across the floor and Rintoul squinted to see who it was. An elongated silhouette of a man against the far wall, shadowed hands stretched like claws, made him catch his breath. There was no point crying out for help for his tongue was scarred from the iron and blood had dried in his throat. And even if he did, no one would come. That he had learnt very quickly since he had arrived here.

But the silhouette softened and a hand appeared on the floor in front of his eyes, a man's face following moments later. Around the newcomer and from the floor, the mist had gone.

Rintoul saw the visitor's eyes were compelling, striking and as pale as the whites.

"You will live," said the man, voice like honey. Those white eyes squinted and the man smiled. "Come, sit up."

Before Rintoul had the chance to indicate that he had no way of changing position, the man had him by the shoulders to pull him upright. Yet there was no pain and the burning in Rintoul's joints had faded, the tightness in his chest easing.

The young soldier made to flinch back as the man suddenly held a grip around his throat. But the hold wasn't tight and the man released it almost as soon as he had moved forward. Fingers brushed Rintoul's throat as if caressing his neck with such tenderness.

Rintoul found he could speak again, clearly and without hindrance.

"How have you done this?" Rintoul stammered, holding his own arms and torso with renewed strength. He could feel his two sharp white teeth catching against his bottom lip and raised his fingers to touch them. Something told him to feel the side of his neck to find two small incisions. "What am I?"

"You are healed," was all the man said and stepped back.

Tentatively, Rintoul stood. There was no need for the caution, however, because his legs were strong, stronger than ever.

"You have the box."

At this Rintoul sagged and leant against the wall. That box! He wished he'd never found it and left it there in the mud. "Do with me what you will. I can say no more about it."

"No," the man purred. "You misunderstand. The box found *you*."

"I don't want it," Rintoul replied, voice rising. "I just want to get back to the encampment."

The man shook his head, long blonde hair rubbing against his shoulders. "That life is over for you now. The Unholy Relic must be kept safe. From hereon, this is your purpose."

"Who are you?" Rintoul gasped. Unholy Relic? In God's name what did that mean? "You're not part of the occupation. You're not a Turk."

"I have larger battles to fight than your petty squabbles."

"Petty?" Rintoul breathed in, chest broad. "Reclaiming our homeland from the invader is no petty squabble. I fight, my brother fights, we all fight, for our homes, our children, our lives. What do you know of this?" Rintoul grabbed the man's wrists and turned his hands over, palms upwards. "Look at your hands, all soft and well-manicured. You have no notion of hard labour, of having to struggle to stay alive every day. To sleep with one eye open to save yourself and your family from the sodomy and rape by the enemy. *Futu-ți morții mă-tii.*"

Rintoul let go of the man and thrust him back. The man, unflinching, steadied himself casually and moved back towards Rintoul. But the last movement, where he had Rintoul back against the wall by one open hand pressed against his chest, was sudden, swift and startling. The pressure on Rintoul's ribcage was tremendous yet he had no issue in taking breath.

"Rintoul," the man began calmly, "I am Ismael. I am the messenger of the Lord of Darkness. To you I bring his gift of immortality."

"But I want nothing from you."

Ismael opened his mouth and Rintoul saw two sharp, white teeth. "The gift is already underway. Can you not feel your own?"

Rintoul ran his tongue across his own top row of teeth. It caught on the extended canines. "What are you doing to me?" he cried. "I want no part of this!"

Ismael ignored Rintoul's anguish. "We have been here before, in this room. Your torturer fed you some potion. You would not remember."

But Rintoul did remember. A haze, an image. Ismael's face coming at him from the darkness. Warm breath on his skin and the feeling of those sharp white teeth plunging into his neck.

And now they pierced him again and he welcomed it. As Ismael drank, Rintoul felt his own blood flow freely across the vampire's lips.

Chapter 7

The locutory was large and, during the day, bright. The tall window arches on two sides made sure of that. But evening had arrived now and as a monk silently lit the massive pillar candles dotted around the room in places to achieve the best light, Shandor made himself comfortable behind a lengthy desk. It was cluttered with papers and parchments that documented the comings and goings of visitors to the monastery.

As the monk eventually left, Apollinari spoke.

"I want to see the casket again, Shandor," he said, preferring to stand rather than be seated on the simple stool placed before the desk.

"What concerns you about it, exactly? Why not wait for its owner to come for it?"

"I recognise the seal it carries."

"I saw the seal too but it means nothing to me. It is clearly the mark of whoever owns it."

Shandor stood, the feet of his heavy chair scraping on the stone floor like fingernails across tree bark. The Abbot looked out of one of the arches and across the island, the blue of the evening pierced occasionally by the braziers alight to warm the air. Beyond the walls, Popescu's entourage was settled for the night, the brotherhood supplying the foodstuffs before they headed back to the army at Prahov. The jetty was burdened with the colourful caravan and its covered wagon as the Zuccos waited for the ferry to come back from the opposite shore to take them away and to their onward journey.

Shandor enjoyed the constant flow of visitors and the subsequent duties they required of them all. He even had little issue with the boyars and their constant requests to hide their treasures. It was when unexpected events occurred that made him feel uncomfortable.

"I know who it belongs to," Apollinari stated.

Shandor turned and faced Apollinari, moving to stand back behind the desk. He knotted his fingers together and raised his knuckles to his lips. A pause – as if considering the response before he made it.

"You will not tell me who, though, will you?"

"You are hiding something from me. I can feel it.

"You must know better than that to ask what an Abbot retains in his own monastery."

"I'm here from the Vatican. I demand to know."

"No!" Shandor slammed a palm down, aggravating the already chaotic array of paperwork before him. He pointed at Apollinari, index finger on his right hand slightly bent. "You are here at the behest of the Bishop Sigmurului. You are a mere messenger. You have delivered the letter and therefore done as you were told. Now you must go, you *and* your novice. You have no authority here."

Apollinari took a deep breath. "I am no one's messenger, Shandor. The Bishop asked me to help."

"I did not ask for your help." Shandor's voice had calmed now and Apollinari noticed the Abbot was shaking slightly.

"Then why show me the catacombs?" Apollinari moved around the desk to Shandor and grabbed his

shoulders. "And why does the casket *in* your catacombs bear the seal of Marise?"
Shandor flinched as if struck, his rotund frame visibly shrivelling in his cassock. "I...don't know what you mean."

"You lie willingly? Shame on you, Abbot Shandor."

"I swear by Almighty God, I don't know what it is you speak of."

"And now you take our Lord's name in vain. Sit."
Shandor fell heavily into the chair as Apollinari went to the corridor and called for some mead. Within moments, a monk appeared with a jug. Silently, Apollinari took it and dismissed him.

"Now you will tell me, Pretorius Shandor, exactly why you have a *moroi*'s possessions in your monastery."

Tanyel and Ekvan stood in the doorway of Rintoul's empty cell. All that was left to tell of its inhabitant's presence was erratic patches of congealed blood on the floor and walls.

"Shall we inform the Governor?" asked Ekvan.

"Idiot," Tanyel hissed. "You're certain no one came through here and no one left?"

"I swear, my Lord. I have been in the guard room for the entire day. Only I have the key to the cells."

"And yet this door is open."
Tanyel moved inside the tiny room and knelt on the floor, noticing something in the blood.

"My Lord?"

"A handprint, Ekvan," Tanyel whispered, hovering his own left palm over the imprint.

"The prisoner's?"

Tanyel stood and rubbed his chin. "Wrong angle, I think. Someone had to be kneeling in the doorway to make this."

"The person who opened the door?"

"Indeed."

"But I had the keys," Ekvan insisted, clutching the bunch permanently fixed to his trouser waist. "I *still have* the keys and the main door to the dungeon remained locked until I let you in a moment ago."

"Your guards...can you trust them?"

"Trust is not a priority. Only I open and close these doors. The guards simply...guard."

"Then there is another set of keys."

"Impossible."

"Perhaps. But you then explain to me how the prisoner escaped." Tanyel leaned in close to Ekvan, examining his expression closely. "Unless *you* released him?"

"I?" Ekvan shook his head. "My allegiance is to the homeland. I would never release a Wallachian dog back into the wild. I would rather suffer the gouging of the eyes."

"Hold that feeling, Ekvan. If the Sultan should learn of this, then that may be both our fates."

Collecting his gloves and cloak from Ekvan's quarters, Tanyel motioned to be let out of the dungeon. "I have a meeting with the Governor now. I will make no mention of this - and neither will you."

"What if he comes to see the prisoner?

"Tarih-i-al-Osman is a cowardly as he is obnoxious. He will not come down here without me to hold his hand."

Tanyel left, satisfied on hearing Ekvan slam and lock the heavy iron door behind him. He knew Ekvan was no traitor and believed he was not responsible for Rintoul disappearing. But how a heavily tortured Wallachian prisoner could have been moved out of the Citadel without being seen was indeed a mystery. It may even be that Rintoul was still *in* the Citadel, the accomplice with the bloody hand print hiding until the time was right to smuggle him out. If he had any sense, Tanyel considered, he would have washed his hand clean by now.

Tanyel passed few people as he walked and it wasn't long until he found himself moving through the dark passages of the Citadel alongside Tarih-i-al-Osman, listening intently as the Governor mapped out an offensive posture against the Wallachian stronghold of Târgoviste. It was an unforeseen move and was Tanyel required recall his troops from the siege on the Shipka Plains. He would make sure they laid waste to the Bulgarian settlements on the Balkans in the process.

"I expect not an ounce of failure, Tanyel," Tarih-i-al-Osman whispered, halting at the top of a wide flight of stairs. "These orders are from the Sultan himself."

That was obvious, Tanyel mused, for such a military stance could not have been dreamt up by this flatulent oaf. He clasped his hands behind his back, the sharp cuffs of his gauntlets cutting into his wrists. This was a better sensation than the repugnance of standing next to his superior.

"There can be but one outcome, Governor. On the morning of the seventeenth, you will be seen as the Governor who saw the downfall of the Impaler Prince," Tanyel said, almost gagging on the words.

"With his head on display at Constantinople, eh?" added Tarih-i-al-Osman.

"Our people of Islam will rejoice the *voivode*'s downfall when we do so."

Tarih-i-al-Osman began to descend, his cloak flowing behind him across the stone steps. Tanyel moved alongside, both men swiftly arriving at the Great Hall.

"What a glorious day that will be, Tanyel. Then Basarab Laiota will be crowned the true *voivode* once more and the Sultan will make us both proud warriors."

"No one more so deserving than you."

Tarih-i-al-Osman seemed to feel aggrandised at that. "How is your prisoner?"

"With your permission, I must take my leave of your exalted presence and make ready for the return of Basarab himself," Tanyel purred, seeing the Governor bathe in the undetected sarcasm and the po-faced theatricality of his words. "The prisoner, in the meantime, can wait." He wasn't about to tell the Governor that Rintoul had disappeared.

"Of course," Tarih-i-al-Osman agreed, waving away his army's captain.

Tanyel crossed the hall to a narrow corridor, pausing suddenly at the mouth of the passage, seeing movement from the corner of his eye.

The huge tapestry hanging down to his left against the cold stone wall gently moved as though caught in a soft breeze.

Tanyel glanced expressionless at Tarih-i-al-Osman watching him from across the room then ducked into the corridor.

Chapter 8

There was a somewhat overpowering aroma of stale urine in the air.

This was from the small open barrels lined along the far wall in Shandor's chambers in which the Abbot's emiction was contained, to be kept and used by the parchmenters in the monastery workshop when preparing the calfskins. It was a common practice in a monastery but nevertheless it was a smell that took a while to get used to.

The chambers themselves, while more expansive than most and certainly larger than his formal office, were no more dressed than the rest of the chambers. Shandor had been party to knowing a handful of abbots and bishops (Sigmirului included) who approached their positions with the view that their wealth should be on display to accentuate the simple needs of the flock. The Abbot did his utmost to maintain the strict rules laid down by the faith and to ensure his brethren was as equal as he. His private chambers, while containing his own chapel and cloister, were always open to the monks if they sought his guidance during the little time his duties gave him to rest.

Nevertheless, Shandor did not take kindly to the military using his rare tranquillity as a place to demand, order and calcify their authority.

Alexandru Popescu had always been near the threshold of atheism and subsequently near the threshold, in Catholic eyes, of being a heathen, a Turk. In his opinion, God was far from revered and in civilised Catholic Europe, having no faith was as punishable as one which deflected the words of the Testaments.

Popescu trod that line, but his dedication to his *master's* beliefs had kept him alive, a master who would die, kill, impale and maim for his faith. Popescu would die, kill, impale and maim for his master.

The Abbot had studied Popescu on the occasions the captain had required Snagov as a refuge. The surprise delivery of Princess Ilona Szilágy two months back now into monastic care and the deceit Popescu had invented to keep her hidden, both shocked and despaired Shandor.

"Tell no one outside these walls of her existence, priest," Popescu had spat to Shandor, "or your fate will not be decided by Him."

Cold, hungry, and frightened, the princess, her bright aspect dulled and wearied by the long journey as well as Popescu's presence, had been left at the massive gates of the monastery. Her flowing wardrobe reduced to the nightgown she was shivering in, the animal fur over he shoulders giving her at least a little decency. A sack by her side had contained two gowns.

The Abbot had not even recognised her until she began to bathe, the dirt and fatigue of abduction sponged away in the petal-scented water.

As she curved her way into a gown, candlelight tanning her softened skin, her royalty returned: back straight, stance elegant and refined.

Shandor had arranged a meal for her, before she was to resume her sleep. As she ate, she told Shandor the tale of her capture. It had been dusk and she had been sleeping for a good while. A sudden drowsiness had taken her early in the evening so her ladies in waiting had assisted in her retirement.

Shandor's opulent knowledge in herbal mixtures told him she had been drugged as she described the way in which the tiredness had claimed her, nausea and the aching of the eyes adding to the forced condition.

She had awoken hours later. To her it seemed like minutes.

Disorientation and weakness had hindered her for a little while into realising she was bound, ungainly, over the shoulders of a steed. The pressure of a gauntleted hand in the small of her back pushed against the horse at her stomach. She couldn't turn her neck far enough to spy her captor but looking down at the stirruped boots, she recognised the spurs: gold, heavy and embossed on one arm of the arch with the Wallachian eagle, on the other the dragon symbolising her husband's power.

Knowing that even the prince with his almost psychotic changes of mood was unlikely to steal away his own wife from their bedchamber, she turned her thoughts the other man capable of carrying out such a kidnap: Alexandru Popescu, the man she had been promised to on her thirteenth birthday.

Then Prince Vlad, the *voivode*, the saviour of Wallachia's freedom, had taken Ilona for his own wife instead.

Ilona was not a witless girl, even at that age and the prince, by many years her senior, was not a man to refuse. So, with her new duty laid out before her, she left the services of the household and became his bride. Much to Popescu's devastating dismay, his anger suppressed through fear of becoming victim to Prince

Vlad's ribald discipline, his love, his child-bride was snatched from him by his own master.

Yet no matter how desperate Popescu became in showing the *voivode* his unwavering loyalty, no matter how often he exceeded his orders and proudly carried the Wallachian flag from battlefield to battlefield, the undying resentment and anger at the wrenching of his heart grew, cancerous, in his soul. It was until he could bear the pain no longer that he dared and proceeded to take back the girl he knew before she became the woman she was forced to be. He took back his *iubire* from the very bed in which she had been made a woman.

It was not uncommon practice for a bride to be taken on her wedding night, not by the groom, but by the earl or prince of the land anyway, so Popescu, certain that his betrothed would one day be his wife, had prepared himself for Târgoviste's ruler and Lord, Prince Vlad, to exercise his God-given right. But his position had allowed him to step beyond his rights and take Ilona for himself at the unwavering approval of God.

What God allowed His subjects to be so vilely deceived, Popescu had questioned to Shandor. Shandor, having no choice in his answer, said it was God's will to let His children seek the paths that their preordained heavenly destiny has laid out for them.

"Even I am penitent in his light, my son," Shandor had comforted.

Driven by his heart and loins, Popescu, in a rage that no whore could ease, became blinded into reclaiming what was his by, so he believed, divine right.

"Divinity has intervened," Shandor continued. He had married the prince to Ilona two summers past now. "Divinity has chosen her path this time. She could not refuse lest she refuse God's will – and then she would be dead. Take comfort in the fact that her heart beats still and accept the Godly truth."

"I cannot. I will not," Popescu had said as the news of the marriage reached him from Shandor's own lips so many months ago.

Popescu had been adamant, passionate when refusing to recount his kidnapping of Ilona, seeing no other course than to do what he did.

"Did you not say yourself that God wills His children to tread their paths? If that is so, then even you, priest, must see that I am doing as my God instructs me to do. As He wills me to do!"

"If you believe that to be true, then may God have mercy upon your soul."

"It is clear to me that you mould your beliefs to suit the situation."

"We are all entitled to our opinions, whether they are from the Jew or the Muslim, but I, as Abbot of Snagov, must instruct my flock in the Catholic faith. I cannot have an opinion that detracts from that."

"You are part of a mass hallucination."

"If that is your opin-"

"Damn you and your opinions!" Popescu raged. "You are part of an order that habit and comfort has determined cannot be changed! It is narrow-minded, sheltered and pointless to believe in something that can neither be proved or disproved."

"But nevertheless provides hope, comfort and strength. That is why religion exists and the day man decides he no longer needs God then God shall, in His wisdom, bring about the Apocalypse. You, captain, are the beginning of that downfall. Humanity is weak, fragile and lost without a fundamental system of unity."

"Prince Vlad is that unity."

"But after all this killing and turmoil," Shandor had said, gesturing around him, "who does your Prince and master bow to?"

Popescu knew where Shandor was taking the argument. Instead of reaching for the bait, the captain had cut the conversation off, demanding again that Shandor's silence regarding Ilona's presence was paramount.

Shandor, realising Popescu's own narrow-mindedness would not allow the soldier to see the futility of his actions, let open the door to his chambers, Popescu nodding once before exiting. Shandor's non-verbal response confirmed to Popescu that Ilona's presence within the monastery walls would remain secret.

And now Popescu was here again in the Abbot's quarters, this time at Shandor's request and the Abbot was not alone. Apollinari was there, standing silently.

"If you have dragged me back up here to spout God's will to me again, I will gut you where you stand," the captain threatened.

"The mere thought," Shandor began gently, "of me reiterating to you a lesson, which you should know so well, hadn't even begun to cross my mind." Shandor clasped his hands together under his habit.

"Why is he here?" Popescu spat, glaring at the younger of the two monks.

Apollinari gritted his, surprised at the soldier's aggressive stance this morning.

"I have told the Abbot that I do not trust you." Popescu turned to face Apollinari. "When I first found you and your novice, I thought I recognised your name.

I sent a carrier and have information returned. I do not believe you are part of any Order."

"Popescu..."

"No, Pretorius, it is fine. Let the man speak," Apollinari said, quite calm.

"Some consider you to be unorthodox, a charlatan. What say you to this?"

"I am part of the Benedictines of Saccargia. I am nothing more than what you see before you."

"At no time has Father Apollinari made any inference that his beliefs are corrupt," pointed out Shandor.

"We live in treacherous times, as well you know, Abbot," Popescu growled. "His beliefs can be bought or burnt into him."

"He is not a heretic. No more than you are."

"What are you implying?" Popescu squinted at the Abbot, but Shandor's peaceful expression met Popescu's glowering stare.

"I imply nothing. Read into it what you will."

"You are nothing but a serpent, Father Shandor," Popescu spat, "sliding from word to word like the reptile moves along the forest floor."

Shandor rose from the single chair and straightened his back. "There are things happening, Alexandru Popescu, that we cannot contain. We need Father Apollinari's help. But for the moment, I believe he needs ours. Please, Father, continue with what you were saying before Popescu joined us."

"Brother Verrecchia did not appear for Prime," Apollinari pointed out, worried that his novice had not been seen for some hours.

Shandor looked concerned. "No one in the order has seen nor heard from him since you both arrived yesterday."

"I left him in our room. According to Prior Alexi, he attended Vespers but has not been seen since."

"Popescu," Apollinari said, turning to the soldier, "surely your men must have seen something of him?"

"He was in conversation with the gypsy."
Shandor mentioned that Zucco had left the evening before, most likely after Vespers, noting that he had seen the caravan leave across the lake.

"What exchanges did he have with this gypsy?" asked Apollinari.

"My men would not eavesdrop but they did mention that it appeared to become heated at some point."

"He is nowhere on the island, my brother," Shandor said, placing a calming hand on Apollinari's shoulder. "I fear he may have left with the gypsy."

"Then I believe it is safe to say that his leaving was not voluntary."

"This casket," Popescu began, noting Shandor shifting uncomfortably where he stood. "My men have moved it as requested."

"I beg your pardon?"

"At Father Apollinari's request." Popescu nodded towards the Sardinian as if Shandor needing reminding he was there.

"You ordered this? You entered the catacombs without my permission?"

"Apollinari has raised his concerns about it with me," Popescu interjected. "But what has that to do with this Verrecchia going missing?"
Shandor was unsure of Apollinari's motives, flicking his gaze towards him for a moment. The other monk was expressionless.

"Shandor," Apollinari said, "you would not entertain a conversation yesterday about the casket and so I let you sleep on it. My assumptions are, for the moment, simply that. I must find my novice. I fear for his welfare."

"Shandor has no horses to spare. Do you seek support from the Prince for this?"

Before Apollinari could answer, a rapping was heard from the other side of the thick wooden door. Shandor bade them enter and the door opened, the candles flickering.

A woman stood in the doorway, head bowed and hands clasped against her forehead. Her dark brown hair was braided tight, a startling emerald band keeping it neatly away from her crown. The clasp complemented the gold and peacock-blue dress she was wearing.

Without full view of her pale face, Apollinari had no way of determining her age but, with the waif-like waist that she had, he guessed she was relatively young.

Shandor called her in and she almost scurried to his side. Dropping her hands, her dark eyes, pupils almost the size of the whites, she glanced up at Apollinari obvious that she was trying to avoid Popescu's gaze.

"Father Apollinari, allow me to introduce Ilona, the Prince's consort."

Chapter 9

The room at the very top of the tower was circular, no larger than fifteen feet in diameter. There was no visible exit save for one single, narrow window, devoid of glass and through which the moonlight freely shone. It contained two simple caskets, empty and their lids cast asunder. The curved stone walls were damp, mould creeping, gaining footholds where no one was able to reach.

It reeked of the dead.

As grey as the walls and as equally as lifeless, Ismael stepped in through the window, motioning for Rintoul to do the same.

The vampire noticed Rintoul's fatigue and offered him his wrist, breathing heavily as the newborn pounced and drank greedily.

After a few moments, Ismael pushed Rintoul away, sensing in his veins that the young man had had enough.

Rintoul was a confirmed vampire now, he too able to hunt and feed of his own volition. But Ismael his maker enjoyed the paternal instincts that turning the Living awakened. Having had no children of his own when he was mortal, these substitute offspring quenched whatever humanistic desire he still maintained and so encouraged the continued feeding.

But, like breathing, such things were really echoes of a life once had, regular reminders of the weaknesses of the flesh.

Rintoul knelt on the floor, the dust gathering around him. He licked the blood from around his lips and gums knowing that these were the last drops he'd have from Ismael for a while, if ever again.

He turned and stood then, his hunger satiated for the moment and left the room, scrabbling back down the outer wall, silent and alert, his new abilities registering little in his undead subconscious.

All that drove him at that moment was his task.

Knowing that Ismael would not accept failure, the threat of staking Rintoul himself if he did, meant that the journey to Tarih-i-al-Osman's private chambers was brief, the Citadel passing beneath him an insignificant blur.

Back in the tower, Ismael welcomed the black shapes that had folded themselves in through the window following Rintoul's departure. Coalescing, reforming, ethereal smoke becoming tangible bodies, three figures came to settle before him.

Together, the four of them, these pale creatures of darkness, were the Vampire Celebrants, appointed by means lost in the annals of undead time.

The oldest of them, it was said, was present at the first Olympiad. But before she had been endorsed as the current elder by the slaying of her predecessor at the hand of Pietro Vincenzo, the Celebrants' wisdom had included the witnessing of the sealing of Hemaka's tomb.

"This Rintoul," the elder began, a thin and gaunt character, "has he proved his worth as the new Guardian?"

"The Unholy Relic chose him, Odalys," Ismael replied. Odalys, her hands skeletal and claw-like, white hair thin across her scalp, glided across the floor, her exposed feet beneath a long white peplos barely touching the ground. "And you believe him?"

"The Greek has grown embittered over the centuries." This was from Kelele, once an Ethiopian prince, his dark features forever preserved.

"If I have, can you blame me?" retorted Odalys. "How many years have we searched for it? It had been in the possession of the Witches for such a time that their incantations may have twisted our perceptions."

"Yet he did bring it to the Living. I was there," Ismael breathed.

"And they do not know what to make of it." Kelele's robes undulated around him as he sat on his haunches. "You cannot deny it is here, Odalys."

"And you, Ismael, you have turned him! Your inexperience of youth is explicit! Rintoul cannot handle the container now." Odalys' features shimmered briefly as her anger caused her form to drift momentarily back into smoke.

"Ismael knows the Living cannot detect its power. Being a vampire is the only way to take it from their grasp."

"And what of the silver?"

"The Witches are sly for encasing it as they have," Ismael said.

Viktor thumped the floor and with gloved hand scrawled in the dust:

Once we have the Unholy Relic, we must seek our revenge on the Witches.

This fourth member of the Celebrants was a pitiful individual, sightless and without voice. He had once been handsome but his Russian features were vague under the scars that had left him the blind mute he now was. He had been made vampire nearly four centuries ago, his eyes and throat ripped out during the turning. His maker had had a vindictive soul and the Celebrants had destroyed him, concerned that the vampire race would become weak by his actions.

But the Celebrants themselves had shown equal malice by keeping Viktor undead, as if to remind themselves of their own perfections.

Odalys folded her arms across her chest. "But the one who kept the Relic from us is dead. Burnt."

Her family still lives, he wrote.

"Be careful," warned Ismael. "Remember our Lord's allegiance. Rintoul will be here before sunrise and he will have the Relic."

"And then? Who will be the one?" Odalys grew excited at the thought. "It should be me."

Kelele nodded. "You are the elder."

"The Unholy Relic must decide," Ismael countered. "You know that."

"Then it could be any one of us."

At Odalys' logic, the three of them turned to watch blind Viktor rocking back and forth on the floor, fingers scrawling shapes and patterns in the dirt, rubbing them through then starting again, over and over, until at last, an image of the Relic itself could be seen in the grooves of dust.

Next to it, he formed a perfect 'V'.

Claudia, the lightest of the group, crouched at the bow of the small boat while Jurat used one of the two oars to guide their way across the lake to the wall of the monastery that touched the water – and where the wheel set into the wall scooped the monks' water into a channel that collected in barrels near the kitchens. The motion of the wheel also allowed the grinding of the grain to make the daily bread.

The wheel was small but its buckets were far enough apart for a lithe-enough figure to squeeze through. The only danger was decapitation or dismemberment if the figure was not quick enough in getting past the ever-turning buckets and out the other side and into the monastery grounds.

Her size meant Claudia was the one who would risk her life to get inside and halt the rotation of the wheel so her cohorts could follow safely.

There was a lantern swinging above the wheel in a separate alcove that gave the bandits a clear target to aim for in the gloom. They hadn't long to get in, search for Popescu's coffers-filled wagon and get out, before the monks woke for their first day's prayers at the second hour of the morning.

Soon the boat was against the wall, hitting the damp stone with gentle thuds. Refik attempted to keep it steady as Claudia stood, leaning against the wooden frame holding the revolving wheel in place. Jurat waited where he was, ready to push the boat back out if they were spotted. The remaining bandits, carrying the weapons for the others, prepared themselves to follow Claudia once she'd locked the wheel.

Claudia counted the rotations, noting the wheel completed one turn every thirty-eight seconds. Taking a deep breath she dived onto the bucket that was raising itself out of the water below her.

The wheel creaked ominously with the sudden weight and Claudia found purchase difficult. The water was freezing and the buckets were covered in stringy algae. Her feet slipped as she tried to thrust them into the next bucket. As the wheel moved upwards, it carried Claudia with it, clinging to the outside like a limpet until it brought her to the summit of its turn and wedged her fast in the narrow gap where the wall arched over the wheel. Claudia cried out in pain as the rough stonework scraped at her skin through her leather tunic, pushing at her lower back as the wheel tried to continue its turn. On the boat, Jurat heard her cry and darted forward to help, upsetting the boat in the process.

Angered shouting and cursing rose up as the bandits all plunged into the cold lake but Refik, spluttering indignantly, urged his men on to clamber through the motionless wheel and into the monastery grounds. They were all still proclaiming their anger, even as Jurat hissed at them to quieten down, swords and daggers clanking against the wood.

All the while, Claudia was tight against the wheel and Jurat climbed up to allow her freedom, but the weight of the wheel and Claudia's position meant it was a struggle to even move her an inch.

"I can't do it, Claudia," Jurat strained, "I can't get you out."

"For God's sake, Jurat, try! It's breaking my back!" Claudia hissed through gritted teeth. "I can't breathe!"

"Just remain calm, I'll try another way."

Jurat clambered back down and pulled, intending to use his weight to force the wheel back.

"That won't work! The wheel's on ratchets and only rotates one way."

Jurat waited for his colleagues to squirm through the centre of the wheel and followed them, hoping an answer could be found inside the grounds. Looking frantically around him, he locked eyes on the lantern.

He stepped up the wheel and smiled at Claudia who was frowning and mouthing some obscenities at him, head poking out from over the curve.

Grabbing at the lantern he pulled at it and it came free in his hands. He almost slipped on the algae - which gave him an idea.

Claudia shook her head as she saw the glowing lantern swinging in front of her. "Don't even think about setting light to me..."

Jurat ignored her and blew the lantern out, examining its base. There was a deposit of watery wax collected in a dish and he reached out and poured it over Claudia's shoulders. She cried out through gritted teeth.

He threw the lantern aside and scooped away at the algae deposits over the wheel, rubbing the green slime over Claudia's waist where he could see and reach.

Below him, Refik shouted to move onwards, eager to find Popescu's wagon, but Jurat waved him quiet, focusing on making Claudia as slippery as possible so she could slide out from her predicament.

Refik padded off to the other waiting bandits, all of them nervous that their leader was causing this unnecessary delay. "Just leave her!" Refik shouted.

"No!" Jurat pushed and pulled at Claudia's shoulders but she wouldn't budge, instead crying out as her body was forced against the stone.

With an irritated curse, Refik stormed forward and pulled Jurat away from the wheel.

"What are you doing?" Jurat cried, stumbling to his feet as Refik unsheathed the axe from the leather harness across his back.

Refik swung the axe, missing Claudia's head by inches, gouging into the wheel. "We don't have time for this, Jurat! You want her out – then we'll cut her out!"

Refik hacked away at the wheel, loosening the bucket under Claudia's chest and allowing her to struggle free.

Jurat reached up and helped her down as Refik gave them a triumphant stare and put away his axe.

Rubbing her neck and shoulders, Claudia's stood upright. "I suppose I should thank you, Refik – but you'd never let me forget it." Jurat tried to smear the algae and crusted wax off her but she batted his hands away. "Come on, we've got treasure to steal."

As they hugged the wall, avoiding the bright moonlight as much as possible while circling the grounds, they failed to notice a solitary guard – one of Popescu's men – watching them from the cover of the stables. He'd sent a colleague to Popescu and the Abbot and was hoping he'd have reinforcements before the infiltrators spotted him.

Claudia halted the group with a raise of her hand, sighing at the clanking of weaponry behind her as the cut-throats ground to a stop. In the gloom, she pointed across the grounds in the general direction of the stables. "The dorms are behind the stables through a narrow door. There's usually a monk in residence there but we should be clear this time of night."

"Why worry about the dormitories?" Jurat queried, changing the subject. "Surely Popescu would either post guards on the wagon or would have moved the coffers to the prison or a crypt?"

Jurat smiled at Claudia, realising what she was after. He knew she wasn't really there for the valuables. He turned to his lieutenant. "Refik, the monks believe monies would be more secure if it is stored in their sleeping quarters. They are not expecting outlaws of our calibre to assault their defences."

Refik nodded, pondering this. "But if the door is so narrow, we must be wary of ambush."

"Don't worry," Claudia added, "there'll be n-"

She snapped her head up suddenly, feeling the rush of air as an arrow embedded itself in the ground next to her feet. There was a soldier atop the stables taking another aim, the fletch already in place. Claudia ducked away and darted around to the side of the stables, Refik following.

The monastery's bell started tolling.

Refik called out, alerting his men to fan out to lessen the target, eyes flicking to the arrow slits and outhouses.

Inside, Shandor rushed to the window but could see nothing in the gloom. Popescu had already left and was racing through the corridors to his men.

A second arrow shot a man down with a cry and Claudia realised their cover was non-existent save for the one door into the dormitories. The narrow window to its side allowed little room to clamber through but it was worth a try.

Rather than be a fixed target, Claudia hurtled past the stables and ducked as a soldier launched himself at her. The man tripped and Claudia was able to jump back and strike him across the jaw with a balled fist. She then changed tack and dived into the stables, testing the mortar on the back wall. It was as loose as she had hoped and it took little work with her booted feet to make a hole big enough to crawl through, out of sight of the enthusiastic bowman.

She felt Refik come up behind her, relishing in the conflict – but neither of them counted on Popescu standing at the hole on the outside of the stable rear, sword drawn.

They landed in a heap of arms, legs and weaponry at Popescu's feet.

"Well, well," sneered Popescu, prodding Refik's shins with the end of his sword. "What have we here?"

Disentangling themselves, Claudia and Refik stood, raising their hands and dropping their weapons in surrender as some of Popescu's men appeared behind him.

"You have either become increasingly desperate or increasingly stupid, Refik, to break into a monastery," Popescu spat, "and with a woman, too! I take it this is your leader's doing?"

Claudia tried to look casually around her, only noticing now that Jurat was not with them.

"We got through the monastic defences; got this far before you realised."

"I had a lookout watching you the moment you started this wasted campaign. He saw you embracing the waterwheel. It made for interesting viewing, so he says." Popescu motioned for four of his men to fasten his captives' hands behind their backs with rope. "But what shall we do with you now?"

"You can throw us to the wolves for all I care, Popescu," Refik retorted as a guard pushed him to his knees. "We've long since decided not to submit to your whims anymore."

Popescu moved forward and struck Refik across the face with a gauntleted hand. "You still cannot see that you will never be better than me."

"Are you going to execute us?" Claudia asked, also now on her knees, feeling a rope tightening around her wrists behind her back. “Do it now to save us the agony of any more of your goading.”

Refik had slumped against Claudia’s shoulder, blood welling from Popescu’s strike above his right eye. “I think I might put Refik back under my service. It will do him good to learn how to act like a soldier, again. And as for you…” Popescu removed his gloves and stroked Claudia’s grimy face. “I’m sure I can find a use for you.”

“Sir!” came a cry from one of Popescu’s men. “The stables!”

Popescu looked up and saw a fire beginning to take hold of the stables’ thatched roof. From out of the hole made by Claudia poked a dark head. At first Popescu naturally thought it was one of his own men until the head lifted.

“Refik! Claudia!” the figure growled, voice oddly guttural.

Claudia pulled at her bonds before the startled guards could secure them. “Jurat?”

Refik pulled himself up and attacked the guards surrounding his companions. Popescu called for more reinforcements as the damp thatch gradually ignited, making easy the collapse of the wooden roof.

Claudia dragged Refik around the side of the burning stables, thinking only of escape now, knowing the idea of this attempt was pointless after all. But her thoughts were broken as Popescu struck against the small of her back with the flat of his sword. Winded, Claudia collapsed to the ground, the sweetness of the damp hay strong in her nostrils. She heard Refik cry out as he realised what Popescu was about to do, feeling tightness across her stomach as the captain raised his sword to decapitate him. The weapon swung down and Refik’s head came cleanly away, blood spraying across her face and hands. Refik's body thudded twitching to the ground, the arteries from the stump that was his neck pumping fresh blood across the snow.

A little distance away, by the raised drawbridge, a shape lit by the braziers caused Popescu to halt. Turning, he caught a breath, the black thing suddenly feet away from him, padding and clawing at the ground. Swallowing, his heart pounding, he raised his sword again.

Then the drawbridge shuddered into motion. Even before the bridge had made its downward arc to the jetty, he heard the rest of the bandits cut down by his bowmen.

Claudia knew she had to escape and at least help some of her companions too, should any of them have survived. She raced back across the courtyard.

The shape moved away from Popescu and howled – it was a wolf! How had it gotten into the grounds?

Shouting, screaming, making as much noise as she could to attract the animal's attention, Claudia ground to a halt, her feet slipping on the mushy hay as the wolf swung around to face her. Her mouth dropped as it moved forward, its form almost translucent in places. Claudia put it down to the meagre light playing tricks. It seemed to be larger than normal, though, a thick neck leading into a long face and muzzle. Its eyes were hauntingly yellow.

Claudia's foot knocked against a bow and quiver. Quickly she glanced down and saw there was one arrow left and she grabbed them, raising the weapon to the wolf. The action was harder than it looked and she pulled as much as she could on the string.

The wolf growled at her. She released the arrow. It thudded into the ground before the animal and she toppled backwards.

An arrow from behind her struck the wolf across the shoulder and it howled in pain, scampering off into the dark.

She turned and saw it was Halil, one of Refik's confidantes. She was grateful and ran towards him but Popescu suddenly appeared in her way. Halil shot another arrow and it glanced off Popescu's body armour, but the blow was enough to cause him to drop his sword. Claudia lunged forward and tried to snatch it from under his grasping fingers.

Halil ducked down and kicked at Popescu's arm.

"Come, we must get to the drawbridge," he hissed, pulling her with him.

"What of the others?"

"They're dead, Claudia."

"Where's Jurat? Where did he go?"

"We must leave!" Halil insisted.

"Stop!"

They heard Popescu's booming cry and spun around. He was standing, a longbow pulled back tight in his arms. Instinctively Claudia threw herself down but Halil stumbled back and then to his knees, a look of surprise brandished across his face as he looked at the arrow that had plunged into his chest.

"Halil!" Claudia cried, watching Halil topple silently to the ground, dead.

Instantly driven by rage, Claudia swung around and hurled herself at Popescu as the captain was reloading his bow. Swiftly, Popescu aimed and carefully fired, intentionally striking her only in the shoulder.

A red mist blurred her vision but she was sure she saw the wolf return and launch itself upon Popescu's back before she blacked out.

Shandor lifted his robes from around his ankles and trotted to keep up with Apollinari and Ilona who had ran out through the narrow dormitory entrance and across the monastery grounds. A handful of monks followed to tackle the fire that was slowly consuming the stables.

Skidding to a halt next to Popescu who was lying on his back in the mud, Apollinari said, "Cat got your tongue, captain?"

"Did...did you see?" Popescu pointed to the space before him. Apollinari offered a hand and pulled the soldier to his feet.

"What is it?" asked Ilona.

"There was a wolf!"

"Are you sure?" responded Apollinari. "In the grounds?"

"Your Highness, please," Shandor said, "I insist you return to your room. There may be danger here."

"My husband sees it fit to keep me here in times of bloodshed. And Popescu clearly believes it to be the safest place for me, too, unless you have other opinions that I should know about?"

Apollinari noticed the briefest expression of annoyance cross Shandor's face but the Abbot simply bowed respectfully and explained that he meant no offence.

"Father Shandor's fears are founded, Princess Ilona," Apollinari soothed. "As your unofficial appointed guardian he has to make sure you are safe here. If I were you I would heed his words."

Ilona opened her mouth to respond as a pained howl erupted from the burning stables.

Apollinari led the way at a run, skidding at the doorway, the heat and billowing smoke holding him back. Popescu, Ilona and Shandor slid up behind him.

"Can you see anyone?"

"No, Abbot," Apollinari shouted over the roar of the flames, pulling his scapular off over his shoulders. "Take this and soak it in a trough. I'm going in."

Shandor carried out the task and handed back the sopping material to Apollinari who flung it over his own head and made to dive into the acrid smoke.

But a dark shape, large and heavy, knocked him back and straight to the floor. The wolf leapt forward, a wound in its shoulder, and placed its front paws on his chest, yellow slavering teeth bared. Its snout twitched as it sniffed at Apollinari's neck. It sensed there was something different about him. Yellow eyes stared out from the black fur.

The wolf raised its head, airing a terrifying howl, and lunged at Apollinari's throat, claws scrabbling along his arms. The monk tried to wrestle the beast away, punching out at the sensitive spot under its throat. The wolf reeled back and came at him again, talons finally piercing the skin. Both Apollinari and the animal cried out, shocking all around.

At about the same time that Claudia and her group had mounted the monastery's waterwheel, some forty kilometres away Rintoul came to rest on the narrow window ledge outside Tarih-i-al-Osman's private chambers.

Wearing just his three-layered ucetek, the Governor moved around inside without any thoughts that he was being watched.

He had not slept well, the worry of the Wallachians' upcoming attack not sitting comfortably with him. He may have had a perfect military commander in Tanyel but nevertheless the *voivode* was ruthless and without mercy – and should their defences be infiltrated, he reasoned Vlad Tepes would not be the sort of man to allow the Turkish occupancy to go unpunished.

He sat and puffed at his pipe for a moment, retaining the smoke in his lungs for as long as he could before releasing it and taking a deep breath. The water in the bulbous chamber bubbled as he removed the mouthpiece, his tongue dry, but he felt the usual sense of comfort as the opium entered his bloodstream.

The small lead casket before him was adorned with a fine layer of gold leaf and images of Mehmed II, both dull now through age and handling. It had been his father's and he had found little use for it except as an ornament. Today, it served as a container for the impenetrable, silver-etched *kutu* that the Wallachian had brought to them, a box within a box.

Sitting on the bed, Tarih-i-al-Osman opened it and stared at the *kutu* nestled tight against the faded blue velvet interior. He ran his fingers over its polished surface but something made him start – something from out of the corner of his eye – so he closed the casket and placed it back on the small table nearby.

There was no one outside the closed window (of course there wouldn't be – they were three storeys up!) and the movement of light coming from under his door was the flickering of the candles, nothing more.

But there was something…

A tightness around his throat!

The Governor gasped for air and fell back on the bed, his ucetek falling open. Then the restriction went and he rubbed his throat anxiously.

More opium and then he moved to the door and opened it.

The guards were there, standing firm as usual. They glanced at him and ignored his flaccid embarrassment as he pulled his gown closed.

The door shut again with a secure, satisfying clunk but the invader was already inside the room, standing at his bed and cradling the lead casket.

"What..." Tarih-i-al-Osman began, but as the invader waved a hand, his voice left him.

"You are not a guardian," Rintoul said, the cuts and bruises on his forever-scarred face white and grey now that the blood had left his skin. "This is not yours."

The Governor tried to speak but no sound came. He rubbed his throat again. Rintoul waved a hand again.

"You!" blurted the Turk, spluttering with the sudden release of pressure on his larynx. "How have you escaped from the dungeon? Guards!"

"They will not hear you. Only within this room can your voice be heard."

Rintoul was still wearing the garb of his trade, the uniform of a Wallachian soldier, and the Governor looked him up and down in distaste.

"That thing you hold. It is not yours, either."

Nervously, Tarih-i-al-Osman didn't let go of the door handle. He tried to turn it but it would not budge. "How did you get in here?"

"My masters made that possible."

Rintoul moved to the window. The container of the Unholy Relic did not burn his vampire skin now that the Governor had so thoughtfully encased it in lead.

"Leave that here!"

The vampire looked down at the casket, as though only just remembering it was there. "You are not a guardian. This is *not* yours."

The window swung apparently open of its own volition.

"How...how have you done that?" Tarih-i-al-Osman cried, aghast as Rintoul stepped up to the ledge and appeared to throw himself out.

For a moment, the Governor stared at the empty window then dashed forward, looking out and down, trying to spot the twisted body of his visitor down below. But of Rintoul there was no sign.

The brief flickering of the moonlight the Turk assumed was clouds, not even remotely aware that it could be Rintoul coursing through the sky, the lead box clutched close to his chest.

Chapter 10

The animal screeched as Popescu's sword sliced across its snout, narrowly missing Apollinari's own face. Bounding off of Apollinari's prone form, the wolf reared up, talons flashing and headed towards the soldier.

"This thing won't die! It is a devil of the Turks!" Popescu staggered back and ducked as the wolf jumped. But the wound across its nose and the arrow protruding from its shoulder had weakened it and assured its fall to the muddy straw with a painful thud. It lay there, twitching and breathing hard, paws curled as though burnt.

Having helped Apollinari to his feet, a pair of soldiers stood either side of him. The monk, blood spreading inside his sleeves where the wolf had clawed him, moved his hands to his waist, open palms hovering at his left hip.

"Destroy it!" Popescu ordered, his men raising their bows with trepidation.

"No! Wait!"

Apollinari's command halted them abruptly but Popescu spun towards him. "It is an abomination. Do not keep it alive."

"No, captain. We cannot destroy it."

Apollinari turned and faced Shandor who was in silent prayer with a group of monks. "Abbot, we need rope. Thick rope."

Finishing his prayer, hoping God would remove the creature from the consecrated ground, Shandor stared, a little bemused. "Yes, we…we do. But-"

The monks looked anxiously to their Father, still unnerved by Apollinari's strange cry. Shandor nodded after a moment's consideration, and they hurried away.

"You intend to examine it?"

"It is injured. *We've* injured it. It needs to be contained so I can take a closer look." Apollinari looked around him and bit his bottom lip. "There." Apollinari pointed to the narrow doorway. "Captain, brothers, keep him out here until we're ready. Then we'll need to take him inside so we can net him in a controlled environment."

"You must be mad, Apollinari," Popescu hissed. "This thing will regain its strength and cut us all down." He brandished his sword. "But at least I know it can be hurt."

The monks soon returned with the rope and Apollinari directed them into securing the wolf. Working quickly, the animal was bound, a length of the long rope trailing to a monk's trembling hands.

The doors to the rooms running off to either side of the corridor had been locked securely, and in a couple of cases where the doors were less sturdy, barricaded with sandbags.

Apollinari, looking pleased with the work, hurried up to Shandor who was standing before the wolf.

"Do you really think we can take it safely inside?" Shandor tugged at the rope as if defying its fastened position and then passed it to a monk. "I assume that is where you intend to move it?"

"Of course," Apollinari retorted, almost sounding hurt that the Abbot had doubted the stability of his idea. "We must be confident."

"It is fate we're tempting, Apollinari." Father Shandor clasped his hands together and shook his head, his thick white hair circling his shaven spot firm atop his crown.

"A word of warning, monk..." Popescu leaned into Apollinari, their faces close. "If you fail at this and the wolf is set free, then I will personally drag you behind my steed all the way to Târgoviste and announce your treachery in front of the council." Apollinari could smell the garlic on his breath, the ale behind it. The man was clearly inebriated having spent the night drinking with his men but he controlled himself remarkably well. "Prince Vlad will be there to welcome you. And then he will impale you."

"I'd better look my best for such a noble audience." Apollinari stepped away from Popescu and returned his gaze to the wolf. "Shandor, I need you to close the rest of the doors and shut off any cloisters or annexes we've forgotten. Should the wolf wrestle itself free, we need to drive it in one direction to the dormitory."

"The brothers are seeing to that now. We will have a clear run."

"Excellent." Apollinari pulled a burning torch from a cradle on the wall and stomped off up the corridor, heading towards the exterior. "Then we'd better get this done and dusted. Let's get this creature in."

Back outside and within the grounds, the wolf was motionless, but a sharp prod from Popescu's sword caused the beast to raise its head and snarl angrily.

"Come on!" Apollinari called back to the monks who had been volunteered to help him. They gingerly lifted the heavy wolf and carried it towards the doorway, but the wolf, sensing it was being taken inside, tensed and howled and the monks faltered in surprise. Shuffling through, the monks stumbled over their own robes, sliding against the rough walls. The wolf twisted out of their grip and Apollinari dashed forward to grab the longer piece of rope, using it as a makeshift lead. The wolf doubled back but Popescu and his men had blocked its way so the only free route was the corridor before it. Apollinari felt the wrench in his shoulders as the wolf broke into a run, grey fur bristling as its anger increased.

"Brother Golick!" Shandor called out, watching the spectacle from the grounds, "help Father Apollinari! Grab that rope!"

The wolf gained speed as it pounded and clawed its way along the corridor as Golick did as he was bade. Alongside Apollinari now, he made chase.

"Come *on*!" Apollinari urged, Golick mouthing a prayer to himself.

The wolf launched itself backwards and landed inches behind Golick's heels. It flashed a claw at his Achilles' tendon, Golick whimpering as he felt the brush. Then the wolf raced off once more, deeper into the monastery.

"Just a bit further, Golick. You can do it!" Apollinari careened into the wall before him, bouncing off to head right, down a wider corridor. Trailing behind, Golick slipped again but managed to maintain his pace and his grip on the rope. He kept his eyes fixed on the burning torch in Apollinari's hand. The wolf's claws clattered and scraped in an eerie percussive rhythm.

A little distance ahead were two more monks, brothers Alexi and Lorimer, standing in the doorway and ready to close off the corridor after the odd trio had swept past. It was imperative to keep the wolf heading towards the dorm set aside for it a few hundred yards further on. If the beast suspected a trap – unlikely,

Apollinari hoped – and it turned back, then the plan would be ruined and they would probably all end up as supper.

Alexi and his quivering companion kept tight against the walls, hoping, praying that the wolf would not notice them and keep on going.

Apollinari and Golick were drawing close now. The shadows on the walls made it difficult the see the wolf in the gloom, but Golick knew it was there at the other end of the taut lead. He could hear the growl, hear the claws, and feel the pull: relentless in its escape from them.

Seconds later, there the wolf was - inches away from Alexi. It ground to a halt.

The thing's bleeding snout sniffed at Alexi, while Lorimer clamped a hand over his mouth to stop himself from vomiting with panic. Smelling worse than when they had found the dead ram at the bottom of the well last summer, the wolf swung its face in Lorimar's direction and snarled. Thick mucous dripped from its jaws.

Lorimer screwed his eyes up tight but the image of the creature was already in his subconscious. At Apollinari's further urging to Golick, the beast clicked its jaws and was gone, leaving Brother Lorimer breathless. Apollinari and Golick let go of the lead.

"Now, Alexi, now!"

Alexi soon knocked himself back into action. But next to him, Lorimer was frozen to the spot. Alexi shoved him out of the way and pulled the little door to the dorm shut, the wolf contained within. Apollinari reached the door and helped Alexi slide the makeshift bar across, wood thundering against wood as the heavy length rumbled down. Alexi, sure the door was tight, slid down against it, panting, trying to ignore his companion who was regurgitating his last meal over the floor.

Apollinari sat next to Alexi, pulling Golick with him.

"Well done," he murmured, the three monks feeling the door behind them shake as the wolf threw itself at it again and again from within its prison. Apollinari didn't even bother to acknowledge Shandor, Popescu and three men-at-arms as they came rushing up.

"You did it, Apollinari," Shandor complemented.

"Yes," Apollinari answered, somewhat smugly. "Yes, I did, didn't I?"

They all stayed there for a while, hearing the wolf howling, growling, and throwing itself around behind the door, until it seemed to grow weaker. Soon there was no noise coming from within and Apollinari stood, satisfied that the wolf had decided to concede defeat.

Chapter 11

Claudia opened her eyes and the pain in her left shoulder reminded her of her predicament.

She looked down. The arrow was embedded there and she knew she had to get it out before the lead tip started to poison her. But even grasping the shaft made her cry out and she wondered with some desperation as to how she would manage to pull it out herself. If only her uncle were here – he'd know. He'd have a way to remove the pain and to heal the wound.

But he wasn't here. She'd led Jurat and his men to their deaths, giving little thought to the lie she'd spun in order to be reunited with her family. She had taken advantage of Refik's greed and the notion that the gold-rich coffers could be theirs, had driven them to their brutal end. How could she ever be forgiven?

She sagged where she sat, against the coldness of the monastery's exterior wall, thinking of the kindness Jurat had shown her, albeit limited and clumsy. There had been no love between them but moments of lust and desire had taken them, taken them away from the camp and the eyes and ears of the bandits.

It had been the first time any man had touched her in that way and it was not an unpleasant experience. Jurat had opened her mind to this knew world and so time and again she allowed him to enter her from behind, to feel his roughness, his animal instinct, as he thrust heavily against her rear, his hands clawing at her arched back or digging into her thighs, until they both collapsed in unalloyed joy.

Across the way, the monks were battling the flames of one of the outhouses. They had no interest in anything else at that time and so Claudia took advantage of the furore and with as much strength as she could muster, yanked the arrow from her flesh.

She screamed and the tears flowed freely down her face.

A monk looked in her general direction but shrugged and got on with his task.

Even the nearby snuffling pigs took little notice of her.

When Claudia's vision cleared, she looked at the shaft in her bloodied hands and whimpered. The arrow head was still deep in her shoulder, the snapped strip in her grasp testament to that. She needed help and ironically she was in the most ideal place.

Perhaps she could convince the monks that she had been a prisoner of the bandits... Yes! That was it! An easy ploy. So there was nothing for it but to cross towards the monks and collapse, the latter something that she was easily able to do.

Rintoul appeared at the window, his form silhouetted by the moonlight. As he stepped into the room, he knelt and thrust out his hands, holding the lead box.

Ismael darted forward, eyes wide with desire but a strong hand on his shoulder made him turn.

"Wait," said Kelele.

"After all this time you wish to delay?" said Ismael, motioning for Rintoul to stand.

"This is a momentous occasion, Ismael," Odalys purred. "We must savour it."

"Four hundred years we have waited. What difference does a few more moments make?" Kelele glided into the moonlight and looked at the silver disc high in the November sky. "There are times when this immortal existence makes us forget where we came from; makes us ignore the delicacies of experience."

"Sentiments for the Living, Kelele, not for the likes of us."

"But remember," Kelele continued, raising a long finger, "without the Living, we are nothing."

"We are superior to the Living," said Odalys. "Kelele, you sound as if you wish to return to their limited world."

"Not at all. I was a prince but now I am vampire. The Living are our cattle."

"Then why do you insist on this dreary reminiscing?" Ismael was growing impatient, the lead box in Rintoul's hands becoming ever more enticing.

"You do not have the experience we do, Ismael. It does us good to remind ourselves of our prior mortality. It allows us to realise the potentials we can achieve." Kelele swung around to face his companions. "To control furtherance! To be able to resurrect that which should be dead!"

"Do not blaspheme, Kelele! Our Lord can never die!"

"Exactly, Ismael," replied the Ethiopian, taking the box from Rintoul. Odalys and Ismael both seemed to gasp at the movement, as if the physical touching of the Relic brought them one step closer to their desires that night. "Only we can bring him back from the jaws of salvation."

"Then do it, Kelele!" Ismael cried.

Kelele looked at the vampires before him. Odalys was anxious, her white eyes boring into him as her fingers wrestled with the cord around her hips. Ismael, ever impatient, needed no further exposition and hissed at Kelele, baring his sharp white teeth. Viktor was silent as ever, rocking back and forth on his haunches, talon-like hands grasping at the thin air. And finally there was Rintoul, calm and penitent - too young to understand the impact that the Relic had on them all and too inferior to witness what was about to happen here. With a flick of his wrist, Kelele flung Rintoul out of the window and Viktor scrabbled in the dirt in reaction. With his other hand, the Ethiopian threw the lead box at the wall. It shattered, hurling the silver-etched container within it to the ground.

As it came to rest as Ismael's feet, the Turk sneered at Kelele.

"Now what?" Ismael said, gesturing at the box. "It is still sealed and we are no further forward."

"Witchcraft protects it," murmured Odalys. "Only witchcraft can open it."

"How?" Kelele asked, this small box seemingly outwitting them.

Viktor shuddered just then and crawled to the box, reaching out as if to touch it.

"No, Viktor," warned Odalys as the mute's fingers hovered.

But instead, he sat on his haunches, held out a wrist and mimed as if to slice it open. He grabbed a palmful of dirt and let it trickle over where he had made the imaginary incision, the dust falling across the box, obscuring the silver.

"Blood..." hissed Ismael.

"But not vampire blood."

"Then who's, Kelele?"

"The blood of the living, Odalys," he responded, understanding, "for the blood is the life!"

Rintoul spun in the air and managed to control himself before he hit the ground. Not that the fall would destroy him, mind, but it would be uncomfortable nevertheless and he'd need fresh blood to regenerate the twisted limbs he'd likely suffer. But it was no matter, for he sank gently to the snow and looked back up at the tower's window many feet above him.

It seemed ages ago now that he could feel the cold through his boots, would shiver in his meagre armour as the biting wind coursed across the Wallachian Plains. As a vampire, Rintoul was discovering that the removal of all feeling save for pain was unnerving. His gums remained sore where his fangs protruded and he was learning when and how to retract them. His limbs ached whenever he woke at night and whenever he drank. Ismael had told him it would pass, these new sensations, as his body adapted to a new way of existing.

But to be dismissed so violently from the tower was something he hadn't expected but he had certainly been warned by Ismael of the vampire hierarchy and its cold handling of those beneath it. The Celebrants, of which Ismael was one of course, had demonstrated that and Rintoul padded through the snow, intrigued as to how the creatures in their high tower would penetrate the box.

His heightened senses alerted him to every noise, every nuance, of the world around him. The powder crunched under his feet as he walked, the breaking of every icicle resonating shrilly. He could hear the Turks embedded in the Citadel talking in their alien tongue as clear as if they were standing without the fortified walls next to him. The forest surrounding Dambovita whispered and creaked against every pressure against it that the wind gave. He tried to drown out the building crescendo by pushing his palms against his ears but it was no use and he cried out, his own voice drowning in the sea of turmoil.

"It will ease."

The voice, stark in its clarity, made Rintoul wheel around.

It was Ismael, laughing gently, the dead breath from his lungs making no issue in the cold night air.

"Are you not required to open the box?" Rintoul asked, frowning.

Ismael shot a glance up to the tower. "We have reached a decision and it involves the Living."

Rintoul did not feel the need to ask any further so nodded.

"You appear troubled, Rintoul. What is concerning you?"

Rintoul was not afraid of Ismael, but he was concerned that his reticence about his new life would anger his maker. "Why did you turn me?"

"Every young vampire asks that question. What you are feeling is no different to anyone else."

"What about you?"

Ismael put an arm around Rintoul's shoulders and they walked together through the snow. "Some of us are old, older than the bricks and mortar that hold up this chariot of man's power. They can only remember how it feels through the eyes of the young like yourself. They have very little recall after all these centuries. Mine are on the cusp, like a dream that pours away forever like sand through fingers. These feelings you have, they make up what you will become. Your body is changing, adapting. It now has little to fear from disease and cold and mortality. It will live forever."

"Forever seems such an awful length of time."

"It will stretch out before you, but do not fear it." Ismael stopped and pulled Rintoul close to face him. "Embrace it, Rintoul! You have been chosen as a guardian of the Relic. It sits up there and the Celebrants fear it. But you and I - we can take the Relic and rise above them - we can be the Celebrants together!"

"But the Celebrants are powerful. How can we take it?"

"They wait for a sacrifice. We will wait until dawn."

"Dawn? But we cannot exist in daylight."

"Why?" Ismael continued to walk and Rintoul followed.

"We are creatures of the dark, we live in the shadows," reasoned the young vampire.

Ismael nodded, a smile playing across his lips. "But are there not shadows in the day as well?"

In the infirmary, sitting on a narrow bed, Apollinari was having his forearms cleaned and bandaged, Brother Jacob careful to wash out any traces of blood and dirt left by the wolf's claws.

Shandor looked agitated as he sipped warm medovina from a narrow bowl. Apollinari had been offered the same but declined. Honey always made him nauseous.

"How long do you intend to keep that animal here?" the Abbot asked.

"As long as I need to, to establish where it came from," responded Apollinari. "Wolves are pack animals yet this one was on its own. So where are its companions?"

"That thought had occurred to me, too," Shandor replied, a shudder caressing his back.

Apollinari winced slightly as his bandages were fastened tight. Jacob suggested a redressing in a few days time. Apollinari nodded and waved the monk away. He had greater concerns at that moment beyond a few cuts and grazes.

Silent until Jacob had closed the infirmary door behind him and careful to ensure no one else was in earshot, Apollinari moved to the edge of the bed and leant closed to Shandor.

"What do you know of the de Blanc Grimoire?"

The question made Shandor tense.

"Nothing," he replied as calmly as he could. "I know only that letter you brought mentioned it. That it had been lost and must be found under all circumstances"

"But you do know what a Grimoire is?"

"Of course. It is not the sort of work I would have in my monastery, Father Apollinari. Why? Is it of importance?"

"Philippe de Blanc was a man who lived something like four hundred years ago. His Grimoire was also his journal, specifically, a log of his journey to and from the Holy Land to obtain a Relic."

"A heathen, then. A blasphemer."

"This Relic could threaten everything we hold dear."

"Relics usually do. But they are nothing more than old, rotten remains of religious extremists who have more influence after they're dead than they ever did when they were alive."

"Normally, I would agree with you. But this Relic is different and de Blanc believed this in the year of 1099. It is still believed now to this very day - and, ironically, life and death have a bearing more than you realise."

"How so?"

"This Relic can bring back the 'extremist' in question."

"De Blanc?"

"No. The enemy of de Blanc, the enemy of Rome. In fact, the enemy of every God-fearing soul on this world. Rome and the Witches share a common foe!"

"I don't know who you are, Apollinari. But I know what Popescu thinks you are. The way you are talking now I should have you arrested, flogged – worse: excommunicated - for such views."

"But you won't."

"No. I won't."

"Why?"

"Because I must know why you are here. And you will tell me what witchcraft has to do with anything."

"It is not witchcraft that threatens us now, Shandor, although I fear it is something we shall have to nevertheless face."

"There are no witches here!"

"Don't be so sure. All the same, we should be more wary of the supernatural."

"The supernatural? We live in daily fear of such things, but our prayers and faith in the Lord keep them at bay. Who are you to say that our penitence is not enough? I would wish you to leave Snagov, to go with your irreverent talk and never return. You are no longer welcome here."

"I will leave, Shandor, gladly I will. But the Undead will remain."

"How dare you!" Shandor spat, the medovina splashing across his chin.

"The Undead *will* remain. And if that Relic falls into the hands of those who know how to use it, the Undead will rise up an army. They will sweep across this land and all other lands and, no matter race, religion or creed, all will curl and wither under their influence. No one will be safe."

"God will protect us."

"No one will be safe, Shandor. Not you, not me. No one. God's enemies will bring about the Apocalypse."

"Hell on Earth."

"Nothing so mundane. Work with me, Abbot. Understand what is happening - what can happen. I was sent here to look for the de Blanc Grimoire. With the book, so tradition has it, comes the Relic. Always together and never apart. And because it is believed the Grimoire is lost, Rome fears the worst."

"But why here?"

"It was in Bistritz that the book was last seen. Its keeper, a woman called Weiss, was burnt at the stake at the beginning of summer. Her belongings were cast into the street and the rabble swooped upon them, eager to own something that once belonged to a witch. It is said that amongst these items the Grimoire sat. Kept safe for centuries by the bloodline of de Blanc only to be cast asunder as if it were food scraps."

"This resurrection you speak of..."

"A resurrection implies something coming from death."

"This is something coming from the...Undead?" Shandor gripped the bowl of medovina as if his very faith depended on it.

"Yes. A restoration, let's say."

"How will it happen? When?"

"That I don't know. But there are those who do. Those already Undead."

"Who?"

"Vampires, Abbot Shandor, vampires! They dare to see their Lord and Master restored. And we have to dare to stop them!"

"You are mad!"

"Am I? Perhaps. But you're still listening to me."

"I feel as if I have no choice."

"We all have choices."

"But at what cost are those choices made?"

And there was the challenge facing Apollinari.

It reminded him of the time he was called upon to marry in secret England's fourth King Edward to his consort, twenty or more years ago now. Apollinari was in defiance of the union but nevertheless was obliged to carry it out – the church hesitant to upset any status quo. It was only years later, as Apollinari plunged a hawthorn stake through Elizabeth Woodville's heart, that his insistence she had not been entirely human were finally met.

Shandor was afraid, Apollinari reasoned, as afraid now as the English Church had been then.

They had known what Woodville was but refused to accept it, instead preferring to keep a vampire at their King's right hand until someone with the courage and sagacity to destroy her had been found. But even then the conspiracy remained: following her demise (which was brutal, Apollinari had to admit) she was replaced by a doppelganger and Apollinari was sworn to secrecy.

Destroying the vampire she had become was relatively easy, especially as Woodville had never turned anyone as far as was known. But the casket in Snagov's catacombs bore the mark to tell of the Relic's presence and it supposed a whole new set of challenges. For Caleb the Undead's influence, even after his demise, meant his disciples could be found in every dark corner and still willing to carry out his posthumous evil.

Apollinari sighed inwardly, the soreness of his arms compounding his fatigue. There was much to do but at the forefront was locating Verrecchia. His novice was young, not even in his second decade yet, and knew little about the world. The wilds of Europe brought dangers and challenges no man should willingly face and so Apollinari had kept close to Verrecchia, determined to protect him at all costs.

It was ironic that here, in a monastery of all places, he should have gone missing.

Forgiveness was something Apollinari found naturally but that didn't extend to forgiving himself should Verrecchia come to harm. He was not willing to let yet another of his apprentices meet such a fate.

But how far could Apollinari push himself before he needed to rest? He wasn't a young man anymore and simply didn't have the stamina like he used to. He needed to rest, if only for a little while, before he made his next move.

And so, as dawn rose, he found himself sitting on a window ledge in the reredorter looking out across the island at this small, self-contained and self-sufficient world which carried on regardless.

He followed the flights of crows in and amongst the treetops and across the lake, heard them calling in their raucous fashion as their day began.

In the inner courtyard below, three gypsies were attaching two horses, hides as black as night, to a flat-bed cart.

Watching them for a while as they darted silently back and forth, Apollinari gave little consideration to the fact that no monks were down there assisting or supervising, assuming Snagov's bustling community meant trader and traveller often came and went. As one gypsy held the horse, the remaining two struggled to lift and slide a heavy crate, covered in tarpaulin, onto the back of the cart.

A sudden gust and the covering lifted for a moment. A glint on the box's top caught Apollinari's eye.

Jumping up, Apollinari rushed to the door and hared down the treacherously worn steps and through the library to a corridor where he collided with Princess Ilona coming in the opposite direction.

She wasn't interested in his apologies, instead desperate to calm her breathing and retain his attention.

"Your Highness, I must pass," he said, hesitant about pushing by in the narrow passageway.

"Please, Father," she breathed, "I need your help."

Her elfin face was framed with the turmoil of anxiety. Apollinari frowned, torn between his mendicant duty and the desire to stop the crate in its tracks. He looked beyond Ilona at the gloomy corridor curling away before him, as if this would will the gypsies to stay.

"Normally," he began, "normally I would endeavour to help you, but..." His voice trailed off and he made to leave.

Her small hand gripped his forearm with a firmness that expressed her unease. "Take me with you."

"Where?"

"Wherever you're going. Away from here!"

"But what convinces you I'm going anywhere?"

"You seem to be in a hurry."

Apollinari couldn't argue with her deduction. "I have business to conclude here before I leave."

She shook her head, her platted tresses swaying against her shoulders. "We must go now."

"Princess Ilona, I..."

He looked down at the silver blade that had suddenly appeared in her hand. "I do not wish to argue or have to force you. I have confronted more powerful men than you."

Apollinari didn't for one moment doubt that statement. He raised his hands in submission. "I have no quarrel with you. But you must understand that I cannot leave here just yet. Now please let me on my way."

"What of your novice?"

The monk gritted his teeth, the cadence of his trimmed beard gentle. "What of him?"

"Surely the longer you stay here the further away he gets?"

Apollinari turned then, quite swiftly, and grabbed the woman's hand. The knife clattered to the flagstones. "Where is he?"

"He has gone, Father, taken by Zucco."

This changed things. "Where?"

"I don't know," she replied.

Apollinari hissed through his teeth.

"But," Ilona continued, seeing Apollinari's impatience increasing, "I overheard the brothers whispering in the frater about the Italian boy leaving with him."

"That gypsy went last night. Did they say where he was headed?"

Ilona said nothing, reclaiming the advantage by folding her arms.

"But you won't tell me unless I take you with me. Is that it?"

Met with further silence, Apollinari bent and picked up the knife. "If you wish to act like a child, then clearly this is not for your hands." The knife disappeared beneath his robes. "So, where do we go from here? Standing in the shadows will not help either of us."

"I told you: away from this place."

"And you will show me where Zucco went?"

"Yes."

Apollinari considered for a moment, worried that her presence would hinder his progress. Admittedly, she could clearly look after herself but nevertheless, she was an important figure and could attract all manner of undesirables wishing to benefit from her vulnerability away from the Royal Court. But Verrecchia was as equally vulnerable now and any chance he had to restore his novice's safety he had to take.

"Very well."

Ilona's posture relaxed then and she stepped forward, her shoulders free of the tautness.

"I ask you to be patient, though, Your Highness. There is something that I *have* to do right now."

"But-"

"Our departure must be swift. Popescu will no doubt be on his guard. Obtain if you can furs. It is treacherous out there and it will be fruitless if we were to die of cold before we catch sight of our quarry."

"Where shall I meet you?"

"Stay within the main courtyard. Keep watch for me."

Ilona looked as though she was about to ask further questions but she saw the restlessness in Apollinari's eyes so instead turned and disappeared up the corridor.

"Why do I get the feeling I'm going to regret this?" Apollinari murmured to himself as he continued his progress.

The narrow entrance to the passageway opened up to a small courtyard, the other side of which the cloisters began. Apollinari darted across, excusing himself as he rushed past a group of monks, one of which expressed his disgust at such a display of impetuousness.

A bit further on and the massive double gates to the main courtyard sat closed before him. He skidded to a halt, the wood under his palms cold as he pushed against them. They were shut tight and the monk in charge of their operation needed some prompting to open them in a timely fashion.

Painfully slowly did they part outwards and Apollinari saw the cart with its burden rumble towards the second set of twin gates and the exterior portion of the monastery proper.

"Stop!" he cried, his voice swallowed by the wind. He called again, louder, harsher, but this only impelled the driver to crack his whip harder across the backs of the black horses before him.

The two other gypsies were at the other gates, pushing them open as the cart was urged forward.

Breaking into a run, Apollinari reached the gypsies as the cart passed through the gateway. How did these people get the casket from the under the watch of Popescu's men? He was sure Popescu had told him he'd moved it from the catacombs.

The men stood their ground, blocking his way, but he lowered his shoulder and rammed his way through, grabbing the rear of the cart with an outstretched hand. Stumbling, his knees striking the wheel nearest to him,

Apollinari regained his balance and reached out again as the cart moved out and down the path to the drawbridge on the island's bank. Again he staggered and the gypsies came up behind him, flattening him into the mud. This was ridiculous! Where was the captain?

Pinned there, the monk watched helplessly as the driver navigated down the stony path, the high walls of the monastery behind him now, waited for the drawbridge to complete its downward arc, then moved the horses and the cart with its dark cargo onto the waiting ferry at the end of the jetty.

His captors' breaths reeked of Tokay as they laughed in his face, aware of his desperation as the cart departed across the lake. The ferry on the other end of the pulley system started making its way across from the far bank.

The gypsies stood, releasing their hold on Apollinari, knowing he couldn't follow now. Apollinari stood and stared after the ferry, the covering over the crate flapping like a bat, almost as if it were taunting him.

Just then, the three men felt the ground begin to rumble and they all turned to see a great grey mare thundering towards them, nostrils flaring, chomping at the bit between its yellow teeth.

On its back was a figure, oddly shaped and concealed, until the massive furred hood was flung back to reveal a delicate aspect framing a rigid expression.

It was Ilona!

The gypsies, startled, hurled themselves out of the way as Ilona turned the horse so that Apollinari could mount it. For the monk, riding bareback was something he had never forgotten how to do. He pulled himself up and onto the steed with surprisingly agility and settled in behind her. His arms snaked around her waist, tiny even wrapped in all the furs she had collected.

With a cry Ilona urged the horse to move, the beast whinnying as it stomped into motion.

She cantered the horse back to the monastery.

"Where are you going?" Apollinari cried, as Ilona headed towards where the monks had collected together the dead bandits. She reached down and slid a sword out from a corpse's sheath. Apollinari clung on as she righted herself, using the heavy sword as a counterbalance, while horse spun back around to the drawbridge that was slowly beginning to rise.

With the horse trotting quicker now, Ilona raised the weapon as they neared the bridge, swinging the blade downwards and through the tar-soaked rope attached to the right wheel. The drum clattered as it came loose and the horse sped on to the pulley's companion, the rope mastering the drawbridge, on the left. The sword made easy work of that too. The bridge crashed back down again as Ilona twisted the steed back in to the centre of the pathway, Apollinari flinging around with them.

Ilona dug her heels into the animal's flank. Apollinari felt the wind take him as the beast whinnied again and broke into a gallop.

The empty ferry had by this time reached the jetty (its companion over the other side of the lake having disgorged its burden onto the mainland). But a fourth gypsy in control of the pulley system on the island's side started frantically turning the great wheel to start the empty ferry on its journey back away from the island.

The gap between the jetty and the ferry widened with every turn and Apollinari swallowed hard at the thought of what Ilona was intending to do. The horse tried to turn its head, distressed that it was being made to aim for such a target. Powering down, Ilona forced the animal on and within seconds they were across the drawbridge and heading onto the jetty.

Ilona encouraged the surefooted horse, which, having launched itself across open air, slid to a halt on the moving ferry.

"This isn't going to work! Look!" called Apollinari as he pointed out that the fourth gypsy was able to pull them back.

Ilona shrugged off the heavy furs from her shoulders to reveal a longbow across her back. A quiver full of arrows lay against her thigh. Apollinari shook his head in wonderment and disbelief, thinking perhaps his concern in bringing her along was unjustified.

Like a marksman, Ilona armed the longbow, turned and fired, hitting the gypsy square in the chest.

The man cried out and fell backwards, dead.

The momentum he had built up with the pulley meant the ferry was free to continue its journey to the far bank unabated.

"And you *really* needed my help to escape?" quipped Apollinari as they both breathed a sigh of relief, the ferry undulating beneath them.

Chapter 12

The huge doors swung back, the resonance as they hit the stone arch supporting them echoing around the phalanx of men. Their way lit by torches and braziers, they moved out through the gateway in perfect synchronicity and along the track.

Yozgatli Tanyel, staying in the shadows of his quarters, watched the procession snake its way slowly out of the Citadel, heading towards dawn and the town at the bottom of the slight hill. The catapulters with their insect-like siege engines, archers with their huge longbows, knights in dull armour and the overseeing Field Marshalls all kept in tight formation.

It would take them three days to reach Târgoviste Palace.

The Governor was sure of the *voivode*'s presence there - the *voivode* having recently received falsified papal orders instructing him to keep a low physical presence at Târgoviste. The Governor would use this ruse to remove Vlad from power and, with their revered leader dead, the Wallachian army would be directionless and easily crushed.

But little did the Governor understand Vlad's blatant disobedience to alternative orders: such orders in the past had led to the Prince's twelve-year imprisonment. Even if Tarih-i-al-Osman's forged letter to the *voivode had* been from the Vatican, he was certainly no more likely to follow its instructions.

Tanyel was not going to bring such a small oversight to his Governor's attention. Damn the fool for even trying to bluff the *voivode* and damn him even further for listening to the sly, ubiquitous Ismael.

His suspicion of this attendant stranger had not eased over the little time Tanyel had been back from Shipka. Ismael had been present at the count's side more or less ever since Tanyel's return and, it seems, feeding Tarih-i-al-Osman with fanciful ideas of razing Târgoviste to the ground. Of course Tanyel understood the need for secrecy and spies. After all, had he not himself once been commanded by the Sultan in person to live as an Egyptian for some years, his infiltration resulting in the successful obtaining of land and treasures?

Yet if this Ismael was indeed a spy, he had most definitely won Tarih-i-al-Osman's confidence but given Tanyel an advantage. He would watch Tarih-i-al-Osman, hawk-like, waiting for Ismael to slip him some untoward falsehood and then Tanyel would watch Tarih-i-al-Osman fall, step in as high commander of the Turkish army and impale Ismael outside the gates of Târgoviste itself.

A knock came at his door but he ignored the call, silently cursing who ever it was to leave him be as they knocked again. The commander returned to his desk and sat, staring long at the maps before him, marked in watery purple to signify potential land clams and detailed ordnances.

If he looked deep enough, what answers would he find? The determined knocking at his door faded into his subconscious.

The day would be long and Tanyel, already tired and weary, closed his eyes for a moment. Just briefly so he could regain his clarity of mind. He would open them again in a moment, focused and alert. He needed no time at all. Just a few seconds. Just discipline and a trained mind.

The knocking at the door had become almost rhythmic now, delicate, relaxing, reassuring. Without even being conscious that he was concentrating, he counted the beats, the gentle taps. One, two, three, four. One, two, three, four. One, tw-

A shout. His eyes snapped open and he threw his hands out to stop himself from falling into his desk that was no longer there.

The room had dissolved around him. He spun and wheeled and the shout came again and again until he realised it was his own voice, his own fear, bouncing back and forth, all around him. Falling, Tanyel saw the ground rushing up at him. What in Islam was happening to him? Even as he descended his mind turned over. Had he done something as infantile as fallen from his window? Was this the courtyard hurtling up towards him? He must remember to reprimand the men for allowing the moss to grow so freely over the cobbles.

The wind whipped over and around his face causing his long hair to flick, like needles, at his eyes and cheeks. Faster and faster he fell, the ground, so far away that he couldn't focus yet so close he could almost touch it, rushing up to meet him. Circles and lights flashed past and shapes that he thought could be many *kutu*s spun by. Willing his arms to cover his eyes, his limbs frozen and almost immobile, he heard himself cry out again from without his body and braced himself. It was pointless, he knew, for the ground, or courtyard, or whatever it really was, would be merciless as he struck.

Then he stopped.

No wind in his hair. No rushing. No sensation of falling helplessly through nothing. No feeling of his chest tightening as the ground beckoned.

Nothing.

Just quiet, still nothing.

Slowly, tentatively, he pulled his arms away. They ached. He dreaded the sight that would befall his eyes as he cracked them open. But if he was alive what was there to be afraid of? Only very recently had he witnessed atrocities on the Shipka Plains that would make even the strongest man weep. He had felt no nausea then, had not shied away from his duties as commander of his forces and chief executioner of the Carpathian hordes – so why the trepidation now?

Suddenly angry, he willed his eyes to open, feeling a churning in the pit of his stomach. How dare he be taken in this way! He demanded to know why he hadn't died in battle, hadn't had a honourable and bloodied death, and not dashed against the courtyard of his spineless master's cuckoo nest.

Who was it that had once said that a running man could cut one thousand throats in a single night? He had meant to prove that wrong before he died. *Two* thousand throats. Two thousand Wallachians.

Now he would never get the chance.

Then his eyes were open, sore from the cold, but wide and alert.

It was a wood in the middle of the night.

Tanyel gasped, clutching at his chest. His breath had suddenly been taken from him, the trees towering above him into the black sky spinning. He shook his head, heart pounding like a hammer behind his ribcage. It was cold and he murmured to himself that he was likely to catch his death, which was ironic because wasn't he dead already? And, if he *was* dead, then the woman standing some feet away must either be dead as well or an astral courtier here to help him on his way.

Striding towards her, he could see she was talking to herself, but the closer he got he realised she were making no sound at all. He called to her, hand playing over the hilt of his dagger hidden in the folds of his cloak. She ignored him and carried on talking.

Surely she must have seen him or, at least, heard him move through the dry, fallen leaves and bracken. Then he stopped and looked down at his boots. They were heavy, leather and studded, but no matter how furiously he kicked at the leaves, no matter how sharply he stomped on broken twigs, breaking them easily under his weight, no crack, rustle or snap was to be heard. He called out his own name, expecting sleeping birds to be frightened from their nests, but nothing moved, nothing stirred, nothing sounded.

What insane afterlife had he ended up in? The notion of permanent and complete silence, except his own voice in his head, briefly gripped him with fear. He laughed the notion away. Silently.

His own voice he heard was only inside his head.

The woman in front of him suddenly stepped in his direction, mouthed something incomprehensible and moved off. Tanyel watched, finding her poise and shape most pleasurable. She wore a white gown, partly translucent in the moonlight, her hair as black as death partially obscuring the curve of her firm breasts.

The sight of the dark, delicate triangle between her legs made his penis stir.

At least his some things hadn't been taken from him.

The vision stepped towards him, hands cupped together to hold the silver-etched box, the elusive *kutu*.

Tanyel reached out to touch the treasure, running his fingers over its surface, noting a strange vibration coursing through his fingertips. It was alive!

He jerked his hand back, initially shocked, and, after a moment, touched the *kutu* again. He did not understand how something could be moving so imperceptibly that he couldn't see it with his eyes, but could still feel the movement under his hand. Neither did he understand the reason for the object itself.

But he knew the *kutu* would explain it to him.

Then without warning the woman pulled the *kutu* away. Tanyel reached out, hands grabbing like a child.

"It will be yours," she said, her voice like silk.

"I want it now." His reply to her was barely perceptible even to himself, yet he knew he *had* answered her out loud.

If no one else could hear him, Tanyel was convinced this woman could. He also wondered if she could hear as clear as he the blood pounding in his ears - and the slow heartbeat that wasn't his own.

"It will call to you."

"When?"

"Soon. It has waited patiently. You will endorse that by being patient yourself."

The woman drifted backwards, away from him, slowly at first but increasing in speed the further back she moved.

"Wait!" Tanyel called out, hands pawing at the air again. But the woman's departure did not cease and

Tanyel watched until she disappeared into the murky depths of the forest.

Tanyel, his desk suddenly before him once more, gasped as if he had swum to the surface of some great lake, the air fighting to get into his lungs.

The Turk rubbed his chest, the tightness easing as he looked around his office.

The knock at the door came again and he called for the visitor to enter.

It was Ekvan. Tanyel stood before his head gaoler had closed the door behind him.

"My Lord..."

"What is it, Ekvan, that you find it so necessary to disturb my peace?"

"The men are waiting below."

"Very well."

Tanyel buckled a luxuriant sheath around his waist then lifted the equally opulent sword which it housed. The commander looked down the sword with one eye, rubbing a blemish clear with a silk kerchief.

"Until we find the Wallachian, I am not prepared to make any sacrifices. Order them back to their quarters."

Ekvan was relieved. Good men were hard to come by during these troubled times and he found the loyalty of his current batch of prison guards to be without question. Too often had he been lumbered with the lame, the objectionable or the traitorous, the army generals not willing to put them among the rank and file on the battlefield. Instead they were distributed among the prisons, kept under lock and key as much as the men they guarded. They were an economical stream of resource.

As Ekvan bowed with honest graciousness, they were soon joined by Tarih-i-al-Osman blundering into the room, cheeks red and a silk kerchief held to his mouth.

"It's gone!" he lisped, breathless and agitated.

"What's that, my Lord?" Tanyel asked and raised an eyebrow, Ekvan noticing the look of distain across his face just then.

"The box! The Wallachian treasure! The *kutu*!"

Tanyel made no mention of his prior vision and the woman who had beckoned to him. Was that where it had gone, the *kutu*? Somehow magicked out of substance and into his thoughts?

He smiled. If that was the case, it was now in the safest place that no man could cast asunder to reach.

"It is a trinket. Nothing more," Tanyel said, waving away any importance in the object.

"But you said it was a key – a way to make our men invincible."

"I was wrong." Tanyel sheathed his sword, coolly nonchalant.

"But what if you were right?" the Count breathed, his windpipe rattling. "What if even now that Wallachian dragon has it and is making his own men as we had hoped to make ours?"

"Vlad Tepes does *not* have the *kutu*."

Even Ekvan, who was used to Tanyel's occasional forays into deceiving the Count - for the Count's own good, Ekvan understood - was surprised at the complacency Tanyel displayed.

"How can you be so sure? How do you know that our troops, marching to Târgoviste as we speak, are not to fall under the curse of Dracul's son? " asked the Count, the same question which Ekvan dared not solicit.

Even as ineffective as the Count could be, Tanyel was not about to reveal where he thought the *kutu* actually was. "No Wallachian would dare infiltrate our defences."

"Defences *they* built!" Tanyel was reminded.

"Do not over estimate their abilities. They may have fortified this place but our foothold makes it invincible."

"But why would they not come for it? It is after all theirs."

"How do you know?" asked Tanyel. "How can you be so sure? Just because one enemy soldier was found with it does not make it theirs by right. It is *meant* to be here – and it *is* here still."

"Where?" said the Count, fussing with his silk. "May Allah strike you down should we be overcome by the Catholic!"

"Don't be so overly dramatic, Count Tarih-i-al-Osman," Tanyel spat, the Count stepping back a few paces in surprise. "The Sultan wouldn't like it."

"How...how dare you talk to me like that!" he squealed. "I am appointed by the Sultan himself and he would-"

"The Sultan would replace you in an instant if he learnt that you considered the might of Dracula to be superior."

"But we are strong!"

"We?" Tanyel considered, fingers drumming the hilt of his sword. "I'm more concerned with *you*."

"The Sultan has faith."

"Perhaps. But faith can be broken. What if he were to learn that the Governor of one of his strategically important occupations was no longer *able* to govern? That the Governor's *own* faith in his men had frayed?"

"What are you saying?" Tarih-i-al-Osman spun to face Ekvan. "Listen to him. He deliberates treason!"

"No, he does not," Ekvan replied. "He deliberates blackmail."

"You see, Governor," Tanyel said, smiling, "I command loyalty. What do *you* have?"

"You listen to this man," the Count screamed to Ekvan, not even aware of his name, "and you will find yourself behind the very prison bars that you maintain!"

"If it means I am at my master's side, then I will go gladly."

Tarih-i-al-Osman shrieked. "Are all your men so insolent, Tanyel?"

"No one will be imprisoned here unless I say so. Now leave and return to your quarters. Remain there and await my command. The *kutu* is safe – safer than being in your hands."

"You will not hear the last of this, Tanyel," the Count seethed, trotting away into the depths of the Citadel.

Tanyel waited until he was out of sight then turned to Ekvan.

"Your loyalty is not unnoticed. Nor will it go unrewarded."

"My Lord," Ekvan bowed.

"There are new things about to happen. A new order is coming. You and I will be part of it."

Ekvan remained stooped and digested Tanyel's words. He didn't quite understand the inference but assumed it had something to do with the exchange had with the Governor.

"I am at your command."

"I expect nothing less. Our men need us as they approach Târgoviste. Let us lead them to victory."

Chapter 13

The Sardinian sun was setting over the fields, glinting through the line of trees to the west. Children played and called, making the most of the last moments before twilight and the impending curfew.

Toes wriggling in the cool, long grass, Roberto Verrecchia could smell the bubbling pasta coming from his mama's kitchen as he stared up at the pinkish clouds, making out shapes: one was a goat and there, over there next to the big one, was an urn. Then the wind blew and the clouds moved on, changing, forever malleable, until they dissolved into the heavens.

A rumbling in the distance signalled thunder.

Roberto frowned, his young face crinkling under his shaggy hair. It had been a wonderfully bright day as he'd played in the stream with his friends, no sign of an oncoming storm.

A cold breeze came over him just then and he shivered.

Without warning, he was drenched in a sudden downpour and he sat up, gasping.

Sardinia had gone, replaced by grimy, rusting bars. The long grass had dried to scratchy hay and the smell of food was coming from a fire nearby.

Zucco stood grinning at him from without the cage. Captive, Verrecchia grabbed the bars from the inside and saw the empty pail in the gypsy's hands, the stagnant contents of which his gaoler had just used to rouse him from his dream.

The manacle around Verrecchia's neck bit into his throat. He felt a flush, his blood pounding in his ears as he realised he was trapped. Mouth dry, he tried to stand but the tiny prison only allowed him to shuffle to his knees. Panic was beginning to set in and Zucco's large face leering at him was not helping.

"Please," Verrecchia began, voice breaking, "let me out."

Zucco broke into a peal of laughter - the young monk not sure if it was a genuine or forced - and flung open the cage door.

Verrecchia was dragged out with such vigour to the compacted snow that the breath was knocked out of him. The young monk lay there for a moment, gasping, but Zucco wasn't a patient man and pulled him to his feet.

Legs wobbling, Verrecchia knew he had to remain standing. The cosh moving back and forth between his captor's wide hands was testament to that.

No verbal exchanges were had for the few moments Verrecchia stood there shaking, keeping his eyes closed and mouthing prayers to himself over and over.

"Do you think that will help?" Zucco finally said, striking Roberto behind his knees. Crumpling to the floor, tears welled up and Roberto pulled his legs up to his chest. Again the rough pull at his neck meant he had to stand. His legs stung where the cosh had struck. "Now get undressed."

The monk looked at Zucco, horrified. He had never even been without his jersey in front of others save for his mother when he was but a boy and the thought of-

The cosh was raised again and Verrecchia had to comply.

The cold that enveloped him as he removed his garments was excruciating but was nothing when compared to the humiliation he was feeling.

Moments later, Roberto stood there naked in the snow, shivering violently, his hands covering his embarrassment. Zucco laughed again and forced him across to the little ladder attached to the rear of the caravan. The ice bit into the soles of his bare feet.

From inside the vehicle, Marta' voice cackled as Verrecchia felt Zucco's palm in the small of his back, pushing him upwards.

To save from falling to the bitter ground, Roberto raised his hands but struck the narrow door with his elbows. It opened and he entered, his thoughts swirling and confused.

Before him on a bed, amidst a tangle of furs, blankets and sheets, was a woman, clearly not Marta Zucco.

She was young – Roberto estimated not much older than he – and astonishingly beautiful. As she pulled her covers free, he realised she was also as naked as he was.

He looked into her eyes, trying his best not to drop his line of sight, but the woman did not make it easy for him. She got to her knees and shuffled towards him, smiling with an almost sensitive air. As Roberto went to lower his hands again, she grabbed his wrists and placed his palms on her breasts, her nipples hardening at the touch. She said nothing to him but tilted her head, nodding at him, as if giving him permission to continue. He looked at her green eyes then found himself caressing her, cupping her firmness under shaking hands.

She guided him to the gap between her bosom and pulled his head towards her with a tight grasp. His fingertips felt the slight moisture of her skin as he brushed the sides of her breasts. Then his lips were against them, firm and heaving. His mouth enclosed an areola, the nipple stiff under his probing, hot tongue.

He gasped and nearly clamped down as she grabbed his hardening penis between warm hands and he ejaculated almost straight away. He shuddered with the intensity and fell into her chest, feeling her let go of him. This felt nothing like his own pleasures late at night in the dormitory of Saccargia - silent, forbidden, guilty.

The woman wiped her hands on the bedding and pushed him back, aware that he had found a place between her swelling breasts that he was reluctant to give up just yet, but she shoved hard and Roberto slumped to the floor, his balls aching.

"Innocent. Truly innocent."

It was moments before he looked up, before he registered that her voice was familiar. His line of sight fell between her legs as she spread them wide but he dared not look anymore as he heard the chilling cackle.

"Done already?" asked Zucco from outside, making Roberto jump, bringing him back to reality.

"All pent up, he was," Marta replied. "Too long with those monks buggering him senseless. Thought he'd enjoy a nice supple female to teach him the true ways of the world. Still, he's young so we'll try again. Won't we my sweet?"

She caressed his neck and shoulders as if he were a lover but Verrecchia burst into tears, unable to control the emotions that had welled up inside him.

It had not been a young woman on the bed, but the vile crone somehow disguised. He had been deceived, lured, seduced by witchcraft and he realised that she had intended him to fuck her.

The caravan door opened behind him and Zucco leaned in, pulling him out and to the ground yet again. His habit was flung on top of him.

"Get dressed."

Whimpering to himself, Verrecchia tried to not look too relieved as he pulled his robes over his head, cold and damp from the snow they had been laying on.

"Ygor," Marta said as she hauled herself off the bed, wrapping a large shawl over her bare shoulders, "I haven't finished.

"Finish yourself off, woman," he said. "This boy's got work to do."

"Let me go."

Zucco glared at Roberto. "No."

"What do you want?"

"You're a priest."

"I am a novice. I do not want to be a priest. I am a monk."

"You speak to Him."

Roberto looked up at Zucco, the square-jawed gypsy, with his skin dark from years of dirt and sun.

"To who?"

"To God."

"We are penitent to him. We pray to Him everyday."

"Does he listen, this God of yours?"

Verrecchia's eyes widened. He had never met anyone before who spoke so disrespectfully. "Do *you* not speak to him?"

"I don't need your God."

"But...you will go to Hell."

It wasn't a threat but an observation, made purely based on the teachings the young monk had received since the day he crossed the threshold of Saccargia's monastery and into a secluded world.

"So you say."

"'There are ways that to men seem right, the end whereof plungeth into the depths of Hell.'"

"And who are you to say that Hell is worse than your Heaven?"

"It is written as such. The words of our Lord God say it to be so."

"Is your God with you now?"

"He is always with me. I can hear Him."

"Then he knows what's in store for you!" laughed Zucco.

Roberto winced, his beliefs pushed at times by Father Apollinari and the Abbot of Saccargia, but he never once faltered in his dedication.

"I'm not scared."

"You are a liar, my young monk. I can see the fear in your eyes. It hides the anger you have towards me. Tell me, is your heart pounding in your chest, so much so that you feel it will burst right under your ribs?"

"It is right to feel fear." This was a teaching by Apollinari but even as Verrecchia said it, he felt foolish.

"And is it also right to do as you are told? Is it not true that if a difficult or impossible task be enjoined on a brother, he is to nevertheless receive the order of him who commands with all meekness and obedience?"

"It's one of the chapters of St Benedict's Holy Rule."

"By which you are bound, I dare say?" Zucco pulled Roberto near the campfire as Marta, dressed and haughty, joined them. "If, however, the monk sees that the gravity of the task is altogether beyond his strength but the Abbot still insists, then isn't the younger to be convinced that it is good for him?"

"Yes," Verrecchia replied, surprised and concerned that this man, so apparently anti-church, was so aware of St Benedict's sermons.

"Then, my dear Marta," Zucco said, turning to his wife, "it seems we have chosen wisely."

"All we need now is the Unholy Relic and we can begin."

"What about Corbiu?" growled Zucco.

"He is fine where he is," cooed Marta, always protective of her boy. "You should trust him."

"He's an animal. He should be put down." Zucco lifted the lid of the pot suspended over the flames and took a deep sniff of its bubbling contents. "Got rid of one and we get lumbered with another."

"You know the spell only works on the innocent. Look what you did to Corbiu. At least this one is pure."

"But his purity isn't yet growing in your womb, is it?" Zucco reminded his wife. "You worked him up too much with that young woman you keep insisting on being."

"It will happen again soon and he will be inside me when it does. As long as his heart remains pure it can be taken from his chest and replaced with the one that we will control. And then the vampires will be wiped off the face of our world for good."

Brother Jacob had his ear pressed firmly against the cell door when Shandor arrived, much to the old Abbot's amusement.

"Penitent to doors now, I see, brother," he said. "It seems your lessons are being learnt at last. Perhaps we can bring the reprimands to a halt now, yes?"

Jacob drew away from the door and looked at the ground, not sure if Shandor was toying with him. His companions nearby kept quiet, talk of Jacob's disgrace some weeks prior having travelled well amongst the monastic community.

"I was listening," he responded quietly.

"So I gathered." Shandor stepped to the door and grasped the bolt. "What were you listening for, exactly?"

"The wolf – it makes no sound."

This was the cell that they had trapped the beast in and it had become the talk of the island. That talk had spread to rumour, Shandor having to quell the gossip before it got too out of hand.

"Perhaps it sleeps – exhausted from all the attention. Let us take a look and we can bring Father Apollinari here for his opinion." Four monks drew up behind Shandor, holding thick nets woven from rope and heavy clubs, prepared should the wolf attempt to flee. "Are we ready, my brothers?"

Murmured responses from the group and Shandor steeled himself as he slid back the bolt, tentatively pushing the door inwards. A flurry of limbs and snarling teeth came at them and the monks all bore down, their Abbot admiring their courage.

Moving in, forcing the animal to retreat to a corner of the cell, Shandor called his monks off. It was clear that it was not a wolf at all but a boy, perhaps nine or ten years of age, clearly feral but obviously terrified and painfully malnourished.

"My poor child," Shandor soothed, slowly walking towards the cowering youngster.

The boy growled, wide eyes darting to each of the men before him. He had long shaggy hair and smelt abominably, nails black and teeth blacker still. Shandor noticed his palms were pink, almost raw, as if they had been burnt, but the child seemed not to notice.

Speaking calmly in low tones, voice gentle and soothing, the Abbot found the boy to be receptive and saw the tenseness about him dissipating slightly.

"Can you talk?"

A cocked head and a frown told Shandor nothing so he tried the question again and, to his surprise, the boy said:

"Yes."

It was guttural, much lower in octave than the Abbot had expected but nevertheless the child was talking.

"Where have you come from?"

Looking around the small room in which he found himself, the boy saw the window high in the wall, the bars casting shadows across the floor. He pointed to the outside.

Shandor nodded.

"And what is your name?"

"I am not allowed to tell you."

"A wise young man," Shandor complemented. "But you are amongst friends here in Snagov. We mean you no harm."

The boy looked around at the men staring at him again but this time his eyes weren't so wild and frantic. "I am Corbiu."

"Hello, Corbiu." Shandor moved closer and sat on the narrow bed in the cell, looking down at Corbiu who crouched on the floor, as if ready to pounce. "Are you hungry?"

The boy shook his head, greasy hair swinging in clumps around his temples and neck. Corbiu's eyes glazed over suddenly and Shandor got the impression that the boy had entered some trance-like state. He snapped out of it but it was only moments later when he went back to that condition.

"What's he doing?" asked Jacob, keeping at a safe distance by the door.

"Corbiu..."

But the child did not answer the Abbot. He remained staring at the wall, through the wall, or perhaps he didn't even *see* the wall.

"Corbiu..."

More firmly this time and the boy twitched, filthy hands wringing together.

"Father..."

"Yes?" answered the Abbot, placing a gentle hand atop Corbiu's matted, dirty hair.

"Father..." Corbiu repeated, voice barely perceptible. "It is gone."

"What's gone?" Shandor leaned in close.

"They have no quarrel with us."

"Who hasn't, young Corbiu?"

Jacob raised a hand and Shandor beckoned him forward. Jacob stayed where he was.

"I do not believe he is talking to you," said the monk. Shandor thought about this for a moment then concurred.

"But who *is* he talking to?"

Corbiu looked down at his hands, turning his palms over as if noticing the welts for the first time. "It is gone and so has he."

The boy fell into silence and no end of coaxing would make him speak again that morning.

Shandor retreated to his office, ensuring Corbiu remained secure in the cell. It was a little cruel, he felt, to keep a child locked up like a common vagabond but with the wolf on the loose it was a just act to make. The monastery too was locked down and, after the Sext recitals, no monk was allowed out of their dormitory and definitely not into the grounds. Only the lookout posts on the exterior walls remained manned. Shandor had even ordered the cancellation of the Nones, stating that Vespers would still be carried out but straight after which everyone would retire until tomorrow's Lauds.

This was unheard of and upset many of the brethren, particularly the lector, but Shandor was insistent and assured the monks that all would be well by morning.

Popescu, however, was having none of it. Even though he rarely attended church while he was away from Dracula's gaze, he still considered Shandor's actions to be extreme and was ready to report back to his superior.

"Prince Dracula will not tolerate this," he spat, pacing back and forth in front of Shandor's desk.

"If you wish to use my cautionary actions as a means by which to depose me, then it is you who will not succeed, Popescu. Remember the princess is here against her wishes."

"You threaten me?" Popescu hissed, stopping directly in front of the passive Abbot.

A knock came at the door and an old monk entered, head lowered and full of illness.

"What is it, Brother Joseph?"

"Pardon me for entering, Father," Joseph said meekly, "but news has just reached us that Father Apollinari has left."

"Left?" Shandor stood. "When?"

"Earlier this morning."

"And how is it that we only know about this now?" bellowed Popescu.

Joseph indicated he did not know.

"Please, Popescu, do not frighten my monks into a stupor." Shandor moved to stand next to the frail monk, the oldest in the monastery and one who had seen many Abbots come. "It is enough that we know now. Tell me, Joseph, in what direction was he headed?"

"The lookout believes it was west." Joseph looked troubled, the cataracts making his glassy.

"I fear you have more to tell."

Joseph nodded and squinted ashamedly at Popescu.

"Why does the old fool look at me like that?" came the captain's gruff response.

Shandor placed an arm around Joseph' shoulders, giving the old man some courage to speak up.

"The princess was with him."

Shandor looked over at Popescu, noting how calm the captain appeared to be as this news sank in. Without saying a word, Popescu spun on his booted heels and strode from Shandor's office, the oak door thudding shut behind him.

"Scorching depths, as you dance give me now the secret glance. Call upon my second sight. Make me intuitive. Make me clairvoyant. Change my mind. Scorching depths, give me now the second sight."

Verrecchia held on the bars tightly, listening to Zucco and his incantation from inside his cage. The large gypsy seemed to be in some sort of trance, staring deep into the campfire before him.

The flames flickered and shuddered as though responding to his words. Across the other side of the fire was Marta, dressed in a white smock like her husband, swaying back and forth, her mouth moving silently, repeating the words Zucco was uttering.

She raised her arms over the fire, hands like fists, then splayed her fingers and the flames erupted into a green geyser before settling back down again.

Between the two gypsies as they chanted, the fire pulsed and writhed further, the words and gestures quickening in pace and complexity. Frenzied now, the Zuccos stood and danced, legs bent and arms crooked. The man stamped and jumped until the fire sprayed green again and they both sank to the ground, exhausted.

Verrecchia huddled in the furthest corner of the wheeled cage, desperately hoping that this was the end of the display. Yet he craned his neck to try and hear what the two witches were saying. It was hard to make out.

"Corbiu is safe," Marta cooed, relieved the flames had been able to tell her about the boy.

"But the casket is gone," added Zucco, more concerned with that than the welfare of the child. "He is too blind to tell us where."

"You are too hard on him, Ygor," Marta chided. "He is only young and inexperienced, too. At least he could say it was headed south."

"If his bitch of a sister hadn't left we'd have both the casket *and* the Relic with us by now. I take it she didn't come through for you either?"

"No," replied his wife, disappointed that Claudia hadn't made contact by way of the flames. "Perhaps she is dead."

"If she brings herself back to us, I'll treat her like she's dead and fuck her wretched corpse."

"That's enough, Ygor!" snapped Marta. "She has her uses."

"That's what you said about God-boy over there," Zucco responded, thumbing in the general direction of Verrecchia's prison.

"And so he will. We have to keep him alive long enough until the Relic is with us."

"And if we don't?" Zucco shook his head and stood, walking a few feet away before raising his smock and urinating on the ground. "That bloody ceremony always makes me piss like a workhorse."

Returning to the camp, Zucco grabbed handfuls of dirt and made a circle around the fire to stop it spreading then, dusting his hands down, shuffled off to the caravan.

"I'm going to sleep."

"What about the casket?"

"We'll set off at first light and meet it on the Cojasca road. Now come on."

Sighing, Marta gingerly stepped around the fire, gave a little wave good-night to Verrecchia and disappeared into the back of their caravan.

Verrecchia sat and watched the flames for some time after his captors had gone to bed, dreading what the day would bring and wondering how his presence would play a part in these blasphemous events.

But fatigue came upon him eventually and he settled down on the dirty soiled straw, sleeping lightly but thinking deeply of Apollinari and Sardinia, both such a very long way away and resignedly unreachable now.

Chapter 14

Isak's knees were beginning to ache and he was glad when Tanyel finally bade him enter into his office.

Tanyel eyed the servant suspiciously.

"I have been attendant at the Governor's feast, my Lord," Isak stated, watery pupils scanning Tanyel's hard expression.

"The fool is always eating," Tanyel spat. "One of these days his guts will explode."

The commander pulled the door open wide and allowed Isak access. The old servant bowed and shuffled in, feeling the air rush behind him as Tanyel slammed the door shut. The tray in his gnarled hands held a decanter and goblet. Moving across the room, Isak noticed the reams of maps and documents strewn in disarray across the huge desk. One in particular, the plans to the palace at Târgoviste, stood out but he made no mention of it. Eyes open, ears pricked and mouth shut he placed the tray on a small side table and wiped his hands on his apron.

"You know I thirst not just for wine, Isak," Tanyel purred as the servant filled the goblet. Tanyel snatched the drink and swilled down the wine in one, drops splashing over his fur tunic. He wiped his chin and mouth with a sleeve as Isak poured more.

"As I say, my Lord," Isak continued, "I have learned of the positioning of your army."

"That is not difficult, old man," Tanyel scolded, finally having his fill of wine. The goblet clattered down on the silver tray. "Are you becoming senile now and gaining information that I already know?"

Isak ignored the cut. "Your army-"

"My army," Tanyel interrupted, "is three hours north-west from here."

"Your army is three hours *north*."

Tanyel sat down heavily on the wide windowsill and rubbed his temples. He decided to overlook Isak's impudence at correcting him. "Am I surrounded by bastard-bred imbeciles?" he said, sotto voce.

"I am relaying the details as I know them, my Lord," Isak said.

"How did this information reach you?"

"Governor Tarih-i-al-Osman made his position very clear. There will be no assault on the Wallachian palace." What was the Governor playing at? It was almost unheard of that someone, in an essentially administrative position, would re-deploy a military force without the approval of the commander-in-chief, let alone going against the orders of the Sultan himself. "Your army is to camp at Prahov before returning to the homeland."

"Further, my Lord, the *voivode* was seen regrouping his men too recently to be now apart from them."

"Where?"

"It is believed they are also at the valley."

"My army is heading into a trap! Who saw the *voivode*?" asked Tanyel, anger boiling in him.

"The visitor from the homeland."

"Ismael," Tanyel hissed, eyes widening, a fire burning behind them. "I knew the man was poison."

"Is he not a Turk, my Lord?" This was unusual for Isak. He was inclined to take orders, give information but never question.

"Can you not see?" Tanyel, briefly angered at his servant's countering, pulled his sheathed sword closer to his hip. "Our foolish Governor is being duped. The *voivode* has not obeyed the orders of the false letter. He will shift his entire contingent to attack us at Prahov and our defences here will be weakened!"

"Count Tarih-i-al-Osman also believes the *voivode*'s consort to be elsewhere other than the Palace."

"Indeed?" Tanyel raised an eyebrow. So the Lady Ilona was not under the Prince's safe guard. "How does our beloved Governor know this?"

Isak was about to open his mouth to reply but the commander waved a glove to silence him.

"Do not tell me: Ismael."

Isak nodded. "The Governor is also of the understanding that the princess is to be found and brought to him and then the Governor will hand her over to Ismael for safe keeping."

"Safe keeping? She is not a gemstone!" Tanyel cried. "Ismael will smuggle her straight back out again!"

"I have heard the Governor say that she is to be used to bargain."

"The dragon prince is...renowned for his *amorous* disposition. Kidnap, kill or rape any number of his women and revenge will find him another equally nubile woman-child to ruin." Yozgatli Tanyel stepped into the corridor after Isak, voice dulled by the low curved ceiling and the close walls. "There will be no bargain."

"What do you intend to do, my Lord?" Isak queried.

"What I should have done a long time ago," Tanyel returned. "That Governor of ours will be rotting in *jahanem* by the time I am through with this wretched campaign. But do not look so worried. Your position as groundskeeper is assured."

Isak bowed. Tanyel thudded away down the corridor, feeling the old servant stare at his back. His powerful form swept along the Wallachian-lain floors, his thoughts not with his army but with the *kutu* buried deep in his subconscious.

His vision had not been one of madness or a momentary lapse of reason, he was sure. This box and the woman with her cold, dead grip had opened his eyes. He felt as though he was a focus now, being focused, a channel through which something could speak its words. He didn't understand the images it had presented to him. It was as if the *kutu* was gradually allowing him to realise certain things, opening parts of his consciousness that had been previously kept from him. Tanyel felt that there was an awareness that had been stagnating in his unchallenged brain.

Tarih-i-al-Osman's door was before him now, the climb from the middle storey of the Citadel to the top easy. Tanyel made a fist ready to pound on the door but stopped. Superior or no, damn the flatulent fool for being drawn in by a spy's falsehood. The Governor didn't deserve respect, Tanyel cursed as he flung open the door to his quarters.

Stirred not in the slightest by the sight of Tarih-i-al-Osman's fat, naked body sweating and thrusting behind a penitent servant boy, Tanyel stepped into the room. His boots were silent on the thick Turkish weave.

He remained there, quiet for a few seconds, looking around the room. It was the first time he had been in here and Tanyel was indifferent to the wealth the count had inherited around him. The carpet under his feet was one of many treasures from the homeland, as well as the incense burners on nearly every ledge. Egyptian cloth draped itself around the huge four-poster bed, which itself was Hungarian by make, as a jewel-encrusted mirror widened the already considerably large room even further.

The smell of the incense: opium, sandalwood and jasmine, the latter a treat from the most Eastern of places, would overwhelm Tanyel if he stayed here any longer than necessary. Already he could feel his nostrils burning.

"I will speak with you," he growled.

Tarih-i-al-Osman, startled then embarrassed, slid himself from the servant and ushered the unfortunate creature away, as though the servant was at fault for being present. The servant pulled his attire straight as he hobbled from the room, eyes flicking up once to meet Tanyel's indifferent stare.

"I demand respect from you, Lord Tanyel," Tarih-i-al-Osman lisped, the attempt at emphasising his superiority lost as he struggled to cover his red, glistening body with its swollen cock under a silken gown. "It is customary to forewarn, or at least, wait for an invitation, before entering your master's rooms. I may not have given you your title but I can take it away."

"Damn your customs and titles, Tarih-i-al-Osman," Tanyel spat, unsheathing his scimitar. "You have spent too long wallowing in the wake of your illustrious predecessor."

"Duke Stanislaus bequeathed my position to me. I am Governor of Turkish Dambovita by mortal right."

"Stanislaus was too wretched to know who you were when he died. The wasting disease that wrecked his body took control of his brain."

"He signed the contract for my position on his death bed."

"You bought, bribed and buggered your way to the top. You are an imbecile and I claim your title by elimination."

"You are you to dictate to me? You are just a timariot! You cannot kill me!" Tarih-i-al-Osman shouted moving his torso to the narrow window in the vain hope that he would be spotted. This window faced away from the courtyard. Only eagles and buzzards would see this high up on the building, they would be the only ones to hear his gargling screams as Yozgatli gutted him – an action that the Governor's assassin did with ease. He spoke no more words to the count, instead ending the fool's life in silence and spilling his bloody guts over the luxuriant flooring.

Wiping his scimitar on Tarih-i-al-Osman's gown, Yozgatli re-sheathed his weapon and stopped over the spliced corpse. He may have just been landowner back home but his position as a *timarli sipahi* had entitled him to unbridled wealth in return for a glorious military career. And who was it now who had killed the Governor as if he were a common animal?

He quickly pulled the linens from the bed, ripping the tapered edges off the frame. He knotted each sheet together, stretching the knots as though a weight had been put to them. Once the makeshift rope was long enough he leant out of the window and rubbed some of the material against the exterior wall, crisp whitens disappearing under grimy ice and moss.

Satisfied that it looked filthy enough to have been used by a fleeing assassin, he tied one end to the bedpost, pulling the bed away a few inches from the wall and the bundle he held in his arms he threw out of the window and then opened the door to the corridor. With a loud cry, he shouted for a guard. Sure enough, two turbaned soldiers came running at his command.

"Count Tarih-i-al-Osman has been assassinated!" he told them. "I saw the infidel escape through the window!"

One of the guards ran over and looked out. He saw the sheets flapping in the breeze against the side of the Citadel wall. The snow below remained undisturbed.

"He has fled my Lord," the guard said bringing his head back in. "Did you see who it was?"

"I cannot be sure but his aspect was similar to that of the visitor Ismael." Yozgatli lied. "Clear this mess away and then find out where he was most recently."

"And when we capture him, my Lord?" the other guard prompted, eyes rigidly ahead.

"Why, interrogate him until he confesses to this despicable crime."

"Yes, Lord," the guards responded simultaneously.

They left Tanyel there, with Tarih-i-al-Osman's body on the carpet and the bedding dangling outside.

He sat in the chair by the open window and looked around him, thinking of the letter he needed to write to the Sultan, to inform him of the Governor's most unfortunate demise and to proclaim his horror at such an incident. The Sultan would declare him the Dambovita Citadel's new Governor.

Governor Yozgatli Tanyel was indeed an honourable name, Tarih-i-al-Osman's most devoted commander-in-chief thought to himself as he turned his gaze to the dark sky outside.

It was a cold night, like every damn night in this wretched country. He missed the humidity of home, the warm shores of Anamur where he grew up, the hauntingly flickering lights of the night boats patrolling the stretch of water towards the land of the Cypriot.

The pulsing light before him now in the distance reminded him of such and he smiled, unusually melancholic.

Then the smile turned to a grimace, angry that he had allowed feelings to take over his mind. He stood and peered into the night, the light watery but enough to penetrate the black sky.

It was coming from the single tower and he was sure that he had ordered it sealed when they had taken control of the Citadel.

He stepped back over the Governor, the blood in the carpet squelching under his tread, and called for another guard. One appeared and followed him through the maze of corridors to eventually end up at the foot of the winding staircase at the base of the tower itself.

Taking the stairs two or three at a time, they passed a number of closed doors that led elsewhere to higher levels of the Citadel until they reached the large archway at the very top, the relatively new stone making up the wall where a doorway had somewhat recently been.

The heavy brickwork was solid but Tanyel knew it was only two layers thick throughout so shouldered the facia with an armoured bicep.

Together, the two large men pushed and thudded again and again at the stone, the cement beginning to weaken. But it was not enough just yet so Tanyel used his curved *jatagan* to dig away at the harder pointing.

Eventually, the brickwork was loose and he lunged at it again with his shoulder, the wall collapsing inwards. He tried to retain his balance and his dignity as the dust and cement puffed around him in great clouds.
Before him, in the previously sealed room, were three men, deathly pale in their own ways. One of them crouched in the corner, deformed and scarred, playing in the dirt with his fingers.

"Who are you?" Tanyel demanded, scimitar unsheathed and swinging between the two standing strangers. The guard behind him also raised his weapon.

"Our means has arrived," one of the figures said - the tall, thin black one.

Shandor's room was entwined by shadows, falling at sharp angles across the cold stone floor and walls.
The Abbot's sleep was intermittent, broken by the concerns of the day just gone. He would never admit to those around him that he was worried, so kept all thoughts to himself, comforted by the knowledge that the Lord would bring solace again before too long. But the belief of a wolf at large within the grounds, let alone the monastery itself, chilled him. The monks on lookout for the beast were as equally as shaken. He would soon be up and about to facilitate with the search and it was important to keep the rest of the brotherhood out of harm's way.
Popescu's sudden exit with his men did not help the situation, but Shandor understood the soldier's reasons even if he did not agree with them.
The woman found in the grounds was an added upset and, while Snagov usually and readily welcomed those injured or unwell, the Abbot could not shake off the

notion that her and this feral boy had something in common. He had been informed of her unconscious presence in the piggery before being taken to the infirmary and so had gone to see for himself what the monks had been concerned about.

As she lay on the straw mattress, a scratchy woollen blanket pulled up to her neck, he watched her twitch and growl in her delirium as if possessed. On waking, her obtuse interactions with the monks, insistent they tend to her wounds but curt enough to define her independence, gave Shandor the impression that this young woman did indeed carry a soul within her that perhaps wasn't her own. Brother Alexi held a damp cloth to her forehead, a fever upon her.

She wasn't one to weep and always considered her pain threshold to be higher than most. But the shaft of the arrow that had protruded from her left shoulder meant even the slightest movement of her arm had caused the most excruciating pain.

The flesh around the arrow had gone black through a combination of clotted blood and infection and Jacob knew that the missile had to be removed to save her life. But even then it was a terrible risk. It was lucky, however, that the arrow head wasn't barbed (many of the Wallachian infantry used arrows fashioned with armour-piercing bodkins) otherwise Claudia would have had most of her muscle and tissue ripped out as the tip was disposed of.

"Will we need to break the bones?" Alexi had asked.

"We're not Vikings, brother," Jacob replied. "There will be no need for such extreme methods. We simply need to snap off the fletch, drive the shaft out the other side then cauterize the two wounds. Hopefully," he had added, holding a pair of thin metal tongs, "we can get all the splinters out, too."

Jacob had tended her well but it would be some days before she was fit enough to return to the outside world. Her shoulder strapped and dressed with clean bandages, she found it difficult to move and still caused he pain. Shandor, even though he was keen to send her on her way as quickly as her recuperation would allow, knew that he could not rush Jacob's treatments and so patiently waited as broths and poultices were delivered and administered one after the other.

He had asked Jacob about her eyes and their peculiar jaundiced colouring, Jacob sure that it was something to do with the foul-smelling seepage from her wounds.

And so Claudia was left to rest and the monastery slept for another night.

His thoughts were distracted by something moving caught the corner of Shandor's eye, a dark shape in his moonlit room. He put it down to his mind playing tricks. He turned on his bed, staring at the elongated shadows across the floor, not registering that a new one had joined the throng.

But the shadow moved again and the Abbot gasped suddenly, a coldness enveloping him as a grey mist formed, hugging the floor like an animal hunting its prey. The mist undulated and drifted from the window where it had entered, Shandor watching it, terror rising in his throat.

The mist rose into a column then dissipated to reveal a man, his face as pale as the moonlight, his staring eyes white and piercing. They seemed to bore into Shandor's own as the Abbot pulled himself up, half sitting half laying now.

The man glided toward him, a hand outstretched - far too stretched, Shandor felt - and talon-like fingers rested on his chest, pushing him back down.

"I am Ismael," the man purred.

"Your hand shall be against every man, and every man's hand against you; and you shall dwell in the face of all your brethren," said Shandor.

"Do you fear me?"

"I do not believe you are the true Ismael, son of Abraham."

"Then why quote scripture at me?"

"I believe you are...*something*."

"Something other than Ismael?"

"Something evil."

"Evil is a point of view," Ismael said. "Do your scriptures also say that I am to be made fruitful, will multiply exceedingly and be made a great nation?" Shandor nodded, swallowing hard. "Then you *must* fear me."

"What are you?" Shandor's voice trembled.

"I am a warning." Ismael opened his mouth to reveal sharp white teeth.

Shandor tried to shuffle in his bed but Ismael's hand, as gently placed as it was, seemed to paralyse the old Abbot.

"We need no warning from the likes of you, *vampyr*," Shandor said defiantly, almost unable to believe that he had even acknowledged what Ismael was and that such a creature had freely crossed onto consecrated ground.

"The warning is not for you," responded the vampire and lunged at Shandor's throat.

The Abbot cried out as he felt the fangs pierce his neck and his own blood flow uninhibited into Ismael's mouth, splashing as it did so onto his habit.

The vampire drank until it could feel Shandor becoming weaker, but Ismael would not turn him nor would he kill him. Not yet.

Pulling away, cheeks flushed with the consumption of the warm, thick blood, Ismael licked the drops of red from around his own mouth with a lizard-like tongue and watched the Abbot breathing fast and shallow.

Ismael stepped into the centre of the room, his undead muscles and ligaments saturated and strengthened with the fresh feed. He spun to face the window with senses heightened and was gone, leaving the old man's body to adjust to sudden attack.

The Abbot had fallen into a deep sleep, sleep that had eluded him for so many hours. He would not waken to help with the search for the wolf and the monks would find it difficult to rouse him the next morning.

Of Ismael's visit itself there would be little sign, only two barely noticeable punctures at Pretorius Shandor's throat.

The flames of the ten thick red candles flickered and quivered as they each rested on their own ornate candelabras. While Tanyel stood rooted to the spot the thought crossed his mind of who had managed to bring them up here.

"He seems to fear little, Kelele," said Odalys.

"More concerned with the décor than us," added Ismael, who had just appeared at the window ledge.

Save his eyes, Tanyel found he could no longer move, arm outstretched with his scimitar still raised, legs and torso immobile. The voice to his left was familiar and he cursed not being able to move his head to see who it was.

Kelele glided forward, orange robes undulating. He circled Tanyel, almost pushing the guard out of the way in the process. But the guard was also frozen where he was and merely wobbled slightly from his ankles as the Ethiopian stepped in front of him.

"They fascinate me," Kelele said. "I can see why you spend so much time with them pretending to still be as they are, Ismael."

Ismael! The damn spy! Tanyel willed his arms to move, his legs to free themselves but there was no movement.

"He is eager, this one," Kelele noted. "He wants to be liberated. The other one, however..."

"He is terrified. You can see it coming from his eyes. Look." Odalys pointed at the tears flooding down the guard's cheeks. "Shall we put him out of his misery?"

The guard's eyes widened further as Odalys moved to caress his face. The guard abruptly jerked into motion and collapsed to the floor, his sword clattering and sliding across the stone. Kelele placed a foot on the weapon to halt its progress. Prising Tanyel's sword from the Turk's grasp, the vampire compared both weapons side by side, testing their weight in his hands.

"We had nothing as cold and crude as these to hunt with," he said. "Nothing was as elegant as the *assegai* with which you could feel felt the power of the kill through one's own body. They are foul representations of the white man's weakness."

Kelele flung them from the tower and turned to his companions.

"Feed, my sister, my brothers."

They pounced on the fallen guard, Viktor scrabbling from his corner to join his vampire siblings.

Tanyel strained his eyes to look down at the horror at his feet, hearing the guard scream as the vampires tore and fed at his throat and chest. Fountains of blood, thick and scarlet, covered the undead creatures.

Within moments the screaming stopped. They had drained the man dry, his skin taught and brittle like autumn leaves. Around him, his spilt blood had already congealed and the vampires stepped back, satiated.

Kelele pulled at Viktor's hair to stop him from consuming the sticky mess. No vampire would lower themselves to take in stale blood, especially a Celebrant.

As Viktor, chided, scurried back to his corner, Odalys noticed the *kutu*.

"Kelele, Ismael...look!"

The frenzied attack had left the box covered in the guard's life-giving fluid and, as they watched, the blood around it and over it was steadily being pulled towards it! It wasn't long before the floor immediately surrounding the box was devoid of any blood, the box itself as equally as clean. The *kutu* appeared to have absorbed it all like a sponge.

The vampires looked at each other then at Viktor, who was rocking on his haunches and scribbling 'C' over and over in the dirt.

"Is this it? Is it the time?" Ismael panted, voice rising in anticipation.

Kelele nodded, somewhat sombrely Odalys thought. Perhaps, after all these centuries, the thrill of their master's return had dulled in the Ethiopian's immortal soul.

"You," Odalys said, gesturing towards Tanyel. "Open it."

Tanyel, movements jerky and loose as though a puppet on a string, stumbled towards the *kutu* and picked it up with trembling hands. It felt heavier than before.

He looked at the creatures around him then down at the *kutu* in his palms. It was here - somehow magicked out of his mind and back into reality! These devils (obviously Catholic heathens) clearly did not realise the power the *kutu* wielded and he found himself compelled to open it, even though he knew previous attempts had proved fruitless. It mattered nothing what they had done to the guard – once the *kutu* was his completely, he had little to fear from demons, Catholic or otherwise.

The Celebrants willed Tanyel on, aware of his thoughts and his twisted rationale and finding amusement in them. Yet they were all equally apprehensive as to who would be the receiver of the Relic. Kelele was convinced it would be him, Odalys desperate it would be her. Ismael hoped it would be neither.

Tanyel flipped open the box to reveal a disembodied heart, swollen, gorged, pumping, and as fresh as though it had been ripped from Caleb's chest only moments before. Yet it was nearly four centuries since that had happened, since the followers of de Blanc had cornered the Vampire Lord outside the Holy Sepulchre and tore it out.

Tanyel reached in and grabbed the heart, fresh blood trickling through his fingers, and dropped the *kutu*. It was just a mere container – it had always been just a mere container - and was of no importance.

Viktor stood, raised himself upright and strode towards Tanyel who had dropped to his knees, the heart outstretched in his grasp. Viktor had not stood since he had been alive and Odalys gasped at the sight – and at the dawning realisation that Viktor was to receive the *kutu*'s heart.

Kelele grew angry. "This is too much!" he thundered. "A cripple is to be our figurehead? Viktor is not worthy!"

Ismael moved forward and placed a cold hand on Kelele's dark, ghostly skin. "No, wait."

Tanyel held the throbbing heart in one hand so that, with the other, he could rip his garments open to reveal his upper body. Using his knife, Tanyel calmly plunged the blade into his own chest, twisting and turning, digging and cutting, blood and flesh pouring down into his lap and across the dusty floor. He dropped the knife and sagged, staring down at his self-inflicted wound as if surprised.

Viktor sliced open a vein in his wrist then placed it over Tanyel's mouth. The Turk coughed and spluttered at first but then settled into a rhythm as he drank the vampire's blood. Viktor plunged his free hand into Tanyel's chest and ripped out the Turk's heart. He dashed it to the floor and took the one Tanyel himself was holding, the one from the box, and thrust it behind Tanyel's rib cage.

Viktor pulled his wrist away and gently laid Tanyel to the cold stone, awash with blood.

He turned to face his brethren, Kelele, Ismael and Odalys, and returned to his usual position, huddled and crouching in the gloom.

At their feet, Tanyel's lifeless form twitched and stirred, thick mist beginning to curl out from under his body and from his butchered chest.

The mist became so dense that it eventually obscured everything in the room, even snuffing out the candles.

Then the mist shifted again, dissolving completely to reveal the Turk's body. The gaping hole in his chest had sealed, leaving no scars.

The body's eyes snapped open, bright and ghostly pale. As it got to its feet, the candles burst back into life.

It had Tanyel's face, it had Tanyel's form and it wore Tanyel's clothes but the thing before the Celebrants was new.

"My children," the creature said, voice harsh, the Ottoman accent watered down from what the vocal chords had produced the last time they had been used. "I am returned."

Chapter 15

The Vampire Celebrants wondered at the sight, taking in Caleb's new aspect with trepidation. Ismael apart, they had all come to know Caleb intimately before his defeat in the Holy Land. His brooding Hispanic features had been as familiar to them as the darkness in which they existed.

But now he stood before them, reborn in the body of a Turk, wiping clean any history or belief Tanyel may have held or cherished.

Kelele stepped forward first, towering over Caleb but still acquiescent to him.

Caleb held out a hand, palm upwards, slit it with a new talon-like nail and pressed it to Kelele's lips. There was not an ounce of hesitancy from the Ethiopian. He knelt with the palm still across his mouth and drank from his resurrected master. The taste of the Turk was faint.

"My Kelele," Caleb said, stroking the vampire's bald, dark head with his other hand. "Your loyalty to me cannot be surpassed."

Kelele released himself from the gift, gasping as the blood pushed its way around his slim body. Caleb looked around the circular room, eyeing the broken stone doorway, his gaze settling on Odalys' firm mouth. His new eyes lit as she moved towards him, eager to share in his blood offering.

But he pushed her away and anger flashed across her face. Yet she knew better than to pressure him.

"Where are the others? Zachariah, Eloise…" he asked, stepping over the guard.

"We are all that are left. There are no others," Odalys replied.

"No others? How can that be?"

"We became displaced after Jerusalem. We were hunted down across the world by the Cult of Marise," added Kelele.

"And how is it you survived but the others didn't?"

"Our collective was weakened and we foresaw extinction if we continued to remain together. So we parted, each returning to our own place, each waiting for you. I went home, taking Viktor with me. Kelele went to the Great Plains."

Caleb turned to face Ismael. "I know you. You are new to us, but I know you."

Ismael's blond hair looked yellow in the glow of the flickering candles. He was expressionless and Caleb could not read him. He had become a Celebrant so very recently and had always distanced himself, like a cat that stays on the periphery of a group. Caleb's powers were indeed great and Ismael wondered to what extent. Was his awareness of Ismael an echo of Tanyel's remembrance carried through to his resurrection or something much greater?

Caleb turned his attention to Viktor who had crawled to be near his feet.

The disfigured creature held Caleb's hands, feeling the rough Turkish skin against his face.

"Zachariah was destroyed first and the others followed," Odalys continued. "Eloise was taken captive under the assumption that we who remained would give ourselves up."

"But you didn't."

"No. Hers was a terrible end. The Cult knew of the strength of her love for you. They used her as an example to us."

"And you let them?"

"We had no choice. We could not risk us all being taken."

"My Eloise..." said Caleb, closing his eyes briefly. But this was not the time to mourn. "Who led the hunt?"

"There was talk that Marise herself had brought their number together but it was nothing more than rumour. De Blanc was the guardian of your remains but we do not know if his capacity went beyond that." This was from Ismael.

"Does de Blanc still live?"

"This was nearly four centuries ago, Master," said Kelele. "Even *his* witchcraft could not keep him alive any longer than nature intended."

"Why did you not take him as he slept?"

"His spells hid him from us," said Odalys, glaring at Ismael who appeared to be about to counter that statement.

"Then we are not to be given the pleasure of retribution," concluded Caleb. "Unless..."

"Master?"

"Does he have descendants? Is the de Blanc bloodline still in existence?"

"We...do not know," responded Kelele, shoulders shrugging slightly.

"You, the Celebrants, the leaders of our vampire kind, have you all grown so old that you no longer desire? What of the Cult? Has your indolence allowed Marise to spread her vile disease?" Caleb spread his arms wide and the vampires grouped together and knelt before him, even Ismael. "We will hunt down de Blanc's legatees and they will inherit our vengeance. There will be none of them left save for the one last born – whose destiny will be to become as we are, our final act of revenge against him and his lineage. Now go and turn others to our cause."

With that, Caleb retreated into the shadows of the circular room with Viktor at his feet. Odalys, Kelele and Ismael launched themselves through the window.

Over the next few nights, the Celebrants carried out Caleb's instruction and they came and went, as dark as the night and as tacit as the breeze.

But to take everyone would induce panic and so their turning of the living was not without forethought or calculation: where the Celebrants went the rats followed, implying the spread of plague. Many outlying villages, some even as far as the Baltics, found their old and infirm remained untouched, not even worth piercing for their thin blood. The young and the strong increased the vampire kind's number.

Reborn from their fresh graves, these new vampires followed the Celebrants back to Dambovita, the Citadel's catacombs swelling with their number. Those living above had no notion of what was massing beneath.

And to a chamber separate from the brood, Odalys seduced and lured the prettiest and the most nubile of the country's virgins for her master's own enjoyment. As Caleb fed and fucked his way through them, the strength of his new body grew, grew to such an extent that before long he had become bloated, his vampiric senses revived and keen. Through his feeding, he felt his victims' lives and times and, while it did no replace the years that had passed since the betrayal in Jerusalem, it allowed him an understanding of where and when he now was.

These were not enlightened times and it appeared that little had progressed since he had been born alive some five centuries before the arrival of the son of the so-called God. Feudal systems had replaced the ordered Roman way of things that he had been delivered into, yet there was still oppression from the hierarchy to those less fortunate. There was an irony to this, however, for the vampire in essence considered itself to be better than its living counterpart, viewing it as no more than mere cattle to be subjugated and consumed. And whether the living subject was wealthy or poor made little difference – to the vampire, if the blood was clean and the body was healthy, that was enough.

There was a common thought amongst those he had consumed these past few days. They feared a battle, or rather the outcome as oppose to the battle itself – the dread that their Turkish oppressors would maintain power and drive out the Wallachian forces for good. For this to happen, Caleb reasoned, the Turks needed to hold fast this Citadel that the vampire horde was quickly inhabiting. Before long, the battle would be brought here and the vampires would feed of the veins pounding with adrenalin. Whoever lived or died, whoever of the living ultimately won, their petty squabbles for power and territory decided once and for all, Caleb simply didn't care.

Marta came screaming from the back of the caravan, skirts hitched around her calves as she trotted ungainly across the compacted snow.

Her furore woke Verrecchia with a start and he rolled over in his cage to get a clearer view as to what was going on.

Zucco seemed vaguely concerned that his wife was making such a calamity. He was more annoyed if anything.

He cursed at her to be quiet but she continued sobbing between bouts of hysteria, so he kept his focus on his breakfast that was cooking before him, waiting for her breathing to steady.

Eventually she slumped where she sat and her husband put down the branch he was using to stoke the fire and turned towards her.

"Have you calmed down, now?"

She sighed with the weight of the world upon her narrow, rounded shoulders and nodded. He asked her why she had been making such a noise and Marta found it hard to respond to him, trying her best to not break down again as she nervously explained the vision she'd received in her sleep.

What he could make out from her erratic description, though, did concern him and he shot a look over towards Verrecchia.

"We need a sacrifice."

Marta wiped thick green snot from her nose and mouth with a forearm and hands and frowned. She saw where he was looking and shook her head frantically.

"Your vision has told us this must happen," he pressured, standing.

She grabbed his trouser leg pleadingly, the act cleansing her hands of the expectoration from her nose having not gone unnoticed by him. He looked down in disgust at her and shook her off.

"No, Marta."

"But he's a boy! He's *my* boy!" she cried.

"He isn't your boy. Just as much as Corbiu isn't your boy, neither!"

"But Blessed Marise hasn't asked for a sacrifice! We've had no sign!"

Zucco spun and grabbed Marta by her hair, the wig coming off in his grasp. She stumbled to the floor, her hand in the embers to break her fall. She cried out again.

"Caleb is back! You saw it! How much more of a sign do you need?" Zucco stomped towards the cage, flinging her matted wig to the ground. "If we're too late in getting Caleb's heart, we'll cut out this virgin child of God's anyway and offer it to the Blessed Mother. She will protect us against him."

"But Caleb won't come for us!"

"Of course he will, woman! This is your family's doing! Why do you think I agreed to take Verrecchia in the first place?"

Marta was shaking, the vision still clear in her mind of a tall, stocky tower, within which was a swirling maelstrom of fire and smoke. The aspect of Caleb, different somehow but undeniably the same, appeared in the translucence of the smoulder, his body clawing its way from the epicentre of the flames as if mocking the way in which the followers of Marise were executed. The vision had given way to consciousness and Marta had woken, sweating and fearful of what she had seen.

Caleb's heart had been missing for so long that they had all begun to believe it existed only as a myth. It was only when one of them had seen the silver-etched box in and amongst the Wallachian camp that had they considered it had finally returned to them, to the rightful owners, the descendants of those who had ripped it from the Vampire Lord's undead chest.

Marta watched her husband taunt the young monk in the cage, rattling the bars, shouting and jeering at him as he collected as much dry kindling as he could.

She knew the boy had to die to appease the wrath of Marise for letting the heart return into the hands of the vampires. She knew the boy had to watch his own heart be pulled from his chest and then be burnt as his body died. It was the only way.

She shivered in the cold, not even the campfire warming her dark soul, as Zucco prepared, sharpening the knife, stacking the wood, becoming ever aroused at the thought of the sacrifice to their goddess.

In the cage, Verrecchia watched in terror, realising that all these preparations were for him. He did not understand why, could not understand why – his upbringing had seen to that – but he knew that there was perhaps little point in even *trying* to understand.

He remained silent as Zucco pulled him from the cage by the chain around his neck, not uttering a sound as the gypsy staked the end of the tether to the ground with a thick, pointed branch and remained completely calm as he noticed the stake was not fixed firm in the icy ground as Zucco had assumed.

All it needed was a sharp tug.

Chapter 16

Approximately one hundred kilometres north of Bucharest, of the citadel called Dambovita, Dracula's army hungered.

They were camped along the banks of the Prahov River, almost twenty-thousand strong. They were diminished but still solid since the sustained attacks on Moldavian territory some weeks before. Above them loomed the Carpathians, shrouded in a mixture of snow, ice and fog. Infiltrators had reported back to Vlad Dracula that the Turks were on the move and so a lookout, one of many, was dispatched to the Caraiman Peak. He had returned hours later, the November weather allowing for little or no views of the valley below. But Dracula gained the trust of his spies through fear alone and knew that, if he had been told that the enemy was marching then, implicitly, that was what they were doing.

A lookout would have merely qualified their progress.

As it was, Dracula had the foresight to keep his army out of Târgoviste, his prior confrontation with Basarab Laiota and the Turks requiring some regrouping and redistribution of troops.

Stefan of Moldavia, eternally grateful for Vlad's success at driving back the Turkish hordes, had given the Wallachian Prince a few thousand men and Dracula was expecting another fifteen thousand from his old ally

Stephen Bathory. Furthermore, Dracula had written to the twelve councillors in the fortress of Brasov asking for their support against Laiota. He promised that all previous customs duties on goods and taxes were to be wiped clean so that Brasovian merchants could trade freely throughout Wallachia. In return he expected their full support and to not shelter his enemies, as they had done before. There was a bitter irony to his supplication for aid, for the denizens of Brasov still acutely recalled the burning and impaling Dracula had dealt them in the past.

Nevertheless, Dracula demanded the arrangement be respected and the Brasovian people had no choice but to supply money, men and arms.

One such subject, Henric, sat with his fellow men-at-arms, his commanding officer having been killed by the Turks three days before.

He moved to the fire, his companions huddling close together. The embers crackled and spat as fat from a roasting pig dripped from the spit and into the heart of the flames. Settling, making his pitiful bedding plumper, Henric refilled his tankard, willing the night away as he drank. It would be colder, he knew, and at least their Lords and their generals had tents to fight the temperature. Henric shook his head. Surely it was the cold making him bitter. Either that or fatigue.

"Henric," croaked Mansi from under a thin blanket, "make yourself warm, or the night will claim you instead of the Turks."

"Soon," Henric responded, leaning towards the spit to tear off a piece of grizzled meat. The flesh was dry and tasteless in his numb mouth.

"Are you sulking?"

Mansi was direct and always had been since childhood. The death of his mother at the hands and groins of Carpathian bandits before his and his brother's eyes when they were but six years old had shown him life had little tolerance for those who stood by and watched.

Henric, on the other hand, still expressed moments of naivety. It angered him that boyars such as his father were made to give their sons as well as their wealth to aide the cause. Young men such as himself had yet to even live their lives, and here they all were, as close to their graves as they would be if they had the Black Death. Henric had heard, though, that hours of prolonged pain with the plague was far more inviting than being captured by the Sultan's men.

"You do know that brooding is the quickest way to get yourself killed in battle?"

"What of it?" Henric threw the meat back down.

Mansi picked it up. Food was rationed and if his pouting companion was going to throw it to the dirt, Mansi had no compunction about eating it instead.

"I want to go home."

"Henric," Mansi said, becoming increasingly irritated, "if we don't stand and fight, do what our masters order us to do, there won't be any home to go back to. The Turk will drive us back, hunt us down. We'll be in Sodom for the rest of eternity. Is that what you want?"

Henric's answer was to stare at the flames, the heat flushing his cheeks. Then he turned to Mansi.

"What about your brother?"

"He is probably already there." Seeing Henric quiver, Mansi shook his head. "What, Henric? You think he's out there trying to find us?"

"He disappeared when there was no battle. He wasn't cut down."

"But he *disappeared*," Mansi emphasised, rubbing his stubble with gloved hands, trying to get some feeling back into his face. "He went. In the middle of the night."

"Don't you even want to find him?"

"Of course I do! Every waking moment I wonder where he is. But how? Where would I even start?" Mansi finally swallowed the stringy meat, considering whether or not to take a second morsel. He dismissed the thought, wiping his greasy fingers on his tunic. "If Rintoul *is* still alive, we'd never find him amidst the occupancy. And if he is dead, he is in a better place than us." Finished with the food, Mansi turned away from Henric and settled back down under his blankets. A tear slowly made its way down his face.

Father Giuliano Apollinari had a sore backside.

He was not used to extended journeys on horseback and was glad when his travelling companion, the Princess Ilona Szilágy, asked to rest.

He had chosen a small clearing within the woodland they had entered some time ago, set within a shallow dip enough to barricade them from the biting wind whipping through the trees.

As Ilona tied their horse to a fallen tree trunk, she watched with some amusement the monk kick and scrape at the cold earth until he had scooped enough away as wide as he was and long enough for him to lay in.

He repeated the action some feet away, eyeing the princess as he did so, estimating her height.

"Are you to bury us?"

Apollinari smiled and set about lighting a fire in the centre of the clearing, so that the two indentations he had made were either side of the flames. He made quick work of collecting and lighting the kindling and, finding another fallen log, dragged it near and bade Ilona sit.

Some time later, the fire had burnt down, forming a circle of hot ash. Using the thick furs, Apollinari gingerly yet efficiently grabbed armfuls of the ash and sprinkled it evenly in both of the indentations and asked Ilona to lay their remaining furs on top.

When the task was done, he relit the fire with fresh branches.

"Our beds," he said proudly. "We will be warm tonight."

Ilona smiled and realised that his hard work would save them from freezing to death.

They both settled down and she watched the fire crackle and pop. Neither spoke for what seemed like ages until a question crossed Ilona's mind.

But Apollinari never answered her. He appeared to have fallen into a deep sleep.

Yet there was a peculiar growing closeness to the air that made sleeping uneasy for her. It was as if it was the height of summer, with humidity sticking in the lungs, pulling her clothes tight to her body.

Believing it was the heat from the ash beneath her making her flushed, Ilona sat up and turned, the forest floor beneath the furs lumpy and uncompromising. Apollinari was laying perfectly still some feet away from her. His eyes were closed.

"Father," she called, gently at first so as not to startle him. But he could not be roused so she sighed and laid back down.

But it was no good. She shifted, turned, sat up, stood up and laid down again for what seemed like hours until the strange warmth in the air gradually began to ease and the November night reclaimed its icy grip over the climate.

The forest was alive, even at night, and every hoot and wail from the dark seemed to echo around her until she noticed, somewhat gradually, that silence had finally fallen.

Looking over at Apollinari, his face half lit by the dying flames from the camp fire, she noticed a small sack not far from his head. It was the same material and colour as his cassock, so it was easy to have not spotted it before.

Waiting patiently to ensure he was sound asleep, Ilona eventually got up and padded over to the monk, tentatively opening the bag. She wasn't sure what she was expecting to find but certainly hadn't imagined the contents to be so…so *strange*.

There were lengths of wood, no longer or thicker than her forearms, cut to sharp points. There was a Bible and a Qur'an, both worn and clearly well-used, and Ilona was taken aback, if not a little horrified, as to why a monk would have a copy of the latter text about his person. She had the urge to wake him, to demand to know his reasons, to even leave him there and return alone to Shandor to explain what she had found.

But that would not help her predicament. Whether Apollinari was a Muslim spy or not was something she had to keep to herself, at least until she had returned to Târgoviste and the protection of her betrothed.

Resolutely, she put both tomes back, unsettled by their presence together.

Digging further through Apollinari's bag, she found great numbers of long, sharp thorns kept in small pouches and a diminutive looking-glass, its mirrored surface bright and reflective in the firelight.

But strangest of all, wrapped carefully in sackcloth, were the glass phials, each filled with the same peculiar effervescent liquid. They ended in points, not unlike the wooden stakes. At one end of every one was some sort of tiny plunger that reminded her of the water pumps outside her city's walls.

She counted at least twenty of these phials and winced as they clinked together. Gingerly replacing them all, she closed the bag.

Apollinari didn't stir.

As she pushed the bag back to him, Ilona noticed it had an exterior pocket and her pluck meant she felt able to reach in and pull out another book, older and more frayed than their religious counterparts.

As she opened it, its black leather cover creaked in indignation. The pages were thick, decades of writing in the odd brown ink adding rigidity to the ancient paper. She thumbed through the book, not recognising the language it was written in, nor understanding the true representations of the hieroglyphs and detailed drawings. Some were of strange basilica, some of animals, stranger still, but many were of symbols, templates she assumed to be copied and enlarged without the confines of the book itself.

Her heart raced as she turned page after page, desperately hoping Apollinari would not wake, but entranced enough to dare to keep looking.

The monk shifted suddenly and she froze, the book clasped in her hands.

Then, a brushing at the nape of her neck!

She dropped the book, hearing its descent to the bag at her knees end with a dull *pop*. One of the phials had obviously burst under the fall.

She stood and spun around as the touch to her neck came again. Not accustomed to swooning, she was taken aback when she found herself some distance from their little camp, fingers clamped in tight fists. It was if she had been magicked there.

"Can you hear them?"

Startled, the voice seemed to come from directly beside her but, when she turned, there was a man standing by the fire, a man who wasn't Apollinari.

He was pushing the embers around the edge with a booted foot. His blonde hair seemed to glow in the fire light.

"Listen."

She was sure it was the man speaking, but his lips never moved and he was too far away to have such clarity in his voice.

"Who are you?" she called but the man didn't directly answer her.

Instead, he gestured at the fire, his gaze facing downwards. "Listen."

Ilona shifted her line of sight and watched the sprites pop and flutter in the cold air. Gradually, they seemed to slow, hanging above the fire like yellow stars, flickering but otherwise motionless. The flames from which they sprung had also ceased to undulate in the way only flames do. She rubbed her eyes, tiredness the only obvious answer to what she was witnessing.

"Listen hard."

The man's voice cut through her and she relented, trying to hear something, anything, in the quiet.

And then she heard them. Voices. Whispering, giggling, hushed. The words they were speaking made no sense, or at least were not in a language Ilona recognised. Were they human? Children? Possibly.

"They are the dead. The dispossessed. The haunted." Nervously, Ilona looked over at Apollinari, wishing now that he would awaken. As she turned back, the stranger was suddenly upon her. She stumbled and her voice stifled in her throat, a soreness at her neck, a taste of iron in her mouth. Then the man retreated back, back near the fire.

"He won't hear us. Your fumbling through his belongings would not have stirred him."

"But I…" Her voice faltered, coldness at her shoulder. She saw there was little need to explain herself to this odd newcomer to the camp. So she asked again: "Who are you?"

"Is he your protector?"

"In a way." Ilona moved back towards the fire, partly for warmth but mainly to allow herself a closer look at the man. She wondered if she should be scared of him but his presence seemed acceptable somehow. "Are you a spirit?"

"In a way," the man mocked. "Where are you going?"

"West," she found herself answering. There was definitely something alluring about him, with his thick blonde hair, bright white eyes and pale, almost translucent, skin.

"For what purpose? You do not seem to be of the traveller's caste." The stranger stepped back from the fire and it continued to behave normally again, the flames licking and curling as before. "No matter. Like the wolf, we are all headed somewhere. What matters is how the journey unfolds."

"You do not sound Wallachian," Ilona said. "Slovak?"

"My name is Ismael."

"A Jew?"

"No. But I may have been once. A long time ago."

"What do you want?"

"Nothing. For the moment. But I will come again."

"Why?"

"Do you fear me?"

"I am Consort to Prince Vlad of Wallachia. What do *you* think?"

"The Princess Ilona?" Ismael's face had all manner of expressions then as he digested this information. "This is a most interesting discovery. You can certainly be assured of my return. You will soon have a purpose beyond your linear duties."

And with that, he was gone and, near the fire, Apollinari stirred. The sudden but distant noises in the forest were not part of his dream.

Rubbing his bearded face with vigour, he rose from his bed, squinting into the trees. The rapping still continued from no discernable direction.

He was about to call out, to ask who was there, but he stopped himself. There was no telling who or what may be watching them or be tempted by his voice.

From the other side of the fire, Ilona made as though she had just awakened herself, a fleece pulled around her shoulders.

"What is it?" she asked, the strange taste still on her tongue.

Apollinari waved her into silence and nodded towards the darkness.

Knock, knock, knock.

Knock, knock, knock.

Ilona scurried up to the monk and held his arm. Apollinari turned and whispered in her ear:

"Be as quiet as possible. Our very lives may depend on it."

Between the trees, at some distance, was a light, flickering and erratic. It seemed to hover, moving left then right and further right still before sliding back towards the left. It was vaguely hypnotic, Apollinari felt, the distant knocking adding to the illusion. The light split into two, then three, four and more, all now moving as unpredictably as each other.

The rapping seemed to be getting louder – no, *closer* – and Apollinari pulled the princess near to him.

The lights appeared to finally fall into some form of patter, fanning evenly out before them. Apollinari circled. There was nothing behind them and so he remained focused on what was ahead.

Silently, he moved to pick up his bag, slipping it over his shoulder and between the folds of his habit. Something glinted as he did so, something against his thigh, but Ilona couldn't determine what it was in the moon-lit and flame-lit gloom.

Apollinari stamped on the fire to extinguish any beacon it projected, ensuring there was no chance of a spark to re-ignite it.

The hovering lights grew in size for every moment they watched and all of a sudden, the quietness of the night was broken by a crescendo of dogs barking at some distance.

Apollinari reasoned there were a considerable number of the animals headed their way.

Accompanying the yapping were the shouts and calls of men, the syntax, even as far off as it was, evidently Wallachian.

"I know who they are."

"Do you know what they want?"

Ilona nodded and began sweeping up some furs, small clouds of ash pluming into the night air. "We need to leave. We need to leave *now*."

"You do know what they want!"

"Father, they want *me*."

Apollinari joined her in grabbing as much coverings as they could manage, enough to still keep them warm in the days to come but few as possible to allow them less cumbersome baggage.

"Are they Popescu's men?"

"I doubt it," she responded. "There are too many of them. More likely they are the Royal Guard."

"Your husband's?"

"Yes, but he will be with his army. These men will be his hunting party."

"How apt that sounds."

"And they always ensnare their quarry. It's me they want but if they find you with me, a stranger, you will be taken before my husband. If he believes and finds you guilty of my abduction, you will be tortured and executed. Whether you are a man of God or not is of no consequence."

"Then as you say, we must leave now."

A shout rose up from the gloom between the hovering lights.

They had been spotted.

"Run!"

And they did, as fast as they could, weaving in and out of the trees, ducking under canopies heavy with snow.

The dogs behind them, realising that the chase was on, broke free from their chains and closed the gap between them and their targets.

They made swift work of the forest, navigating with ease where Apollinari and Ilona struggled.

It was mere moments until they were at their heels, snapping and clawing as they ran.

Ilona stumbled - her long dress not designed for this - and Apollinari supported her then grabbed her furs, flinging them away and to the side.

The dogs were distracted and changed direction to investigate.

Ilona could hear them growling and snapping, the furs ripping. She realised that if the animals caught them, there may not be a chance that Apollinari would even survive to be taken before her husband. Her own end seemed horribly near as well, but she wondered what the outcome would be for the men following them if they allowed their dogs to rip her apart too.

Not satisfied with the cold, musty animal skins, the dogs resumed their chase, the brief pause giving no respite to their prey.

Apollinari threw his own furs away, hoping the trick would work a second time, but the dogs never even broke their pace. They kept coming, relentless, determined.

And there it was, a claw at the hem of his cassock, bringing him crashing to the ground.

The ice was hard and it stung his hands and knees but the dog on his back soon made him forget about the floor. He turned over and kicked out, the dog jumping away then launching back at him, its companions doing likewise.

The dogs, six in all, attacked as one but what happened next took Apollinari a few moments to register.
There was an immense spray of red, almost black in the moonlight, a cacophony of painful yelps and the tearing of flesh – then a series of thumps hitting the ground.
A mist had suddenly formed, rolling in on itself.
Apollinari checked himself over in somewhat of a panic but found no injuries. His forearms from the previous wolf attack did ache, though, but the bandages had held fast.
But where was Ilona? Had the men taken her? Their pursuers had suddenly gone very quiet and if anything they should have easily caught up with them by now.
As he pulled himself to his feet, he saw the dogs, all of them, maimed and dead, scattered around the trees near where Apollinari had fallen.
A sickly-sweet aroma filled the air, only noticeable to a select few. It was a scent that he had never gotten used to and it chilled him to the bone because he knew what it heralded.
Dropping his hand to his upper right thigh, flicking back his cassock, he revealed the silver rapier strapped there. It gleamed in the moonlight.

"Come on out, show yourselves," he called into the darkness.

Something stirred behind him but he remained steadfast. It was probably a woodland creature, disturbed from its nocturnal sojourn by all the commotion.
Whatever it was, Apollinari knew it was too small to be what he was expecting to appear.
Before him, a little beyond the dismembered bodies of the dogs, the mist curled and thickened, rising up from the forest floor.

It lost its formless shape, shifting into four distinct columns, which themselves started to move independently of each other.

And from out of a column each stepped a pale figure, all with eyes burning and lips drawn back to reveal sharp white teeth.

"It's been a long time, Giuliano," said the one with the blonde hair.

"Not long enough, Ismael," replied Apollinari and drew his sword.

The infirmary was positioned some distance away from the main building complex, simply to avoid the spread of contagion and bad humors.

In the large single room, sitting by a bed hidden from view by off-white drapes, Brother Jacob wept.

Father Shandor had collapsed in his private quarters some hours ago and Jacob, diagnosing a peculiar loss of blood, initially feared an outbreak of plague. But apart from two tiny marks on the Abbot's neck, his body was mercifully devoid of buboes.

Shandor was the bedrock of the monastery and Jacob was hard pressed to keep concealed the fact that their spiritual father had become ill, many of the brotherhood linking this with recent events as the coming of the day of reckoning for them all.

Jacob didn't know how to treat Shandor, the patient refusing to eat and hiding in the shadows as if even the briefest glimmer of daylight was abhorrent to him.

So Jacob had brought him to the infirmary and made him as warm and comfortable as possible.

Shandor, on the other hand, was more than conscious of what was happening to him. Of course it was no sickness – and he even considered the fact that Jacob knew exactly what ailed him but dared not speak it.

There was an ignominious end in store for Shandor: he was becoming a vampire.

Ismael was prolonging the process, a typically malicious act of the undead, knowing that Shandor was not capable of suicide – for that in itself would send the Abbot's soul to Hell.

The bite marks were sore and throbbing but in some way Shandor accepted the pain they gave: it reminded him of how damned he now was and how that damnation could only be lifted with a stake plunged through his heart or his head removed from his shoulders.

He knew Jacob was sitting on a stool nearby and could hear his sobbing. Normally, he would have chided such a display of emotion but now there seemed little point so instead listened to his spiritual brother mourn him and let his mind wander, something he had not allowed it to do in nearly thirty years.

But it was as clear as day when Shandor reflected on his decision to enter into monastic postulancy, one of a number of attempts.

Since no vows had been required of him in those early days, he had found it hard to truly conform, yet the thought of returning to England filled him with dread. The succession of weak kings allowed the Church to exploit their continuous assault on alleged heresy, even within the Church itself, and Shandor's family were forced to leave their home after his father was executed as a lollard.

His mother did not agree with his decision to enter into a monastic life, fearing that one religious commune was a corrupt as the other, but the young Shandor's continued faith meant he was determined to find the ordered lifestyle that the violent background his childhood had witnessed now required.

Three successive monasteries rejected his application for novitiate until he found sanctuary in Karlsbad and from then on his career dedicated to God was secure.

And now, so many years later, he had fallen here at the hands of an ultimate heretic, condemned and humiliated, where even death wouldn't offer a release.

Chapter 17

Her scream stifled by a bloodied hand across her mouth, Ilona found there was little point in struggling. Her abductor was not about to lessen the grip around her chest until Ilona was calm and prepared to stay where she was.

"If you run they will find you," the voice hissed in her ear and she was sure it was female attempting to be disguised as a man's. "I cannot help you then."

It was as if this person was trying to save her from the men who were talking to Apollinari.

Ilona nodded and her captor tentatively released hold.

The princess spun to see who her apparent saviour was and her assumption that it could have been a woman was correct.

Except the woman crouching before her was naked save for the dirty bandage over one shoulder and congealed blood and strips of flesh hanging head to toe from the rest of her body. Only her eyes shone out.

"Dear Lord," Ilona whispered, "what happened to you?"

The woman seemed initially surprised then gave a semblance of a smile through the mess.

"Don't concern yourself. This isn't my blood," she said, looking down at herself. "If you wish to survive, you will do the same."

"I beg your pardon?"

The woman pulled from nearby the remains of some form of animal. It was dismembered to such an extent that Ilona had no way knowing what it once was. "Take your clothes off."

"I will not," Ilona replied, folding her arms. This was intolerable. She would not humiliate herself in this way. And as for the cold!

"Then you will die," came the simple answer.

"Are you threatening me?"

"No." The woman started scooping the animal's entrails into a neat pile. "But they will."

Ilona looked across to where Apollinari was, seeing he was deep in conversation. Was it the same man who had appeared to her by the campfire? She couldn't be sure. She looked back at the woman before her.

"Who are you?"

"My name is Claudia and you must do as I say if you want to live."

"I...I don't know..."

"If you want to live?" Claudia responded. "Who are *you*?"

"I am Princess Ilona."

Claudia nodded, recognising her name. "Then trust me, Your Highness. Take off your dress. You won't be as cold as you think you will."

Ilona squinted at her strange companion who looked back at her, looked *into* her, and was surprised to find that she was willing to have the corset of her peacock-blue outfit unlaced. Her undergarments too were to be taken off, Claudia indicated, and Ilona was surprised that she was complying. She was also suspicious when she found Claudia staring intently at her breasts.

She turned, trying to retain some element of dignity as she removed her short braies.

Covering her groin with one hand and her other arm her breasts, Ilona turned to face Claudia. She almost gagged as Claudia proceeded to smear the blood and entrails over her, leaving no part untouched. Even her hair was covered. It was vile.

"The vampires will not be able to smell you now."

"Vampires!" Ilona retorted, aghast. She tried to stop Claudia from continuing with the disguise, convinced she was insane.

Claudia growled at her to be quiet. "They can still hear, you know. They're senses are heightened. Our heartbeats will still be detectable but these animal guts will confuse them. They will not hunt us."

"How do you know this?"

"I've been...*involved* with vampires for as long as I care to remember."

"*But vampires do not exist!* They're tales to scare children."

"If you continue to talk as loudly as you are, you will soon find out your childhood fears are indeed standing over there."

Claudia was allowed to finish her task in silence and her attention to Ilona's rear and inner thighs did not go unnoticed by the princess. The animal skin itself was flung over her back.

"Are we ready now?"

Claudia nodded and pulled Ilona down with her and they both crouched in the snow.

Neither of them could clearly make out the exchange being had between Apollinari and Ismael but both women noted, Ilona in particular, that there seemed to be some familiarity between them.

"Am I dreaming? Is this some nightmare that I cannot wake from? What would a monk have to do with a vampire?" she whispered.

Claudia tilted her head and raised a hand, leaning to hear what the men were saying. Eventually she turned to Ilona. "Apollinari isn't what he seems."

Ilona thought about the objects in Apollinari's bag. "You know him?"

Claudia nodded. "I know both of them - the blonde vampire only by reputation, mind."

Ilona watched the men, but one minute the vampire was there, the next minute he wasn't.

"They're quick," Claudia said, sensing Ilona's confusion. Apollinari had collected himself together, sheathed his sword and was heading off into the night. "Come. We must follow him."

Chapter 18

The pungent smell of sweat and vomit hit Popescu's nostrils as he pushed open the door. This place known as the *Okruh Kráľovnej* had never been somewhere he could tolerate for too long, but he knew most of the Wallachian principality's less than agreeable population passed through here one time or another.

Information, then, was readily available – at the right price.

He was an officer and his presence here could end in a number of ways so he intended his visit to be brief.

Crossing the low, crowded room to the long bar at the far end, ignoring the woman on her knees practicing fellatio on a well-endowed but unconscious customer, Popescu wasn't sure whether he should risk having a drink. This place was infamous for its potent *tuică* and sour wine which seemed not to deter anyone from coming here. In fact there was never a time when this place was empty, some patrons staying for days before shuffling out the door, easy prey for the child pickpockets waiting outside to relieve them of the few coins they had left.

"I need information," Popescu snarled to the unshaven brute behind the bar.

The man pretended not to hear. Popescu repeated his question.

"Information is expensive. How heavy is your purse?" the landlord eventually replied.

"Heavy enough."

"That may not last long here, friend. Drink?"

Popescu shook his head. "I need a clear head."

"Perhaps you didn't understand the question." The landlord reached for a tankard, not as clean as Popescu would have liked, and sloppily filled it with *Tokay*. "I take it as a personal affront if my clients leave here without sampling what's on offer. Your drink."

He pushed the tankard towards Popescu who grudgingly threw some coins across the bar in return. "Now: information."

The man drummed his dirty fingers on the bar and raised an eyebrow. Popescu shook his head and handed out more *leu*.

"Thank you, *sir*," said the landlord, sliding the whole lot into his apron pocket. "In the corner. That's where you'll find your information."

Popescu's gaze followed the landlord's nonchalant thumbing motion. He lifted his tankard in acknowledgement and weaved across to where he had been directed. Two men ignored him as he approached, their game of knucklebones in full swing.

He used their ignorance to take in their appearance.

The man to his left was swarthy, shaggy-haired and well tanned, a hood half on and half off his head, face obscured. His hands were like paws, fingers thick and strong. They swamped the small pieces of carved bone they were using in the game, yet he moved them with surprising grace, catching the jack before it had time to land.

His companion was squat and Popescu wondered if he was a dwarf. His wide-brimmed hat sat at an angle on his head, the hair protruding from his scarred ears typical of that of an old man's. Arthritis claimed his joints and he winced every time he moved his arms. The volumes of *tuică* he regularly consumed made the pain easier but it never truly went away.

Popescu wondered why the old man would be playing such a game that involved the quick use of fingers and wrists.

"Do you intend to stand there all night?" the dwarfish man said between swigs.

"I need information."

The larger, hooded man kept his eyes on the game. "You're from the Palace."

It was definitely a statement.

Popescu frowned. "Do you know me? Look at me."

The hood ignored him.

"I said look at me!"

"Easy, my friend," the shorter man said, calming their visitor. "No disrespect was meant. Your people have your own spies and we ask why you bother us with your intrigues?"

"It is for the Palace that I am here," Popescu lied.

"Târgoviste offers a reward for information you require?" the hooded man asked, spying the purse about Popescu's waist.

"Do not push your luck," Popescu warned, hand darting to his hilt as the man went to stand. It was only the man's elder placing a gnarled hand on his arm that stopped him. He glared at his companion. "Do you know who I serve?"

"We're not afraid of Vlad the Impaler here," the man in the hood replied caustically. "That *is* what they call him, isn't it? What is it that you want?"

"I need to know if two people have been here recently."

The man to Popescu's left snorted and gestured to the room about them, smoky with the fireplace that was burning fiercely. "I should say so."

"Ease up," chided the old man. "You need to be more specific."

"I'm looking for a monk. He is with a woman."

The hooded man squinted into his own tankard. He downed it, making Popescu wait. He then stood and the old man did not stop him this time. Popescu was ready to draw his knife but was pushed aside.

"I need to piss."

Popescu let the man pass, frowning again. He was *sure* he knew his face, obscured as it was. The squat man offered him the vacated seat opposite him. Popescu took it and sipped his *Tokay*.

For a while both men sat in silence, Popescu absorbing the inn around him and the comings and goings of the far from salubrious clientele. He looked back at the dwarfish man on the other side of the table, uncomfortable with the way he was being stared at.

"Have you something to tell me?"

The dwarf, not breaking his gaze, swilled the *tuică* around his tankard in measured circles. "When the wolf is at your door, do you let it in or do you let it out?"

"What is that supposed to mean?"

"There are wolves everywhere. Always hunting. Always watching. Out for blood."

"For survival."

"Or for sport."

"Sport? I've no time for this. I am not looking for any damn wolf. Have you seen this monk or not?"

The man shrugged with indifference. "There *was* a monk here, a few days ago. He played a determined game of chess. He also drank like a bull. I'm not sure he had a woman with him. Is that normal for a man of the cloth? To have a woman?" The man wiped his mouth with the back of his hand following some lengthy gulps of drink. "I haven't been to prayer for a while so it may all have changed, of course."

"Father Apollinari is his name, Sardinian. Arrogant." Popescu knew better than to reveal the identity of the monk's companion.

"Most are," the man guffawed.

"Raudúlfr!" the hooded man called from across the crowded room.

"That's your name?" asked Popescu, the dwarf nodding. "You're a long way from home."

Raudúlfr looked at Popescu. "It is not through choice."

"Do you know where the monk was headed?"

Shaking his head, Raudúlfr drained his tankard dry. "He was here to get supplies."

"What sort of supplies?"

"I don't know," the man said, rather too quickly.

"Did he speak to anyone here?"

"No." Raudúlfr stood, and wasn't much taller in height as a result. Clearly agitated, he straightened his hat and gave a short bow. "I need to join my friend. Good luck in your search."

Popescu couldn't press the man for more information. He would soon be overheard and subsequently outnumbered.

The dwarf scurried off into the crowd, leaving Popescu with his thoughts, his *Tokay* and the retention of his money.

Reaching the door, Raudúlfr followed his companion outside.

"It was lucky you called me, Jurat," he said. "He was beginning to ask questions."

"It's been years and we both look different but he nearly recognised me. A few more moments and he would have known."

"Thank the *Einherjar*. I bet he thinks I've come out here to hold your dick for you while you piss."

Jurat gave a great laugh and slapped his short companion across the shoulders. Raudúlfr nearly toppled over.

"I'm not ready to face him yet and I think I know who this woman is who he says was with the monk."

"Who?"

"The wife of his great leader."

Raudúlfr's eyes widened under his bushy eyebrows. "This could be to your advantage."

"Of course. I may yet be able to ruin him completely."

Jurat looked up into the night sky. The moon was out and no sign of any snow. "I need to run. When Popescu leaves, I will follow him."

Raudúlfr shuffled over to the wall and slid down it. "Go. Do your hunting. I'll wait here."

"Don't run off with my clothes," Jurat replied, smiling, as he began to slip out of his hooded tunic.

"Don't you worry, my friend. I've seen the size of your claws."

Whether her bare feet were bloodied from the animal entrails she was covered in or the raw woodland floor didn't matter, for Ilona felt as though she had Hermes' wings at her ankles as she and Claudia tore through the deep parts of the Vlasie forest.

They were following Apollinari, the monk maintaining a good speed through the snow some yards ahead.

The icy wind stung their face and shoulders as they matched his pace, yet Ilona wondered if he would tire soon, not registering the fact that she herself had yet to feel fatigued.

The animal skin she was wrapped in seemed to mould itself to her back and before long she found she no longer needed to clasp it around her.

Claudia was still naked and unperturbed by the intense night cold, the snow that had begun to fall heavily melting as soon as it landed on her blood-covered body. Her hips were wide above full thighs, calf muscles taught as she traversed the ice. She motioned for Ilona to stop, pointing in silence at Apollinari who had paused at the edge of a rough track up ahead.

The monk was deciding which way to go, turned left, walked a few paces, thought better of it and turned to head off in the other direction.

"Does he know where he's going?" whispered Ilona.

Claudia shook her head. "He's using his inner sight. This is the first time he's been in the Vlasie."

"How do you know this? Have you been following him? Following *us*?" Ilona suddenly felt a chill. "Or do you have this 'inner sight', too?"

The women remained at a distance behind Apollinari, following him along the road until he turned off again into the trees.

They lost him briefly but caught sight of him entering an old ramshackle cottage that seemed to loom out of the darkness.

It was dark and solitary but clearly this had been Apollinari's destination.

Waiting until it seemed he would not be leaving the single storey building, they crept up, Claudia peering through a gap in a window's broken shutter.

"I think it's time he welcomed his guests," Ilona said and pushed open the door just as Claudia made to hold her back.

But Ilona stepped through and stumbled backwards as Apollinari launched himself at her from behind the door.

Realising who she was, he made a mess of his apologies, and tried to help her up. It was only as she stood that he realised her state of undress.

"Good Lord, Ilona, what has happened to you?"

Shy once more, Ilona tried to cover herself as best she could as she introduced her companion. "Father, this is Claudia. She says she knows you."

"That may be so," Apollinari replied, not giving Claudia even the briefest of glances. "I suggest you both get yourselves tidied up. There are some clothes in the parlour. They may not fit properly but it's the best we can do."

As the monk lit the fire in the tiny grate, the women disappeared into the next room.

They returned a little while later to find Apollinari sitting in a large wooden chair to one side of the fireplace. He looked up and smiled, seeing beyond the dark bloody stains on their skin and their matted hair. They were wearing heavy trousers each and grey woollen shirts. Leather boots, a few sizes too big, kept their feet warm. Ilona looked uncomfortable.

"This is a huntsman's cabin," Apollinari said, "and the garments you're used to at Târgoviste are far removed from what is available here. They'll do."

There were dry meats and some stale bread on the hearth and Apollinari served then a meagre portion each on grubby metal plates.

"I can't remember the last time I ate a meal indoors," Claudia said, hungrily consuming her share.

"You persevered in following me," Apollinari said. He looked at neither of them as he spoke but Ilona felt the statement wasn't directed at her. Strangely though, he seemed unwilling to actually acknowledge Claudia's presence.

Claudia didn't reply so Ilona spoke up.

"You know of vampires."

"Yes," Apollinari responded calmly, "I do."

"How?"

"How?" he queried. He pushed the bread around his plate. "How do any of us know the demons that surround us? Surely a man in my position should be wary of evil more than most."

"Your position?" spat Claudia.

"Ilona, there are many dangers in this world, many terrible things that by rights should not exist. But exist they do. Do you know what Claudia is?"

So he *was* willing to concede she was there!

"No."

"Did you not ask yourself why you didn't feel the cold? How the animal skin clung to your own like it was part of you? Like you felt you were gliding across the forest floor?"

Ilona looked between Apollinari and Claudia. They *did* know each other, they *had* to.

"I know it was strange but I saw *you* talking to a vampire. And those things in your bag..."

She hadn't meant to let it slip and dropped her eyes to her meal.

Apollinari chuckled. "I didn't have the heart to stop you looking through it. You seemed quite determined to find out what was in it."

"You knew I was looking through it?"

"Yes."

Ilona felt sick. Sick and embarrassed and wished for that moment that the snow would fold in on over her. "I'm sorry. I didn't mean-"

"It is fine, Ilona. You were curious about me. You had every right. I would have done the same."

"But what were they, all those strange things?"

"My employ takes me far wider than the norm for a monk. They are tools, nothing more."

"Do you have it with you?" Claudia asked suddenly. Apollinari put down his plate and bridged his hands together, staring deep into the fire. "I do."

Claudia tensed, excited yet fearful.

"Can I see it?"

Apollinari kept his eyes fixed firmly front, unblinking, unwavering in his gaze. Then after silence had fallen in the little house, he moved suddenly, making Ilona jump.

From out of his bag, still snuggled safely within the folds of his cassock, Apollinari drew the old, leather-bound book.

Ilona leant forward, her heart beginning to quicken as she recognised its worn appearance. "What is it?"

Apollinari held it flat between his palms, deep in concentration. Ilona repeated her question.

"Hmmm? I'm sorry, Your Highness, what were you saying?"

"It is something very special," Claudia said. "It's the lost de Blanc Grimoire."

"It was never lost," Apollinari corrected. "But it is important that it is *believed* to be lost."

"You had it all the time?" Claudia asked.

Apollinari nodded. "Your mother made strict instructions before her…death."

"Were you there?"

The monk sighed. "Some weeks ago I received a letter from Bistritz's bishop. He told me your mother was dead and that the Grimoire had gone. I was instructed by Rome to search for it. It seemed they feared Sigmirului would speak openly of it. I did not tell the bishop that she had sent the Grimoire to me at Saccargia before she died."

"I cannot imagine your Abbot was pleased to receive that at his monastery."

This drew a gentle chuckle from Apollinari. "De Bricassart has learnt to turn a blind eye at such things."

"Was my mother's end typical?"

"All flames, chanting and holy water?" Apollinari nodded. "I'm sorry. Yes, it was. But she died knowing the Grimoire was safe."

"Why is it so special?" Ilona wanted to know.

"You've looked through it. You tell me." Apollinari continued eating his bread.

"It was full of drawings…of nonsense."

"It has in it the key to destroying Caleb."

"And you would be wise," Apollinari added, "to remember that."

"But this means nothing to me! Who is Caleb?"

Claudia turned to the princess, seeing the firelight flickering in her eyes. "Caleb is a monster, the ancient vampire enemy of our kind. He is the Lord of the undead, ruler of the damned!"

"Your kind?"

"I am witch, Ilona, like my mother." Claudia was proud of the fact.

"Her mother, Agatha Weiss, comes from a long bloodline of powerful witches. She was chosen to keep the Grimoire safe. Before she died, she instructed me to find Claudia so she could inherit the responsibility."

"But you're a monk!" exclaimed Ilona. "Why would you be involved in witchcraft? In vampires? In *any* of this? I don't understand!"

"We should be working for opposite sides, you mean?" Apollinari leaned forward, his face suddenly darkening. Ilona felt that same chill again. "It is not as straightforward as that, Ilona. Claudia is my niece."

Chapter 19

The single, shrill note rang out in the distance, slightly off-key and like a banshee screaming to its children.

A call to arms, the noise bounced and spun from the valley walls, giving the impression of being everywhere at once.

It triggered the Wallachian army into position, dragging itself into ranks that it had spent months becoming familiar with, yet all the time diminishing in size as more men failed to survive each conflict.

This time it was different: something in the air that made it feel inimitable, final.

The sound called out again. It was the enemy and they were headed around the curve in the valley some three miles east, announcing their advance and their impending attack on the defending forces.

Mansi's nerves were beginning to shred but he knew he had to stand fast. He was at the front line and it would be him and his fellow men-at-arms who would be the first to see the Turk, to engage with them.

Barefoot (his boots had long ago fallen apart), he kept deathly still, the mud ice-cold between his toes and licking at his ankles. His throat was coarse because he dared not swallow, his eyes front and unblinking, even though the bitter wind sweeping down the Prahov made him weep. Unable to lessen his grip from his lance, he simply let the tears freeze on his cheeks and hoped no one would notice.

And no one did, for they were all like him, all fearful of the death knell that the Turkish trumpeters were sounding but far more terrified of their commanders-in-chief who remained at a safe distance behind the thousands-strong mass of young men.

Stephen of Moldavia was one such leader and, from atop his ride that was easily eighteen hands, he had a clear view of the army below.

Moving his mount, the beast stomping and snorting on the solidifying slush beneath its great hooves, Stephen faced Vlad Dracula.

"Are you waiting until we see the yellow of the Turk's eyes before we react?" he asked.

"God is patient," came Dracula's reply, "and so must you be, my ally."

Such an order did not sit well with Stephen. His treacherous defeat at the hands of the Moldavian army, nearly two years past now, could tell of that. He had not listened to his generals, did not listen to their advice to wait until the enemy was on the move before striking. Had he done so, then the town of Vaslui would have been his. After two defeats, he had ordered his generals executed and, on their deaths, news reached him that they had purposely betrayed him to the Moldavians. For what gain he never knew but Dracula was different.

He was a formidable opponent yet it was the loss of Vaslui that had made him approach the great prince with the suggestion of an alliance.

It was well known that Dracula had been desperate to increase his weight against the Ottoman Turks and he willingly accepted the olive branch. His influence still strong, Stephen was able to convince the King of Hungary to reappoint Dracula as Prince of Wallachia and Vlad, in his gratitude, made Stephen a general in his army.

So, if Dracula told him to be patient, then for good reason.

Dracula's own résumé in itself gave Stephen the confidence to follow his instructions. After all, Stephen was now under his command and technically unable to question his leader's authority. Dracula, on the other hand, allowed Stephen a certain amount of leeway and held back his infamous temper whenever his valuable ally angered him.

Stephen knew Dracula would never recover from the defeat if he decided to retract his troops, thereby cutting down the weight of the Wallachian might. The Turks would win, of that all of them had no doubt, so it would be churlish to premeditate that eventuality. Yet the dangerous game Stephen was playing with Dracula lingered at the back of the Moldavian's mind and he was fully aware that, as soon as the Turk had been driven out of his land, Dracula would have no qualms in cutting out Stephen's two-faced heart.

But allies they were, here on the slopes of the Prahov Valley, ready to cut down the oncoming enemy.

This would be a good battle and Stephen's blood pounded in his ears in anticipation.

Suddenly a cry came up from the ranks but Dracula bellowed them into silence almost immediately. Stephen moved his horse back around to face the troops beneath them, adrenalin surging through him as he caught first sight of the surprise Dracula had prepared for the Turks. The general grimaced, careful to make sure Dracula did not see his expression, but the prince was taken by prayer, eyes wide and his voice a coarse bellow as he shouted out across the heaving army.

"God of power and mercy, maker and love of peace, to know you is to live, and to serve you is to reign! Through the intercession of St. Michael, the archangel, be our protection in battle against all evil! Help us to overcome war and violence and to establish your law of love and justice! Grant this through Christ our Lord and may He protect us as we strike out for our freedom! The Turkish invaders have taken our women, our land, our homes – and this day will see their banishment from our country!"

The unanimous cheered response, albeit delayed in places as Dracula's words were repeated around the men, floated up towards the mounted leaders.

"You, every one of you, are saviours of our land! No longer will we cower and hide in the fields. We will till them again, we will reseed our honour. You are all protected by the grace of God and His might will see us the victor in this campaign. Now be ready and drive the invader from our homes!"

As the army grew to a frenzy, Dracula smiled. He leaned over to Stephen. "Now we advance," he hissed.

Relieved they were finally getting underway, Stephen nodded and out flashed his sword high above his head. As Dracula gave the order for his surprise to be shown, Stephen turned away.

Evenly spaced in a line before the front line and tethered by four ropes each, were fifty wooden poles, blunted and greased. A man at each rope end manoeuvred the huge lengths, thirty feet each if not more, into upright positions. As they dropped neatly into the holes provided, the poles righted themselves, shuddering into place as the four men to each pole kicked and pushed them secure.

The movement also meant that the individual Turk at the very top of each own pole slid down further, the rounded ends pushing their way without remorse through the impaled victims' bodies.

If they made any cry, Stephen could not tell, for the frenzied yelping of the Wallachian army drowned out any other voice.

Beneath the vicious line of poles, Mansi didn't dare look up. He didn't join in with the hollering of his countrymen, finding that his fear had left him speechless.

And then, through the mist in the distance, he could see the Turkish army pounding towards them. The wind had changed so he couldn't hear their advance just yet.

Even though he knew they were the enemy and his orders and his heritage meant he had to defend his home, he couldn't but help think just then how the Turks would feel as they realised what was atop the fifty thin trunks of wood.

But he dismissed it from his mind as a battalion leader cried out the motion to advance and advance they did, lances horizontal and ready to stake the invading hordes as the battle was met.

Ilona had knees drawn up under her chin as she perched on the wide windowsill. She stared through the crack in the shutters at the snow outside. The moonlight reflected and bathed everything in a blue-white hue.

The night seemed to go on, endless and cold.

She had never been comfortable with soothsayers and alchemists. They were banished from Dracula's official residences and so the intolerance had become second nature to her.

But Apollinari was still a monk and their journey from Snagov had not given them much time to rest, yet she had noticed that he did pray as often as he could.

And as for Claudia, Ilona should have realised as soon as she had appeared naked and covered in animal guts that she wasn't the average peasant girl.

What would they be doing now, she wondered, as they sat over the other side of the main room in this little cottage, by the roaring fire. Would they be casting their runes, sifting through rats' entrails to see signs of forthcoming events? Or would they be deep in incantation, placing curses upon those who had the misfortune to cross their paths? Would she, Ilona, be the recipient of such blight, falling into a deep sleep never to wake, or *to* wake and find herself buried alive?

"Why don't you join us in the warm?"

She tried to ignore the monk but it was not easy in a room that sparse. A heavy farmhouse table was between her and them, with Apollinari still sitting in the wooden chair and Claudia curled up on the floor at his feet, her head resting on his knees.

From his initial reticence, Father Apollinari seemed to welcome her presence.

He repeated his question, voice gentle, reassuring. How could he possibly have links to witchcraft?

"I'm sorry I never told you. You don't need to be scared of me, of us."

"I'm not scared of either of you. My husband has dealt with hundreds of your kind over the years. Be thankful he doesn't know of your existence or that we are here together."

"We are no threat to you," said Claudia. "You willingly came with Giuliano."

"Before I knew he was a bloody witch!"

"We have no quarrel. It is you who experience discord," reasoned Claudia.

Apollinari stood and Claudia moved to give him space. "What do you wish us to do, Ilona?"

Ilona turned to look at the monk, his face almost yearning for some form of forgiveness from her.

"I want you to leave."

"Leaving you alone here?" he replied. "There are things out tonight that we must protect ourselves from."

"Surely it is better than being in your company."

"We will not leave," Apollinari said firmly.

"Then *I* will leave!" Ilona retorted, not really having any true desire to do so. She swung her legs around and to the floor. She tried to ignore Apollinari's raised eyebrow. "Does your novice know he is being tutored by a blasphemer? You seem little bothered that he isn't even with you!"

"Roberto is constantly in my thoughts, Ilona. I do not necessarily need to air those thoughts."

"How is it that Rome even lets you sermonize?" she said acidly.

"Rome and I have not seen eye-to-eye on occasion but that has worked in both our favours. They are hesitant to truly acknowledge the darkness that walks this earth and therefore willing to have someone like me, someone less conservative by their teachings, to help defend against..."

Thump!

"...them," Apollinari finished, as they all looked upwards.

Thump!

The dust, settled over decades, shifted from the rafters and floated down like individual clouds of ash.

The three looked at each other.

The dull sound came a third time, albeit stronger. A bulbous bird, an ornament carved from local wood, wobbled on the mantelpiece and fell to the hearth, a crack in its beak.

Something struck at the shutters and they clattered in protest.

"They can hear us," Apollinari breathed.

"They can smell us," Claudia added.

"What are they?"

"Vampires," Claudia confirmed.

"But we're safe, though. Don't they need to be invited in?"

"That's a myth, Ilona. If they want to come in, they will. There's no politeness involved when it comes to wanting our blood. But they can still be stopped from crossing the threshold. Claudia, take these…"

He threw the witch, who appeared to be muttering to herself, a handful of the small bags from his pack and she set about sprinkling their contents across the window sills and along the bottom of the two doorframes – the one for the main door to the outside and the one that led to the parlour. The thorns were sharp and she didn't finish the job without at least receiving a few scratches.

Apollinari moved to the parlour but came back almost instantly, shuddering slightly. He caught Ilona's stare and composed himself, rooting back through his bag to pull out handfuls of the stubby, sharpened lengths of wood. "'Hath the whitethorn many virtues, for he that beareth a branch on him thereof, no manner of tempest may dare him...'" A thought then occurred to him. "Where is the longbow you had?"

Ilona frowned, having forgotten all about them. "Oh no...I think I left them in the woods." She looked almost sheepish. The wife of a seasoned warrior and she broke the first rule of defence – never lose your weapons.

"It's no major loss. An arrow wouldn't necessarily kill a vampire but it would have slowed them down for us."

Thump.

Thump.

Thump, *thump*.

"They're all over the roof," said Ilona, voice quivering.

Claudia agreed. "They're looking for a way in.

"It'll be dawn in a couple of hours. If we can hold them off until then..."

"Do you think we can, Father?" Ilona stared at the thorns, seeing how pitiful they looked dotted around.

"We don't have much choice in the matter."

The main door, bolted tight from the inside, suddenly shattered open, splintering wood everywhere. Ilona screamed as Claudia dragged her behind the table.

In the doorway stood a creature, not unlike a bat – had such creatures been upright and standing taller that the average man. Nevertheless its face, with its upturned nostrils and slavering tongue between sharp white teeth, was terrifying.

It faltered, as if unable to cross the threshold. Its great snout twitched as it scented the thorns amidst the wood fragments, unsure, it appeared, as to what it should do. A second monstrosity appeared behind it, hissing, head tilted.

"I've never seen anything like them!" Claudia called. Apollinari mused over this. "They're vampires, make no mistake!"

"Are they human?" Ilona asked, her throat beginning to feel restricted.

"No vampire is human, but they were once." Apollinari stood firm in front of the fire, a stake in each hand, the rest tucked in his belt. "Some have the ability to change shape, become other things. Abominations every one."

The first vampire flashed out an elongated arm. Leathery skin, a vile interpretation of a wing, attached it to its torso.

Claudia dived across to the window nearest her, picked up a handful of the thorns (ignoring this time their sharp caresses in her palm) and launched them at their unwelcome visitors.

While it had the desired effect, for the vampires screeched and reeled as the thorn pricked their skin, her actions had cleared the path for others and they came crashing through the shutters, three of them, all as hideous as the two in the doorway.

The ground trembled as the Turkish cavalry pounded around the curve in the valley, the mist obscuring for the moment its target.

Behind them stormed the foot soldiers, ready to mop up the stragglers after the mounted troops had mown down the initial Wallachian infantry.

But the sight that met them, looming out of the morning fog, filled them with horror and the brutal determination of the twisted mind of their enemy was never more apparent.

The fifty Turks impaled on their own poles were still alive and still horrifyingly conscious.

The twenty or so horsemen pulled back on their reins, the steeds whinnying in protest, some falling to the ground, others flinging their riders clear.

The Wallachian lancers scrambled forward and spiked many of the fallen enemy, disabling the horses in the process.

Behind the riders, the Turkish foot soldiers met the Wallachians, fierce and unforgiving. Steel flashed in the sky, in that time just before twilight. Moonlight still shone bright but its effect decayed now that the night around it was beginning to fade.

Chapter 20

Apollinari made quick work of two of the vampires, their twisted abominations of human form exploding as soon as he had driven whitethorn stakes through their undead hearts.

The third one retreated to the parlour as Apollinari followed it, his silver sword drawn and gleaming in the firelight.

"What is dark be filled with light, remove this evil from my sight," intoned Claudia as she raised her hands. The vampire hissed and spat blood as she came up behind Apollinari. "The whitest flame burns bright, bringing power to my fight."

The room seemed to flash with red and white and Ilona was blinded for a moment. When her eyes re-accustomed themselves, the light had faded and the vampire was on the floor, writhing and burning, the flames holding it at bay.

Apollinari swung his weapon in an arc, neatly removing the vampire's head from its shoulders. The creature's body altered, shifted, and it looked human once more, the flames doing their work and turning it to cinders. The head rolled to a stop at Ilona's feet. Dead eyes looked up at her and she clamped a hand over her mouth to stifle her horror.

It was not the face of a demon, but of a boy, perhaps no older than ten.

Apollinari turned to leave the parlour. He pushed past Ilona. Ignoring her expression, Claudia sagged, exhausted by her spell.

"Claudia, we don't have time to rest."

The two other vampires outside had grown frenzied by their companions' destruction and had scrabbled around to the window. They were already climbing in when Apollinari reached them, sword still sticky with blood. The sword flashed down and struck one of the vampires in the shoulder. Its silver burnt the creature and as it writhed, Apollinari drew another stake and drove it through its heart, guts and blood showering his hands and face.

As Apollinari stopped to wipe the mess from his eyes, the remaining creature lashed out a great talon and caught the monk clean across the throat. Startled, Apollinari staggered back then fell as the weight of the attacking vampire landed upon him.

Fangs bared, the vampire shifted back to human form and sunk its teeth deep into Apollinari's neck.

"It feels like I'm rotting from the inside."

"Did you think you'd sparkle in the daylight?" Ismael laughed, his rank breath hitting Rintoul's nostrils. "It will pass. Your limbs have stopped aching, yes?"

Rintoul nodded, holding his forearms as if to demonstrate. "But my throat is sore."

"It's the blood you drink. You need to consume it while it is fresh. The staler it is, the sicker it makes you feel. You are experiencing nothing more than any other newborn vampire has been through." Ismael pulled Rintoul close to him. "Look at them, see how they run. They fight for their lives, for their souls."

"They fight for their existence. I have betrayed them."

"How so?"

"I used to be them."

"You are better than they are now."

Rintoul squinted across the valley from their vantage point, watching for two days the massive armies collide.

The sound of steel clashing against steel, forged metal through flesh and the falling thuds of fresh corpses, both man and steed alike, against the ice-cold mud had rang up the valley walls for the last two days.

War cries from both sides and the wail of the Turkish janissaries rallied the battle on. Wallachian arbalests fired over the heads of the men and the bolts rained down, embedding into armour and flesh.

Ismael grabbed Rintoul and launched them high into the air, carrion crows fleeing in terror. They were motionless in the sky for a while, like a pair of hawks far above the two mighty armies, hearing the thousands of hearts beating, gallons of thick red blood pumping through endless lengths of pulsating veins. Some said that vampires couldn't feel, but only a vampire knew what it was to *be* a vampire, to be truly undead. Ismael held Rintoul by the back of the neck and brought them back down to land amidst the chaos and the blood.

Around them swords still flashed and lances spun, Turkish soldiers falling dead at their feet as Dracula's men stood their ground.

"They can't see us," Rintoul noted.

"No, they cannot. We are but shadows to them, drifting through the darkness of the light. They can only perceive us if we wish it."

"The shadows in the day that you spoke of..."

"Smell the blood! Is it not glorious?" Ismael exclaimed, flinging his arms wide, the rank odour of death stirring his desires.

Rintoul's senses were afire, not just with the mud, the blood and the sweat but with the very tears of the soldiers who saw their lives about to end.

"I'm hungry," realised Rintoul.

"Then we shall feast well in the blackness of this human conflict!"

Together, the two vampires tore through the killing fields, tearing and biting and greedily drinking. If it were Turk or Wallachian, it made no difference.

The trail of corpses they left went unnoticed for the humans were leaving behind their own imprints of slaughter, the reddening snow testament to that.

The passing of time for a vampire is not what it is for the living and soon the two undead creatures had covered the majority of the valley, fresh blood in their veins.

The battle raged on around them and they retreated to the very edge of the valley a few miles north. Even from this distance the noise and smell was extraordinary.

A sudden jerking motion caught both their gaze and they focused on a large blur slicing through the soldiers, some toppling like trees as it passed.

Solidifying before them, both Rintoul recognised the form as it finally came to a halt. For him, it was still Tanyel, the Turkish commander who had so cruelly tortured him. His eyes and gums were red with blood, teeth bared. He was dressed in black, having shrugged off the cumbersome armour of his host body's former self. The cold of course didn't affect him so gone too were the furs, leaving the leather tunic and braies visible.

Yozgatli Tanyel's treasured riding boots finished off the ensemble.

For Ismael, it was clear who this newcomer was.

"Skulking around the weak and injured, Ismael?" Caleb spat. "Did you not learn your lesson at the hands of Morgan ab Owain?"

Ismael turned away from the vampire, disturbed. Some said that Caleb's powers were beyond that of other vampires. Were these skills part of that strength? To know Ismael and to be conscious of events that had happened *after* his destruction in Jerusalem? Whatever the case, Ismael was not willing to acknowledge the reference and so did not answer the senior vampire.

"You are his," Caleb stated of Rintoul, nodding in Ismael's direction.

"He turned me," Rintoul replied acerbically. His new vampire powers gave him the courage to answer the man back. "What concern is it of yours?"

Like lightning, Caleb was upon Rintoul, claw-like fingers pressing at the newborn's throat. "You must learn respect. Your maker clearly has neglected that in his teachings."

"Caleb," hissed Ismael, sharply enough for Caleb to ease the pressure on Rintoul's throat and move back.

"It seems my absence has allowed free thinking amongst us. This will not do."

"You still lead us, Caleb."

"But not by your choice, I feel, Ismael?" Caleb responded, wary of the blonde vampire's demeanour. "Who would *you* have to lead us? You?"

Ismael looked at Caleb, the ancient vampire's new eyes boring into his own. "Yours is superior," he responded simply and bowed.

Rintoul watched this exchange, beginning to understand who Caleb probably was. Had Tanyel also become a vampire? It seemed so, yet he still appeared to be a figure of some authority.

"I take it by your progress through the battlefield that you are fed?"

"We are."

"You still have room for more, you and your sprightly bitch, here?" Caleb seemed to fold in on himself for a moment and swept into the throng of soldiers from whence he had appeared, returning in the blink of an eye with a bruised and battered Wallachian hanging from his grasp.

For a moment, Rintoul remembered how he himself had been dragged into the company of the enemy, *in front of the aspect of the very man standing before him.* This poor wretch was no different – isolated from his fellow men and too weak to retaliate.

Just then, Rintoul made to dash forward, suddenly recognising the captive under the thick layers of blood and dirt. But Ismael was quicker than Rintoul and held his arm, holding him firmly back.

"Eager to taste him, are you?" purred Caleb, looking down at the soldier.

"He's..." Rintoul's words caught in his throat.

"What?" taunted Caleb.

"This is his fellow countryman. Rintoul is newborn and still clings to the frailties of human emotion."

Rintoul shook his head in disagreement.

"Then you must feed from him. Purge these feelings."

Caleb threw the soldier to Rintoul's feet, the poor soul landing like a rag doll. Rintoul looked down at him, desperate to speak but feeling as if Ismael had somehow taken his voice.

"Feed!" Caleb roared.

Rintoul knelt, holding the soldier's head in his hands. Prone, the Wallachian was far too young to be where he was, deep in battle and fighting for his country's freedom.

He had no boots on, his bare feet cut and bruised. The welts on his soles were compacted with congealed blood and soil.

His armour was meagre, missing in places where it should have been at its most secure. The boy had a broken arm, twisted and held tight to his body by its own tension. Rintoul wondered how he had been able to defend himself. He was no swordsman, no mounted cavalry. The youngster's wounds were clearly and ultimately going to be fatal. Then Rintoul looked up and towards Ismael. If he turned the boy, then surely that would save him..?

Ismael seemed to be aware of the thought. *Do as Caleb has commanded*, Rintoul seemed to hear him say.

"But I can't!" cried Rintoul, bloody tears splashing over the boy's face. "He's just a child!"

"We are all children, Rintoul."

"Listen to your maker, Rintoul," Caleb said and wrenched the boy out from under the anguished vampire. In a swift and overly brutal moment, Caleb struck, sinking his fangs deep into the neck below the lolling chin.

"No!"

Rintoul launched himself at Caleb but, even as the old vampire tore out Henric's throat, he flung out an arm and hurled Rintoul far across the snow.

"For your mother's sake!" Ismael shouted. "Stay back!"

Rintoul ignored Ismael and, collecting himself like a cat, flew back across the ice - but Ismael appeared in his way and they both thudded in a heap not far from where Henric's shredded corpse now lay.

Caleb stood over Rintoul's brother, fresh blood glistening on leather. Rintoul had never felt rage like it before and his breathing became shallow, growling in his throat. Animalistic, his vampiric senses took hold. He clambered up from under Ismael who, while the stronger of the two, still could not keep him down.

"*Rintoul...*"

The warning was ignored, blood behind his eyes now.

"Caleb!" spat Rintoul.

Caleb bared his fangs, Rintoul doing likewise. "You dare defy me? You, who is not yet even fully aware of what he now is?"

"Rintoul doesn't know his limitations, Caleb."

"Should I be scared of this puppy?"

"You sound like a Turk," said Rintoul, pacing back and forth like a caged beast.

"You sound as if you have no sense."

"You killed him!"

"What concern is that of yours?"

Rintoul wanted to rip the vampire's head from his neck, but something in Caleb's voice sounded oddly reassuring, like it made perfect sense. Rintoul shook his head, trying to dislodge the feeling.

"He was alive and now he is dead. No matter how you perceive it, you are beyond such constraints. You have entered a new world. You are part of a superior order. These weak creatures are but cattle to us. See them as such and treat them as such!"

Caleb slid forward, cutting through the air that was thick with death and decay. His eyes were white, as were all vampires' of course, but there was a presence behind his that no other vampire seemed to have.

Alluring and intoxicating, Caleb touched Rintoul's face. "Bloodlines now are with your new brethren. The blood of the living has no value except as nourishment."

Rintoul dropped to his knees, his joints weak, undead heart pounding in his chest.

"Yes…master…" the newborn whispered.

Ismael remembered how that felt, the caress of an elder's fingers across his face. He raised a cold hand to his own cheek and closed his eyes.

Even though he had made Rintoul, Rintoul was Caleb's now and Ismael had to accept it to be so. He disappeared into the air, flying higher and higher over the weakening battle until Rintoul and Caleb were mere specks below and he could see the morning sun creep out from behind the horizon of the Orient. The day wouldn't reach them here in Wallachia for another couple of hours yet, so he still had time to savour the night and consider his position amongst the Celebrants.

"Come away from it! Let it die!"

Ilona wasn't sure what to do, but Claudia's words did make sense.

As the witch gently tended to the bite marks on Apollinari's neck that had taken hours to stop weeping, Ilona couldn't help but feel drawn to the vampire that was lying on the cold stone floor of the cottage.

The vampire looked up at her, white eyes filled with tears of blood, scarlet oozing from its mouth.

She couldn't help but think of him as human. He looked so normal, save for the blood and the pale skin. His hair, cropped almost to the skull, was black, greying at the temples. His fangs protruded down over his bottom lip and he breathed hard, laboured and painful.

"What's happened to him? What did you do?" Ilona asked, frowning at Apollinari.

"Do not get drawn in by its hypnosis. It will render you useless then strike."

"But look at him, Claudia. He can barely move!"

"The poison in it will make long work of its destruction – deservedly so!"

A poison? "One minute he was so powerful, then the next..."

Ilona reached out to touch the vampire's forehead whose eyes followed the movement of her hands. Under her fingertips, he was ice cold.

"He is not like us, princess. Claudia is right. You must keep away from him." Apollinari stood, thanking Claudia for her attentiveness to his wound. "He will not last much longer."

"But he *bit* you! He drank your blood! It should be *you* dying!" Ilona held her head in her hands. "I'm sorry; I didn't mean it to sound like it did."

Apollinari rested a hand on her trembling shoulders. "It's fine. I know what you meant."

"But you have to tell me! How is it *he* is dying?"

As Apollinari went to open his mouth, Claudia spoke over him. "It is not for the likes of you to know such things."

"*For the likes of me?* You mean someone who isn't a bloody profane witch?"

"Claudia," soothed the monk, "it is fine. Perhaps the princess *should* know."

"Know what?"

Apollinari moved to the chair, shifting it so he could keep one eye on the prone vampire, even though he knew the undead creature wasn't going anywhere. It had been there for two whole nights now, slowly and painfully disintegrating. Apollinari sat.

"In Rome's fight against the demons of this world, they have tapped into certain...*areas* that would usually be off limits. I am one such area. There are powers which are at my disposal that I use to oppose the darkness." He rifled through his bag and pulled out the clinking, glass phials. Holding a couple up to the firelight, Ilona could see that the silvery liquid inside was almost translucent.

"You drink this?"

Apollinari nodded. "I have been consuming it for many years. It is said to be fatal but with the right spell, it can be the ultimate protection from the vampire."

Claudia laughed. "So that's your secret! That's why they didn't attack you in the forest."

Apollinari nodded. "Yes, and also that particular vampire in the forest is an old acquaintance of mine. Our paths have crossed before."

"You are a man of God," stated Ilona. "How can you sit there and talk so calmly of such things? You sound as cold as the vampires."

"The vampires made me cold. I find it hard to feel. If I did so easily, my work would be hindered."

"Your coldness becomes you, Father Apollinari. It is as though you haven't lost anyone close to you at all!"

"I have lost more than you can imagine because of the vampires, Ilona. It had made me who I am."

"I know what you are," spat the princess.

"You cannot know what I am! You cannot begin to comprehend what I may be!"

Ilona looked long and hard at Apollinari's face, the lines etched around his eyes and across his forehead telling her so much. As he broke her stare, she picked up one of the phials. "How does it work?"

"It is a remedy passed down to me, down the family line. But too much and I could become ill. Taken in the right dosage however means that any vampire who bites me and drinks my blood is destroyed from the inside."

All three turned to look at the vampire as it lay there, panting like a thirsty wolf. Its eyes flicked to look back at them as if to ask for their blood, to save it, to make it strong again.

Ilona looked at the phial in her hand. The colloidal silver seemed odd, unreal. Perhaps it *was* witchcraft. She thrust it back into Apollinari's palm, shuddering.

"I am surprised you are not aware of this, Claudia," said Apollinari.

"I know it as a method but I never believed it to be practiced."

"You...you can conjure spells and poisons but it still won't stop us," the vampire suddenly gurgled.

Apollinari stood and walked over to the monster. "What do you mean?"

"Ignore it, Giuliano; it is trying to get inside your head."

"Caleb is returned. He lives again!"

Apollinari's shoulders tensed. The Grimoire, his ancestor's book of shadows, explicitly told of Caleb's death, of how the Holy City had been sacked by the Templar knights, how the skirmish had driven the vampires out of hiding and how Caleb had been executed at the very spot where the Christ had suffered a fate not unlike that of impaling one thousand years before. Only Caleb's heart remained, his body quartered and burnt.

"You are wrong," was all the monk could say, knowing he wasn't.

The vampire laughed like wind through trees. "The Celebrants have come together once more. They do his bidding."

"Where is he?" Apollinari spat. The smile the vampire gave as a response made the monk pull at his collar. "Tell me!"

"You'll never find him!"

Apollinari struck the vampire clean across the jaw but it had little effect. The smile remained: cruel, knowing. A stake appeared in Apollinari's hands and the vampire's eyes widened.

"End my existence if you will, monk. But I will not tell you!"

"Father," Ilona said, tentative. For all the spells this Grimoire contained, it all seemed to come down to a physical battle in the end. She knew the raising of that stake in the monk's shaking grasp meant only one thing.

"His casket is secure, watched over by one darker than any of us. The battle between your kind and ours begins again. No Turk, no Wallachian – no one - will stand in our way. We are rooted. Cut us down and we will spring up again and again and again! You efforts will never penetrate the walls!"

Apollinari brought the stake down.

"Don't!" Ilona blurted but not before the sharpened wood pierced the vampire's ribcage. Even before the stake had hit the floor underneath, the creature had exploded, the expression on its face unflinching 'til the last.

The monk stood, dazed, staring coolly at Ilona. "You think me mad? Perhaps I am." He knew the casket signified something of Caleb's return but he had chosen to dismiss it, choosing to believe that it was the *idea* of Caleb that has resurfaced, not Caleb himself. Perhaps that was what it was – this vampire was deluded into believing through rumour and myth that their great undead leader had somehow returned. The fact that Apollinari was here, trying to find the damn thing as well as his own novice, told him that deep down he had accepted the fact that the war never ended – perhaps would *never* end. "We're going to Dambovita," he whispered.

"But the Turks occupy it," pointed out Ilona. "Why there?"

"Because that's where Caleb's influence resides."

"Are you certain?" Claudia was cautious.

"This man was born a Wallachian. He mentioned 'the walls'. It is an achievement all Wallachians used to be proud of until the Turks breached them. The walls he referred to must be those that encompass the Dambovita Citadel." He looked between Claudia and Ilona, wondering how he had ended up with two such different characters: a princess from an aristocratic background and his own sister's daughter, born into witchcraft and relative poverty. "Let us rest. We go at first light. If we are lucky it will take us no more than a day."

"And when we get there?" Claudia asked.

"The Turks will surely recognise me," said Ilona. "I will jeopardise your welfare."

"I don't believe the Turks will be in occupancy when we arrive. But if there are any left, they will be vampires and will care little about whose loyalty you hold."

"And *when* we get there?" Claudia asked again.

"We find Caleb's disciples and destroy them."

Chapter 21

Mansi's forearms ached as he swung the bastard sword over his head, its own weight bringing it crashing down on a Turk's head, splitting his skull.

He had been trained in combat with the lance but, following its fracturing as easily as this unfortunate combatant's head, Mansi had to find another means by which to defend himself.

Littered with the dead, their weapons cast asunder, the reek emanating from the Prahov Valley could be smelt (it was said some years later) from as far south as the banks of the Danube.

Mansi knelt in the soft earth around him, so little energy left in his body. But he had to call on his reserve strength for sitting here made him vulnerable, and vulnerability meant death.

He had long ago stopped looking for Henric, had ceased calling out for him as he sliced and pummelled his way across the battlefield. He had to conclude the boy was dead.

Pulling himself to his feet, legs trembling, he left the heavy sword where he had dropped it, in the mud, finding a lighter scimitar in amongst the debris and congealed body parts.

Renewed, he cried out and ploughed on, cutting and stabbing, Turks falling around him. One lucky strike against him knocked him face down in the mud but he rolled away from the blade heading towards his neck. Thrusting upwards, Mansi caught the Turk under the ribs, the scimitar stuck hard with suction. But a sharp twist and a boot in the chest freed the scimitar and the Turk fell away, dead.

"Aceasta este pentru mama mea, tatăl meu, sângele meu."

Trampling the mountain of corpses, Mansi kept going, somehow maintaining the pace for the next few hours, felling men and receiving his own share of flesh wounds. The valley was wide and the expanse of the battle meant that before long there were considerable moments of calm, where no one person was confronted or met, not from either side.

The Wallachian generals on their horses had disappeared from their vantage point high up the valley's slopes. Mansi deduced they had joined the battle proper, Dracula never being shy of standing shoulder to shoulder with his men.

Where were they now though, he wondered, even considering that the battle had somehow ceased. If that was the case, was there a victor? Mansi could never imagine it to be the Turk, for he was sure he had seen more bloodied turban than helmet dotted around him.

A toppled caravan, Turkish by design, made good cover and he was sure he felt rain upon his face as he settled up against it. The scimitar dropped from his grip.

He was cold, hungry and exhausted in equal measure. He drank from a flask found by a torso without limbs or head. It contents were rank and he spat the stagnant water out across the slush, tossing the blood-stained container away.

A great crack of lightning ripped high over his head and the heavens finally opened, the downpour merciless and ice cold.

Great drops of rain hit the ground, scarring the mud and slush with little round craters.

Mansi slumped as the freezing water rose around his legs, fatigue taking hold of him. His eyelids drooped.

"Come...we have more to do."

The voice was strong and direct and made Mansi's spittle catch in his throat.

He looked up, alarmed.

Standing over him, legs astride and a long-sword held tight in his gauntleted hands, was Vlad Dracula.

Snagov's bell had been tolling during the daylight hours, each slow and solitary strike of the clapper producing a mournful sonority.

Father Shandor was dead, passing over two nights ago and leaving a cold, lingering pallor across the island.

Jacob sat at the Abbot's desk, staring at the masses of documents and correspondence that would now go unanswered by Shandor. Jacob had sent word to Sigmurului by rider, inviting the bishop to the monastery to see to the Abbot's business and, of course, his burial. It was a task too substantial for the monks to carry out themselves and Apollinari's departure meant the bishop was the most senior member of the faith in the general locale. Even the paperwork seemed too daunting for Jacob.

The chapel had been full day and night, the monastery struggling to come to terms with what had happened. Two younger monks, seeking release from the anguish in the stables, were discovered missing from the dormitory and found swinging from make-shift nooses. They were quietly cut down and buried at a crossroads on the mainland. News of their suicides was never announced, implying instead that they had been sent on church business elsewhere and would not be returning.

These were bleak times indeed for Snagov and Jacob knew their united strength in their faith would be the only chance they would have to see the coming days through.

The door to Shandor's office was flung open suddenly and Golick, distraught and breathless, floundered in.

Trying as best he could to emulate Pretorius Shandor's approach, Jacob stood and attempted to calm Golick with some soothing words and upturned palms.

"The bishop..." breathed Golick, shaking his head and pointing towards the high-arched window. "He's here!"

Panic crept to the nape of Jacob's neck but he maintained a serene exterior. "We must welcome our most exalted guest, my brother. See that his way is clear. I will meet him at the main gate."

A flurry of robes and sandaled feet for the next few minutes as all rushed to prepare for Sigmurului, the bishop's entourage crossing the lake and eventually coming to a halt at the opened main gates, beyond which was the interior courtyard of the great monastery.

Jacob dropped to one knee before the wizened old bishop as Sigmurului extended with firmness his right hand. Jacob took the offering and kissed the jewel on the bishop's ring finger, detecting the scent of stale wine on the dry skin.

Sigmurului retracted his hand and Jacob was sure he saw the bishop wipe it slyly against his hip.

"Where is the body?"

Taken aback by the question, for Jacob was expecting a more formal and less direct opening conversation, the monk stood.

"In the infirmary," Jacob replied.

"Move it," came the response, directed to Sigmurului's own men.

"Your Excellency, I..."

Jacob's distress continued as the bishop's entourage set to work removing Shandor's body from the monastery, Sigmurului retreating to the chapel at noon to hold Nones. All were expected and non-attendance was not an option.

As Sigmurului proceeded through the service, his priests remained outside, their orders to quarter the Abbot and remove his teeth and his eyes once he had been formally buried.

As far as Sigmurului saw it, Apollinari's reasons for visiting their country had brought with him a curse, qualified by Shandor's untimely death. By removing his teeth no witch could attempt to resurrect the body and without eyes, any actual reincarnation would mean the corpse would be sightless. To be even more secure against the forces of darkness, Sigmurului wanted the Abbot's dismembered body was burn and thrown in the lake.

Such an ignominious end. But superstition and religion blurred in these heady days.

After Nones, Sigmurului made himself comfortable in Shandor's office.

"It is *my* office now, Brother Jacob," the bishop intoned and dispatched the bemused monk to his usual order of business.

Sigmurului looked down at the stack of papers on the desk before him. One caught his eye and he pulled it to the top of the pile. It was written in scrawling black ink and dated two months prior, before the Russian snows had arrived.

> *Your holiness, Father Pretorius Shandor. Herewith we let you know, as we did before, that a messenger from the Turk has now come to us. You should understand well and keep in mind our former agreements for brotherhood and peace. The Turks intend to put great burdens, almost impossible to bear, upon our shoulders, forcing us to bow down before them and work against the Catholic faith and against you. As we make ready the protection of our homes, you will protect our riches, our inheritances, for they will be plundered and our strong desire is to keep safe that which we hold dear. As I have told you, for your and our wellbeing and defence, prepare as quickly as you can the means by which you will offer this protection because, we swear before God, we are thinking more of your welfare and security than of ours. Târgoviste, the Friday after St. Mary's Day, in the year of our Lord 1476*
> *Vlad, prince of Wallachia, and ruler of Făgăraş*
> *Your brother and friend in all.*

The bishop's digits tingled with anticipation, with the knowledge that he was potentially sitting on a glorious amount of wealth. Collected from the boyars, who were most likely either dead or mourning their dead in the aftermath of the battle at Prahov, it was Sigmurului's now. This Vlad, this warlord prince, he was nothing compared to the power of Rome and the bishop would have no qualms in reminding him of such.

It had to be a considerable size, this hiding place, but finding it was another matter and no amount of searching and sifting through Shandor's files and correspondence revealed a layout of the monastery. It would either be a case of taking his priests and physically looking for the fortune or interrogating the monks one by one until one of them told him where it was. The first method was more direct but the second far more enjoyable.

The rain pounded down on the canopy, like a thousand scurrying insects.

Mansi was so weary that the noise was almost hypnotic, echoing around inside his skull. But he daren't show his fatigue, for his Lord would never tolerate such a display. Instead, Mansi fought his exhaustion with determination, standing like a rock on the canvas that made up the floor of the tent.

The tent, itself a deep red, was spacious inside, lined with heavy wooden benches, and stands supporting highly polished swords and shields. The air was warm, thick with incense as a multitude of burners plumed out great clouds of smoke, making Mansi's nostrils twitch.

Before him on a chair positioned in the very middle of the tent and flanked by two powerful guards, sat Dracula, eyes as black as night and long hair equally as dark about his shoulders. His face was clean shaven save for a long black moustache, and he was clad in the same rich, dark red as the tent about them, the only difference in shade being the black riding boots with solid silver spurs at the heels.

His face was strong and aquiline, with a high bridge to a thin nose and arched nostrils. A tall forehead accompanied thick eyebrows, almost meeting over the nose and with bushy hair that seemed to curl in on itself. The mouth, so far as Mansi could see under the heavy moustache, was fixed and rather cruel-looking. The chin was broad and strong, either side cheeks firm albeit thin.

Long fingers grasped the handle of the massive sword, its blade pointing downwards and puncturing the canvas at Dracula's feet. With his other hand, Dracula motioned for Mansi to kneel.

As he dropped to one knee, a shaking hand resting on the other, Mansi noticed for the first time a woman standing towards the back of tent, face covered by a yellow veil, hands across her bare breasts. Whether she was naked from the waist down he could not tell for a great black casket before her obscured his view. His eyes flicked back to the man seated before him, who gave no indication that he had seen him staring at the woman.

"You have survived," Dracula said, thick Wallachian fleck to his words. "How is this so when many of my generals did not?"

Mansi kept his expression firm. Was Dracula testing him? Was he accusing him? He had to plot his words carefully.

"Speak," Dracula commanded. "Has the battle ripped out your tongue? Or perhaps I should rip it out for you?"

Mansi swallowed hard. The infamy of his leader's cruelty was not without reason. "No, my Lord," Mansi said firmly.

"Then answer me: how is it you have survived?"

"I used my wits. I defended when I had to and attacked when I was able to. Those of us less experienced should not have died."

"Are you saying I deployed an immature army?"
Mansi's breath caught in his chest, sending a cold sweat to his shoulders. "N-no...I meant that they deserved to live their lives."

"You would have died in their place?"

"Yes, my Lord."

"Would you die if I commanded it?"

"If you commanded it, yes."

"Noble," nodded the great warlord, "and sentimental."

"Yes, my Lord."

"There is no place for sentiment on the battlefield."
Mansi nodded at Dracula's words, thinking of his brother. "Nor in my army. It makes you weak."

"Yet I have survived."
Mansi saw Dracula's hand that gripped the sword tense, as if angered by his words. *Oh dear God, what have I said!* In hindsight perhaps Mansi's response was not the wisest.

"News has reached me," Dracula began, clearly altering the subject much to Mansi's relief, "that my wife is not at the Palace. You will go out to the Principalities and bring her back."

"My Lord?"
Dracula stood. He was a tall man and walked with the grace of a mountain lion, arriving at the black casket. A strange silver symbol was etched in its side. The veiled woman retreated into the shadows as he leant across the great box. He turned back to Mansi, in his hands a striking blue dress covered in dried, congealed blood. His wife's, Mansi reasoned, and clearly she had

been taken by force. Dracula shook his head and explained that no guards at Târgoviste had reported such an event.

"This was found two days ride from the Palace."

"Do you believe she..."

"...still lives?" Vlad Dracula returned to his seat, the sword back in his grip like it was of comfort to him. "Rue the day for the man who took her from me if she is not."

Where do I start? Even the thought of looking for dear Rintoul is too great a task, yet I dare not fail in this for my master. The outcome was too hideous to contemplate.

"With respect, my Lord, but why me? Am I worthy of such a responsibility?" Mansi hoped that Dracula would reconsider and appoint someone else, but that long mane of dark as night hair shook again and Mansi inwardly sagged.

"You have proved your mettle by staying alive. The battle here is not yet won and I cannot leave my army. Dambovita is now our target. You will deliver Princess Ilona to me there as we reclaim our occupancy."

"But what if she *is* dead?" Mansi carefully asked.

Dracula's eyes dropped to the floor, staring at his boots. Mansi felt for a moment that Dracula had already concluded that that was the case but still had to cling to some vague hope that perhaps she did still live.

"Take these two men," the prince said, gesturing to the guards who stood as statues. "Use them as your eyes and ears. Fresh horses await you. Go, Mansi, and do not fail me."

With that, Dracula suddenly moved out of the chair and to the back of the great tent, swiftly and with determination. The veiled woman fell into his arms as he lifted her up on to the casket, spreading her legs wide. It was of course the Prince's right to take any woman for himself when and where he chose and it was not for Mansi to moralise against his master's actions. The young man stood and spun, leaving the tent and his Prince's carnality as quickly as he could.

The rain fell heavy on to the phalanx of horse-backed troops as they cut their way through the forest.

The sudden downpour made the going more treacherous, the snow turning to muddy slush, rivulets of water rushing between the horses' hooves. The heavy rain drops struck the back plates of each soldier under their cloaks, sounding like a percussive roll.

The men, helmets heavy for their necks, found it difficult to maintain a light disposition in the deluge for they were already cold and now they couldn't see beyond their own noses. They nearly walked their horses into each other as Popescu, up ahead, unexpectedly raised a gloved hand, halting the entourage.

His lieutenant, Seneslav, cantered his horse as best he could up alongside his captain.

"Sir?"

The question was initially met with a glare from under the captain's helmet. Popescu returned his attention to the track ahead and the expansive clearing it slid into. "Take the men and fan out along the pathway."

"Are we expecting company, sir?"

"I don't know," Popescu responded. "But I have a very strange feeling. Stay alert until we cross the clearing."

The lieutenant passed on the orders and the men dismounted, spreading out as they entered the gap.

The trees formed a circle around them and the path could easily be seen continuing into the woodland over on the other side. But open like this, even for a short distance, left them vulnerable to attack by either the Turks or Carpathian bandits and the captain wasn't about to look foolish in front of his men. Yet his caution was not wasted as a sudden shower of arrows came out of the rain, felling two of his men. With a cry of alarm, the men spread themselves wide across the clearing to reduce their size as targets. A second batch of arrows rained down up on them and Popescu saw three more of his men fall to the ground, speared through their hearts. He urged the remaining soldiers onwards to the safety of the trees, but, in the confusion, they had turned and fled back to where they had come from.

The attacking Turkish infantry took advantage of this mistake and came from out of hiding to join the skirmish man to man.

The metallic resonance as sword met sword made Popescu realise how far he was from his men and, as he made to turn back to join them, a Turk spotted him alone and veered his horse towards him. Popescu had no choice but to turn back around and continue his flight, soon leaving the clearing and finding cover in the trees. He could hear the pounding of the Turk's horse behind him then a distant *thwack* as an arrow embedded itself between his enemy's shoulder blades. Popescu pulled his horse to a stop and swung the beast around.

The Turk's animal had stopped of its own accord once its master had fallen.

Dismounting, Popescu unsheathed his weapon on the assumption that the Turkish soldier could still be alive but, on approaching the form, he saw no movement from the body, the arrow's quiver still.

The icy rain stung at Popescu's face as he pulled his horse around, silencing its whinnying with a sharp tug at the reigns. One of his men came up alongside.

"I detest twilight," Popescu murmured, squinting into the gloom around them.

An arrow whistled past Popescu's ear and embedded itself into the back of his man. Wilhelm screamed and fell heavy, and quite dead, to the ground.

"Regroup! More infantry!" he called.

"*Izleyin! Onları öldürmek!*" Popescu heard over the pounding of hooves and clanking of armour. Turkish reconnaisance or part of the army at Prahov – it didn't matter. Popescu needed to reduce the enemy's advantage before he could continue the fight. Moments passed before he spotted something on the other side of the clearing. Was that a cabin he could see?

He remounted and urged his horse on but, darting quickly to his left, he immediately jumped back off and slapped its croup hard. The animal kept on running and he could hear Turkish voices calling to follow it. Popescu drew his sword and headed for the cabin, two of his remaining five men doing likewise.

But the Turks saw them too and made to follow.

Popescu crashed through the door that looked like it had seen better days. It was already half off its hinges before the captain pounded through it, splinters and debris already in the room. He spun on his heels and laughed as his three other men, still on horseback, came up behind the Turks and decapitated one and slashed at two, swinging their weapons around to fell another four.

That left two Turks still alive and heading for the cabin. But on realising they were now outnumbered, they changed direction and fell back to the trees and out of sight.

Popescu called his men together inside the cabin.

"There are another three following my horse, but I would assume by now they have found it to be a decoy."

"Five of them, six of us? Those odds aren't fair," growled Seneslav, his blind eye glassy. "Bring on a whole contingent of the Turkish *nemernici*."

"I encourage your dedication," Popescu sneered. "They have seen us. They will not leave until we are all dead. But we will kill them first and then continue with our search. Bring the horses around to the rear. I spotted a trough there."

With one man on lookout, another broke the ice across the surface of the water trough and the horses drank thirstily.

But the Turks saw the advantage and a series of arrows felled most the animals.

Another deluge of arrows, this time alight (Popescu wondering where they had got fire from in this damp morning), hit the thatch of the cabin, some entering through the open windows and door.

Treading on something he took to be animal entrails, Popescu stamped out the flames but another attack came from more arrows and took two men down. They fell to the floor, the blood soaking into the wood.

Then the Turks arrived at the cabin's weak spots, wielding *kilij* and heavy shields. Drawing their own swords, the Wallachian soldiers stayed firm for as long as they could. Seneslav took two Turks down where he stood, Popescu another one. But the Turks were relentless and killed two more of Popescu's men, leaving just himself and Seneslav inside the building and trying not to trip over the floor that was beginning to buckle in peculiar ways beneath their feet.

Back to back, the two Wallachians attacked, parried and defended, their heavy-set enemies strong and unforgiving. But Popescu was not about to let the death of his men go for nothing and in a show of strength, he forced the two turbaned soldiers from the cabin and into the misty clearing outside.

Slice after slice, Popescu kept going but it was only the unexpected cry that came from back within the cabin that removed his advantage. Seeing the distraction, the Turks pincered Popescu, bringing him to his knees, his sword falling to the ground.

Raising his sabre, one of the Turks started to bring it down to cleave Popescu's skull in two but his companion suddenly let out a horrified gurgle.

Popescu looked up and saw a bloodied, skinless man-shape at the Turk's neck. The Turk with the lifted sword spun to help his fellow soldier but the apparition reached out and snapped his neck as though it were dry wood – all the time drinking from the neck of the Turk it had hold of.

Popescu watched, not sure if his eyes deceived him because the thing's skin seemed to grow and spread over its raw flesh. It was as if the act of drinking from the Turk was somehow making the thing look less like a monster. The Turk's corpse, drained and pale, fell to the floor and the creature, now clearly a man, dark haired and pale, turned his attention to Popescu and smiled.

He held out a hand, fingers long and bony. "Drink from me and live forever."

In response, Popescu got to his feet and shot towards the cabin.

"Seneslav!" he called but there came no answer, instead the sound of fumbling and thumping.

As Popescu entered the cabin, he saw Seneslav fending off another of the skinless creatures but this time he could see it was probably a woman, sharp white fangs as bright as the whites of her eyes and as outstanding as the paleness of her pupils.

"What in God's name is it?" screamed Seneslav as the creature snapped its teeth at him, trying to reach his neck.

Popescu picked up a broken chair and slammed it hard against the gruesome vampire's back.

The dead Wallachian at Seneslav's feet twitched and shifted, skin becoming discoloured and brittle like autumn leaves. Around the body, spilt blood drained into the floorboards, into the very wood itself, until there was not a drop left.

With a dry crack, the Wallachian's corpse seemed to spring into the air, forced up from underneath by a scarlet tendon-covered hand, to collapse in a twisted heap nearby.

Attached to the red raw arm and a complete body to match, the hand felt for purchase and dragged itself from under the cabin's floor, the whole abomination standing tentatively like a newborn calf.

The thing was hideous and stank of rotten meat, a parody of a man all bone and muscle. White eyes stared out of the bloody face, sharp teeth bared.

Popescu swung the sabre over his head to bring it down across the half-formed vampire's neck but the vampire, now stable on its feet, raised an arm and parried the blow. A spray of glutinous serous fluid covered Popescu's face.

Popescu struck again but this newest vampire slammed the soldier into the ground, lunging forward. Popescu fumbled around for a sabre and brought it up, slicing the creature's arm clean off.

With a screech, the vampire fell away as Popescu scrambled to his feet.

The one holding Seneslav seemed to falter, as if not sure whether to help her fallen comrade. Seneslav picked up on the hesitation and flung himself around, assuming the vampire would regain her composure and follow. This it did, but years of fighting alongside his captain meant he knew that Popescu would understand what Seneslav was doing.

The vampire now had her back to Popescu. Seneslav ducked just as Popescu swung the sabre a second time and decapitated her.

The first of the vampires, the healed male, appeared at the doorway, enraged that his skinless companion had found death again so soon.

"Live forever will you?" cried Popescu. "I don't fucking think so!"

"Take them!" the vampire roared. "Rip out their throats!"

There was an arrow still burning in the corner and Seneslav dived towards it and threw it at the vampire who batted it away. It clattered against a window ledge and nestled under a shutter, smoking to itself.

By this time the third creature was on its feet, its missing arm forgotten, and heading towards Popescu. The Wallachian had the sabre at his command and slashed out at the skinless apparition.

They had been resurrected from the spilt blood of the fracas and were thirsty for fresh, living veins.

Seneslav and Popescu were not prepared to become their victims and between them they managed to edge away from the two vampires.

"There is nowhere for you to go. Succumb to us and your suffering will be short-lived."

"You do not belong in this world!"

"And you are to banish us?" laughed the vampire, canines glistening in the flames that had suddenly leapt from the arrow to the shutters.

"I remember the stories my grandmother used to tell me," said Seneslav suddenly, eyes flicking to the open doorway and the sky outside.

"Stories? We are not from a child's nightmares. We are *real*."

"Real or imaginary," Popescu's lieutenant continued, "there is one thing that I know you fear."

The vampire looked at the flames. "I fear nothing."

"It is daylight, foul creature. Where will you go now?"

In the distance, a cock crowed and the vampire's eyes widened as he realised his predicament. He stepped back towards the door, the one-armed half-formed vampire nearby reaching out to him. The vampire snarled at his pitiful companion and spun away, out of the door and into the dying night.

Popescu and Seneslav looked down at the remaining vampire. It had begun to emit wisps of pungent smoke from every orifice as the night dissipated and a guttural wail was born in its throat.

"Help me!" it quavered.

Popescu threw down the sabre and knelt at the thing's head, grabbing under its armpits.

"What are you doing?" asked Seneslav, having no wish to touch the creature.

Gagging, Popescu lifted and dragged the vampire out into the open. Struggling pitifully, it lay there and watched the day begin to creep through the trees, a shaft of sunlight falling across its face. It screamed and tore at its own raw flesh with its one hand and Popescu gasped as the vampire burst into flame, as bright as starlight and as brief as a gunpowder flash.

The vampire was no more, only a charred outline on the forest's ferny floor to tell of its hellish existence.

Popescu dropped to his knees, exhausted, Seneslav at his shoulder and the cabin in flames behind them.

They looked at each other then great waves of laughter came over them, more from relief than anything else, their guffaws rising up into the fresh morning sky.

Chapter 22

The Slovak's grasp of Wallachian was such that he was unable to keep up with the conversation being had over his shoulder. Instead, he pulled his heavy hooded cloak tighter and held firm to the leather reins. His eyes were fixed on the road ahead, seeing the banks of the Caldarusani tributary and the narrow bridge that spanned this particular section.

On the back of the open cart, Apollinari and Claudia were huddled together to keep warm. Ilona sat as far away from them as the small vehicle would allow. She would not speak, refused to eat any of the food kindly offered to them by the merchant and complained of severe pains behind the eyes. At the moment though she appeared to be asleep.

Claudia had little time for her.

"She's spoilt. Too used to being waited on. Why did you bring her with you?" she murmured so only her uncle would hear.

Apollinari looked at Ilona, seeing the traumatic look upon her face, even as she slept. "She is troubled."

"You have taken her under your wing?"

The monk shook his head. "No, that's not it. Ever since we left the cottage, she has been listless. Distant."

The cart rocked as the merchant navigated around a ditch.

"Musíme tam byť pred zotmením. Tieto cesty sú nebezpečné," the merchant said.

Apollinari did not speak Slovak so instead made a noise in agreement to whatever it was their driver had said.

He had found them, the merchant, traipsing at the side of the path, soaked and cold. Through a series of animated explanations, they had managed to explain that they were heading for Dambovita. Beckoned onboard, Apollinari and his two companions had hoped that they had been understood. A conversation had followed, the man talking in fast and heavy-accented Slovak, accentuated by pointing here and there and fist-shaking as if to the world around them. His passengers nodded and smiled politely. But the one-sided conversation had to eventually cease and so it was that they all soon sat in silence watching the forest go slowly by.

"Perhaps she needs a spell," Claudia suggested. "If something distresses her, we can magick it away."

"She told me she knew where Verrecchia had gone. I believed her."

"Do you think he's there?" she asked pointing ahead of them.

"She said he'd gone with some gypsies. I have to believe that the Citadel would be their destination also."

"Have you been there before?"

"I have been to this part of the world before but not for many years. Not since I was a novice." Apollinari clasped his hands together on his lap, swaying gently with the motion of the cart. He found it difficult to look at Claudia. She was so much like her mother, the way she held herself, played with her hair at the ends, her sometimes dry and accusatory tone.

Claudia made Ilona comfortable under the blankets that were on the cart. They smelt musty but they were warm and Ilona's shivering seemed to have abated. "You want to say something to me, Uncle?"

Intuitive, too.

"It wasn't easy for me."

Claudia sighed, not sure this was a conversation she was willing to have. "You abandoned us."

"It wasn't like that. You must realise that."

"Realise what? That your Order, with its penitence and abstinence, would not welcome us?"

"The Order is based upon the removal of sin and encompassing the word of God."

"And that precludes your own flesh and blood?"

"When your mother was arrested it was not possible for me to act against those who had imprisoned her. You know full well that our heritage already allows me certain privileges in the Church. If I had spoken up about her arrest, we would have all been condemned."

"Corbiu and I *were* condemned! The Zuccos weren't exactly welcoming. And don't you dare tell me we had to accept being with them because they are family, too!"

"You know I don't think that!"

"Do I? Tell me how! Should I have been grateful?" Claudia's cheeks flushed and she shifted uncomfortably. "You told me to my face that they would look after us like their own. They kept Corbiu in a bloody cage! And you haven't even asked after him! Is this how you treated Verrecchia too?"

Apollinari looked down, knowing what she said rang true. "Where is he? Where is Corbiu?"

Claudia broke down into tears, the release of anger after all these months too much. "I don't know," she sobbed.

The monk reached out and placed a hand on her shoulder, feeling her shaking. There was something to be said, he felt, about the segregation that a monastic life forced upon a man. For him it had removed all familial roots, discarding the need for blood ties. It had made him cold and he knew then that all of them, Claudia, Ilona, Corbiu and Verrecchia needed him, for he was the only one they should be able to turn to. Yes, he was out here on a road in an attempt to find his novice, but how far would that search go? When would he give up? Should he give up? Should he even be questioning himself?

Claudia nestled against his shoulder, feeling the chill in the air more than ever. „Do not let my mother‘s death be for nothing," she said quietly. "She was burnt for trying to warn others of Caleb‘s coming resurrection - and you would sit here and feel sorrow! My mother, your sister, deserves better than that."

Apollinari breathed out slowly, his mind in disarray.

The trees thinned out to nothing either side of them, adding more light to the day, as they approached the banks of the murky river and the bridge it flowed under. Everything was grey now that the rains had come to wash away the snow – the land under their feet, the sky above and the water before them.

Without the trees to shield the full force of the weather, the wind was intense, pulling the air from their lungs. On the other side of the bridge the landscape seemed to go on forever, monotonous and uninspiring, ringed by a flat horizon and broken only by the occasional hillock in the distance. Further away still the tallest spires of the Dambovita Citadel could just be seen, standing like thin fingers beckoning to the morose cloudy sky.

It was a lonesome place, of restless spirits and lost souls, and Apollinari could feel the touch of death in the air. The cart reached halfway across the rickety bridge when the horse began to stamp and protest, bringing the little party to a halt.

"Poyhb! Poyhb!" the merchant cried, whip cracking across the agitated animal's back. But no amount of encouragement or force would convince the mare to take another step. Even getting down from his seat and pulling the horse across the bridge would make no difference.

It snorted and whinnied, clearly distressed and refusing to budge.

The merchant turned back to his passengers, explaining in his own tongue that they were going no further, pointing at the horse, the bridge and the expanse of land ahead of them.

Apollinari clambered down and approached the horse, all the while whispering under his breath. Holding gripping the animal around its neck, he caressed and cooed, Claudia coming up behind him.

The horse's eyes were wide but the stamping had ceased. Apollinari's voice was low, soothing, and he moved his fingers in a strange pattern over the animal's snout. A brief jerk and the cart slid on a patch of ice that still remained on the bridge. The merchant looked worried, concerned that this monk was talking strange incantations into his horse's ear.

But the horse exhaled loudly and raised its front legs, bringing them down hard. The bridge shook and Claudia feared it would collapse. The horse began to sidle backwards, back onto land. Apollinari's efforts had been in vain.

"If we continue it will be on foot," he said matter-of-factly. He let the animal go. The merchant guided it safely back to the bridge's edge.

"But what about Ilona? She is in no fit state to..." Claudia's words hung in the air.

At the far end of the bridge, where the horse had refused to go, a series of blue flame-like rings appeared, one on top of the other, a gap of maybe two or three hands between them. It was a most extraordinary sight. An unnerving hissing, like a grass snake, accompanied the vision and the effect it had on the merchant was extreme. He screamed and wailed, joining his horse in the distress of the moment, and flung Apollinari's bag at the monk, who managed to catch it before it hit the ground. With a great leap, the merchant was once again upon his perch and urging his horse back along the path from whence they had come.

Ilona still remained aboard and Apollinari dashed forward, calling to the merchant to stop. But the horse had picked up speed now and the cart rattled and bounced away. Apollinari knew he could not keep up.

"Can you not cast a spell?" Claudia asked but Apollinari seemed unwilling to do so. "Then I will!" She raised her hands, directing rigid fingers at the retreating cart.

"No!" Apollinari bellowed. "No spells!"

Claudia stopped immediately, the commanding tone sounding strange coming from her uncle's mouth. She dropped her arms.

They both caught sight of the unearthly rings of fire dissipate and fade into nothing, turning back to watch the merchant and his sleeping cargo thunder away down the path.

Snoring loudly enough to wake the dead, he squat little man with the loose-fitting hat lay asleep outside the door to the *Okruh Kráľovnej*. He didn't even stir when Mansi raised the brim to peer underneath, the Wallachian noting the heavy-set features and bulbous nose.

Letting the dwarf sleep, Mansi motioned for the two burly guards to join him and they peered inside the building's greasy windows.

Expecting a calamitous noise usually associated with raucous inns, at least in his experience, Mansi had been cautious in approaching, having watched the place for a while in secret behind a garishly painted gypsy caravan. He was surprised to discover that the residents appeared to be either unconscious or subdued.

The three men entered, the door creaking like a rack in the dungeons of their prince's palace. The fireplace contained embers now, vestiges of smoke curling pathetically up the flume and servants and drinkers alike had fallen where they stood or slumped where they sat.

"They are all too pissed."

"But that's not the reason they sleep. Look…" Mansi pointed to a small strange sculpture that sat on by itself on the beer-soaked bar. Made of entwined willow and moss, it was a doll no more than half a foot tall, vaguely female with arms raised and legs bent as if kneeling.

Mansi's associates tensed, recognising the charm and what it symbolised.

"They are bewitched!"

Mansi nodded, agreeing with one of the guards. "But why? What would be the purpose of silencing a place such as this?"

"They have seen something," the first guard said.

"Then the spell must be broken. These people between them can tell us much more than any interrogation would produce."

"I will not tamper with any witchcraft."

"Nor I."

"And the pair of you would return to the prince empty handed," Mansi pointed out. "That surely is a fate worse than any incantation and one that I do not wish to experience."

"Then *you* break it."

"I am afraid, just as you two are. But we must succeed in our quest."

"We are not afraid," the second guard growled, all the while knowing that the failure of this mission would mean impalement.

Mansi had grown up amongst those fearful of the spirits, wrestling often with the superstitions built into the family belief system. The desire to turn and run from the scene before him was almost too much to bear but worse still there would be no escape from Vlad Dracula if he did.

A wolf howled in the distance.

"Listen to them," the second guard said, voice quavering. "The night breeds its own horrors, its own children." The howl came again. "It's as if it's singing."

"And what music they make," Mansi agreed, not wishing to get drawn into thoughts of what terrors might be rising up outside. Upsetting the spirits was not something he was ever eager to do. Had his mother not been raped and killed by spirits posing as Russian dignitaries? Yet Mansi realised he had little choice. He had been tasked with this mission by Dracula and he knew he had to succeed no matter what the cost.

Stepping over the sleeping throng wherever they lay in his path, Mansi reached the bar, took a deep breath, and grabbed the wicker doll.

Even though he had been expecting some sort of repercussion, Mansi wasn't prepared for the terrible noise, like a thousand skulls being crushed at once, to reverberate around the inn. Ears bleeding, he found himself rooted to the spot and unable to release his grip on the doll.

The inn disappeared around him in flashes of light and dark and he was standing in the centre of a gloomy space, the stone floor under his feet cold, almost as cold as the air against his skin.

He looked up and saw a vaulted ceiling stretching far above him. It made him feel dizzy it was so high.

Looking back down he squinted, trying to make out the shapes in the distance. Were they moving or were they just shadows? The place was empty, empty and huge because he could see no walls around him – yet the ceiling was definitely there suspended above.

If this was a church it was unlike anything he had ever seen before.

Mansi looked down at his feet and it took a moment to register that there were markings on the stone, specific geometric shapes intertwined and crossing over each other. What they were he could not make out for they seemed to stretch in equal directions all around him. Neither could he determine what kind of ink they were drawn with but he imagined it to be some form of molten silver.

In his hand, he still clenched the doll and no matter how hard he tried, he could not shake it free.

"It is part of you, Mansi."

Startled, he looked up to where the lilting voice had come, but a confusing mass of light and shape dazzled him. He reached out but there was no heat, no sensation to speak of. It was if there was nothing really there, the flashes of red, yellow and azure green taunting him from behind his own eyes.

As the tumult began to ease he saw, finally, a woman form, cradled by the branches of a great thick tree that had risen silently from the ground before him. The sweet scent of the tiny red flowers hanging from the tree's bows like droplets of blood overwhelmed him, stinging his nostrils and catching at the back of his throat.

He made to speak but no sound came.

The woman uncurled herself from the tree and snaked down the massive trunk, fronds and tendrils undulating and caressing as they eased her descent.

She stepped elegantly to the cold stone floor, its strange silver etchings pulling and dragging together to collect at her bare feet and slide up around her ankles and beyond.

Yet, Mansi could not see her face at first, even though she was standing directly in front of him. He rubbed his eyes but could not focus on her features. It was as if her face was obscured, clouded by his own determination to know what she looked like.

"Who are you?"

The face veiled from his sight began to clear and then Mansi saw her.

She was astonishingly beautiful, he thought, her dark hair cascading down her shoulders, contrasting with the pure white samite gown she almost wore.

Her eyes were beguiling, dark pools of black framed by a white face. Her lips were full and as blood red as the flowers from the tree behind her. They parted delicately as she smiled at him.

"I am known by many and unknown to all. I am Acco. I am Rhiannon. I am Marise. I am what you perceive me to be. You have crossed the boundary by attempting to break the spell. Did you not understand the fears your mother held all those years ago? Was it still not enough to stop you tampering with that which you do not comprehend?"

"You sent them, the spirits...sent them to my mother?"

Marise laughed. "No, I didn't. They *were* just men. The spirits would have been much gentler."

This still made no difference to Mansi, real or supernatural, for his mother had undergone a terrifying and humiliating ordeal moments before her life was taken from her.

Something had made the Russians do what they did and it was not inconceivable that they had been at least *influenced* by the spirits. Even if this Marise denied it, Mansi still finally had someone tangible to blame.

"If you need to project your anger on to me, then so be it."

She'd heard him! He hadn't said that out loud but she'd heard him!

"I can hear everything," she said.

What secrets could a man keep if such women now existed?

"None at all." She was enjoying this, enjoying the taunting. Perhaps she should push him more. "Are you scared of me?" Mansi shook his head. "Yet you told your two companions that you were all afraid. Do not try to deceive me." Marise circled Mansi, her fingers brushing his back and chest. She stopped directly in front of him and he could detect a faint odour of wine on her breath. "How far would you go for your beliefs, Mansi?"

"What do you mean?"

"You acknowledge that spirits exist yet I can hear your thoughts. You are telling yourself over and over that I am not real. Would you like me to prove that I *do not* exist?"

Mansi frowned. If Marise proved to be real, it could open up a world to him that he would *never* be free of.

"Yes."

He closed his eyes, willing himself to be back at the *Okruh Kráľovnej*. But when he opened them again, he was still in the same strange place. This time the tree had gone to be replaced with an altar draped in a black cloth. Lying prone atop it was a boy, perhaps a teenager, with the hairstyle typical of a monk. He was enshrouded in a robe made from the same dark material. Open to the waist it was, his bare torso rising and falling as he breathed.

Marise held a knife, which she pressed into Mansi's free hand.

"Sacrifice this boy, this child of God, and prove that I do not exist."

Was this it? Was this really all that was required of Mansi to dispel the spirits from his history? He felt the cold steel of the weapon in his palm and looked at the wicker doll in his other. Compelled, he walked with a stiff gait to the altar and stood over the boy. He didn't even feel his own arm raise, but with horror he saw the knife blade hovering over the young monk's neck. Who was he, this boy?

"Bring the knife down! Slice into his throat! The blood that will spring forth will prove that which you are afraid to know!"

Mansi hesitated. He had killed many on the battlefield, felled many an enemy as a foot-soldier, but this time it seemed wrong. Here was a boy, defenceless and penitent to a higher power and Mansi was expected to sacrifice him to...to what? *For* what? What if *he* were being deceived?

"Do it! Do it now!" Marise screamed.

Mansi began to shake, to convulse, as the awfulness of taking an innocent's life coated his very thoughts. The knife was so close to the monk's neck and Mansi forced his hand back up, looked at the doll, then with a terrified scream plunged the blade into his own hand, piercing the wicker figurine and showering it in his blood.

A great crashing noise filled his head.

With his good hand, Mansi reached out and grabbed the arm of the monk as the altar crumbled away, the floor opening up before them. There was nowhere else to go and so Mansi and the young monk fell through the hole that was widening with every second, until a final flash of pain found them in a crumpled heap on the floor of the inn.

The knife was still embedded in Mansi's right hand, the doll impaled thereon.

The young monk, covered only in the black drape pulled himself to his feet and moved over to his executioner-come-saviour.

"Who are you?" asked Mansi as the monk removed the knife from Mansi's hand, placing it and the doll on the bar before them.

"My name is Roberto, Roberto Verrecchia."

All around them the drinkers and the servants were beginning to wake, the spell broken. Amongst them was a man known to Verrecchia and who the monk had thought he'd escaped from.

Recognising Verrecchia, Zucco could not resist shouting out the monk's name, bile and poison lacing his exclamation.

Verrecchia spun to grab Mansi's good hand and pulled him to his feet.

"Run," he said.

Ilona opened her eyes and saw nothing, heard nothing. Yet she felt a pressure all around her. It was close and confining but not unpleasant. In fact as she got used to the blackness, a wave of comfort and protection seemed to wash over her.

"I said I would come back for you."

It made her jump, the voice in her ear, the voice in her *head*. But to flinch was simply not possible. The heavy soil pressing down on her restricted her movements to such an extent that she couldn't even stretch out her fingers.

She was buried alive.

But why was she not panicked? How could she breathe? She realised the answer to the second question was even more perplexing than the question itself, for she realised that she wasn't actually breathing.

She swallowed hard, the smell of the dirt in her nostrils and clogging the back of her throat. She closed her eyes again for there was little point in keeping them open in here.

As she lay there, like a foetus in a womb of earth, she could clearly recall now reaching this point, how she had been on the back of the merchant's cart, dazed and confused and calling to him to slow down.

But forever they had travelled, the horse's hooves pummelling the ground beneath it until Ismael had appeared in the road ahead, the Slovak pulling on the reins. The cart slid to a halt in the mud and Ilona heard the merchant's pulse pounding through his veins as Ismael just stood there and watched him.

A mist had developed, hanging low in the air, lingering and thick.

From underneath the blankets, Ilona stood, stretching thin arms into the air. The back of the merchant's neck was revealed to her as the man removed his lengthy scarf. She heard him gulp hard as Ismael padded towards them, the vampire's boots making no sound on the muddy track. The jugular in the Slovak's neck undulated, full with sweet, red blood and Ilona suddenly felt hungry, perhaps even ravenous.

She moved forward and placed a hand on the man's shoulder as Ismael continued watching.

There was something alluring about this heavy vein, something which triggered a desire in her to prick it open and drink the blood that would gush forth.

"Do it," Ismael whispered in her ear but still standing some feet away. "It yearns your every thought. Give yourself up to it."

Ilona looked between Ismael and the merchant's neck, the merchant himself rooted to his seat. Only his eyes moved, wide and terrified. A bead of sweat trickled down his left temple and Ilona dabbed it with a fingertip, tasting the salty liquid between full lips.

Like a hammer blow to the back of her head, Ilona's mouth was suddenly forced on to the Slovaks' neck by

Ismael's powerful grip. *But the blonde-haired vampire was still standing before the cart!*

Ilona could smell the merchant's stale, unwashed skin as she opened her mouth wide, an unnerving *click* ringing in her ears. Sharp white canines flicked from her gums and pierced the man's neck. The blood flowed. Warm. Satisfying. As the red liquor coursed down her throat she orgasmed, intense and unexpected. She gasped and cried out but Ismael, like a dominant lover, was upon her to keep her mouth tight over the Slovak's open vein. With his other hand under her clothes he caressed and kneaded her throbbing clitoris.

Ilona drank until her stomach ached and she could take no more.

Ismael finally pulled Ilona away and savagely licked the blood from her lips and her ejaculate from his own fingers.

The merchant sagged in his seat, weakened but still alive.

Then something happened. She couldn't tell what. A flurry of blood, of flashing swords and cries of pain and defiance. Then the cart was on the move again.

Ilona huddled back down amidst the blankets, feeling inebriated and woozy. For ages she rocked with the motion of the cart, not even realising Ismael had gone, until the cart pulled into a small courtyard set back from the road.

They were at the *Okruh Kráľovnej*, and the merchant feebly motioned towards the rear of his cart as a flurry of figures, haloed by the light from the doorway, scurried out to attend to their latest arrival. Amongst them was the landlord, a short stocky man with thick grey hair and kindly eyes who went by the name of Grozăvie.

The servants attended to the horse as the Slovak dismounted, clearly weakened and in need of a drink. He stumbled inside as Grozăvie followed, carrying Ilona who had willingly allowed him to pick her up in his arms, heading straight to the rooms towards the back of the inn. Grozăvie's wife shouted down the jeers and lewd comments the resident drunks directed at the landlord as he had weaved through the throng. The merchant disappeared into the crowd at the bar, exhausted and unwilling to talk about his passenger or how he had come to have her on the back of his cart.

Once the door was shut to the back rooms, the noise was muffled. Grozăvie took the damp cloth offered by his wife and dabbed Ilona's forehead.

Dressed in the garb of a woodsman and drifting in and out of consciousness, Ilona revealed nothing to show her true background. But as Grozăvie wiped away the grime and dried blood from her face, his wife considered that perhaps she was gentry. She put the candle down, the flame casting long and twisted shadows against the walls, and took hold of one of Ilona's hands, tracing her soft palms with the roughness of her own fingertips.

"See? She has not done a day's work in her life."

"Who is she?"

"She must be from the Palace."

"We can't keep her here." Grozăvie was a fearful man, having lived in the shadow of the Târgoviste Palace for all his life. Even though his inn was always frequented with those not always welcomed elsewhere, by vagabonds and the dispossessed, Grozăvie never harboured or concealed fugitives or the condemned. The place was a veritable sluice gate, collecting all manner of undesirables but never keeping hold of any of them long enough to afford unwanted allegiances.

But this evening he had just broken his first rule and got involved. And if this young woman *was* from the Palace as his wife believed, then they were bringing trouble to them all – not least his customers, who welcomed the anonymity of the place.

"We must get her cleaned up and back out that door. The Slovak can take her away with him."

"I don't think he wants anything to do with her."

"She's not our problem. She *mustn't* be our problem."

Grozăvie turned Ilona's head to wipe away a line of dirt under her chin and spotted two small welts on her neck above her collarbone. They were red, sore, weeping. He tried to cover the twin punctures under Ilona's hair but his wife caught him and pulled his hands away. As they watched, the marks faded away. She gasped, a shaking hand over her mouth.

"That settles it. She has to go," she said.

Grozăvie nodded. "Get my knife. We need to free her from the evil."

"You'll do it here?"

"We have to. Her marks have gone. She is dead but if we don't do this now she will soon rise to walk the earth, forever cursed and drinking the blood of the living."

The landlord's wife hurried away as Grozăvie cleared the table and hauled Ilona's murmuring figure atop it. He pulled open her shirt to reveal her curved breasts, small nipples erect and pink.

His wife returned with a large hunting knife and he grasped it firmly between trembling hands, the point hovering inches above Ilona's barely moving chest. A swift plunge into her heart then a firm slice to remove her head and the task would be done - and another soul would be saved from eternal damnation.

"NO!"

The booming call stopped Grozăvie from bringing the weapon down. Instead, he dropped it in panic, its blade impaling itself at an odd angle in Ilona's arm.

A blur at Grozăvie's side and the landlord felt himself being hurled across the room. He heard his wife scream then gurgle into silence as he hit the wall, the breath knocked from him.

He looked up to see a blond haired man standing over the young woman, pulling the knife free to fling it away. The old man tried not to break down, tried to hold back the tears that were building behind his eyes - for at the newcomer's feet lay Grozăvie's wife of fifty-one years, neck broken and quite dead.

Grozăvie slumped where he had landed, dazed and nothing but revenge in his mind yet with no way of serving it.

"Ilona, wake up," Ismael said.

Triggered by his voice, awake the princess did. She sat upright with all the grace of a bird in flight.

Grozăvie looked at Ilona, his chest tightening as her piercing eyes bored into his skull.

Ilona, Grozăvie whispered to himself. *Dracula's wife.* How could she have become a vampire?

Ilona felt a wave of elation as her dulled mind finally registered that Ismael had come back for her. Without acknowledging her, Ismael beckoned another man into the room.

"Zucco," Ismael hissed, distaste in his voice clear. The newcomer, filthy and with an evil eye, licked his slovenly lips as he spied Ilona's bare breasts.

Zucco and Ismael, their voices low and unclear, seemed to be well acquainted but grudgingly respectful of each other in a way that spoke of a history, an animosity. A hate.

The gypsy's eyes widened as Ismael explained what was required of him.

Then in the beat of a heart, Ismael was at Ilona's side, pulling her out into the dusk, the cold air biting at her face and tugging at her hair as they travelled far, above the treetops and to a place deep in the sylvanian landscape unreachable by man.

And she lay there, buried in the earth with Ismael's voice inside her head, until it was time to awaken, reborn as a true creature of darkness, a bedevilled swan floating upon a lake of blood.

Chapter 23

Verrecchia's attempts at supporting Mansi were short-lived and his innocence and naivety soon revealed themselves to the more seasoned solider.

Initially dazed by his confrontation with Marise and his extreme action to rid himself of what he assumed was a vision (but in fact had been reality judging by the gaping wound still in his palm), Mansi had allowed the young monk to lead them out of the inn and to the thick forest beyond. But it was clear by Verrecchia's desperate endeavours to lose Zucco that they would soon be caught if Mansi didn't take the lead.

Whatever spell Zucco had cast over the inn's clientele had left some form of hold, for the gypsy was accompanied by a number of militant companions who would normally have found solace in a frothing tankard.

The forest wasn't Mansi's natural surroundings, having been raised between the straight lines and angles of the politically-driven town of Sebes. But years on the battlefield under the command of such leaders as Hunyadi and Dracula had given him the knowledge to understand the land around him.

He stopped Verrecchia and pulled him close to a tree with a wide trunk, obscuring them both from their pursuers.

"What do you plan to do?" asked Verrecchia, voice quavering as he breathed hard. They had been running for a while and his throat was pained.

"We've got no weapons and there's the added problem of your friend back there being a witch. So at the moment the plan is to keep one step ahead at least."

"He's not my friend," came the indignant sounding reply that proved Verrecchia's age.

"He seems to know you, Roberto. I'm not sure I want to know why just yet." Mansi looked at the monk, his young face framed by shadow. "Where are you from? I don't recognise your accent."

Verrecchia told him, giving a brief description of the life he had left behind at Saccargia and the journey he and his mentor Father Apollinari had been on when they had been split apart.

"You seem to have had a rough time of it," Mansi said, noticing the dark scab on Verrecchia's shin. "You stink like shit, too."

"Zucco kept me in a cage. They covered me in their... their toilet."

"How did you get to be in that place with the Marise woman?" Verrecchia frowned, not sure what Mansi meant. "You do remember being on the altar?"

"I...I remember it being cold and I do recall a woman's voice. I thought I was at Snagov. I'm confused."

"It'll be clear in time, I guess," said Mansi, looking at his hand.

"You need that cleaned and bandaged or it will become infected," pointed out Verrecchia, his basic apothecary training telling him as such.

Shouts and cries from the party hunting them reverberated through the trees.

Most of the group appeared to be armed and the small knife that suddenly imbedded itself in the tree trunk missed Mansi's other hand by inches.

"We need to get moving." Mansi wrenched the small weapon from the wood and pushed Verrecchia forward, urging him to run ahead.

Initially hesitant, Verrecchia complied as he saw Mansi's reassuring single nod.

Mansi watched the young monk dash off then moved to the left. He waited in silence and on his haunches by some fallen logs for the first of their followers to catch up, presumably the one who had launched the dagger.

It took him seconds to secure his hand with a makeshift bandage ripped from the hem of his tunic, finishing the job just as a large beast of a man thundered into view.

Clutching a falchion in a paw-like hand, the barbarian padded towards Mansi's hiding place, oblivious to the attack that was about to come. Within moments, he had been overcome, overwhelmed and disarmed, the knife in his throat revealing his windpipe to the cold air. Mansi's further attack brought the man's own weapon to his stomach and the weak resistance meant the smaller, lighter Wallachian soldier could gut his weightier opponent with comparative ease.

The barbarian thudded to the floor and Mansi sneered. He was armed now, the falchion heavy but comfortable in his grip. He had been trained to be ambidextrous when it came to sword play so one hand out of action wasn't too much of a hindrance. The small dagger he slid safely into his belt.

"I see you!" cried the gypsy but Mansi knew he lied. Nevertheless he pelted after Verrecchia, both amused and concerned that the monk had not got far. In fact, Verrecchia had come to a grinding halt.

"This isn't a damn walk in the country, boy!" Mansi snapped. "Get moving or we'll be dead. Or worse."

Verrecchia's eyes widened. "Worse?"

"Yes. Now move!"

Verrecchia's expression dropped. "I can't."

"What do you mean you can't?" Mansi followed Verrecchia's gaze to the monk's feet. They were entwined in slippery black tree roots that seemed to undulate like snakes. "Hold still."

Mansi began hacking away at the tendrils, Verrecchia convinced he could hear them squeal under his owned panicked breathing.

Soon Verrecchia was free and the two unlikely companions tore through the forest, branches and peculiar vines grabbed and slapping at them.

As they ducked and darted through the writhing forest, they didn't realise they were being herded to a specific point, the very trees and vegetation around them pushing and guiding until Verrecchia realised that the path was getting narrower. The branches were thicker and less malleable. Their flight was slowing down.

"We can't get through that," Roberto said, trying to prise the branches aside. Mansi couldn't break through even with the falchion.

The hunters had come up behind them, Zucco at their head.

"You can't escape," the gypsy spat, the effort of the chase as sweat upon his brow. "You're back in my grip you little shit."

"Not if I have anything to do with it you won't," responded Mansi and sliced the air in front of Zucco's face.

Zucco laughed, teasing the soldier by flamboyantly offering him his neck, withdrawing and doing so again. Mansi was beginning to grow tiresome of this brute and gave an almighty swing with the falchion, knocking the gypsy back and striking him across his lower jaw.

Mansi took advantage of the reeling man and jumped over him, Verrecchia in tow, careening through the mob behind like they were *kegeln*.

Taken aback, the mob didn't quite know what to do. Zucco's pain had somehow released his hold over them.

"You won't get far!" Zucco gurgled through a mouthful of blood.

"Don't look back!" hissed Mansi as he felt Verrecchia drop back briefly. "Come on!"

The forest ahead was thinner now, Zucco's influence over the trees gone. But what was that ahead? Mansi squinted as he navigated them through the woodland.

All of a sudden, a mass of branches and evergreen leaves reared up before them and Mansi and Verrecchia stumbled in a heap. Mud and mulch flung up around them.

Mansi couldn't believe his eyes as the branches looped and curled together to form, quite clearly, a man, devoid of any facial features to tell of but, undeniably, a man.

Verrecchia crossed himself and mouthed a prayer as another of the strange creatures rose up, then another and another, until Mansi and Verrecchia were surrounded - golems, made not from mud and dust, but from the very woodland around them.

Mansi breathed hard, channelling his fear into adrenalin, not allowing his mind to accept these creatures as invincible or even that they truly existed. If they had ascended from nothing then they could be cut down to nothing. They were, after all, only made of wood. The creatures moved into action as Mansi and Verrecchia renewed their escape.

"Până la moarte!" Mansi cried rising and spinning, falchion flashing and slicing.

Verrecchia was aghast at the unnatural life that had sprang from God's own earth, but perhaps more taken aback at the gusto with which his new-found protector tore through the creatures, their onslaught as a group relentless.

Yet as soon as one of the creatures was felled, it appeared not to be able to rise again. Even the smallest of cuts was enough to wound them. With bravery that surprised even himself, Verrecchia called to Mansi for the dagger and it was flung in his direction. He took it up and stabbed at the monsters. They were quick and easily came within touching distance.

Creature after creature fell and, even though Verrecchia had not the agility that Mansi showed as he darted through the trees spinning around trunks and bracken with falchion flashing, steel striking wood, he still stood his ground.

Between them, Verrecchia and Mansi drove back the fearsome visions until none were left.

Zucco's spell was defeated yet again and Verrecchia was beginning to realise that the magic in the gypsy's fingertips was less spiritual and rather more in line with nature. For if Zucco was a powerful witch, why would he simply not turn them both into mountain weasels?

Back at the road, the forest and its demonic uprisings behind them, Mansi gained his bearings and headed south, Verrecchia exhausted but keeping up with the soldier's cealess energy. Where Zucco was Verrecchia did not wish to know, more at peace now with the knowledge that here was a man who was able to see them both safe.

The island of Snagov, with its high walls enclosing the grandiose monastery, was a formidable place to those who had not visited it before. Yet once within the confines of the mighty fortification, the calming air of the brotherhood could be felt in every corner.

But today, a weight of gloom could not be lifted, could not be turned. The rain pummelling down reinforced the pall. For today was the burial of Abbot Shandor, spiritual father and mentor to so many of the monks who had joined the order, whether it be through family crisis, a turn of faith or the desire to be part of a unique community, fully penitent to God. In any case, the Abbot had welcomed them all, taking them under his wing and ensuring they received the fullest religious teaching possible.

Some of the monks had been here for decades, seeing numerous Abbots come and go, burying many and saying goodbye to others as their appointments at Snagov came to an end.

But for all, the passing of Shandor was different, mainly due to the fact that Sigmurului, the tyrannical bishop of Bistritz, was here to carry out the burial himself.

As Jacob stood next the bishop, he could feel the thoughts of his fellow brothers weighing heavy upon his decision to bring Sigmurului here. Some accused him of wanting the Abbotship for himself, hence their belief that his inviting the bishop was a sycophantic move so that the bishop would acquiesce to his desire.

Rather they believe that, Jacob concluded, than the fact that the Abbot had died the most unnatural death.

Shandor's body had been washed by the three priests who had accompanied Sigmurului from Bistritz. Redressed in fresh sacerdotal vestments, the Abbot's face was covered with an Aër, embroidered with fine pale silk thread. In his right hand a cross was placed.

The casket had remained open all the time it sat in the monastery's chapel, a procession of senior monks reading psalms one after the other once the Requiem Mass had been said. This was to ensure that Shandor's body was never left without prayer, especially as no last rites had been read: no penance, no unction and no receiving of the Eucharist.

Jacob was not included in this, Sigmurului aware that he had seen the vampire's mark on the Abbot's neck. Jacob, as distraught as he could be, insisted to the bishop that he would keep this revelation to himself, desperate to pray for Shandor's soul. But Sigmurului would only agree to have Jacob present at the burial itself, simply to save questions being raised if the monk were to not attend.

They stood now in the rain at the grave, itself open like a maw into the very bowels of the earth. It waited silently for the now-sealed casket it was soon to receive.

"*Sanctus Deus, Sanctus Fortis, Sanctus Immortális, miserére nobis*," intoned Sigmurului as Shandor's body was eventually lowered into his hopefully eternal resting place. Scented oil was sprinkled across the lid of the casket and, unusually for the burial of an Abbot, whitethorn was crushed and dusted into the grave.

Jacob closed his eyes at this point, knowing the significance. It was intended to stop Shandor's undead corpse from rising.

A chilled wind suddenly beat at them with its biting force, as if the spirits were being kept at bay.

Jacob looked into the grave.

"It is done," Sigmurului said after a lengthy silence. Turning away, the old bishop motioned to his three priests, murmuring to them. Jacob strained to hear but could not. The three priests kept glancing back at Jacob and the monk was sure the conversation being had involved him somehow.

Then the four from Bistritz retreated into the monastery and to Shandor's office. Whose office it now was still remained to be seen but there was little doubt that Sigmurului would have some sort of say on the matter.

Jacob clasped his hands together under the folds of his cassock, in the way that Shandor used to do, hood pulled over his eyes. He glanced at the faces of the other monks still at the graveside and suddenly realised that he didn't recognise any of them. In fact none of the brotherhood except a meagre handful was actually present.

Pulling his hood back from his head, Jacob moved to the nearest of the unknown monks. "What is your name?"

The monk, a large man, swarthy and with an out-of-character dueling scar across his left cheek, squinted back. "Brother Robert," he growled in an accent rare in these parts. He was an Englishman.

"And you?" This was to the man next to him.

"Brother William," the shorter man replied, also English.

"What are you doing here?" Jacob stood at their side. "Have you come with the bishop?"

"We have come *for* the bishop. We are here at his request," said Robert.

"To what end?"

William looked furtively at his companion. "We are... protection."

"From what? Against whom?" Jacob was becoming agitated. "No one needs protecting while at Snagov."

William made to speak but closed his mouth as Robert glared at him.

"How many of you are there?"

Robert breathed in deeply, the cold wind reddening his cheeks. "The bishop will answer any further questions you may have."

"You will answer me here, now!" demanded Jacob but his attempt to command the situation fell flat as Robert and William kept their silence. Something under the neck of William's cassock caught his eye and he leant forward. William tensed as Jacob grabbed his collar and tugged at it.

Beneath the brown garb of the monk Jacob saw a glint of chainmail. His eyes widened as he realised what they were. "You're knights! Both of you!"

The streets of the Dambovita Citadel were bustling, always bustling, day and night. The shrill tones of the stringed *iklig* gave an atmosphere to the market that was unlike any other north of the Sea of Marmara.

It was a little part of Turkey set in the heart of Wallachia, a brusque cuckoo made from incense, music and spice. Light-fingered child pick-pockets, buxom whores and bartering merchants abound, occasionally these three professions overlapping. Nevertheless it was a society based on hospitality. As a cornerstone of their culture, the Turks believed that visitors should be treated 'as guests of God' and, even though their occupancy of the Wallachian Citadel was obtained by force, it hadn't taken long for Constantinople's influence to take over.

From out of the solitary window of the solitary room atop the solitary tower, Caleb, Kelele and Odalys watched the life below them weave itself in and around the populous.

"They don't even realise what is beneath their feet," said Odalys, referring to the catacombs swollen with new-born vampires.

"Perhaps it is time we showed them," purred Caleb. "They annoy me, with their limited outlook and short existence."

"Yet they are useful," Kelele pointed out. "A rich source of blood."

"Long gone are the days where we could farm them," said Odalys, melancholy in her tone. "I wish to walk amongst them."

Caleb didn't stop the vampires from sweeping down out of the tower and to the cold, icy streets of the Citadel.

Here they could feel the hearts beating in hundreds of warm bodies, could smell the blood pounding through the veins of every one of them.

In one man, his pulse quickened as he took advantage of the available prostitute down a side alley, and another - a trader - whose heart thumped harder still as he harangued a passer-by for a sale.

The vampires moved among them freely, the people not even truly conscious that they were there. It was a trait of the undead, to be able to go unnoticed until it was time to strike or seduce. Even Kelele, nearing seven feet tall with his dark skin and its ghostly sheen, walked without the perception of the living.

"Take them," Caleb said suddenly as he joined them amid the market stalls. "Take them all."

The Vampire Celebrants needed no further prompting, picking out and picking off suitable donors one by one. The streets began to thin out as the residents became victims, slowly enough so no one would notice.

Viktor, still in the tower, rocked back and forth on his haunches as he heard the throats of the living being pierced, torn and gouged by his vampire siblings.

The blood flowed freely. Kelele sliced open a woman's neck with his teeth. A man, an overweight, asthmatic individual, suddenly noticed the Ethiopian standing before him. He cried out in horror and then mass panic followed. As far as the living were concerned, Odalys, Caleb and Kelele had abruptly appeared from nowhere. There was screaming and shouting as the crowds scattered and Caleb breathed in deeply, sensing the terror in their veins. This was how the feed *should* be, he thought – fear in the blood made it that much sweeter to drink.

The flashing of sharp talons. The biting with white teeth. The Celebrants gorged themselves, leaving no one they touched alive.

From the depths of the Citadel's catacombs, the frenzied hunting could be felt by the multitude of newborn vampires.

Caleb willed them, these desperate and savage infantile undead, willed them to join him and his Celebrants. Like rats from the hovels, the vampires swarmed and soon the streets were a mass of black shapes, drinking and killing. The *iklegs*' songs fell silent, the braziers upturned, hot coals spilling over the icy ground and around the market stalls. Canvasses and silks, flapping in the November wind, felt the touch of the heat and smouldered, wisps of smoke curling as the flames caught. Within minutes the fires had spread, jumping from stall to stall, ferocious and unrelenting just like the vampires on this cold and uncompromising night.

In the dark hours that followed, the undead had done a far more efficient job in claiming the Citadel for themselves than any amount of Turks could have done.

From his vantage point many feet above, defying the buffeting wind and ice air, Caleb hovered, arms spread. The sight below him sent liberated waves of contentment through his centuries-old heart. His children born of darkness, through their feeding and their slaughtering, were becoming stronger night by night.

The huge fireplace in the Great Hall was as cold as the grave, its fire long since burnt out.

Rintoul sat at one end of the long table in the centre of the hall, directly opposite Ismael. It was loaded high with cold meats, fruit, wine and bread by the basket-load.

Between them, down each side of the table and on elaborate chairs padded with cobalt velvet, sat the corpses of the Elite Guard, their skin as dry as autumn leaves and just as discoloured. Their stomachs were full from the feast but their veins were empty.

The two vampires had watched them from the shadows as they ate, the soldiers apparently little perturbed that their Governor had been slaughtered only very recently and that their commander in chief Lord Yozgatli Tanyel had disappeared. Rumours had begun to spring up of sightings of Tanyel yet no one could pin point when or where. Many dismissed it as some sort of psychosis.

Some feared he had been killed in battle and his *hayalet* had returned to haunt the corridors.

Rintoul and Ismael had struck with such speed that the soldiers had no chance to defend themselves (even though it would have been futile had they even been able to grasp at a sword hilt).

The last man Rintoul had drank from tasted like goat's milk and he remembered from his living existence it was not a flavour that he had enjoyed. Ismael, however, had long ago learnt to ignore the after tastes that his victims' diets left in their blood. But he did enjoy drinking from those who were inebriated. The alcohol had a similar effect on the vampire as it had on the living but to a somewhat lesser extent.

Like some undead parody of upper nobility, Ismael sipped from a gold goblet (the silverware long since removed), full with blood drained fresh from the wrists of one of the soldiers.

"Did you ever imagine you would be sitting here at the table of the rich?"

"No. Neither did I imagine I would be a vampire!"

Ismael laughed, the blood thick in his throat. "Do you like it?"

"Being a vampire?" Rintoul toyed with the edge of the wooden bowl before him, stomach churning at the thought of once having needed to digest all that solid food. "What I think really makes no difference. You saw to that."

Rintoul's scarred face looked back at Ismael, the disfigurement from his torture made permanent by Ismael's bite.

"We vampires are meant to be free of the constraints of emotion. But I do not believe that to be so." Ismael replaced the goblet on the table and leant back in his chair. "Do you hold it against me that I turned you?"

Rintoul pursed his lips, fangs protruding. He traced their sharpness with the tip of his tongue. "You call me a newborn. You consider me to be immature. Immature for a vampire, that is."

Ismael nodded, a curl of blonde hair falling across his forehead. "Perhaps."

"Yet you expect me to have a measured response, not driven by the fact that you made me like this only a matter of days ago?"

"And therefore you cannot answer me. Is that what you are saying?"

Rintoul considered. "I agree that without you I would have suffered a cruel death at the hands of the Turkish commander. Yet what has *he* become? Is he any different?"

"He is Caleb now, Caleb in every way."

"What does that mean?"

Ismael stood and walked slowly towards Rintoul, bringing his goblet with him. "You saw Caleb out there on the battlefield. You saw how he took that soldier. What did you make of him?"

"He is a monster. Blood-thirsty. He is like us."

Rintoul tensed as Ismael stopped behind him, feeling a cold undead hand rest upon his left shoulder.

"He is not like us," Ismael said coolly. "He is *nothing* like us."

Rintoul frowned. Ismael sensed his companion's confusion.

"He is neither living nor vampire. He was destroyed by witchcraft so many years ago and yet the spell still sits inside his rejuvenated heart like a cancer."

"If he is no vampire, then what..?"
Ismael clenched his teeth, finding it almost unbearable to say. But if he did not reveal this to Rintoul then his goal would be even further out of reach. "He is *tertium quid*. Not pure enough to rule us."

What was Ismael saying? Even as a newborn, Rintoul felt the allegiance to Caleb. He was their father in darkness and the link all vampires had to him, irrespective of their generation, was innate. For Ismael to talk like this was tantamount to blasphemy.

"But he is our *master*."

"I know you feel it too."

"No," replied Rintoul, a hand to his temple. "I...I don't know what I feel..."

With the strength only a vampire has, Ismael grabbed at the back of Rintoul's chair, shattering it like matchwood. He tossed the goblet aside, its contents splattering across the floor behind him.

Rintoul tumbled to the ground, startled. Tensed, he was ready to spring back up but Ismael stood over him, blocking his ascent. Wary of Ismael's sudden unpredictability, Rintoul wondered what he had been like when he had been alive. The blonde hair, the fair complexion – he was not from this part of the world.

Ismael placed a booted foot on Rintoul's chest and pierced the palm of his own left hand, flicking the ensuing blood across the floor, the table and Rintoul.

Much like the beasts in the forest, the vampire marked its territory. But unlike the feral animal, the vampire's reason for scenting its chosen surroundings was purely hierarchical.

The prone newborn wiped the scarlet emission from his eyes.

"I made you, Rintoul. You are mine to command!" Ismael's eyes squinted, his voice lowering to a harsh whisper. "You will obey me."

Rintoul frowned, unsure if the sudden ringing in his ears was real or an illusion. He tried to break Ismael's deep gaze but found himself transfixed. It was as if Ismael were seducing him all over again, just as he had done so in the dungeons many feet beneath them, just as he had done so when he was alive.

Feeling a terrible wrench between his instinct of penitence to Caleb and intimacy to the one who had made him, Rintoul tried to bow his head but his companion's stare was strong, unwavering. The dark shadows of blood-filled tears collected in the corners of his eyes. Rintoul wanted to lash out, to bite and claw his way clear but the incessant ringing in his head altered in pitch and became much more soothing.

For life it craves your soul.

A voice! Inside his head! Replacing the whine. But it wasn't Ismael's: it was a woman's, lilted with a peculiar accent. Rintoul found it similar to that of the olive-skinned merchants from the distant east who had often come to the Citadel to trade before the Turkish occupancy kept them away.

But just as swiftly, the noise returned and the voice did not come again. Suddenly overcome by a wave of exhilaration, Rintoul shifted onto his knees in front of Ismael and watched as Ismael bared his own chest and sliced it once, diagonally, with a sharp fingernail. A welt of blood followed and Rintoul, like a sanguine dog, waited until the delicacy was offered him. Then, pouncing on the blood, Rintoul lapped until his thirst was slaked.

Ismael smiled and placed a hand on top of the young vampire's head. "Now go. And spread word amongst our kind of Caleb's impurity."

"To what end?" gasped Rintoul, Ismael's blood clotting around his lips.

"Why, my coronation of course," Ismael purred, pushing Rintoul to the floor. "Don't you see? I intend to replace him."

Sigmurului had been burning the disarray of paperwork in Shandor's office for the last two hours, the ochre glow flickering from the high windows.

Jacob had been forcibly removed from the room by the priests, having received no explanation as to why English knights would be guarding Shandor's grave.

Warned to stay out of the way, Jacob knew that the bishop would have no qualms in banishing him. Sigmurului was infamous for cutting many peoples' ties with the Church, those who crossed him, essentially. It was a punishment in this God-fearing age sometime greater than any imprisonment.

So Jacob had returned to his cramped dormitory and lay on the hard cot, the sack cloth pillow aggravating the back of his neck more than usual.

"You've said nothing since you returned, brother," Yazid said from the bed along the opposite wall. Jacob's eyes flicked to his fellow monk and back again to the ceiling. He did not answer. Ages seemed to pass before the middle-aged monk spoke again. "I lay here sometimes, staring at the mould on the walls. It's as if it creeps out from the corners to smother the goodness of this place."

"Then it echoes my mood," said Jacob flatly. "Go to sleep."

"I think it is you who needs to do that," responded Yazid, his bearded chin twitching. "I understand that you are troubled. The Abbot's passing has affected us all, but y-."

"You know nothing of which you speak, Yazid," interrupted Jacob, somewhat unkindly.

The older monk ignored Jacob's venom and sighed. "Who are the monks standing at the Abbot's grave?"

Jacob shifted on to his side so he was facing Yazid. They'd shared quarters for nearly three years and they often aired their thoughts when Compline had been read and all had retired to their rooms for the night.

Yazid seemed to not be concerned when Jacob told him what the strangers were. He nodded thoughtfully.

"But why come all this way?" Jacob wanted to know.

"Perhaps they are stationed at Bistritz. With talk of the Turk being at large in the forests and on the roads, now more than ever, it would make sense that Bishop Sigmurului would have an armed escort."

"Surely he would use the Prince's army?"

"Not necessarily. The Hungarians control most of the north."

"And destroying Father Shandor's documents? You know I am not one for idle conversations, Yazid, but this clearly indicates the bishop is ridding all signs of the Abbot."

"Perhaps the bishop is concerned about..." Yazid's voice drifted off as he heard the quiet shuffle of sandals on stone in the corridor outside.

Immediately alert, Jacob slipped to the door, trying to hear through the heavy wood. As the footsteps moved away, he shook his head. "Why should we feel like prisoners in our own monastery?"

From the depths of the maze-like corridors, a plaintive wail echoed up. Yazid stood to be near Jacob. "It's the boy."

"Corbiu?" Jacob was concerned. He had grown fond of the child in the last few days, tending to him, listening to his stories of him being on the run. He was such a lonely young boy that it aggrieved Jacob to not be able to visit him some days. "Was that a cry of pain?"

"It was something." A further sound came, more distant, like… "A wolf!"

"It's that one that was loose! The one that attacked the monk from Saccargia!"

"But that's coming from without the grounds of Snagov," Yazid pointed out.

"Better out there than still in here with us."

As the wolf howled again, so Corbiu replied in his own strange way.

"He is peculiar, that boy."

Jacob nodded. "He displays habits that are almost feral."

"And now he talks to the wolf," Yazid said quietly. "Do you wish to go to him? To see if he is upset?"

Jacob thought for a moment. "I should but it will soon be the second hour of the morning."

The nocturnal readings, that of the Night Office as it was known, was the beginning of the vigils leading up to the dawn prayers. As the most senior member of the monastery, it was up to Jacob to lead the psalms. Bishop present or not, Jacob was not about to let his duties falter.

Yet the events of the next few moments, during which Jacob and Yazid made their way through the monastery, meant that the Night Office would not begin, the first time ever that such an thing had happened in the long and complex history of Snagov monastery. But it was a night of firsts: never before had an Abbot's grave been so keenly guarded by knights from a far off land; and never before had the monastery itself come under attack from the very things that it had been designed to spiritually keep out – creatures of Satan, spawned from the very depths of Hell itself, the vampire horde.

Chapter 24

"This is madness, Alexandru. We'll never find her."

"Your familiarity should be reprimanded, soldier," smiled Popescu as the two men on their respective horses travelled south along the Brasov road. "But I do begin to feel the same."

"If the Prince finds that it was us who took her from the Palace you know what he'll do to us. Why did I let you talk me into this?"

"Because you are loyal. Our years together have proven that."

"What were those demons back there?" Seneslav nodded his head backwards to emphasise the question.

"Exactly that, my friend. Demons or something else."

"They took the Turks, too. It seemed they were not fussy."

"You wished them to drink from the veins of Turks alone? I wouldn't wish that on anybody!" Popescu laughed, but Seneslav couldn't make light of what had happened to them. Two opposing contingents of soldiers brought to their knees so swiftly by such monsters was a horrifying image and one likely to stay in the minds of these two seasoned warriors for many years to come.
The rain had stopped, and everything was still, silent. Even the birds had stopped twittering in the trees around them. The road, still treacherous, would take them right

to the heart of the Turkish occupancy and Popescu knew they had to convince the enemy they were not Wallachians. He had had the foresight to take uniforms from the fallen Turks back at the cabin and, even though they were caked with blood, they would suffice. Ilona had to be there, it would be the most logical place. He had to believe she was still alive, being such a valuable bargaining tool on the part of the Turks. The wife of their sworn enemy! Who wouldn't take advantage of that!

Seneslav brought them to a stop, his bladder full and a pain in his gut. Dismounting, he motioned to his captain that he would be but a moment and darted into the trees to relieve himself, leaving his sword hanging from the saddle.

Popescu waited, Seneslav the only man, save for his own leaders, that he would be so patient with. Giving Seneslav some privacy, he too dismounted and sat at the edge of the road, picking the mud and slush from his spurs.

Seneslav tramped through the undergrowth, finding a suitable spot, muttering to himself about the bad food an army was expected to consume. It was only after he had managed to settle his stomach that he realised he wasn't alone – at least not in the vicinity.

There was a voice, quiet but definitely distinguishable amidst the gentle rustling. It was female to be sure so Seneslav tightened his belt and squinted into the trees. It was difficult to determine where she was but, on a breeze in his direction, he thought she was ahead so stepped into the thicket. Branches and leaves slapped into his face as he went deeper into the forest, all the while listening to the voice. Yet he could not make out the words, just the sounds and it was definitely- Seneslav stopped. The voice had changed position. It was behind him. He turned.

It was now to his left. No - to his right. He removed his helmet and pushed his wet fringe away from his eyes. He could hear the voice clearly now. It was like a song, beckoning him forwards and so he broke into a run, ignoring the branches scraping at his face. Salty blood trickled across his forehead as he dived into a clearing, the ferns bowing under his steps. He didn't even consider he was alone and unarmed because there she was, crouching only a few yards from him, her damp hair moving gently in the wind. She looked up and their eyes met.

Delve within the depths of your mind.

Her lips hadn't moved, but he'd clearly heard her say it. Seneslav stepped into the clearing. The woman was wearing, surprisingly, the garb of some backwoodsman. It didn't suit her in the slightest, Seneslav thought, appreciating the fact that she was now curling out of it. Her back arched as she removed the heavy trousers. The white shirt, three sizes too big, fell to the ground behind.

See the image breathing there.

The woman's smooth shoulders moved as she raised her hand, beckoning hi to join her. Seneslav shook his head and rubbed his eyes, not entirely sure what it was he was seeing.

Waiting to take control of your being.

She moved to sit on her haunches, kneeling in the wet grass and held a hand out to him. With her other she caressed her neck, her breasts, moving down to between her parted legs.

"Ilona..." he said, voice so quiet he wasn't even sure if he made a sound.

Seneslav realised she was even more beautiful than he knew and understood in some way his captain's obsession with her.

A form based upon your sweetest desire.

Seneslav closed his eyes and breathed in, opening them again moments later. She was still there, so she had to be real. Didn't she? He felt something at his temples. It was if she were inside his head.

For life it craves your mind.

The whole forest melted away around him and his vision saw only her. He felt that he would die if he couldn't touch her, so took a step forward. She stood.

Yearns your every thought.

Her nude form curled towards him, a slight movement as she drew her hands over her hips. Seneslav needed to cry out but his voice was caught in his throat. His manhood was swelling between his legs. Captivated, he didn't care that he could no longer move, was not concerned that his heart was pounding so fast he felt faint, because she was coming towards him all the while her haunting call inside his head.

Give yourself up to its power.

She moved slowly towards him and he reached out, his thoughts touched by hers as his fingertips brushed her shoulders. She moved closer still, bringing her lips to his. They touched and Seneslav felt as though his skin was prickling around his mouth. Trembling in her arms as she enveloped him, he gasped as if he had taken a blow to the chest. As if a breath had been taken from him.

And breathe the existence of the moroi.

Ilona smiled, drawing her delicate lips apart to reveal long canines, white and sharp. She hissed and immediately Seneslav reeled back, as if stumbling from a dream into a nightmare. The rank odour of death from her open mouth watered his eyes and he fell to the floor, vision blurred. She landed on top of him, long black tongue flicking out, licking at his face and neck. He tried to get out from under her but she had him pinned between her legs, her body glistening with rain water. Pushing her face away from his, he saw, through stinging eyes that her lithe body was twisting and shuddering.

"Seneslav!" came a cry, laced with venom and unalloyed anger.

Stunned, the man looked to his left to see Popescu pounding towards him, sword in his hand. Even at this range Seneslav could see his captain gnashing his teeth.

He turned back to Ilona, suddenly realising the situation he was in. But had she really just bared sharp, white teeth?

Ilona leapt into the air.

Seneslav wiped his eyes and gagged, struggling to stand but his legs still wouldn't work properly. Popescu slid to halt next to him and dragged him to his feet.

"What in God's name do you think you're doing?" Popescu snarled, sword tip at Seneslav's throat. A drop of blood appeared where he had nicked the skin.

Above them, the vampire Ilona could smell the fresh life-force, even the tiny amount that had been spilt. She flitted in and out of the trees.

Popescu threw Seneslav back to the floor.

The lieutenant raised his arms. "My Lord, she is not alive! She is one of them! A *vampyr*!"

"I will gut you, Seneslav! First you betray me then you say she is a monster!"

"It's true, I swear it!" Seneslav stumbled to his feet.

Sick, Popescu felt tears form behind his eyes, but what was he to do now? He squinted up in the sky but saw no sign of her.

"See? You look up there for her! You *saw* her fly!"

Dropping to his knees, Popescu could no longer control

his emotions, wracked with anguish and pain. The thing that had been Ilona bore down from directly above them but he stood his ground and lashed out at her with his sword, tears streaming down his cheeks.

Ilona knocked him flat on his back and, as if taunting him, landed in front of Seneslav, naked and ripe.

"Get away from him! You are mine!" Popescu hollered. But Ilona ignored him, responding instead with a fanged smile - then ripped Seneslav's throat out with a single shocking and brutal bite.

Bravery was never a requisite to becoming a monk, not that every monk was a coward. Yet in the face of God, they were all fearful, humble. Jacob, however, embraced the penitence, seeing it as a way to relinquish all personal doubts and anxieties. But it was never as straightforward as that, as Jacob had learnt, particularly today.

His breathing was fast and hard, the silver crucifix tight in his grasp and clutched close to his chest.

He stood flush against the south wall of the cloisters, Yazid at his side. Together they had made their way through the monastery, scurrying and hiding from the vampires. It had not been easy: many of their brothers had been cut down and ripped apart in the feeding frenzy. Yazid, his bones objecting to the exercise, had stumbled a few times, partly due to the atrocities he was witnessing around him and partly down to the arthritis in his joints.

Jacob had urged him on, knowing he was being slowed down by the old monk but staying with him nevertheless. Jacob wasn't entirely sure where to go next. Nowhere in the monastery seemed safe and in fact being inside was potentially more dangerous, with any number of dank, narrow corridors and locked heavy doors to be trapped in and against. So outside was the most likely place to go yet it seemed futile to willingly find the open air.

A vampire suddenly landed in the centre of the cloisters, twitching and scrabbling insect-like, hearing the hearts beating around it and the blood coursing through living veins. Sixty when she had been turned, the female moved with such strength. For a brief moment, before he remembered what she was, Yazid felt envious of her agility.

As if aware of this, the grey-haired vampire dashed forward, stopping inches before the two monks, head tilted. Her eyes, strikingly white but forever incurable of the cataracts, blinked at them. Her pointed teeth were bared as she drew back her lips. Her breath was rank, of rotten meat and rotting gums.

Jacob swallowed hard, raised his crucifix and thrust it in her face! She screamed and gurgled, the silver leaving a bubbling wound across her forehead.

Angry now, she went to bite Jacob's neck but stopped, transfixed for a moment, before she exploded before them.

Both Yazid and Jacob, gasping in terror, saw standing on the other side of the cloisters Robert, devoid of his monk's habit and revealed in black and dark green tunic and breeches. A longbow, just fired, was firm in his left hand. He nodded once at the monks, pulled a hood up over his head, covering his long dark hair, then retreated into the shadows.

Yazid looked down at the mess of blood and bone and hair at their feet and saw, glinting, a silver arrowhead affixed to a thin shaft of whitethorn. He tried to speak but could not form the words.

"It seems our stranger-knights are well versed in the art of despatching vampires," said Jacob, picking up the projectile. "I understand now what they meant when they said they are here to protect. But where's the bishop?"

Renewed, Jacob grabbed Yazid and the two of them weaved and ducked their way towards the main courtyard by the shortest possible route, through the kitchens. But even the destruction of a vampire at their feet and its fellow creatures' inflictions wherever they turned was no preparation for the sight that met them as they eventually entered the high-walled expanse.

Right arm outstretched and standing in the centre of the courtyard, was the vampire Pretorius Shandor. Entwined between his cold, pale fingers was the matted hair and scalp of the knight called William. The knight's head proper was in Shandor's other hand, held by the lower jaw, casually swinging against the vampire Abbot's thigh.

Where William's body was never occurred to Jacob for the monk vomited where he stood, the sight of his beloved Father's undead form too much.

Shandor looked at the monk as if trying to remember who he was. A vampire's initial steps were always faltering. Disorientation was an added complication and further it was unusual for the recently turned to rise so soon.

The coming of the vampires had woken Shandor early and he knew he had to feed but, like a child, found the act of finding his own meal somewhat beyond his capabilities for the moment.

Shandor had once had a kind face, full of wisdom and a hidden sparkle. But now he was undead, all vestiges of placidity had been wiped away, leaving in its place a pale, vacant expression. His eyes were not yet the striking white characteristic of all vampires: they still retaining the glassy, soulless appearance of a typical cadaver.

And that was what made it worse for Jacob, if that was at all possible. If Shandor had stood before them, conscious of his surroundings and of what he now was, it would have been easier for Jacob to deal with the situation. As it was, Shandor appeared to be a veritable zombie, resurrected and mindless.

His cassock was caked in mud and specks of whitethorn dust, not enough to keep him still. His fingers were black with dirt, compacted under the nails where he had clawed his way out from the ground.

Shandor dropped William's scalp and threw the knight's head, like a child throws away something that is of no interest to it anymore. It rolled down the gentle incline towards Yazid and Jacob, the older monk trying as best he could to comfort his companion.

Around them, the battle between living and vampire continued, with the knights loyal to Sir Robert hacking and slicing their way clear. The blood drinkers fell as easy as stacked dice. Of Sir Robert himself there was no sign.

All Jacob and Yazid felt they could do was watch from the sidelines and pray to God that their protectors would be victorious. They were shortly joined by six other monks.

The number of vampires that had descended on the monastery was probably less than was apparent. Moments of calm were interspersed by bouts of flurrying black shapes, decapitation and staking; only a few of Sir Robert's men falling in the process, William, of course, included. But even these Englishmen, as well-equipped as they were, could not hold them all back and soon the surviving creatures had cornered the monks and their protectors, only a narrow door some yards away the only potential way clear.

The biggest of Sir Robert's men, as tall as he was broad and an unkempt beard obscuring his features, herded the monks along the wall to the door. His quarterstaff swung out to keep the vampires at bay. The other men used their swords and arrows, picking off a couple of the creatures here and there. But one broke through and sunk its claws into the shoulder of the slowest monk, pulling him clear, ripping his head clean from his body and lapping at the resultant blood flow.

Yazid cowered, the acts of evil around him incomprehensible. What had they done to deserve such torment? They prayed day and night, they kept the crops, they welcomed the lame and the infirm. What more could they have done?

"It's the boy," Yazid whispered into Jacob's ear. "It has to be. He has cursed us with his feral ways." Jacob was terrified at the events occurring but still shot Yazid a look that meant he was not prepared to accept the old monk's conclusion. "He must be cast out. 'By your many sins and dishonest trade you have desecrated your sanctuaries.'"

"He has done nothing!" Jacob insisted, hoping that it were true.

The air closed in around them as they entered the corridor, the Englishmen both at front and rear. The door was secured from the inside, leaving them in semi-darkness.

"Where to now?" Jacob asked the big man.

"The chapel," he answered and Jacob nodded, leading the group further into the monastery's interior.

On the other side of the door came a powerful thud. It sounded again and again once more.

"Brother Jacob!" came a shout in a timbre that Jacob knew so well. "Let me in! Don't leave me out here with these demons!"

"Keep going. It's trying to tempt you," the bearded giant growled.

"But it's..."

"I know who it is, Yazid," spat Jacob, trying all he can to void from his mind the familiar tones. "Keep going."

The calling came again, plaintive, almost desperate. But it was a ploy, a ruse to make the loyal Jacob turn back and unbar the door.

Pretorius Shandor had found his voice and wanted to get in.

The dragons flew proud in the grey morning sky high above the Wallachian army that had massed near the bank of the Southern-most tip of the Cernica Lake.

The striking image of the mythical creature that symbolised the Dracula family had been weaved in pure gold on the narrow scarlet flags. They curled and snapped in the wind, the squall catching and pulling at them.

The same icon was repeated on the chest plate of Dracula himself and on the shields of his innermost circle of troops.

It was a formidable representation of the Wallachian military might.

Dracula had ordered his army to rest here in preparation for the battle that was about to ensue, his encampment re-erected from that which was at Prahov only two nights before.

From his retreat, Dracula had ordered word of Mansi to be brought to him but none had yet come back. Angered, the prince had raped one of the wenches in his entourage and, some believed, ripped out her heart to feed it to his dogs. Still incensed, he'd had two soldiers brought to him and killed them in hand to hand combat.

There was a bloodlust curled inside the prince that took extreme actions to satisfy. The witches knew it, the werewolves avoided it and the vampires appreciated it.

Dracula himself, however, would dismiss the notion of supernatural and elemental forces yet, upon a hill due south and some distance away from the lake, Jurat watched the Wallachian army. His sight was keen, his sense of smell more so. Padding impatiently on all fours, his fur bristled as the wind whipped around him.

Jurat did not need a full moon to transform. Neither did it need to be dark. These were the advantages of being born a lycanthrope, as oppose to being turned by one. Otherwise, he shared the same traits and abilities as the rest of his species.

He'd followed the army as soon as he'd picked up their scent (the aromas from an army on the move were second to none), his assumption that they were headed for the eastern side of the Citadel confirmed. Where Popescu was he had no idea, having lost that particular track somewhere in the Vlasie forest: there were many strange and confusing trails these last few days, many of which he identified as being of the vampire. Over the centuries, there had always been an uneasy alliance between the undead and his own kind: neither party fed off of or hunted the other, yet trust was still a fragile commodity, their existence side-by-side strained at the best of times. The lycanthropes put it down to the class structure some vampires were prevalent to, while the vampires blamed the werewolves' 'vile' pack instinct (thereby reinforcing the realisation of a hierarchical vampire society).

From his vantage point, he had seen a reconnaissance party go to and from the Citadel, relaying to Dracula on their return what they had found. Jurat didn't need to be amongst them to hear what they said, for the smell of death from the other side of the gargantuan walls was thick in the air.

He threw his neck back, heavy with his dark mane, and howled, long and deep. It was instinctive, warning those around him that he was present, that he was hungry and that his hunger would soon be satiated. It would take no time at all to infiltrate the camp down by the lake, pick off the weakest soldier he could find and fill his stomach for the night.

Whatever slaughter had taken place inside the Citadel was not for him to become involved in. Whatever battle was about to unfold once Dracula's army stormed the Turkish stronghold was of little consequence to his existence.

He would feed and he would move on, as he had always done and would continue to do.

But he would have considered a different path had he realised that Claudia was crossing the boundaries of Dambovita - and into the very depths of Hell itself.

As Jurat bounded unseen to the rear of the army, the mighty force seemed to develop an intensity that chilled Jurat as much as the wind. The sound of the chanting and stomping throng bubbled into a chaotic mass, the thump of sword on shield adding to the frenzy.

The party had reported the area immediately within the confines of the walls as derelict but Dracula wasn't convinced. It would not be unlike the Turk to use cadavers to disguise the true strength and so, after much debate with his surviving generals (for none of them were prepared to use their costly ammunition for an easy offensive), the prince of Wallachia had finally decided to storm the Citadel as originally planned (when they had expected it to have still been fully occupied).

So the order to advance was given and the trumpeters surged forward, the wailing call of their raised instruments igniting the artillerymen into motion first, the men at arms and mounted cavalry to follow.

Jurat would have to make haste. He honed in on a figure who appeared to be struggling with the already quickening march. He was a standard bearer, one who carried the icon of the dragon into battle – but such images did not strike terror into the heart of the predator at his back.

Rolling mighty siege engines forward, the Wallachian army waited until it was within range. Lit and fired in unison, great thunderclaps followed as the forged iron spheres spun and hurled across the November sky.

The crack of the artillery quietened the army and it was only when, some breath-held seconds later, the balls hit their targets or fell short, that the wordless chanting resumed. From their vantage point atop their horses, Vlad and his generals could see that it would take more than a few hits from the catapults to weaken the walls that Dracula himself had seen to strengthen. Again the catapults were loaded and fired, again the delayed slap of iron against air. The booming of the spheres as they struck the Citadel echoed back up the rise, drowned out by the tumultuous cheers from the attacking soldiers.

Coldly, silently and without remorse for the boy's fears or family, Jurat took this moment to strike, felling the standard bearer with one massive claw. It would be a mediocre feed for the kill was undernourished and grisly.

The scarlet flag fluttered in a declining curve as the wooden pole it was atop was loosened from the bearer's grip and bounced to the muddy ground.

The army surged on, oblivious that it was one man down. Sadder still, the boy wouldn't even be missed.

Jacob was quietly enjoying the role of Abbot, even though the reason for him being in this position was sometimes unbearable. But he knew it would only be for as long as it would take to find a replacement for the late but very undead Father Shandor.

Yazid, however, had found it difficult to stay put in the chapel, his obsession with Corbiu being the cause of all this evil smothering him.

He had not listened to Jacob, who had tried to tell him that being here, at the monastery's focal point for their faith, was the safest place to be. Instead, Yazid had convinced once of Sir Robert's men to hand him a sword and he had scurried off, like some ancient knight, on a quest of his own.

The bearded giant sat at the steps of the iconostasis, his quarterstaff across his knees and at an angle, touching the cold stone floor. Jacob noted that one end had been sharpened and was stained dark with blood from countless battles.

The monk turned as he heard another of Sir Roberts's men come up behind him. Jacob clasped his hands together and smiled.

"My son," he began. "I cannot thank you enough for all that you are doing."

The stocky man had a grizzled expression, enhanced by a permanently half-closed right eye, giving him the appearance of a drunkard – something which the giant clearly used as bait.

"Careful, Father, he's after the communion wine!"

The man glared at his big companion then turned his attention back to Jacob. "I am Sir David of Doncaster," he said, voice light and in contrast to his appearance.

"You seem troubled. How can I help you?"

Jacob led Sir David away from the ears of the handful of monks who were kneeling in the pews.

"We are a long way from home and I fear that my crops are suffering as a result."

Essentially a yeoman, Jacob did not query how David had become knighted or what he had done to attain a high status. Rather, he focused Sir David's mind on the loyalty of his faith, assuring him that God will see him clear to a successful harvest. But there was one question that Jacob had to have answered before this day was over.

"Sir David, how do you know Bishop Sigmurului?"

The knight frowned. "You do not know? He was with us at Not-"

With a crash, the main door to the chapel burst open, in its arched frame stood Shandor, flanked by the remaining vampires.

Huddling behind the undead Abbot was Sigmurului, his white robes caked in blood. Shandor grabbed the bishop and flung him down the nave.

The giant stood, his quarterstaff ready. Sir David's sword was out and in his hand in a flash.

"Father, let us handle this," Sir David said and motioned for Jacob to step out of the way.

"I knew you'd retreat here, Jacob. Ever faithful." Shandor's voice echoed around the chapel as he stepped forward. Ahead of him, the bishop struggled to his feet. Jacob felt driven to watch him rather than help, but his years of service would not allow him to do so.

He sat Sigmurului down in the nearest pew. The old bishop wheezed and groaned like a punctured bellows but still had the strength to speak.

"Shandor, your time has passed. You are not what you used to be. Your soul is bedevilled now."

"I am enriched!" called the Abbot, arms raised. "*Your* God was wrong. All those years I was penitent to him, waiting for the immortality once my earthly life was over. But now, Lucifer himself has seen fit to give me *both*!"

Jacob shook his head, tears welling. "But what have you become?"

"Allow me to show you," Shandor purred and glided forward.

The giant was suddenly in front of Jacob, quarterstaff out, its sharp tip inches from Shandor's chest. "No further," his deep voice sounded.

"How have you come back? I saw the whitethorn on your casket! I ordered your body to be dismembered!" screeched Sigmurului then thrust a bony arm outwards. "He's evil! Kill him! Kill him now!" The giant looked over to David, who seemed hesitant. "Do as I say! You are here at *my* command!" That was true, but David and the giant only took their orders from Robert. The bishop did not understand. These men refused to do as he said and as for his own priests...they had been instructed to destroy Shandor's body to stop his undead resurrection. *But there he stood!*

Shandor grabbed the quarterstaff but the giant's grip was firm. Shandor moved again, his superior vampire strength winning out, and the giant stumbled to the chapel floor, the quarterstaff clattering to his side.

Jacob pulled out his crucifix but the Abbot merely sneered at the symbol, instead crouching to lunge at the giant's neck.

"Enough!"

Ismael was standing on the balcony. Shandor hissed, hungry and wishing to be rid of these God-fearing things. "I need to feed!"

"I said enough!" Ismael swooped down and landed between the pews, some knocked over by his weight. "You do not command here!"

"It seems more than one of us would like to be," growled Sir David, glancing at the prone Sigmurului.

"Stand, all of you," commanded the blonde vampire. "*I* am superior here."

Sir David held tight to his sword, eyeing up the newcomer. "You are one of the Celebrants?"

Ismael almost looked haughty as the knight realised his position.

"David," the giant growled, "if we take him alive..."

David nodded. "For years we've been looking for one of you."

"And now that you've found me, you want to keep me as your pet?" Ismael laughed. "I think not."

David and the giant stood firm together, weapons ready. Ismael alone would be hard enough to capture - but there were other vampires in the room including Shandor and so Ismael would prove almost impossible to ensnare. A Celebrant, though, would be too much of a prize to let go.

As if knowing of the futility of their plan, Ismael motioned for the vampires behind him to gather together, stalking slowly up the nave to the steps. Jacob, David and the giant, who Jacob was sure he'd heard being called Johann by David, backed up into the iconostasis. Jacob crossed himself and clutched his rosaries so tight that the blood was draining from his gingers.

David's eyes flicked to the left, seeing the light outside change, grow brighter. Dawn was upon them and all they needed were a few more moments.

"The font..." whispered David and the giant nodded, waiting until the vampires were almost upon them. Then with a mighty lunge, the giant threw his weigh against the font and the stone container tumbled and cracked to the ground, spilling holy water down the nave and between the pews.

Taken aback, the vampires stood rooted to the spot. They hissed, they spat, they cursed. But they did not move! Ismael had launched himself back up to the balcony, however.

"It's water! Just water!" Ismael screamed, seeing the first shafts of sunlight creep up the walls from the arrow slits. "Move! Move out of the way!"

But like children, they would not, their fear keeping them where they were. Whether it was the *idea* that it was holy water or not, Ismael didn't know, but he knew the liquid, blessed as it was, could not harm them.

"Take them! Leave none of them alive!" cried Ismael, his fangs bared. "Do not be afraid of the water!"

But it was no use. The vampires, Shandor included, would not move. And resolutely, the sun moved up in the sky, throwing its great beams outwards and in through the arrow slits.

Like daggers of light, they struck the immobile vampires and it was as if God himself had finally fought back in this most holiest of places. Each of them burst into flames, clawed hands outstretched, writhing in the heat. Shandor fell to the floor, muddy robes turning the water dirty brown, caught in the sunlight. Tears of blood coursed down his face as he reached out to Jacob. The Abbot new he was no longer part of this world and opened his mouth to speak. But the sun had fried his tongue and no sound came.

Yet Jacob, knowing that face so well after so many years, knew that even now in his death throes, the once-proud Pretorius Shandor wanted forgiveness, his last rites, his soul saved.

But it was too late.

For he and his siblings in darkness exploded, showering the chapel and its terrified living in sticky, burnt undead flesh.

Ismael threw a hand over his eyes, enraged, and spun around, the darkest exit away from the day his goal.

Chapter 25

The north gateway of the Dambovita Citadel looked out across the austere plains of Wallachia, the great peaks of the Carpathians rising through the heavy clouds far in the distance.

Either side of the gateway, itself an arch made of pentelic marble, the mighty walls stretched along in each direction and disappeared into the mist.

Apollinari and Claudia, weary and chilled to their bones, moved under the cornice, above which the central tablet sat, bearing a dedicatory inscription written in Wallachian but defaced now by the vicious chisels and axes of the Turkish cuckoos.

The frieze along the cornice depicted a line of both military and civil officials, along with sacrificial animals. Flanking the central arch, the side bays each contained a shallow niche-like aedicular doorway that led into the guts of the defence walls themselves.

Once within the Citadel itself, they saw the wood and iron gates torn from their hinges and laying shattered across the ground.

A usual afternoon here would have meant such bustle and frenetic activity, but today the streets and market squares were deserted. Upturned braziers and smouldering stalls greeted the newcomers and not the typical oppressive traders coercing and convincing unwary passers-by that their lives would be unfulfilled without the wares they were pushing.

"Where has everybody gone?"

It was a question from Claudia's lips that echoed the thoughts running around inside Apollinari's head. "If there was a man who was here to answer that, I would very much like to meet him."

Claudia paused at a gloomy alleyway, sensing it was not entirely empty. "In the shadows, there are assassins standing still. The bond between darkness and evil must not be underestimated. We are not alone, uncle. The undead are stirring."

They walked with great care, the shadows moving around them, shapes in the dark side streets moving back out of view. Apollinari could feel eyes watching, scanning them for threats and danger. He clasped his bag close to him under his cassock, feeling the reassuring shapes of the glass phials against his hip.

"There's hope," said Apollinari, seeing a flurry of dark shapes moving along the battlements. "Not your shadows, but men."

"Turks? They would surely kill us."

A thunderous boom from without the Citadel shook the ground beneath them. "I fear their enemy may do that for them."

The Wallachian catapults were breaking through Dambovita's easterly perimeter and Apollinari hurried them deeper into the ice-covered fortress.

He ducked instinctively, pulling Claudia close to him, as the sound of collapsing masonry rang out across the inner city. His boots made the ice creak as he carefully trod across the cobbles and down a narrow street.

"We'll be entombed if the walls collapse!" said Claudia.

Up on the precarious slush-filled battlements, the only remaining Turkish infantry in the Citadel saw, in the distance along the brow of a hill, a line of their impaled comrades. It was a signal more terrifying that any embroidered dragon of Dracula's viciousness and they valiantly tried to ignore the sight, instead concentrating on showering the advancing enemy in arrows and hot oil. But the razed north gates and the collapsing of the eastern wall meant that no matter what they did or how many men they had (in fact it was a pathetic eighty compared to the one-thousand heading their way), Dracula would soon be back inside the Wallachian-build Citadel.

The dark figures of Apollinari and Claudia went unnoticed beneath them, as the monk had thought.

Pausing at a corner, Apollinari raised a finger to a dog that had come barking at them from a building. Glaring at the mange-ridden mongrel as it fell silent, the monk continued to lead on, turning this way and that to reach the exterior wall of the main building itself. With still some braziers lit, the heavy doors finally came into view – and in time, Dracula's catapults would soon make easy work of them and Apollinari wondered if it would not be logical to simply keep out of the way and let the Wallachians make entry for them.

Claudia grabbed his wrist tight, startled by a waxy-looking skeletal figure in a leather apron huddled against a damp wall. In twisted hands the old man held a clump of whitethorn.

Apollinari knelt and felt his neck for a pulse. It was so weak that the monk had to try more than once to find it.

"I think his time has come," Apollinari whispered, a hand on the old man's feeble chest. But grey eyes flickered opened and looked around to see who had come."What happened to you?"

It hadn't been the Wallachians who had left him here for they had yet to penetrate this far. And why would it have been the Turks? He was clearly a servant here.

Isak raised a hand weakly, the whitethorn falling to his lap. "Leave here..." His voice was almost a whisper and Apollinari leaned in. "The vampires...they rule here now."

"How many are there?"

Isak shook his head. "My master did not survive. He is like them now."

"Your master is a vampire?"

"He sits at the head. But he is not who he was."

Apollinari's knees began to ache so he shifted to a more comfortable position. Claudia kept a look out at the edge of the alley.

"What does that mean?"

"His heart...is not his own." Isak's head drooped so the monk gently held his chin.

Apollinari knew what the gnarled old man was referring to but was still cautious to ask. "Does your master call himself by a different name now?"

A nod. Another question that Apollinari already knew the answer to.

"Caleb."

The monk sank to the floor and looked at Claudia. *It's happened*, he thought. *Caleb had been resurrected as the Grimoire foretold.* Apollinari would be little surprised if the vampire had not turned most of the Citadel's residents and killed the rest. And if that was so, the vampire horde would indeed be of huge numbers now. How was he expected to destroy them all?

"Was you master a Turk?"

Isak nodded. "He was a good man. Loyal to his people, to his Sultan. Now he is of the darkness. Please," begged Isak, focusing on Apollinari's cassock and grabbed it weakly, "can you redeem his soul?"

"Your master no longer exists, my friend," Apollinari said sadly. "But I will restore his faith to his God. You have my word."

Isak seemed to be content with that and leant back against the wall. He never moved again.

Apollinari stood and returned to Claudia. "Anything?"

Claudia pointed into the sky. It glowed orange. "It won't be long until Dracula and his army arrives. They have set light to most of the outer buildings." She glanced behind her uncle to the old man. "What do you intend to do?"

"Caleb *is* in there," Apollinari said, gesturing to the mighty building behind them.

"He is a vampire. Kill him as he would be killed. A silver blade to the neck then burn the *pizdă*."

Apollinari disagreed. "The *Tertium Quid* cannot be disposed of quite so simply. We have to get to the heart and break the spell that binds it to the chest in which it sits."

"Hmm. And the other vampires?"

"Well," replied the monk, a smile playing across his lips, "for them, it's the old fashioned way. Come on, let's go."

The frieze above Dambovita's west gate was all but obliterated: the result of the invading *bashi-bazouk*. It was scorched too now, the fury of the recent Greek

Fires adopted by Dracula's army also having done their work. The gate itself had been re-erected and barricaded from the inside.

Mansi pushed hard against it, feeling it give a little. With some determination and brute strength, he reasoned he could move it enough to allow Verrecchia to squeeze through.

After a while and some angry pauses, Mansi had managed to get Verrecchia over the threshold and into the Citadel's grounds.

"Is it clear?" asked Mansi.

Unlike the section that his mentor Apollinari had arrived at not so long ago, the western quarter was rather more residential, reflecting the lower number of foreign visitors in this area during the Wallachian rule. Most visitors to the Citadel arrived by the north or south gates.

But like the rest of the area leading up to the central building, it was devoid of people and there was a distinct aroma of burnt flesh in the air.

"There's been some sort of battle here," Verrecchia called back. "I can't see anybody but there are fires burning everywhere." He peered through a gaping window of the nearest building. His sheltered upbringing meant that he didn't recognise the mass of dark red and sickly yellow across a little table for what it was: a shredded corpse, half-consumed and possibly female. "Are you coming?" Verrecchia listened out but no reply came. He repeated the question then, worried, nipped back to the barricade. It was closed again. He pulled at it but it would not budge. "Mansi...are you there? Mansi?"

On the other side, Mansi was on his knees, a sword at his throat. At the other end of the weapon, Popescu pressed a finger firmly to his own lips, signalling to Mansi to keep his silence as Verrecchia's muffled voice came through the gate.

Popescu was motionless and clearly able to stand there for as long as necessary until the monk had decided to give up.

But it would not be Popescu's decision this evening.

"If you can hear me," called Verrecchia, "I'm going to see if I can get help."

Stupid child, Mansi thought, guessing Popescu considered the same judging by the raising of his thick eyebrows. Where the boy would go Mansi had know way of telling. He himself had only been to the Citadel a couple of times before but that was as part of military convoy and so his geography of the place was limited. And if he ever did get in, it would be hindered further by the mist that was rolling inexorably towards them.

Eventually, Popescu lowered both his sword from Mansi's windpipe and his finger from his own lips.

"Who the fuck are you?" Mansi spat, recognising Popescu's uniform. Mansi was dressed quite similarly but that didn't seem to have deterred Popescu from suppressing him.

"Alexandru Popescu, captain in the Wallachian army, loyal to the rightful Prince of Wallachia, Vlad Dracula."

Mansi respected the chain of command but here it seemed worthless. He had no compunction to maintain it, especially with this pompous fool. "Why are you skulking around here?"

"Who are you?" Popescu asked instead. "You are dressed as I. Have you lost your contingent?"

If Popescu was showing his feathers then so would Mansi. "I am here at the direct request of the Prince himself."

Popescu tensed. Mansi noticed.

"Why?"

"I am not at liberty to discuss that," Mansi retorted, enjoying the verbal sparring.

"What is your name and rank, soldier?" Popescu was becoming riled.

Mansi motioned to stand and Popescu stepped back, his weapon still drawn however.

Now on his feet, Mansi was a little conceited to note that he was nearly a head taller than this captain.

"My name is not important. My mission is none of your concern – unless you wish to assist me?" Mansi realised he had spoken before he had thought. But he had to get into the Citadel for he was convinced Ilona *was* in there. As puffed up as this captain was, an extra resource (and, arguably, one with more strength than young Verrecchia) would be useful. It was just a pity that it was Popescu, the reason that Ilona was outside the safety of the Târgoviste palace in the first place. But Mansi wasn't to know that.

It would only become apparent in the desperate hours ahead of them.

In a thin part of the Vlasie, the erratic rhythmic tapping of the pots suspended from either side of the painted wagon signalled the frantic motion of the small procession cutting a desperate trail through the forest.

Zucco had been unsuccessful in recapturing Verrecchia and his brief allegiance with Ismael had left him anxious of the repercussions. So, like the coward he was, he fled, determined to get as far away from this part of the world as quickly as possible. But his affright meant that he never even considered for a moment that She who must be worshipped could never be out-distanced!

Zucco cracked his whip hard across the wide back of his horse, urging it onwards. The mare was not used to a canter let alone a gallop but the gypsy was relentless and so the horse struggled on.

In the back, Marta clung on as the caravan swayed sickeningly. She spat a few insults in her husband's general direction but he ignored her. He had done for years. He always would do.

The road ahead - north to Ploieşti then Bistritz and eventually Rădăuţi, their home town – would be fraught with danger, none more so than from the vicious Carpathian bandits who frequented the Borgo Pass. But the mist that had descended startlingly quickly was soupy-thick and Zucco could feel it clinging to his lungs. It had already slowed them down, the horse not able to see beyond its own nose. It became jumpy and it took all of Zucco's considerable strength to keep the caravan straight and on the road. Even one wheel hitting the ditch that rang along either side of the track would spell the end of their-

The horse lurched and reared up. The caravan crunched and twisted, its right front wheel locking in the deep trench. With the horse panicked (Zucco could not see what it was that had caused such a reaction), there was little he could do and he called out to Marta as he felt the caravan topple. He jumped clear, his heavy frame landing awkwardly on the rough path. Heard his ankle *crack* as it broke, the pain a red mist behind his eyes. It even drowned out the screeching wail as his wife tumbled within the caravan, the transport coming to rest on its side, roof titled downwards and all four wheels freely spinning to a stop.

As Zucco cradled his leg he knew, even without the break in his bones, that he would never be able to right the caravan again.

But that wasn't his most immediate concern. Neither was the salvation of his wife from the upturned wagon.

The wolf, head larger than normal and with a thick black-grey mane that hid broad shoulders, stood in the middle of the road and stared at him.

The horse, half-on and half-off the road, whinnied and snorted as it struggled in its twisted harness that had snapped free from the caravan. The wolf growled back, yellow eyes glowing.

Jurat considered changing back into human form but as a werewolf his fur kept him warm. And it also meant he was more powerful this way, stronger to wreak his revenge on this gutless gypsy.

Zucco swallowed hard, his throat dry. The fog was dense, denser than ever and all he could see of the wolf was its snout back to its shoulders. For all he could tell, the damn beast could have been huge.

A low growl and Zucco tried to shuffle back. But his shattered ankle shot incredible waves of pain up his body. He gasped in breathless agony.

"Go...go away!" was all he could muster, waving an arm as if to frighten the creature.

But Jurat stood deathly still, the rumble in his throat continuing.

"Cast a spell! Can you not cast a spell?" cackled Marta as she pulled herself from the wreckage. Zucco didn't need to turn around to see the state she was in. She looked a bloody mess most of the time anyway and a somersault inside the caravan would have made no difference. Stomping on to the road, she stopped and huffed. "I can't see a thing! Where are you, Ygor?"

"Stay where you are!" he shouted over his shoulder. "Don't come over here."

"This fog – I've never known anything like it!" As Marta waved her hands around, the fog seemed to follow then re-coalesce, as if it were conscious of her movements. "What's going on?" As she shuffled forward on bunyoned feet, she heard Jurat's growl. She inhaled sharply, the fog burning her tonsils. "Is that my boy? Corbiu, you come home to mummy?"

"Don't be soft, woman," said Zucco. "This here wolf is no boy."

Jurat's ears pricked at the mention of Corbiu's name, his canines slavering at the thought that she considered herself to be the boy's mother. Angered further, he loped forward, massive paws silent on the stony track.

Zucco clutched his chest. "Stay back! You keep away from me you fucking werewolf!"

Use your magic now, gypsy, if you can, Jurat thought. He knew the man had no power over him while his ankle was broken. It was almost as if it had taken his spells from him. The man was weak and the woman was slow. This would be an easy kill – and sweetest of all because it would be retribution for the caging of Corbiu, his were-brother.

That thick mane was flung back and Jurat let out an almighty howl. Then he pounced.

Zucco threw his arms over his face but his flesh was sliced like paper, Jurat making his way through to the gypsy's face – and tore it clean away. Marta, heading to the sound of screaming, loomed up out of the fog, a spell at her hands. Jurat staggered back as Marta weaved a protective chant around them but her concentration was broken as she saw her husband's head. Jurat took that moment and jumped, swiping at Marta and slicing her throat open.

She gurgled and twisted, eyes wide as the air entered no further than her gaping neck. Blood spewed thick and red from between her lips. It was more than enough for Jurat to resist the temptation to feed, the scent of the kill was that strong in his snout. Yet he would not feast, not on these pathetic creatures. He padded back out of the way to watch them die, knowing it would be enough that they would cease to be.

But the fog had other ideas.

As he sat there on his hind legs, the thick grey gumbo hanging low in the air and clinging to the ground, the trees, the backs of those caught in the middle of it, seemed to move and grow even thicker – if that was possible – around his prey.

By this time, the Zuccos had fallen in a heap on top of each other but they were becoming obscured by the fog, as if *becoming* the fog.

Before long, Jurat could see nothing of them and wondered if they were still dying. He could certainly still smell them.

A dual scream gave him his answer. The sounds that came from the larynx of the dying human body were unique: his friend Raudúlfr would have said it was to warn the dead of Valhalla that more fallen were to join them.

But whatever the reason, this time it felt different, like the beginning of something new.

He snarled as the fog seemed to grow brighter for an instant, then it simply…dissolved.

And there before him in the clear, cold air, all tall and elegant, was a woman, olive-skinned and robed in fine white silk.

He didn't know how but he knew that she had been borne from those dying screams, had somehow formed into reality as the Zuccos left theirs. He also knew that his purpose now was to follow her. There were no other thoughts in his head.

"You are pure now," she purred, gliding towards him, leaving the finished lives of the Zuccos behind her to evaporate into the air.

Jurat realised what she had done. There was no panic, no fear. Just acceptance. As she had found solid form, so he had *become* a solid form. He was no longer a werewolf. He was lycore – a once-man. This woman had taken the ability to transform from him and made him permanently one shape – and as a result he had to obey her. His human voice forever gone now, he could only communicate as the true giant of a wolf he now was and licked her outstretched hand.

Marise smiled and stroked the lycore's generous mane and together they walked into the night.

Still bathed in the azure light of a few upright braziers, a row of stables came into view as Verrecchia turned a corner. It was a welcome shelter from the biting cold winds that whipped through the streets.

He had been creeping through the Citadel's ground for a good while now and hadn't seen another living soul. Only the battle cries from the battlements overhead had told of any life here – yet here was a place, warm and still occupied! The young novice monk only hoped that whoever was in there was friendly.

He sidled up to a half open door. There was a man inside preparing a steed.

What was he to do? Ask for shelter, using his religious position as a bargaining tool? Bearing in mind most Turks were Muslims, would he take kindly to a lone Catholic without the protection of the Wallachians?

Verrecchia decided to play it safe and backed away, but tripped over the brazier. He cried out as his forearms met with the hot metal drum.

Immediately, the man came out. Verrecchia, cradling his burns, tried to smile. The Turk looked him up and down a few times, glanced in the general direction of the west gate as a another missile met its target.

"You must be one of the last left," the man growled.

Verrecchia tried to stay calm. His stomach was churning and his arms were agony. "I thought I was – until I found you, that is."

"I've got standing orders to remain here to see that the gentry makes it out of here safely. The Wallachian cunts won't keep many of us alive. Why the Governor feels it necessary to waste a good horse on the likes of you is not for me to say," the horse master snapped. "He knows we need all for the battle – unless you intend to ride ahead of the cavalry?"

"But there's..." What would be the point in telling this man that the only Turks left were the handful futilely defending the Citadel up on the battlements? "No, I don't," Verrecchia responded instead.

"I thought not. You've been ordered to flee then, have you?"

"You are...very perceptive," Verrecchia said, sounding as forthright as he could.

"Like his doctor," the man drawled, "the Governor's wrangler knows much and says little."

Verrecchia jumped into the stables as a body fell from the battlements into the snow at his feet.

"Quickly," the man said, grabbing Verrecchia and pushing him towards a large black beast of a horse. The man said not another word, instead ensuring the fastenings of the saddle were secure, attaching a dagger to the harness. In silence, Verrecchia mounted the steed and eased her out of the warm stables. The creature whinnied as debris landed nearby from above but the monk urged her on into a gallop into the maze that was the Citadel's inner city. A bell started tolling in the distance. The rider and mount ploughed through the narrow streets.

Behind him, he heard the man cry out as a troop of Wallachian soldiers descended on the stables. But he daren't look back, instead crouching low behind the horse's neck.

Some streets and alleys later, Verrecchia slowed his mount down. Where he was headed he knew not and he felt a tightness in his stomach that was hard to ignore. It hurt even worse than his singed arms.

Suddenly, the wall beside him exploded, throwing the horse into a panic. Verrecchia held on to the reigns for fear of being thrown. Deeper into the inner city he was now, but the battle was truly joined, the Wallachian cannons rumbling through the streets at the hands of their masters.

Black shapes began appearing and Verrecchia would have sworn that the very shadows themselves were coming alive! But they were vampires, at last released from behind the locked doors of the catacombs. They swarmed out and over the invading army. It was a challenge to keep out of sight but the monk valiantly hugged the walls, even though the horse was bucking under him. The cries of battle, the sound of metal upon undead bodies and teeth ripping into living flesh meant that neither side noticed Verrecchia dismounting in the shadow of a huge building.

The horse bolted and Verrecchia sadly mused that its life was now virtually over. He realised why the wrangler had kept it back from the battle, why it hadn't been allowed to join the others waiting on the other side of the Citadel, for it was untrained, terrified, and useless.

Verrecchia would be lucky to survive himself if the Wallachians took any interest in him as they thundered by. He had ducked into a narrow side street. The clatter of the armour and weaponry faded as the Wallachians scoured the streets. Peering ahead of him, Verrecchia saw all was clear and so continued his journey. As he reached a turning a devilish cry made him break into a run but he soon came to a halt. There was nothing at the end of the lane. A dead end! No way through. Panicking, the boy staggered against the wall before him. He pulled himself around so his back was flush against the cold, damp barrier.

A vampire was hurtling up the alley towards him.

Verrecchia froze, not able to muster the courage to pray for his own salvation. In a futile gesture, he raised his arms and curled, foetus-like, against the ground. The creature fell dead, quite unexpectedly, at his feet. Its head rolled free from its shoulders.

Verrecchia clutched a hand tight to his mouth, stifling a scream. A shadow fell across him and he feared that one demon had simply been replaced with another. Yet he was alive! Surely it wasn't just to allow something else to slay him instead? Craning his neck up, he heard the snow crunch near his head.

Dracula was standing over him, dark and menacing, the blood of battle on his hands. A sword was in his grip, its tip wavering at the monk's throat.

Verrecchia's eyes widened as he drew a breath.

"You are not Turkish." It was a statement, not a question. Verrecchia shook his head in agreement, the rest of his body joining in for good measure. "Leave here. This is no place for those in fear of God." The man squinted at Verrecchia, laying there in the ice, and retracted his sword. He stepped back and was gone.

From his prone position, Verrecchia breathed out sharply and clambered to his feet. With some tentative steps back the way he had come, he took a few moments to consider his fortune and his faith.

Soon, after a few furtive glances and frozen steps in the winding streets and curling shadows, a massive door met him. It was slightly ajar.

This was the entrance to the Citadel's central building complex and, as he pushed the heavy door back further, the smell of stale incense and spices distressed his nostrils. He could not imagine that his teacher and friend, Giuliano Apollinari, had crossed the same threshold only a little while before.

Chapter 26

Dracula's own entry to the main building some time later was far less sedate. His elite guard swarmed into the massive reception hall, candelabras cold and dark, thick columns stretching to the vaulted ceiling easily able to obscure any number of vampires. The last time Dracula had stood here was when he had been arrested for high treason and taken to Buda for imprisonment for so many years. Within that time, some twelve years, this Citadel had fallen to Turkish might but now the rightful Prince of Wallachia was back and stronger than ever in his bid to reclaim the throne.

The journey to the Great Hall was difficult, fierce confrontations with the demons that lurked here.

Dracula's religious upbringing made this quite straightforward for him: they were creations of the Turks. The fact that they were actually vampires was beyond his comprehension.

How they could be cut down so easily was due to the strains of silver Dracula had ordered his blacksmiths to weave into his and his elite guards' weaponry as a sign of their superior standing. It was this alone that allowed such an easy entry here. The loss of the foot soldiers was to be expected and he paid it no mind.

The vampires had become wise to the forging of the weapons and so had begun to fall back, cowering in the shadows.

Burning torches soon arrived and Dracula ordered the Citadel's occupancy to be brought to its knees once and for all as he reached the double doors to the Hall.

On the other side, Kelele sat in the largest of the three seats, ordered there by Caleb. He had heard the Citadel around him fall to the grip of Prince Vlad's army. He wasn't surprised, of course, for the Prince had fortified this city and instructed his troops well in its secrets.

The Turks had buried themselves deep in this place to seal the mark of Constantinople forever on the landscape of Wallachia – but they hadn't accounted for the superior vampire might, humanistic power struggles and conflicts of no interest to Caleb and the Celebrants.

From his position in the Great Hall, Kelele was easily able to hear all the commotion from the rest of the Citadel and had grown angry at the slaughter of so many of his kind by this brazen Dracula. He had brought the last of the vampires up from the dungeons to surround him. They had fed, not fully, but satisfied enough to remain patient.

Kelele flicked his head towards the huge doors as a great thud came from the other side. The bolted entrance held fast as the thud repeated. Dull voices soaked through the wood and Kelele's Wallachian was not good but good enough to understand that the doors were to be broken down. The thud that came next was different – louder and more forceful. It came again and again, repeated until the doors buckled inwards and fell under the wheels of a battering ram.

The vampires hissed and chittered, waiting for their master to command. But his order was for them to retreat back up to the rafters.

Suddenly, from over the top of the ram, armoured figures swarmed in. In reaction, Kelele staggered back into his chair.

In the doorway, flanked by too many guards for even Kelele to count successfully in a short space of time, was the Prince of Wallachia.

Sword in hand, the Prince stared at the Ethiopian and their dark eyes locked.

Dracula's taut expression never wavered – but who was this man standing at *his* throne? He was not a Turk! But still, there would be no need for words, no need to tell this bastard invader what his punishment would be. This infidel deserved not to be told. To come to his land, to rape the wives of innocent Wallachians, to make sport of the Boyar and to banish the Lord from his home, for all these crimes and more, Prince Vlad would cut open the man standing before him and let rabid dogs eat at the wounds. He would impale his body on a stake outside the Citadel walls to warn any other would-be invaders. And just before death claimed the pathetic form, Vlad would take the Ethiopian down, sew his eyes and mouth shut and keep him, barely alive, in the bowels of Dambovita, in the Citadel's dungeon. Prince Vlad's justice was, without question, the most brutal of any of the Wallachian principals. It gave little room for redemption but ensured that a man could leave his worldly wealth out for all to see without fear of it being stolen.

Kelele, face to face with the person that the whole of this land and of that beyond the forest viewed as a terrifying, blood-thirsty tyrant, reached out and beckoned Dracula to step forward as though he were here as a guest.

"Welcome home, Prince Vlad," Kelele said, opening his arms wide. "Have you to see how insignificant you are to us?"

In response, the *voivode* snapped his fingers and four men double marched from behind him and to the vampire's sides.

Kelele smiled, infuriating the Prince.

"An escort?" Kelele mused. "An escort from the great Vlad's own men? I am honoured indeed."

Prince Vlad motioned again and his men made to hold Kelele fast, but the vampire raised his arms defiantly.

"No."

The deepness of the voice, the harshness with which he spat that simple word, caused Vlad's men to stop, but their prince barked an order at them and, reluctantly, they shuffled forwards.

"I said: *no*."

Casually, as if wafting away an irritating insect, Kelele motioned with his hands in the direction of the soldiers. Dracula repeated his command but his men never moved, never even twitched. Spinning, his long hair following under his helmet, Vlad saw that the men in the doorway were still also.

"There is little point, Prince Vlad," Kelele purred, "for they are quite incapable of obeying any command you now give them."

The Prince hissed an obscenity at him and raised his sword.

"I do not fear you," the vampire stated. "We have little to fear from anyone."

"I demand your life, demon!"

"A demon! Is that what you think I am?" Kelele laughed. It would have been infectious if it wasn't so chilling.

Vlad decided not to maintain this dark-skinned devil's torturous existence. The impudence of the man before him boiled the Catholic's blood and he would take his head from the man's shoulders and claim back the Citadel in the name of God.

And the demon just stood there and laughed at him.

The Prince lunged forward, swinging the heavy sword over his head in a skilfully executed complex whirl. The thick blade came plummeting down, ready to cleave Kelele's skull in two, but the sword thudded to a halt in mid-air, literally a paper-thin distance from the Ethiopian's scalp. Using both hands, Vlad tried to shift the weapon but it was held fast by the invisible grip of the vampire's will.

"You will die at my hand for the blasphemies that your demon-kind have unleashed here today!"

"I am no demon"" Kelele hissed. "I am driven by forces undead and you, warrior Prince, will *never* defeat us."

The Prince's eyes flicked to spy his men rooted to the spot. He looked back at the sword suspended in mid air and let it go, the blade remaining aloft by an invisible grip, snarling at Kelele as the vampire smiled at him.

Like lightning, Vlad unsheathed the two pure silver daggers kept hidden under his breast plate and plunged them deep into the sides of Kelele's torso.

Surprise was not really the right word for what the vampire felt for the scorching of the silver was unlike anything he had ever felt before. Mercifully, it would also be last thing he ever felt – expect for a sudden wave of unalloyed sadness, of regret, of a life long gone. He could smell the African plains once more, feel the hot wind rolling across the flat, relentless landscape;

could see his children gather around him at sunset as he told them stories of the gentleness of Laibon, the first Maasai prophet-magician and the terror of the evil giant Oltatuani.

The Prince removed his knives with a twist and thrust them in again at different points in Kelele's torso. But the odd slapping sound from behind him made him leave the daggers embedded so he could whirl around to face the noise.

Four skinless man-shaped creatures, clearly born from the satanic faith these infidels worshipped, dropped like giant bats from the rafters of the Great Hall, to sway, hypnotically, before the Prince.

Never one to be fearful, except for matters concerning His will, Vlad did not understand why there was a tightness forming in his chest. If he was becoming cowardly in the sight of these demons, he would overcome them and prove his superior might. Spinning back around, the voivode grabbed at the suspended weapon over Kelele's head, nearly toppling as it came free from the unseen grip. Such unholy apparitions would be overwhelmed once the demon's head had left his body. He had to wipe away this veil of blasphemy and exorcise the demons now, before it was too late. His priests could perform the sacred rites after if they so wished.

And so it was that the Prince of Wallachia decapitated the ancient vampire's head from his shoulders in one calculated swing.

Kelele's body folded, turning with the motion to face the Prince, and exploded as he hit the floor.

With the Celebrant gone, the newborn vampires, in blind confusion, began to snap and hiss at each other.

Vlad, breathing hard, had almost forgotten the creatures were there, but was nevertheless angered that they still existed in his Citadel. He batted at them with his sword and noticed his men slowly returning to normality, waking as if from a deep sleep.

With a heightened thrill, the vampires sensed the multitude of hearts beating, one of them even pouncing on Kelele's fleshy mass, lapping at the raw meat. In a flash, two of the creatures launched themselves at the nearest soldiers, while the third...

Prince Vlad felt himself hammering to the hard stone as one of the vampires pounded into his chest. With a cry that would wake the dead and the strength worthy of five men, the Prince flung the creature off but it scrabbled back before the man could stand. Rolling underneath the vampire, Vlad cracked his head against the floor as he tried to retreat from the snapping teeth.

This creature was different to the others, lighter, almost female.

With great horror, Dracula looked deep into the twisting face of the vampire on top of him and finally recognised who she was.

"Ilona!" His body shook, unable to comprehend the vileness of it all. He wanted to scream, to run, to impale the fucking animals that did this to his beloved wife! How had she even got here? "Where is my God? Has he forsaken me! Why has he done this to me?"

He struggled underneath Ilona. He managed to push her away even though her strength was unnatural.

As if broken from a spell, she suddenly focused on him and his eyes widened as she appeared to return to a state to which he was accustomed. Her fangs clicked back into her gums and she swayed, as if drunk.

"My Prince?"

On his back, Dracula reached up to cautiously touch her beautiful face. "There can be no better prize on this earth than one of true love," he said.

She smiled. Ilona smiled! She remembered. Dracula was relieved and his heart jumped. Perhaps she could be saved after all!

"I am a river filled with tears of sadness and heartbreak," Ilona whispered, bloody tears trickling down her face. She knelt before her Prince and stroked his thick black hair, remembering how it used to fall across her shoulders and her breasts as they made love in the summer fields outside Târgoviste. But then her smile dropped and her eyes glowered, bewitched again by the cruel curse of vampirism. "I am sorry, my love. I am truly sorry."

With an undead screech, she flung her head back. White fangs reappeared longer than ever and she sank them deep into her husband's neck.

Dracula cried out in pain and despair and grabbed at her hair.

The flames took hold of the Great Hall around them.

Popescu had lost a good man today. But worse still, he had lost him to the only woman he had truly loved – and she too had gone, turned into the same vile creatures that had attacked them in the cabin.

The captain could have very easily turned around and disappeared into the woods himself, a broken man. But that was not his way. He had spent years under the command of Dracula and, even though he had carried out the ultimate betrayal by stealing Ilona away in the first place, he would not succumb to emotion. Not today.

Perhaps this was retribution, punishment for his actions against his leader and his beloved. With no religion to protect him, he had left himself vulnerable – something which no warrior should ever do.

Mansi stopped suddenly as he realised Popescu was not by his side. Turning back, he saw the man on his knees in the gloomy passageway, hand clasped and mouth silently moving in desperate prayer. The candles along the wall flickered twisted shadows around them.

"Come on, we haven't time for this," Mansi whispered. "This place is crawling with vampires."

Popescu ignored him. If this was a turning point in his life, to finally acknowledge and accept that he was to do God's bidding – in this accursed place more than anywhere – then pray he would.

"Popescu!" Mansi grabbed his companion and hauled him to his feet. "What's the matter with you?"

"What is your mission?"

"What?"

"Your mission. You were sent here by the Prince. Why?"

"Will this get you moving again?"

Popescu nodded, readjusting his sword. "Tell me."

Mansi licked his dry lips. "I am to find and return to Dracula his wife, the Princess Ilona Szilágy."

Popescu's hand was still at his sword and he gripped it hard. *Ilona!* His heart pounded at the sound of her name. This man knew of her. "To what end?"

Mansi shrugged. "To restore their marriage, I assume. I am to do as am I am bid. Why would I question my Lord Prince Dracula?"

Popescu felt then as if he'd been running for eternity for his breath had caught in his chest. "And what are you to do with those who are responsible for taking her from him?"

"That is not my concern. If Dracula demands the lives of those who have done this, let his wrath be merciful."

Popescu let go of the sword hilt. "You and I both know he will never show mercy. Remember the Eastern visitors who had their turbans nailed to their skulls because they would not remove them from their heads? If he considered their own beliefs a sign of disrespect, what would he do to the man who had taken his own wife from him?"

"Perhaps that man should have thought about that before he did it," Mansi replied calmly.

Popescu thought the same, yet did not regret his actions. But at what cost? Ilona would never be his now, not after what she had become. His eyes fell to his hands. There might as well have been her blood on them for all his actions had been worth.

"And why would you be so concerned?" Mansi asked. "You're making me start to wonder if it was you."

And then Popescu's sword was out and back at Mansi's throat, his heart in turmoil and his fear of Dracula's wrath pounding in his veins.

"Popescu, we've been here before. Put it away. I am not your enemy."

Popescu's shoulders sagged a little and he nodded. His sword disappeared back into its sheath with a gentle *swoosh* that was satisfying to Mansi's ears.

"If we find her, we'll both take the credit," Mansi said.

Popescu did not reply but walked ahead. If they did find her, as Mansi hoped, there was little neither of them could do to ensure Ilona would not slaughter them both.

There was a ringing in Apollinari's ears, one that wouldn't stop no matter how much he shook his head. There was a *drip drip drip* to add to the tone as water hit the flagstone by the narrow door to the catacombs. Claudia was chained to the wall as he was, both in a tiny cell in the guts of the Dambovita Citadel. Orange glowed all about them as flames and hot coals burned in grates and fire pits.

The abduction from the dark passages above them three nights ago had been swift and silent and Apollinari was surprised that they had not been harmed, apart from the strike about his head to stop him from struggling.

Three vampires stood before them now, eyes white and teeth bared. They were either hungry or angry – or both. Apollinari mused that sometimes it was difficult to tell.

The blonde one toed the hot coals in the fire pit near him. The embers popped and floated as if sentient. "We are at a stalemate, Giuliano."

"I was of the belief that stalemate meant equal footing," said Apollinari, the chains biting into the monk's wrists. "But you seem to have me at a disadvantage."

"Is this Ismael?" asked Claudia.

"Does my reputation precede me?" Ismael traced Claudia's jaw line with a strong index finger. "Why, Giuliano, I am embarrassed that you speak of me."

"It is not on favourable terms. It has *never* been on favourable terms." Which wasn't exactly true.

There had been a time when Ismael and Apollinari had almost been inseparable. But that was a long time ago and Apollinari could no longer see anything beyond that pallid skin and those pin-sharp fangs. Ismael had always had pale eyes, so his becoming a vampire had not really changed that, but they were white and soulless now, cold and unfeeling.

The night Ismael was transformed, the same night that the Church essentially turned its back on Apollinari, the monk would never forget. If he'd only gone through with the task that had been set before him and not hesitated, not been cowardice, then Ismael would still be alive today.

"I *am* Ismael," the blonde vampire said to Claudia, politeness as impeccable as his outfit. "This is Rintoul and he," he continued, gesturing to a brute in the corner with his evil eye on her, "is your gaoler. Ekvan, I believe his name is."

"What do you want with us? Don't you ever tire of this feud between you and Giuliano?"

"This is not about us," Ismael replied. Whether he still held Apollinari responsible for the events on the banks of the Towy river nearly twenty years ago, the monk did not know, but he would have been surprised if the vampire had been truly exonerating. Certainly it was not the vampire manner and Apollinari had learnt the hard way that to expect forgiveness from something so vilely undead, irrespective of the bond that had been during a living friendship, was pointless and, worse, devastating.

Pulling from his velvet cloak the battered, leather Grimoire, Ismael thumbed the thick pages open. "You bring this here? You expect to use it?"

"I've never seen that before."

"What is it?" asked Claudia.

Ismael looked between his two captives. "Have you rehearsed this little routine?" Neither of them answered. "Do you know whose blood this is which inks this book?

No? Then I'll tell you." He came up close to Claudia's face. "It is the author's. Philippe de Blanc. A relation of Apollinari's, I believe."

"If you say so. It makes no difference to me."

"It makes no difference to *me*," mimicked Ismael. "But to my master it has everything to do with *you*, isn't that correct?"

"Like I say, I don't know anything of which you speak. Apollinari is simply a monk from—"

"He is part of the de Blanc family: Father Giuliano Apollinari *de Bianco*." Ismael slid close to the monk. "Do you not share your life history with your friends? You bored *me* about it often enough."

"Father Apollinari's business is his own," Claudia spat.

Ismael frowned as a thought crossed his face. "You are familiar." Claudia snorted at him. "No. You are *very* familiar. You remind me of..." Ismael raised a finger. "Are you Agatha's daughter?"

Claudia's expression gave the vampire the answer he was looking for. Apollinari grew concerned.

"Leave her be, Ismael."

"Do you have silver in your veins, too?"

"It's not hereditary," interjected Apollinari. "But all the same, I guess that makes you rather scared of us."

Ismael threw back his head and laughed, blonde locks moving. "Far from it, my friend."

"Then what stalemate do you refer to?"

"I cannot spill your blood. You cannot spill mine."

"I wouldn't be so assured with that latter statement, Ismael. And surely it is up to your resurrected master whether or not I live or die. I assume it *was* him who ordered our incarceration?"

"Caleb has not seen the night sky for something like four hundred years. He does not know you but he knows you exist. Both of you. He sits in this Citadel and he rules. But I am empowered."

"By knowing things he doesn't know? That's rather a weak argument, I think," Apollinari said calmly. He sighed and considered for a moment. "Unless you mean to overthrow him?"

That laugh came again but this time Apollinari could sense nervousness beneath it. He knew Ismael well.

"You are to be taken before him. He demands an audience with the surviving de Blanc bloodline. This book will tell him all he needs to know."

Ismael tossed it into the fire pit.

"No!" exclaimed Apollinari as the Grimoire popped and crackled amongst the coals, its ancient pages curling into ash: de Blanc's life's work gone within seconds

"An anti-climax? No one will ever know now what it truly contained. The first act in the final destruction of the de Blanc curse upon our kind!"

"And the means by which Caleb could have found true perpetuity, beyond the whitethorn and the silver. And you could have had that before him! You could have been the Vampire Celebrant Eternal!"

Ismael's face hardened with what Apollinari was saying. "You lie."

"It wasn't just about how to destroy the vampires, the demons, and the undead of this world. It was also how to call them, tame them, resurrect them, *immortalise them.*" Apollinari winced as Ismael struck him across the face. He was lucky, however, that the vampire hadn't unleashed his full fury for the monk's head would have been knocked clean off his shoulders.

"And now you have to remain at his right hand, in his shadow."

"No..." Ismael hissed.

"It appears I was right. You did intend to replace him with yourself. Is vampire society so maladjusted that you would assassinate to take office?"

"It is no different to your own kind's twisted control of power," Ismael snarled. "Get them down." Ekvan and Rintoul moved like lightning and the two prisoners were freed from their shackles. "Take them to him."

Chapter 27

There was no need to hide, thought Mansi. They would not be noticed, two extra figures amongst this throng. He stepped out of the shadows, pulling Popescu with him and strode purposefully in the direction that the people were headed.

"Why is this place not deserted? We were led to believe it was," said Popescu over the clamour of shuffling bodies.

"Look at the state of them. They are prisoners here."

"The vampires take *prisoners*?"

"It seems so."

There were something like a hundred or so all headed in the same direction: soldiers, servants, anyone left, even the senior ladies-in-waiting. All moving resolutely and at a pace too fast to be interrupted or spoken to, Popescu ignored the throng and instead stepped in the way of an old woman, spine bent with work and age.

"You," he began, dropping a hand behind her neck. The crone stopped and strained to look up and back at him.

"What is happening here?"

"We have been ordered to the Great Hall," she said, snorting at Mansi's concerned expression behind

Popescu. "I wouldn't get too excited. These things are usually of no importance to the likes of us, being from the seraglio, but we have to be seen to be there."

The old woman hobbled off, but before she was quickly lost in the tide of people, Mansi grabbed her shoulder. "Do you know who it was who has summoned you?"

The woman turned. "The Governor, of course. No one else makes the whole Citadel move so suddenly."

Mansi was amazed. "The whole Citadel? But there's only..."

Popescu pushed the woman away and she disappeared into the crowd. "The vampires have twisted their minds. They believe the Citadel to still be under foreign rule. But why?"

"Because it seems the vampires need them alive for a bit longer. And deceiving them means they can control them better. Let's find out."

Before Popescu could object, Mansi joined the flow. Down a few more widening corridors and the towering doors of the Great Hall came into view. The throng began to slow as each and everyone filed into the chamber. Mansi and Popescu stayed at the rear.

Soon all were inside and, with a great, final thud the doors shut behind them. The echoes of mumbling voices were solely contained within the high-vaulted room. Mansi was unsure if the additional thuds he heard weren't great bolts sliding across the exit on the other side.

Around them, the walls were scorched and charred and the roof was weakened. The huge table was blackened and on its side. The fire started by Dracula had burnt itself out but the damage was not just at the surface.

The sudden call of two trumpeters from the far end of the hall, behind the raised dais, culled the congregation into silence. And, as the sound of the shrill fanfare dropped off, Ismael stepped up to the main throne and raised his arms.

"By the power of Allah and all that Islam is power of, I give you His Eminence the Lord, Count and Governor, Yozgatli Tanyel!"

At this, hushed whispers whipped around the hall. Mansi, as intrigued as the rest of them, remained quiet. The sting of smouldering wood reached into his nostrils. *Where is Tarih-i-al-Osman?* The confused congregation soon fell into silence again as the Governor took his position at the largest of the three seats.

Popescu recognised Tanyel from previous skirmishes elsewhere but was taken aback by how deathly pale he looked. There was something about him that wasn't quite right, like a painting that had been copied over and over until it vaguely resembled the original but was still nevertheless recognisable.

"*Tamahkarin gozunu toprak dozurur*," the man said, arms raised. His accent was not that of a Turk.

Death puts an end to greed? What did this mean?

"Allah has seen it necessary to give your allegiance to me. Your former Governor Abdu Tarih-i-al-Osman has gone to tell of his learnings to the devil himself and so I now rule here, in the land of the blasphemers."

Whispers raced around the congregation. So the count *was* dead – but by whose hand?

"It is my right that I now pass judgement on to those who would see fit to harm the cherished among us.

"I have been sent forth as a witness and as bearer of news and warnings, so that you may have faith in Satan now instead, and that you may assist Him, honour Him and praise Him morning and evening. You are bidden to serve Satan and worship Him alone. I am bidden to be the first of those who submit to Him." The man caressed the lip of a large highly-polished bowl that stood before him. The golden cradle that held it was firm tall and solid. "You will obey me and only me."

In unison, the congregation said:

"I will never disobey, my Lord, for I fear the torment of a fateful day."

"I am your only Lord," the man continued. "I am Caleb and you *will* serve me! It is ordained that every nation we have destroyed shall never rise again and I will bring that to you that you have been promised: when we can walk freely across His earth without the fear of our children being hunted down by the living!"

A slow panic began to wash over the congregation. This man, once Tanyel but now Caleb, used the right words they would expect to hear but had twisted them. But because Tarih-i-al-Osman had never been so passionate about his people as this Caleb was, they still wanted to listen, to understand and to believe.

"You, all of you here," Caleb said, right index finger hooked but pointing, it felt, to every individual in the hall, "you all have predestined for Hell many *jinn* and many men; they have hearts, yet cannot understand; eyes, yet they do not see; ears, yet they do not hear. They are like beasts, indeed, yet less enlightened.

"Such are the heedless.

"Remember that *your* God first created man from an essence of clay, then placed him, a living germ, in a safe place. The clay he fashioned into bones, then clothed the bones with the flesh from the germ, thus bringing forth the Creation: the Golem! I, Caleb, have been blessed, in the name of Satan the Benevolent, Satan the Gracious, with the gift of the *new* Golem: the right to create the creatures with which Satan intends to wipe clean His earth of the diseased and the living!"

So it was clear. Mansi felt his chest tighten. Caleb was not the Governor. He was not a Moslem Turk. He was something else.

"Behold the vessels who will do his work! Behold the *vampyr*!"

A tremendous screech filled the air and the congregation all looked upwards, tracing the sound to the beams of the tiered roof. As the giant candelabra swung gently, they saw huddled shadows. They pointed and they gasped. Some of the men and women uttered panicked screams. As if triggered by the fear, the horde of vampires dropped, bat-like, from the fire-scarred beams to swoop and curl their way across the heads of the undulating mass below them.

So many veins. So many hearts beating.

By the doors, Mansi cursed, using a blasphemy only a Catholic would in a room full of Moslems. But even the vain mention of the Christ's name did not stir those nearest Mansi and Popescu against them. The vampires had them in fits of near hysteria, Mansi increasingly concerned that they would be crushed in the stampede to get out. He and Popescu shuffled along the wall to a corner. A beast of a vampire landed on the wall above them, swinging its skinless head in their direction. Its talons clicked on the bricks in time with the movement of its jaw.

Popescu froze, his hand unwilling to move to the sword at his hip. Suddenly a man, a large Turk, heaved into him. Popescu gasped at the pressure, feeling the man's great elbow against his chest. The vampire swung out at the man, a claw tearing into his shoulder. The Turk shouted something at the creature which used both elongated hands to grab the man by the neck and heaved him up out of the crowd and to the rafters. Popescu felt Mansi urge him on and, forcing his starched joints to move, threw himself to the floor, his breath catching in his lungs as he felt more vampires swoop over their heads.

And so it continued around the Great Hall. Vampires dropping like spiders onto the backs of writhing bodies, pulling up men and women alike, and those unfortunate enough not to be battered against the exit as the congregation desperately tried to claw the huge wooden doors open.

Mansi stayed low, edging his way behind the upturned table to the raised dais in an attempt to avoid the erratic swinging of swords as well as flashing talons. He realised Popescu was no longer with him.

Glancing around him, he saw that Caleb was the only person in the room standing tall save for a monk and a woman, bound and terrified. Yet the vampires ignored them.

Mansi crawled around the back of the dais, keeping his field of vision as wide as he dared. He felt his hands and arms trembling as he heard the creatures do what came naturally to them but still managed to overcome his terror to see Caleb, hands and arms moving like he was conducting the vampires in a danse macabre, commanding the swooping, screeching, biting and tearing at the frantic congregation before him. There were less people screaming for help now than there were corpses, some of them left where they had been felled. Some, cut but alive, were pulled into the beams. Mansi had not seen vampires before today yet he wondered if the sacrifices weren't an aside and not actually relevant or important to whatever reason Caleb was here. It was quite possible that the sacrifices were merely a sadistic pleasure for none of the vampires actually appeared to be feeding.

A rumbling and shaking filled the room then, as the rafters, weakened by the flames, could no longer support the weight of the roof above and the burden of the shifting vampires and their prey. The roof itself also struggled to cope under the pressure of the ice and snow laying thick across its surface.

The result was obvious.

Great clouds of snow and thick blocks of ice and masonry came crashing down, crushing the corpses and the half-dead. The vampires shifted like lightning, avoiding the collapsing roof, but it meant that they now no longer had any fresh blood to feed with except for...

Against the wall, Mansi coughed and spluttered, dust and ice clogging his throat and momentarily blinding his eyes.

On the dais, Apollinari and Claudia had thrown themselves to the floor. Caleb had fallen backwards over the thrones that could not cope with the weight of the roof sections. Incredibly, the bowl remained positioned on the cradle.

In the confusion, Mansi crawled towards the dais. Apollinari waved him away as Caleb began to rise. Mansi frowned but indicated with raised eyebrows and a subtle nod that he was headed onwards. He had spotted a narrow door leading out of the hall. This second exit was concealed from the rest of the chamber, more so now with the rubble and dirt. Desperately wishing it was unlocked, Mansi closed his eyes briefly then rose up, shooting forward to the door, clambering over the destruction. He thought he felt the rank breath of a vampire at his ear for a moment but never slowed his pace. He slammed into the door and, after a momentary struggle with the stiff bolt, he pushed it open and threw it shut behind him. He could bolt it from his side too, so did so eagerly. There was a dull thud against the wood from the side he had just come from. It came again. Mansi fled down the narrow corridor, sheathed sword at his waist clanking against the wall. Then a panic began to grip him as his vision blurred. A sharp sting was at his wrist and he feared he had been bitten. Legs collapsing under him, he folded into a heap in the gloom, trying to see the dark shape that was leaning over him.

Back in the Great Hall, Apollinari was helpless, yet bemused that he and Claudia had not been slaughtered in the same way as these Turks (and was relieved the ceiling had not brought them to a messy end). Was Caleb aware that he had silver in his veins? By what Ismael had said in the dungeon that seemed unlikely. Yet Caleb did know of Apollinari. He could have done nothing but watch the people die before him: the vampires had only been slaughtering. The difference, the viciousness, had been startling, even for Apollinari who had seen similar events many times before.

With the frenzy brought to an abrupt end, the vampires sunk back into the shadows, likely returning to the catacombs to rest.

Caleb, his Hispanic features pale, beckoned for Apollinari and Claudia to stand before him. Ismael appeared and stood to Caleb's right. Caleb looked more than comfortable in his position of absolute power, even amidst the ruined hall.

"Father Giuliano Apollinari," the vampire purred.

"I don't believe we've met before," snapped Apollinari, dusting his cassock down, not easy with bound wrists. He glared at Ismael who seemed reluctant to return his stare.

Caleb was expressionless as he looked at the monk before him, his eyes flicking briefly to Claudia. Swiftly, Caleb glided down the few steps, to stand level with Apollinari.

"Apollinari the Debased. That is what they call you?"

"I'm sure I've been called worse."

Caleb waved a hand as though batting away an insect. "I have no interest in the petty squabbles between you and your God."

"Then I should be honoured that my *petty* consternations have found their way to your ears."

"I have seen empires rise and those same empires toppled by the likes of you."

"Then I scare you?"

Caleb laughed, like oil across water. "Such empires are built by the mortal. I have nothing to fear from you. I was there at the Battle of Compiègne, I witnessed the Crusaders defeat Prince Redwan of Aleppo at Antioch and welcomed the Abbasid army to Damascus. What can you, with your weapons of whitethorn and book of God, do to me?"

"I have my faith."

"And what has that done for you?"

"I have no regrets. I know my methods have attracted many who do not wish to acknowledge that there is evil in this world. I'm not here to prove them wrong. I'm here to protect that which we, the oppressed, seek so much – the path of the right and the just."

"Spare me your preaching, monk. You have no concept of the world beyond that which you know."

"I know that it can give me peace – once your undead existence is doused."

Caleb swept into the air just then, his cloak of midnight black flapping around him like immense wings. Apollinari followed the vampire's journey with a determined gaze, the coldness of the Great Hall with its roof burnt away enveloping him. High in the sky, the brightness of the night washed the place in white and darkness, Caleb's gliding form silhouetted against the moon.

"What would you have me do?" came the question from above Apollinari's head. "Impale you like a commoner, a heathen, as would the infamous Tepes? Or put you through your ultimate humiliation and turn you?"

A gust of icy air coursed down into the Great Hall, bringing with it new snow.

Caleb held out a hand and watched as the flakes settled in his palm, not melting, not moving, the vampire's skin giving no heat.

The cold stung Apollinari's cheeks. "How many have you killed? How many have suffered at the hands of your satanic rites?"

"We serve similar causes."

"We have nothing in common!"

"I am penitent to a being much greater than myself, as are you. But I will consume this world and be His representative upon it."

"Until what? If you consume all, what will be left?" Apollinari moved his hand down to his waist. "You would be master of a dead world."

"I would be master of the *un*dead, commanding all and answering to no one!"

"Except Satan himself. And I will not let you get that far."

Caleb saw anger flash across Apollinari's face and landed silently back on the ground before him.

"And by what means do you intend to dispatch me?" Caleb paused for a moment, as if contemplating. Then: "Do you know what it is like to live forever? To only feel warmth and sunlight as a memory? It is different here, in this place of eternal winter. So still, so silent – even for a vampire.

"Incessantly, day after day, night after night, the rocks at the foot of our garden where it met the sea broke the waves. And as the sea retreated back into itself, it washed over the pebbles, leaving behind a gentle hiss. Inland, tree frogs croaked and insects chirruped after the sun had gone down. It was a glorious symphony of the night.

"And one night in particular was uncannily hot. I remember it well. My clothes, as thin as they were, stuck to me with the humidity. I could not sleep.

"My master, Faustinus Livius, was one of the wealthiest of the Empire's commanders stationed outside Rome and his land and property stretched for acres.

"It was not unusual for visitors to come from as far afield as Gaul, Hafnia and even the land of the Afri, so often the villa was home to strangers, welcomed by Faustinus' unparalleled hospitality and generosity.

"Once such visitor - I cannot recall her name but remember her mass of long thick black hair upon her head and a body that even Venus would envy – had been with us for about a month. She never left the villa, never accompanied my master on his hunting trips but always joined him in the evenings for the orgies. As I watched from the sidelines, waiting to refill the decadents' their cups and restock their platters, I saw that she had experience which left nothing to the imagination.

"After a few successive nights, the number of other guests became sparser and those who continued to attend seemed to be more lacklustre, as if they wearied of the hedonism. And then my master himself began to show signs of a funk, to such an extent that he began to cease any activity during the daylight hours. His beloved horses became lame in their stables and the dogs remained ever hungry.

"The woman left as quietly as she had arrived and of her I never saw anything again.

"But she left a legacy that I bear to this day, some two thousand years later.

"For she was a vampire and she had fed on her host's friends, eventually turning on Faustinus as her bloodlust dwindled the easily available numbers.

"The night of which I speak was the night that I was turned, when my master entered my room by the usual means – but this time he was undead, risen for the first time and with an insatiable blood lust about him. He sodomised me, as was his want most nights, but as I felt him deep inside me so he dug talon-like claws into the small of my back and sunk his new vampire teeth into my neck.

"I was enraptured. The feeling of such a violation was beyond anything I had experienced before. He made me drink from him and for hours, for all the time the sun was beneath the horizon, we made love and exchanged our warm, sweet blood.

"But the next morning I woke and, with an effect not unlike having had too much to drink, the cold light of day reminded me of the hideousness of what had happened.

"I felt the incisions in my neck, could taste the blood upon my lips. What had he done to me!

"Enraged I tore through the villa, finding his filthy retreat in the bowels.

"And there he lay, swollen with my blood and a look of such content over his sleeping face that I had to pause for a moment to admire his beauty.

"But he was an abomination. *A vampire.* And he had taken me, used me. So I raised the stake in my hand that I had fashioned with tears and shaking hands from the whitethorn tree in the garden and plunged it into his chest.

"His scream tore into my very soul and he descended into a vile, sickly mess, his eyes the last to go. They stared at me, blaming me, begging me until nothing was left but dust and congealed blood.

"But worse was to come.

"I suddenly grew so very weak. I had to sleep but there was nowhere to go.

"My master's casket seemed so inviting, so warm. Without a second thought I had climbed in and laid down, his remains congealing under me.

"And so I fell into the deepest and longest sleep I had ever had only to wake some nights later, the desire for blood strong in my heart.

"I was a vampire. *Made by my master who I had destroyed in a fit of such anger.*

"There was no one to teach me. No one to guide me and for months I wandered the land, poaching, stalking. Rats and mountain cubs were my quarry. I longed for the taste of human blood but was unable to trigger the instincts which I knew were in me.

"But learn I did - the courage of my convictions too strong to remain buried forever.

"And so you, with your talk of righteousness and light, mean nothing to me. You have not suffered, been forced to become something against your will and lost all faith in the world around you."

"You know nothing of my life, Caleb. Yet you wish me to believe that you have a conscience and that I must feel sorrow for what you have become?" Apollinari shook his head. "Cold runs the blood from a vampire's veins. And you are no more and no less than a walking cadaver with delusions of grandeur." He held in his palm a stake of whitethorn. "I would have no compunction about dispatching you in the same way you dispatched your maker. In fact, you would surely be relieved that I offer you the true death!"

"You are either brave or stupid."

"Both, occasionally."

Caleb brushed Claudia's hair. She pulled away.

"Don't touch me, vampire."

He ignored her. "Do you know why you are both still alive?"

Apollinari sighed. "Enlighten us."

"I am told that you are the last of your line. The last of the line that brought chaos to our kind."

"If that is so, then I am proud to be."

"And I will rip that pride from you as easily as if I would tear out your eyes!"

"So you *do* intend to destroy us."

"Perhaps not in the way that you think. You will become vampire and every day you will be reminded of that which Philippe de Blanc had done to us – to *me*. Your immortality will mean I can inflict this upon you forever. You will pay for my Eloise's true death and you will suffer for my humiliation at the Holy Sepulchre."

"Then do it. Put me at your mercy but leave Claudia to the fates."

Caleb frowned. "You wish this?"

"I clearly have no choice. Do it now. Bite me. Drink from me. Turn me."

Apollinari turned his neck to give Caleb his throat. Suspicious but entranced by the thought of de Blanc's blood coursing through his own veins, Caleb lunged forward, teeth bared.

This was it, Ismael knew, the moment he had been waiting for. Caleb would find death here and take the meddling monk with him. Then he would step forward and take his place as the Vampire Celebrant. Kelele had been his biggest threat and now he was gone only Odalys stood in his way. What could *she* do? She was older than any of them and out of touch with the modern world. And as for Viktor, the undead cripple wasn't even worth considering.

"Stop!"

Chapter 28

Caleb wasn't used to being given orders but the force of the command made him halt.

Ismael felt a cold pulse throb in his ears. He knew that voice. Young, impetuous. Not unlike himself as he used to be.

Rintoul stepped out of the gloom into the moonlight shining down through the shattered roof.

"Ismael, control your animal."

"What are you doing, Rintoul?" Ismael asked.

The scarred young vampire tossed a crumpled bag towards the dais. It clinked as it slid along the floor that was slowly being covered in delicate snow flakes. And wrapped safely in sackcloth (which even still made Rintoul's hands ache) was Apollinari's other possessions: his dagger and his sword, both cast from silver and both deadly to the touch for Caleb and his kind.

"The monk. He comes here to destroy us."

"I would have thought that was damned obvious," Caleb snorted. "Ismael, your bitch is a simpleton."

"My Lord Caleb," Ismael began but Rintoul was at his throat, sharp nails pressing his windpipe.

"Say nothing or you will condemn yourself."

Caleb turned and watched this exchange. "Entertainment? And from one such as you, Ismael? You are not as stolid as I was led to believe. I *am* impressed."

"Silence," hissed Rintoul. "This man, this vampire, means to usurp you."

"Enough, Rintoul," growled Ismael. "You have been drinking spoilt blood. You are delirious. Get back."

"Let him speak," Apollinari called, a sidelong glance towards Claudia. Ismael looked almost worried.

"I have to agree with de Blanc's representative," said Caleb.

Rintoul stepped away from Ismael and bowed respectfully to the senior vampire. "He betrays you. Apollinari holds a secret in his blood, a secret known to all of us except you, my Lord Caleb. Your absence for all these centuries has made you unaware of the dangers he brings." Caleb roared with laughter as Rintoul went on to describe the colloidal silver that the monk had been consuming for most of his life. "One bite from his veins and you would have burnt to nothing from the inside out."

"This is nonsense!" blurted Apollinari. "Do not listen to him! I deserve everything you intend to do to me. The only poison I carry in my blood is because I am *of* the de Blanc family. I see that now! Drink from me! I implore you!" The monk dropped to his knees, faux tears at his eyes. "End my life. I can do nothing to harm you."

"Rintoul lies, my Lord," Ismael said. "I grow weary of his constant childishness. Now he is turned, his outlook will never mature. Pay it no mind and destroy this monk whose ancestors have brought so much shame to us. Even the monk realises himself that he is weak and can live no longer."

Caleb looked between them all. He sighed, his mind turning over and over. Rintoul was a new born and clearly deranged if he dared to speak down to his superiors in such a way; yet Ismael was sly and treacherous and Odalys had told Caleb of the blonde vampire's ways. Caleb suddenly remembered his old life with Livius, and the food-taster the senator had employed to avoid the poisons any would-be assassin cared to serve.

"*You* will drink from him."

"My Lord?" Ismael stepped back. It was the smallest, most imperceptible of movements, but to a vampire it was almost a leap.

"If he is harmless, then what do you fear?"

"I fear…nothing," responded Ismael. "I am vampire. I *cannot* fear."

"So sure are you?" Caleb had turned to face Ismael, in one hand Apollinari's neck, pulling the monk close. Apollinari gagged and struggled, his breath impeded. "Vampires *feel*. Of course we feel! We are passionate creatures, born from the most intimate association between the living and the undead. Now drink from this man or I will rip out your throat over and over until the end of days."

Ismael could not break free from Caleb's superior strength and so found his mouth being forced towards Apollinari's neck. The jugular looked so full, so warm and rich, but he knew the silver it contained. He was torn in so many ways: to drink, to satisfy his bloodlust but to ingest the metal that would bring such an agonising true death. Or the eternal torture at Caleb's hands: for he knew his Lord would see his threat clear. Was there another way? Could he spill Apollinari's blood perhaps and somehow make Caleb ingest it? Apollinari: his one-time friend and confidant reduced to a bitter enemy on the side of light while Ismael himself kept to the shadows. And then there was the bag down there at their feet, the bag which contained the phials of silver... Yes, that would be the way - grab one of the phials and force it into Caleb's eyes! If it didn't destroy him it would permanently blind him!

But he couldn't break free from Caleb's vice and so he cried out, pathetically. "It is true! What Rintoul says is true! Apollinari's veins are filled with silver! I wanted you to drink from him so I could replace you!"

Caleb released the men and they both crumpled to the floor, one breathless, one defeated. "You dare to take my place? You who are so weak that you even admit your betrayal at the first sign of defeat?"

"You are *tertium quid*! You are not true vampire!"

"Ismael!" warned Apollinari, a hand on the vampire's arm and surprise that in his own heart concern for him remained.

But Ismael ignored the monk and looked up at Caleb. "You are an abomination, Caleb, and you have no right to stand as our master!"

Caleb tilted his head and nodded, as if a decision had been made. He glided to the bowl on its golden cradle and dipped his hands in the blood that would not clot. Raising them, he washed his palms gently, the blood pink against his own skin and between his fingers. With the silk he cleaned them.

Ismael knew what this meant. Had seen it before. He tried to stand. Found his legs had numbed under him.

In a flash, Caleb was upon Ismael and had ripped his arms clean from his sockets. Ismael screamed, the agony beyond measure. He shook as he saw Caleb fling one limb to Rintoul, who greedily consumed the blood that flowed so freely from it, and kept the other for himself.

Apollinari scrabbled back, horror in his eyes. Ismael looked back at him, pitiful and useless.

"I have no need for the Celebrants," Caleb roared, as he tore into Ismael's right arm, the flesh between his sharp teeth. "Odalys will be banished from this land, never to return. I have no need for her. Rintoul will become my only companion, he who would wish me to remain undead – unlike you, Ismael, you traitorous cunt."

Apollinari's dagger, his athamé, suddenly found itself in Rintoul's grip, placed there by Caleb. The silver blistered Rintoul's palm but Caleb motioned to the young vampire. "Quickly! The honour is yours!"

Rintoul glided over to Ismael who had by this time fallen to the floor, blood gushing from the roots at his shoulders, and brought the athamé down into the dismembered vampire's chest. With a scream and a gurgle, Ismael soon exploded and Rintoul fell backwards, hands burning. The silver knife skidded halfway across the Great Hall.

Apollinari's shoulders began to shake as tears came upon him: salty, bitter and regretful. And flowing for Ismael. For a vampire!

Marise's grip on Mansi's psyche was strong. He found he could not cry out in response to the sudden sound of his brother's voice coming from the other side of the door.

Not yet, Marise said, her voice nowhere else except inside his skull. *Rintoul can be of use to us. But call out to him now and he will turn on you. He is vampire and we must be cautious to trust him.*

Mansi's eyes were panicked and wild, his tongue desperate to form the words his vocal chords were producing. But the only sound that came was a series of stunted moans, not unlike those which his father used to make in the last years of his life, when the brain fever had gripped him.

He nodded, understanding and wishing to be released from her spell. He had a coughing fit that came upon him quite suddenly, and as his eyes stopped watering he realised he had voice again. Tongue feeling less swollen, he cleared his throat.

"Please do not hurt me," Mansi said, a pitiful-sounding request from such a seasoned warrior. But this woman had skills it was unwise to ignore. She was a witch, powerful and blasphemous and Mansi feared her as much as he feared his God. "I will do anything you command."

"Is that so?" Marise's olive skin looked even richer in the corridor's half-light. Her eyes, great pools of black, glinted and her delicate, ruby red lips parted as she smiled. "Your brother in there: what would you offer me if I said I could bring him back to you?"

"You have the power to do that? Can you restore him?"

Marise nodded. "But not without your loyalty to me."

Mansi's temples tingled with the thought of Rintoul back to normal. How far would he go? What would Marise demand of him?

With trepidation, he reached out to touch her, the white silk clinging to her curves. But a growl came from nearby and he retracted his hands. Yellow eyes appeared and brought into the view the lycore.

"Jurat," warned Marise, sensing the beast was about to demonstrate his dominance. "Mansi, I expect nothing less than complete loyalty to me. You will do as I say at all times."

Her black eyes widened and Mansi had no other compunction but to obey. It was as if his own mind was no longer fully his and he even accepted the presence of this huge wolf-thing without so much as a second glance.

Marise cast a spell and enveloped Mansi in a shroud from head to toe, thick and grey like a pupae. Jurat carried him over his broad shoulders as they moved down through the corridors, a long way back around the huge doors to the Great Hall.

The doors swung open with a great *clang* and the wooden candelabra that hung desperately to the last of the rafters came thundering down, shattering everywhere.

Apollinari, Claudia, Caleb and Rintoul were startled in unison as Marise and her small entourage entered.

Caleb gasped as he recognised the woman's aspect, her manner and superior air. But he could not remember her name. It was *so* long ago.

With Yozgatli Tanyel's body hosting his heart, Caleb was perfectly hidden - but Marise's powers meant he would not stay concealed for long. Not only that, his own arrogance would soon reveal him to her.

"I want the *tertium quid*. Bring him to me," she pronounced.

The cocoon across Jurat's back slid to the floor. Jurat sat.

"Yours is not to command here," Caleb spat back. "For you nor your…menagerie."

"Giuliano, which one is it?" asked Marise, looking at Apollinari.

"You know this woman, monk?" Caleb growled as the memory of her aspect began to register in his mind. It was her! The woman who had come to Livius' villa!

Apollinari shrugged resolutely, hands still shackled.

"You would bind my flock?" Marise waved a hand and Apollinari's and Claudia's shackles burst into bright flame and fell to the floor, smoking in the melting snow. The rains had come again and were gently pattering the ice into slush. "I demand the *tertium quid*! It is mine by right!"

The diktat reverberated around the devastated hall but no one seemed to be willing to deliver what the witch wanted.

A silent command from Caleb and the vampires in the shadows rustled into movement, ready to bring down this woman.

But Marise was not to be trifled with.

Suddenly, Apollinari's sword wobbled and raised itself into the air and began to spin and undulate. Around and around it went, a blur forming a silver disc which glowed bright.

"Duck!" Apollinari hissed as he pulled Claudia to the ground.

Caleb overheard the monk and realised in a split second what was about to happen. He took Rintoul down with him just as the sword splintered, a thousand shards of pure silver spraying into the dark recesses of the Great Hall where Caleb's vampire army lurked.

Chapter 29

Showered in the undead flesh and blood that spewed back out, Caleb roared in anger and dismay, his children in darkness – save Rintoul - having been destroyed with just this one spell.

"How dare you come to this place and commit such an act against me! I, who have commanded thousands on the battlefields between the undead and the living, who have drank from a hundred throats in one night and left not a soul alive! And you, who took my master from me! The only person who I have truly loved! Will you now take everything else from me? What have I done to *you*?"

Marise knew then who he was. Could see behind his eyes those of that slave from Livius' villa – but more so could feel the heart that once beat inside another chest.

"You are the *tertium quid*! Livius' personal sodomite. How far you have come! Your master would have been proud."

"Who is this woman, Caleb?" asked Rintoul, blood from his destroyed vampire siblings dripping from his arms.

"This is the vampire who killed my master."

"*You* killed him! You drove that stake through his heart, not I!" Marise said.

Apollinari's skin prickled. He stepped forward. "She is no vampire," he said.

"You are wrong, Apollinari. She turned my master."

"Marise, tell him he is wrong. You are *not* vampire." Apollinari didn't know what to do as Marise stared coldly at him. While his Wiccan heritage had wavered on occasion, he had always known that Marise, the dark mother, was the bitter enemy of the vampire horde. That had been enough to spur his beliefs on, to work with the Church and bring an end to the undead disease that stalked the world.

But what was now being said? Caleb seemed convinced of what he thought he knew and Marise did not seem to be too eager to counter him.

"She is undead, monk. I can smell others' blood coursing through her veins." Caleb swooped down and stopped in front of Marise. "If I am *tertium quid*, then what does that make you?"

"You are resurrected by a curse. The heart inside a body that it does not belong to. You are an abomination, Caleb, not her! A creature that believes itself to be vampire – yet slays those it demands to be like with such ease." Apollinari began to walk slowly down from the dais. His bag was not far away.

"My disciples are loyal to the last," Marise said.

"Disciples?" Caleb raised his arms and gestured to those before him. "Am I to believe that these brethren of yours could overthrow me?"

"They did so before," Marise pointed out.

"But your numbers were greater then. This is all that remains of the all-powerful Cult of Marise: a monk and a girl!"

"Do not mock me, Caleb," replied the woman, the rain moulding her samite dress to her. She was naked underneath and she saw Caleb's gaze linger over the curve of her large breasts, her full hips and the delicately rounded labia between her legs. "You wish to fuck me? No, of course you don't. I'm not your type."

"I wish to destroy you."

"Vampires never used to kill vampires," she said. "All that changed once you slaughtered Livius."

"I loved him."

"Yet if you had let him remain undead, you could have loved him forever."

Caleb did not wish to be reminded of that which he knew so well himself. He was in another body now, but he had brought all of his guilt and regret with him. "You made me do it."

"I can mould free will. I can control a mind. But you, Caleb, have nothing left. Your soul is as undead as you are."

"What can you control that I cannot?"

Marise motioned for the lycore to step forward. "An example."

Caleb did not seem impressed. "You control the beasts. A trait from your vampire heritage. Your meagre cult is made from those you condition."

What in God's name is she? Apollinari's mind was churning over and over. Was it true that he had been penitent to a vampire all this time?

"Is that not what all cults ultimately are? Living or undead?" Marise motioned to Jurat without looking in his direction. "Kill the girl," she said and Jurat padded around the room, Claudia's scent filling his nostrils.

As a werewolf, he had easily hunted and killed. It was part of his nature, what kept him alive. But now to be *ordered* to kill...

Marise sensed him hesitate. "Lycore, do as you are commanded!"

Lycore! Apollinari tensed. Marise had powers indeed – far more than he had assumed. As a witch she was powerful. But if she was what Apollinari feared she was – a *moroi*, a *living* vampire - then the limit of her powers would be unknown. Perhaps Caleb shouldn't be so nonchalant after all.

But for all her strength, Jurat could not obey her, even as he stood inches from Claudia, smelling the girl's fear as he bared his teeth.

"Leave her alone, Marise!" shouted Apollinari, having picked up his bag and swung it swiftly over his shoulder.

"This is a lesson for Caleb's benefit, Giuliano. Stay out of this."

"The girl is my niece. Surely you should know that what with all your powers. Silver runs through her blood." A lie, but it may have just made Marise think on it. And what was it he said to himself about Caleb's apparent nonchalance?

"Watch yourself, Giuliano. You may be useful to the Church but I have no such need for you."

"If you *are* vampire - and I hope that you are not – then what you have taught me about killing vampires should make what I am about to do so much easier."

In one motion, Apollinari had brought out from his bag and thrown into Marise's stunningly beautiful face a handful of silver-filled phials. She howled as the liquid burst over her eyes, her hold over Jurat lost for a moment. But the lycore's loyalty to his mistress' safety was unalloyed and he launched himself at Marise, protecting her from any further harm.

Marise cast a spell and the room spun for all of them. Apollinari was flung back but in the centre of the growing maelstrom remained the witch, the lycore and the cocoon that contained Mansi. Squinting, shielding his eyes from the rising glare, Apollinari was sure he saw Marise's form mould into someone new, some startlingly familiar to him. Agatha, his sister, seemed to reach out to him, mouthing his name, skin blistering until she was a blackened, charred, writhing figure. Her hands clawed, begged, pleaded but as much as Apollinari tried to crawl towards her, the heat pushed him back.

"*Sciocco*!" he called out, his name for her when they were just children. But her skull now devoid of skin rolled back, jaw in a hideous grimace. He flung more of the silver phials, purely in desperation, as if that would quell the vision before him. Whether it worked or not he did not know. Nevertheless, the whirling light and smoke turned in on itself, into a thin, tangible spinning pillar of ectenic force. Then it suddenly forced itself upwards, up through the shattered roof of the Great Hall and dissipated in the cold, black sky, leaving nothing but a battered and bloody Mansi in a heap not far from where Apollinari had stumbled.

"And so she has gone," Caleb announced, as if he had dispatched Marise himself.

"I wouldn't be too sure, Caleb," gasped Apollinari, tears flowing down his cheeks.

"*Mia madre*," whispered Claudia as she wept too, hands shaking as she tried to comprehend what she had witnessed. If it had not been real, how cruel had Marise been to inflict this upon them.

Apollinari lightly held his niece by her shoulders. He had never been overly affectionate to her as she had grown up, not through want of trying, so Claudia rightly took the tentative contact to mean so much more. She smiled as best she could and wiped his tears from his cheeks. Apollinari flinched briefly but then smiled sadly back, grateful for the interaction. He composed himself and helped Mansi to his feet.

The soldier's eyes stung and he could see very little.

"Her demonstration of control was pathetic," the vampire said.

He clicked his fingers and Claudia tensed.

"Uncle..."

"Claudia...fight it!"

But Caleb was an ancient vampire and his powers were strong, probably more than a match for Marise had she remained. Claudia tried to hold herself back but Caleb had impressed a desperate longing for him inside her head and she could not dismiss it. She walked entranced towards him, wishing she could cast a spell to ward him off but he was too strong.

Within moments, she was on her knees in front of him.

But Caleb didn't want to feed. He wanted to prove a point.

He grabbed Claudia's head between his strong hands – he could thank Tanyel's years of sword training for that – and pushed her face into his groin. Her hands raised up and he could feel her fingers tearing at the material, desperate to reach the swelling prize underneath. But he laughed and pushed her back and twisted her head clean off her shoulders. As if it was a ball, he tossed it down the hall to Apollinari, blood spraying as it tumbled.

"I do not need animals to do my work for me."

As if he had been stabbed in the heart, the monk clutched at his chest, rage bubbling up inside him and he cried out.

"You bloody monster! You fucking bloody monster!"

"Such language for a man of the cloth," Caleb chuckled, bloodied hands clasped together.

Claudia's face looked up at Apollinari from between his feet, her brief moment of agony frozen on her features. Poor, sweet Claudia! There was no time to grieve for her brutal end – instead he channelled his emotion to one purpose. Grabbing a whitethorn stake from his bag, Apollinari hollered out and rushed towards Caleb, ready to wreak his vengeance for poor Claudia.

"I am made to relive my sister's terrible end and now you make her daughter suffer equally as hideously before me!"

The monk had nearly reached Caleb however Rintoul was in his way in a second. But Rintoul had not accounted for Apollinari's fury mixing with his Wiccan blood. The monk was not about to let something as insignificant as a supernaturally strong vampire get in his way.

Apollinari raised the stake and plunged it into Rintoul's chest.

"No…" Mansi croaked, too weak to intervene.

The effect on Rintoul was not unlike that of an impaled snake, the young vampire writhing and hissing as the whitethorn was worked deeper into his body.

"What you deserve," hissed Apollinari as he struggled, the stake held tight in his left hand. The monk pushed forward, feeling Rintoul's ribcage split and widen further. Blood, thick and putrid, splashed out and down over Apollinari's chest.

An angst-scented cry and a final shove and Apollinari knew the stake wouldn't be going in any further. Rintoul's eyes widened and he screamed at his killer before him, arms flailing, catching Apollinari across the face. Gashes appeared across Apollinari's cheeks and, even though the stake was held fast in the creature's chest, Rintoul's senses were raised and excited by the sight of the fresh blood before him.

Apollinari twisted the stake and Rintoul grabbed it with both hands in agony, his dead palms burning as he touched the whitethorn.

"Brother!" screamed Rintoul, a look for terror upon his face as he swung his gaze towards Mansi.

"Will you just *die*!" cried Apollinari as Rintoul fought for as long as his undead strength would let him. The two of them circled and twisted, hitting walls and pillars, stumbling across the floor, all the while Rintoul's jaws snapping and slavering.

After what seemed an eternity but was probably only moments, Apollinari could feel the vampire's struggles beginning to weaken. Apollinari brought the silver athamé up from where he had snatched it from the floor a moment ago and sliced out at Rintoul, keeping a tight grip on the stake.

Rintoul's head rolled from his shoulders, a twisted echo of Claudia's fate, and the body crumpled to the floor as Apollinari released his hold. It turned to a sticky mass of flesh and bone before it settled.

Rintoul's spinning head had hit a nearest pillar and exploded, pieces of hair, skull and brain sliding downwards.

Apollinari sagged back to the floor, the remains of the vampire having splattered his cassock and covered his feet. He looked at Mansi but what could he say? His face was burning where Rintoul's talons had cut him but there was no time for respite.

Caleb was on the move, enraged.

Finding strength within him, Apollinari raised himself up to face Caleb, fury flashing across the vampire's face. As Caleb glided, the darkness around him seemed to pull and drag, following him as he moved.

Apollinari looked around him, unable to determine if any more vampires – ones that had avoided Marise's trick with his sword (*his* sword that his father had given him!) – were in the shadows. Exhausted, the monk had the sagacity to know that this could be his very last stand.

"Caleb..." Apollinari returned, breathing hard and fast and the silver knife back in its sheath at his waist.

"You now wish to end my life?"

"You are not alive. You have *never* lived."

"And yet here I am, talking to you." Caleb opened his arms and Apollinari noticed the lack of body armour across his chest. "Does that make you delirious? Are you having visions?"

"Perhaps. I was separated from the Order for less."

Apollinari summoned more strength and hurled himself at the vampire's chest but Caleb moved like lightning at the last moment. Apollinari skidded across the floor, striking his elbows against the steps. As the monk turned, fumbling in the slush with the athamé, Caleb launched into the air again and landed at the prone man's feet.

Pulling Apollinari up by his scapular, Caleb drew back his lips to reveal his fangs and lifted the monk into the air, only to hurl him across the Hall. Apollinari landed heavily and awkwardly against a wall, Rintoul's remains squelching under him.

The athamé was still in his grip.

Caleb, cloak billowing and deep red satins black in the half-light, swooped down upon Apollinari and dragged the battered monk back to the thrones.

"I wish you to be at my right hand when I turn you, Apollinari." But Caleb hesitated. Could he smell the silver in the monk's veins?

"I will not become like you!" Apollinari cried and, with all the strength he could muster, thrust the blade towards Caleb's chest. "You can drink my blood! But the silver in my veins will eat you from the inside! Do it! Do it now!"

The vampire snarled and struck Apollinari's wrist. As the athamé fell from the monk's grasp, the tip of it touched Caleb's skin and the vampire snarled in pain. The silver *hurt*.

The athamé skidded away and far out of Apollinari's reach.

These, then, were Apollinari's last moments, he realised. As he lay in the snow, flakes settling on his cassock, he looked up at the Vampire Lord and silently mouthed a prayer, readying himself for the fate that Caleb was about to place upon his soul. He could not be turned, but at least he would take Caleb with him.

Caleb smiled, finding amusement in this disgraced holy man talking for a final time to his God. The vampire had little time for sentiment, though, and revealed the glistening white fangs again. He could not take the risk to drink his blood – so why not deliver to him the same fate that which he himself suffered? Rip out his heart and dash it into oblivion!

"You can't turn me – and that *burns*! Burns you to the very depths of your putrid core! Yet is it enough now for you to kill me? You want to humiliate me, to make me pay for everything my bloodline has done. But we won't let you! We have seen to that."

"You are human. A disciple of the *moroi* bitch but human nevertheless...therefore limited by mortality and trapped by the claustrophobia of life. Perhaps I will let you live, not through an act of mercy but so that you can feel pain. I need not turn you but I can still bring you to your knees. Can you live with the humiliation?"

As Apollinari was about to answer, a hideous screech came from the vampire's open mouth and Apollinari was taken aback by the sudden exclamation.

Both the monk and Caleb looked down simultaneously to see the silver athamé hovering in the space between their chests, the blade pointing up slightly and towards Apollinari.

Around the knife's black handle, now covered in thick dark blood, was a hand - the wrist and arm protruding from Caleb's chest.

Caleb seemed to want to speak as he looked confusedly back at Apollinari and briefly the monk believed he saw something in the vampire's expression that had grown lighter, as if the vestiges of Yozgatli Tanyel had surfaced at that moment. Or was it Caleb's true self before he had become undead?

The knife dropped, bounced off Apollinari's labouring breast and clattered to the floor.

The hand that had wielded it disappeared back into Caleb's body and out the other side, out from his back.

Caleb reached out towards Apollinari, white eyes suddenly aglow again, and spat, the release hitting the monk across the forehead.

Moments later, as Apollinari watched agog, wiping the bloody expectoration from his face, the vampire seemed to wither and curl in on itself, face contorting and displacing, until the undead creature exploded, gummy flesh and bone spraying everywhere.

Standing there, with Caleb's shriveling heart twitching in his bloodied right hand, was Verrecchia.

Chapter 30

A flock of ravens swooped high, casting brief, flickering shadows over the island of Snagov as the sun shone brightly in the chilly blue sky.

Down in the kitchens where the bread baked, the heat coming from the huge ovens warmed those sitting around the heavy table.

"It seems we are turning into an asylum for the unfortunate," Jacob said as he sipped mead from a bowl. His hair had flecks of white, Apollinari sure they hadn't been there before. "Brother Golick found poor Yazid with a blade through his neck. No one seems to know how it happened. Golick lost his voice and now sits in silence in his cell."

"And the bishop?" asked Apollinari.

"He too seems to have lost the will to continue, yet does nothing to end his internal conflicts."

"You know that suicide is not an option. To have the path to Heaven taken away from you is a notion that some people cannot deal with. They would rather endure a life of suffering. What does Rome say about it?"

"I wrote to them but they have yet to reply. I fear they will turn a blind eye and let us deal with him." Jacob put down his bowl. It was time for Vespers and the whole monastery was to meet in the main chapel. "My worry is young Corbiu."

As Apollinari gathered his belongings, ready to depart after the prayers, he followed Jacob out of the kitchens. "What of him?"

"The ravens that amass in the main courtyard fascinate him. He spends hours staring at them."

"Not an unhealthy past time, by any means."

"He wants to catch one – just a small one, he says."

"Can you trust him to keep it as a pet?"

"I had considered it. He'd even been collecting insects ready to feed it, but..." Jacob's voice tailed off as some of the brotherhood met them on their way through the monastery. As they moved away, Jacob resumed his story. "I caught him eating a fly."

Apollinari raised an eyebrow as Jacob shuddered. "Has he shown these tendencies since?"

"It was a big fat round thing. He gobbled it down like he hadn't eaten for weeks!"

"And when you confronted him about it?"

"He said it was his master's doing but he still seemed remorseful. Do you have any idea what this means? What master is he referring to?"

Apollinari pulled Jacob close as they turned a corner, the chapel a few hundred yards away from them at the end of the gloomy passageway. "Keep a close eye on him."

"Will you be able to call in on him before you go?"

Apollinari did not answer. Jacob detected that there was little point in pressing him for a response. Instead:

"What of you? Where will you go now?"

"To Spain. I have to give Caleb a proper burial. Or at least what's left of him." Apollinari thought of the long journey ahead of him, of the cargo he was to carry: Caleb's shrivelled heart wrapped in black linen, and a task started by his ancestor Philippe de Blanc nearly four hundred years ago. And it would be a journey he would undertake alone

Apollinari's young novice, who had been through so much these last few weeks, had lost much trust in his mentor and his faith. Long discussions over the last few nights since they had returned to Snagov had not made Apollinari change Verrecchia's mind. Verrecchia, seeing his future elsewhere and without the Church, had decided to help rebuild the Citadel. The Turks had been excised, albeit by the vampire invasion, and so it was now free to be reclaimed by Wallachia once more. Mansi had been appointed by the Wallachian generals to oversee the reintegration of Dambovita into their society and he had asked Verrecchia to assist. Whether it was because he saw Verrecchia as a replacement for his brother, Verrecchia didn't know. Verrecchia's loss of faith had mingled with his guilt for his mentor's actions that had led him to want to help.

Apollinari, ultimately, could not argue and had always seen in Verrecchia the desire to help those less fortunate. So perhaps this was the right path for Verrecchia, not some stuffy monastery with its stolid ways and harsh regime but an environment where he could breathe and truly make a difference.

Even though Verrecchia had not asked for it and did not need it, he accepted Apollinari's blessing in the manner in which it had been intended. They would not depart on difficult terms.

Apollinari had pulled Verrecchia close to him, hugging him uncharacteristically tightly, using the tactility to say goodbye to Claudia too and, perhaps, Agatha. Verrecchia felt the tightness of the clutch and had pulled himself away, unable to look Apollinari in the eye again. Both monks were desperately melancholic that such a companionship, as fraught as it had been recently, was ending.

Verrecchia gave no parting speech and, declining to attend Vespers, had left for the Citadel. It was easier for him to leave first than watch Apollinari go.

As Jacob and Apollinari reached the chapel, the Sardinian asked, "Will your appointment be official?"

Jacob looked almost embarrassed. He hadn't been appointed Abbot of Snagov but had taken on the duties it required. That was something else for Rome to decide upon. "There are great challenges ahead for all of us."

As Jacob took his place at the front, facing the brotherhood. Apollinari slid into a pew and used the service to reflect on his own days to come, saying prayers for the only family he had known – and cruelly lost - and wondering on Marise. That she was a *moroi* did not sit easily on his shoulders. But he had no wish to dwell and so, once Vespers had been completed, a fresh horse and cart was made ready for him.

He left Snagov, intending never to return. There would be many days on the road to the Spanish territories where solitude would allow him to reflect further. He had grudgingly accepted Verrecchia's choice and felt remorse in leaving him behind. Ismael, however, was a burden that had always sat between his shoulder blades like a crouching spider, heavier now that his old friend was truly dead.

Bran Castle is a fortress situated on the border between Transylvania and Wallachia.

The Bran Gorge, at the mouth of which it sits, is one of the most important trans-Carpathian passages: the trade routes of its crossroads, and the recurring military invasions that utilized them. A natural amphitheatre, guarded from the east by the Bucegi Mountains and from the west by the Piatra Craiului Massive, the Bran Gorge offers a wide panorama both to Tara Bârsei, and to the hills and valley of Moeciu.

Prince Vlad Dracula was not interested in such views and meditative ruminations. There had been times past where he had sat on the balcony of his rooms and simply stared but today light was beginning to hurt his eyes and his bones.

He had found the journey back from Dambovita long and arduous but he was safe now, ensconced in the catacombs of one of his royal abodes. They stretched into darkness in all directions, dust piled thick across the cold earthy floor. Mould and cobwebs appeared to hold crumbling architraves firm.

A constant nagging was in the Prince's head, as if someone was talking to him, fanatical about blood and insects and domination.

But it hadn't been his prisoner, for *he* was bound and gagged and terrified for his life.

Dracula hadn't said a word in the time they had taken to get to Bran, the prince knowing that his silence spoke more to Popescu than any other threat or comment.

Dracula had found the Wallachian captain tearing through the streets of the Citadel, catching him like a rat in a trap, bleating of vampires and Turks, and when he mentioned Ilona, he gave the game away. A sword tip pressed simply against Popescu's groin made the captain tell all: how he had stolen the princess away from

Târgoviste and how he had replaced her with a mutilated peasant girl to make Dracula believe his wife had been murdered as she slept. But Dracula had known it had not been Ilona in that bed and he never even asked why Popescu had taken her from him. It was enough that he had admitted the crime. Then Dracula ripped out his tongue.

Yet that had no real impact on any forgiveness Popescu could expect from Dracula, especially not now that Ilona had become a thing of unspeakable horror.

The prince could not comprehend that. But he would, in time. Just as he would come to accept he would no longer share with her the glorious dawn over the Danube delta. And this realisation would take him down a path that would forever shape his destiny.

Wearied and dabbing the blood that continually seeped from his eyes (only while the sun was up, he noted), Dracula slumped against the great black casket that seemed to have obsessed him since it had been delivered into his possession back at Prahov. He pressed a hand against its side, feeling its coolness and wondering if it would protect him from the daylight that he had somehow become allergic to.

On the other side of the crypt, Popescu was bound to the wall, iron chains cutting into flesh. The stump that was the reminder of his tongue twitched at the back of his throat. He sobbed as he watched his Prince, with all the strength he could muster, wrench open the heavy lid.

Epilogue

The last sanctuary for Odalys and Viktor was still the room at the very top of the tower at Dambovita.

The battle, the sacking of the Citadel by the Wallachians, had meant the stairway, the single route from inside the fortification, had collapsed away and so the window was the only way in and out once more – just as it had been when the doorway had been sealed up.

With Caleb gone and Kelele missing, Odalys had to assume she was the last Celebrant left, apart from Viktor, of course. Ismael had not returned either. Was the impetus on her now to rebuild their kind? She hoped not for she would be quite content to disappear herself, return to Greece and live out her undead existence in solitude.

Viktor was annoying her, with his scribbling in the dirt. She'd leave the damn grotesque behind but he was insistent and pulled at her hem, gesturing to the marks he was making.

Without a tongue, he couldn't speak but she had a connection with him. She'd always had and it was something the others hadn't understood.

Of course she wouldn't *really* leave him behind.

"We will go now, Viktor," she said. "Enough."

But Viktor pushed at her ankle and started drawing again.

"The Celebrants are no more. We must away."

But Viktor knew otherwise.

There is another coming. One who will become the most feared of us all.

In the dust, he had drawn an elaborate 'D'.

Shaking her head, Odalys grabbed him and brushed the sign away with a sandaled foot and they swept out into the darkness. Not so long ago she would have believed him, would have wished that their power, their influence would never end.

Once upon a time.

Lightning Source UK Ltd.
Milton Keynes UK
UKOW04f1811230913

217779UK00001B/12/P